The
Importance
of Being
Wicked

Center Point
Large Print

Also by Victoria Alexander and available from Center Point Large Print:

The Perfect Mistress
My Wicked Little Lies

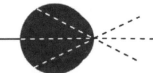

**This Large Print Book carries the
Seal of Approval of N.A.V.H.**

The Importance of Being Wicked

Victoria Alexander

CENTER POINT LARGE PRINT
THORNDIKE, MAINE

This Center Point Large Print edition is published
in the year 2013 by arrangement with
Kensington Publishing Corp.

ISBN: 978-1-61173-653-3

Library of Congress Cataloging-in-Publication Data

Alexander, Victoria.
The importance of being wicked / Victoria Alexander. — Center Point
    Large Print edition.
pages cm
ISBN 978-1-61173-653-3 (Library binding : alk. paper)
1. Nobility—England—Fiction. 2. England—Fiction.
    3. Large type books. I. Title.
PS3551.L357713I47 2013
813´.54—dc23

2012046422

This book is for Lizzie,
Jenn and MaryKaren

Thank you!

The
Importance
of Being
Wicked

Prologue

March 1887

It could be worse.

The phrase repeated itself over and over in his head like the irritating refrain to a little-liked song.

Winfield Elliott, Viscount Stillwell, stared at the façade of Fairborough Hall and tried to ignore the leaden weight in the pit of his stomach, a weight that had settled there since the moment late in the night when he and the rest of the household had been roused from their beds by cries of fire.

"It doesn't look nearly as bad as I thought it would," his cousin, Grayson Elliott, said in what he obviously meant to be a helpful manner. It wasn't. "A bit scorched around the edges perhaps, but not bad, not bad at all."

"No, it doesn't look bad." The two men stood some ten yards from the house at the foot of the circular drive that linked the long drive to the main gate. And from here, given this precise angle and in the cold light of late afternoon, there was indeed little to indicate the destruction within the stone walls of the hall. Certainly what was left of the front door was charred and the glass in most of the windows in the center section of the house had shattered, but the east and west wings appeared untouched. All in all it really didn't *look* bad.

"Appearances, cousin, are deceiving." Win started toward the house, barely noting the puddles of soot-laden water or trampled, filthy snow or the chunks of charred wood lying about. Nor was he especially aware of the pervading aroma of smoke and acrid burned matter or the brisk breeze and his lack of suitable outer garments. "It is much worse than it looks."

It could be worse.

"Fortunately," he continued, "everyone in the house escaped unharmed. And no one was injured battling the blaze."

"Something to be grateful for," Gray said at his side.

Any number of people still milled around the building, mostly male servants: the gardener and undergardeners, the stable hands, the footmen. The hours since the fire had been discovered blurred together in an endless moment or day or eternity. Win had lost track of the time (although it was now obviously late afternoon), as well as exactly who had been here. The fire brigade from the village had responded and help had arrived from neighboring estates, but the snow had made the going slow. Still, it had also helped put out the blaze. While it was certainly cold, the lake was not frozen and the estate pumping station had supplied the water needed to fight the flames.

Win stepped over the threshold and gestured for his cousin to join him. Gray had been in London and Win had sent word to him shortly after daybreak. After all, Fairborough Hall was as much Gray's home as it was Win's.

Gray stepped up beside him and sucked in a hard breath. "Good God."

"I should think this was the work of a hand considerably lower than heaven," Win murmured. It was indeed a scene straight from hell. Or perhaps it was hell's aftermath.

Haphazard heaps of blackened wood littered what had once been the grand entry hall. Here and there a whisper of smoke drifted upward from still-smoldering debris. A blackened skeleton was all that remained of the magnificent center stairway. The glorious ballroom ceiling with its intricate plaster moldings and painted scenes from Greek mythology was little more than a charred memory, open now to the floors above them and all the way to the scorched roof timbers.

Gray started into the house, but Win grabbed him and pulled him back. "Careful, Gray. The integrity of the floor is still in question and will be until we can get in there, start cleaning out the debris and assess the destruction." He ran a weary hand through his sooty hair. The aroma of smoke drifted around him. Odd, he would have thought by now he was immune to the smell of smoke.

"Of course." Gray's shocked gaze scanned the

damage. "I can't believe how much is gone." He glanced at his cousin. "Were any of the furnishings saved? The paintings? Uncle Roland's books?"

"We did manage to get the family portraits and most of the paintings out, those hung low enough to reach, that is. Thanks to Mother, really." He forced a wry smile. "While Father and I and Prescott and the other male servants were trying to prevent the spread of the fire, Mother was directing the housekeeper and the maids in rescuing the paintings and whatever else she could think of." At this point he didn't want to consider how much had been lost. Time enough for that later. It had been nothing short of chaos, and the fact that they had rescued anything at all now seemed something of a minor miracle.

"It looks like the fire was confined to the middle section of the house." He glanced at Win. "So the library was unaffected?"

It could be worse.

"With any luck, given its location," Win said. "The east and west wings appear untouched although I fear there might be a great deal of smoke damage. Oddly enough, the stone walls between the wings and the main portion of the building were widened at some point in its history, providing a fire break all the way to the roof. Father mentioned something about that when we realized the fire had been contained, but it's not original to the building of the house. I had never given the width of those walls much thought—indeed, I'm not certain I ever noticed—but they kept the fire from spreading."

"Wasn't a previous earl a witness to the Great Fire of London in 1666? And was terrified of fire from then on?"

"Perhaps we have him to thank then." Nonetheless, it was difficult to manage any semblance of gratitude for a long dead ancestor. Win was fairly certain allowing any emotion, even one as simple as gratitude, would open the floodgates for despair, and for that he simply didn't have the time. "I had always thought the house was essentially unchanged from the day when it was built by the first earl. I can't remember when."

"Fifteen ninety-two," Gray murmured.

"You always were good at dates."

"I know."

Under other circumstances, Win would have replied with something appropriately sarcastic and witty, but, at the moment, he didn't have the strength. The fire had awoken them some fourteen hours ago. It seemed like forever.

"At least the roof is still intact," Gray said.

It could be worse.

"That's something, I suppose."

"Any idea how it started?"

"It could have been anything. A spark from a fireplace. An untended lamp." Win shrugged.

"I daresay we'll probably never really know."

"How are Uncle Roland and Aunt Margaret?"

"Bearing up. Mother is made of much sterner stuff than I had imagined. She and I insisted Father rest. I sent them to the dower house." Win managed a slight smile. "It is a testament to the serious nature of the day that Mother did not protest although it was all she could do to make Father leave."

"How is he?" Gray's worried gaze searched Win's.

"As well as can be expected, I suppose. He's getting older and all this . . ." Win's throat tightened. He shook his head, turned and stepped outside.

Gray followed him. His parents had died when he was very young and Win's parents had raised him as their own. Even though Gray had left England for more than a decade, he was still Win's closest friend and very much his brother. Gray grabbed his cousin's arm. "Win."

"He's tired, Gray, that's all." Win blew a long, weary breath. "We're all tired."

"I hope he looks better than you do." Gray studied him closely. "You look like you've been through hell."

"I can't imagine why." He glanced down. His clothes were filthy; there was a tear in his coat sleeve and a nasty burn on the back of his hand. Odd, he hadn't even noticed it.

14

"So . . ." Gray looked back at the house. "What happens now?"

"There's nothing more to be done today. I have men here who will stay the night and make certain the fire does not reignite. Tomorrow, we'll assess the east and west wings to determine the damage. Hopefully, it's minimal."

It could be worse.

The refrain echoed in his head. He ignored it. "For now, most of the servants have family in the village they can stay with. Mother, Father and I will stay in the dower house, along with whatever servants need a bed. It will be overly crowded, but we shall make do, at least for tonight."

"Prescott will love that." Gray smiled. "He's never approved of making do."

Even the thought of their eminently proper butler making do in tight quarters with the Earl and Countess of Fairborough failed to ease Win's mood. "Will you be going back to London tonight?"

"Absolutely not." Indignation sounded in Gray's voice. "I know I haven't lived here for years, but this is still my home, Win. I intend to stay right here for as long as you and Uncle Roland and Aunt Margaret need me. And, given the looks of it, that will be for some time."

"The dower house is already overcrowded," Win said wryly.

"I'll stay the night at Millworth Manor." He

paused. "Aunt Margaret and Uncle Roland would probably be more comfortable there as well, as would you. And it's only a half an hour carriage drive from here."

"That is something to consider for tomorrow, but as for tonight, we'll stay here. I'm not sure I could drag Father away as it is." Win gestured at the destruction. "I don't know that he's really accepted all this."

It wasn't easy to watch your heritage—the house that had served as your family's home for nearly three centuries as well as all those treasures one didn't realize were treasures until they were gone—go up in smoke. Win had known, in a rational sense, that his father was growing older, but Win had never seen his father as aged until he saw the fire reflected in the older man's eyes. And the sorrow. Win had known as well that one day he would be the next Earl of Fairborough, but last night that inevitable inheritance had for the first time been very real and all too close.

He shoved the thought aside. Father was in good health and there was no need borrowing trouble. They had enough already.

"Have *you* accepted all this?" Gray asked.

"I don't know." Win's gaze drifted over the house once again. The overcast skies only added to the dreary scene. It was as if all color had vanished from the world, leaving everything gray and black and dull and dingy. He wasn't entirely certain it hadn't all been a dreadful dream brought on by something he'd eaten that disagreed with him or some odd story he'd read that lingered in the back of his mind. "I shall have to, I suppose." He glanced at his cousin. "Have you?"

Gray stared at the house for a long moment. "I was able to prepare myself, I suppose, after I received your telegram. Waiting for the next train and the hour-long trip here, I had the time to imagine the worst and ready myself."

Win started down the drive toward the dower house. "You should see Mother and Father. They'll be pleased that you're here."

"I wouldn't be anywhere else." Gray took a last look at Fairborough Hall, then shook his head and joined his cousin. "It could have been much worse, I suppose."

"That's what I keep thinking."

A crash sounded behind them, reverberating through the air and the ground beneath their feet. The two men swiveled back and stared at the house. A cloud of ash and dust hung directly above the mid-portion of the building. Win winced.

Gray's eyes widened. "What on earth was that?"

"I'm fairly certain that," Win said with a weary sigh, "was the roof."

Yes, indeed it could have been worse.

And now, it was.

April

Chapter I

Three weeks later . . .

". . . and you will not believe what I was told about Lady . . ." Mrs. Bianca Roberts continued without so much as a pause for breath. And why should she? The latest on-dit about Lady Whoever-she-was-talking-about-now was entirely too tasty to keep to herself.

Under other circumstances, Miranda, Lady Garret, would be alternately amused or annoyed at her inability to get a word in. Today, she appreciated her sister's ramblings. She had entirely too much on her mind to pay any attention at all, and Bianca's enthusiastic and incessant chatter made it unnecessary to do so. All Bianca really required in terms of a response was the occasional nod or murmur of surprise or clucking of the tongue. In recent years, Miranda had become quite adept at it. It did seem she did some of her best thinking when Bianca was confident she had her rapt attention.

". . . can imagine my surprise, of course. Particularly when I heard, from a quite reliable source mind you, that she had had quite enough . . ."

Miranda sipped her tea and smiled with

encouragement. She had long gotten over this particular deception. It did no real harm and kept her sister from prying too deeply into Miranda's activities. Activities she would much prefer to keep private. Who knew how her family—especially her brothers—might react? The Hadley-Attwaters considered themselves a fairly proper family.

Adrian, of course, would be the most disapproving. Her oldest brother and the current Earl of Waterston was a great stickler for propriety even if, on occasion, he could also be most surprising. Miranda suspected that was due to the influence of his wife, Evelyn. Still, one couldn't count on *most surprising*. Her next older brother, Hugh, was a barrister and, as such, all too cognizant of proper behavior. Her remaining brother, Sebastian, who had always flouted tradition in his own life, might well be her greatest ally given his wife Veronica's outspoken tendencies and penchant for support of various rights for women. Although, on the other hand, what one overlooked in one's wife, one might not accept in one's sister.

As for the female members of the family, one never quite knew on which side of a debate her mother and her oldest sister Diana would fall. Mother could be startlingly progressive when she wished to be, and Diana had always had an independent nature. Even so, this was not the sort of thing with which one wanted to test them.

Bianca might think it rather exciting, but she had never been particularly good at keeping a secret. Precisely why Miranda had gone to great pains not to reveal so much as a hint of her activities. There was nothing Bianca liked better than ferreting out secrets. Her cousin, Portia, who was as much a sister to her as Diana and Bianca, would certainly be shocked. Why, it was one thing for a lady to dabble in the arts or to take up the cause of charitable works, and quite another to become involved in business. This simply wasn't the sort of thing a Hadley-Attwater did.

The fact that this was Miranda and not another member of the family would only add to their shock. Her family considered her the quietest of the lot and the most reserved. She was the youngest and the others had long felt she needed their protection. It was a source of annoyance even if she had never said anything. It had always been so much easier to avoid confrontation than to exhibit outright defiance. John had recognized, and indeed admired, her strength of character, which was yet another reason why she had loved him.

". . . given that it was her fortune after all . . ."

Not that her family had any say in the matter, not really. Miranda was, after all, twenty-eight years of age and financially independent, and she had been a widow for nearly three years. She was used to making her own decisions now and

make them she would. Besides, she enjoyed—
no—loved what she was doing. While she did
appreciate her family's advice—and as the
youngest of six children, advice was in abun-
dance—she would follow her own path. A path
that had begun innocently enough. Indeed, one
could say she had taken the first step upon that
path when she had first met her late husband.

". . . and needless to say, at first, I was shocked
by the mere thought . . ."

Miranda had met John Garret, younger brother
of Viscount Garret, at a lecture on the influence of
Palladio on English architecture. Miranda had
been one of the few women present, but she had
always had an interest in the design of buildings.
Indeed, she had drawn houses—both practical and
fanciful—for much of her life. So she had
summoned her courage, enlisted the assistance of
an elderly aunt as a chaperone, and attended.

The lecture had been fascinating but not nearly
as interesting as the dashing Mr. Garret. He was
handsome and amusing and of good family. To her
eyes, he was very nearly perfect. He encouraged
her interest in architecture and a good portion of
their courtship consisted of attending lectures and
viewing exhibits. Years later he admitted his
encouragement had as much to do with being in
her company as anything else. He quite swept her
off her feet and they married within a few
months. Shortly after their marriage, John opened

his own architectural firm, thanks in part to funding from an anonymous investor who wanted nothing more than repayment and his name as part of the business. Thus was born the firm of Garret and Tempest.

Miranda had a good eye and an innate grasp of design, and when John brought home drawings she would make a suggestion here and point out a problem there. Before long, she was quietly working by his side. John was proud to admit she was much more creative than he was. During the six years of their marriage, he taught her everything he knew and she gradually took over most of the design work, whereas he was the public face of the firm.

". . . could scarcely avoid the comparison, as it was so annoyingly obvious . . ."

When John died in a construction accident, along with his construction supervisor, Mr. West, Miranda inherited the company, and its debts, and the firm continued with the projects already under way. Miranda hired Mr. West's sister, Clara—who had a clever mind with figures—to assist Mr. Emmett Clarke, who had been John's assistant. But in the second year after John's death Clara pointed out the firm would not survive without new business. For that they needed a chief architect. Upon reflection, Miranda still wasn't entirely sure how it had happened, but there had been a void in her life and doing the design work she had done with John filled that emptiness.

Now, Emmett was the liaison with clients, Clara ran the company and Miranda produced the designs. There were a handful of additional employees as well. Garret and Tempest had endured and Miranda continued to make regular payments to Mr. Tempest's financial representatives. While the firm was prospering, Miranda, Clara and Emmett knew if Miranda's role became public knowledge, the company would not survive, no matter how good its reputation. The world would simply not accept a woman doing work that was thought best done by men. But Miranda had an obligation to the people who had worked for John, and now worked for her, to avoid failure at all costs.

Keeping her work a secret, even from her family, hadn't been easy, especially when it came to Bianca. She wasn't merely Miranda's sister but her dearest friend. But Bianca hadn't seemed to notice that Miranda was unusually busy these days and that the sisters were meeting more and more often here at the Ladies Tearoom at Fenwick and Sons, Booksellers. It was convenient to the Garret and Tempest office, was a favorite of Sebastian's wife, Veronica, and, more importantly to Bianca, had become quite the place for ladies of society to frequent.

". . . and I thought, if she could, why couldn't I? After all, it's not . . ."

Miranda had just come from a meeting with Clara and Mr. Clarke about a lucrative new commission to redesign and rebuild a manor house that had been devastated by fire. While they couldn't afford to pass on the job, taking it would be difficult. Fairborough Hall was an hour away from London by train and the work would require the presence of someone from the firm nearly every day during construction. But Emmett's wife was with child and she was having difficulties. She had already had two previous miscarriages and her doctor was insisting she stay in bed. Emmett did not want to be away from London should she have need of him. Miranda and Clara could not fault him for that although the two women acknowledged between themselves, if his employer had been male, his reluctance would not have been tolerated. The three decided there was no choice but to have Miranda meet with Lord Stillwell and, should they get the commission, she would present the plans and represent the firm during construction. They agreed that there was no need to reveal the true architect.

". . . which, of course, will prove difficult as I have not heard from him for more than a year now. Nor have I wished . . ."

Aside from the obvious difficulties, Miranda wasn't at all sure she was up to the task of dealing with someone like Lord Stillwell. He had a reputation that could only be called, well, wicked.

She'd never met the man, but she had seen him at one social event or another. He was quite handsome and dashing and reportedly most charming. He did seem to laugh a great deal and he inevitably had the most devilish glint in his eye. She thought he was around Sebastian's age and had skated remarkably close to scandal in his youth. Of course, so had her brothers. And while, from what she had heard, he had reformed somewhat with maturity, one could not discount his history. Why, the man had been engaged three times and had never once made it to the altar. Surely toying with the hearts of not one but three women was the very definition of wicked. One failed engagement might not be his fault, but three?

". . . will be scandal, no doubt. But it does seem to me, in these circumstances, scandal is the lesser . . ."

She'd never really met a man with quite as wicked a reputation, which did, in hindsight, seem rather a pity. Her brothers, of course, had all been *enthusiastic* in their younger days, but one did hesitate to think of one's own brothers as wicked. John hadn't been the least bit wicked. Now that he was gone, there had been moments, late in the night, when she had wondered what it might be like to be with a wicked man. In his arms, in his bed. She would never dare say it aloud, never admit it to anyone, but for Miranda Garret, wicked had a great deal of appeal. She was at once apprehensive and rather excited at the thought of meeting the wicked Lord Stillwell.

"Then you agree?"

Certainly the man wouldn't throw her to the ground and have his way with her on their first meeting. Nor would he run kisses up the inside of her arm or pull her into his embrace and press his lips to hers. The very idea was absurd. He was a gentleman, after all. She'd never truly been seduced although that too had a certain amount of appeal. Not that she would allow him to do so at any rate. Not on their first meeting, or ever. After all, she was a woman of business. And, even if it wasn't known to more than a handful of people, she rather liked the title. And a woman of business would never allow herself to be seduced by a man with a wicked reputation. Resolve washed through her. Why, the very thought that she could not handle Lord Stillwell was absurd. She was more than up to the challenge. Still, she couldn't deny her anticipation in regard to meeting the disreputable lord equaled her apprehension, even if there was—

"Do you agree or not?" Bianca said sharply.

Agree to what?

"There is a great deal to consider," Miranda said cautiously.

"That is exactly what I have been doing." Bianca's eyes narrowed. "You haven't listened to a word I said, have you?"

"I most certainly have."

"I get the distinct feeling more often than not that you pay absolutely no attention to me whatsoever."

"Don't be absurd." Miranda shrugged off the charge, ignoring a twinge of guilt at its accuracy. "You have my complete attention."

"Do I?" Bianca studied her closely. "Then tell me, do you or do you not agree with my decision to seek a divorce?"

"Divorce?" Miranda gasped in spite of herself. For once, Bianca's incessant chatter was important. Who would have imagined it?

"I knew you weren't listening," Bianca sniffed. "This is an enormous decision. The biggest decision of my life thus far aside from wedding that beastly man in the first place. And, as I value your opinion above all others, I should like to hear it."

"A Hadley-Attwater has never been divorced."

"I believe I mentioned that."

"Mother and Adrian and, oh, well, everyone will be shocked. And horrified really."

"Yes, I said that as well." Bianca's tone hardened.

"Absolutely no one will support you in this."

"I am prepared for that." Bianca's gaze met her sister's. "What I want to know is will you? In spite of its shocking nature, do you think I'm doing the right thing?"

"Yes," Miranda said without thinking. "I do."

"Really?" Bianca stared. "You don't think I'm being rash or foolish?"

"No, I don't. You were rash and foolish when you married Martin. This decision is far wiser than that." Miranda shook her head. "The man has virtually abandoned you."

"We did not suit," Bianca said under her breath. It was more than simply not suiting, but Miranda knew better than to bring that matter up. She was the only one Bianca had ever confided in. Partially because she had felt so very stupid at her choice of husband and did not wish for the rest of the family to know and partially because her brothers would have more than likely killed the brute.

"You have been separated and living apart for nearly four years and you haven't even spoken for a good year or more."

"I don't know where he is." Bianca set her lips together in a firm line. "I fear I shall have to track him down before I can do anything at all."

"You do realize society may never forgive you."

"Nonsense." Bianca scoffed. "It has been my observation that society forgives anything if one is not involved in outright scandal or—"

"Divorce is generally considered outright scandal."

Bianca ignored her. "Or if one has enough money."

"And Adrian and Hugh were clever enough to

take the legal precautions to make certain your money remained your own."

"I resented them a bit in the beginning, you know. The fact that they didn't completely trust the man I was to marry." Bianca heaved a heart-felt sigh. "One of the worst parts of this is having to admit they were right and I was so very wrong." She wrinkled her nose. "I do hate to admit I was wrong."

"That, dear sister, is a Hadley-Attwater trait. It's in our blood."

"Hopefully, they won't rub it in my face."

"I daresay they will all be most kind. Once they get over the shock." Miranda took her sister's hand. "Why, I suspect they won't even gloat for some time, perhaps even years."

"Something to look forward to, I suppose."

Miranda was not at all the kind of person to consider her own needs at the expense of others and she did not do so now. But she couldn't ignore the thought that the impropriety of her business pursuits paled dramatically in light of her sister's decision to seek a divorce. Indeed, if she timed the revelation of her secret correctly . . .

"Then you think I have made the right decision?"

"Oh, my dear Bianca." Miranda cast her sister her most encouraging smile. "I don't know that you can do anything else."

Chapter 2

"You have me at a disadvantage, I'm afraid." Win peered around the woman, who had introduced herself as Lady Garret, at the carriage he had sent to fetch the representative of Garret and Tempest from the train. The carriage had stopped at the foot of the circular drive, discharged the lady and appeared to be empty of additional occupants. "Lady Garret—" He glanced down at her or rather where she had been a moment ago. She was now striding toward Fairborough Hall.

He hurried after her. "I say, Lady Garret, I was not expecting—"

"You were not expecting a female," she said over her shoulder. She carried a paperboard tube and a satchel and was pretty enough in an ordinary sort of way. The kind of woman one would glance at approvingly but might not look at a second time. Her clothing, while obviously of quality, was a few years out of fashion, and nondescript in color and style. She was a good six inches shorter than he with hair a warm shade of walnut worn in a severe manner under an entirely too sensible hat and eyes that were neither green nor brown, or perhaps a bit of both. An intriguing color—hazel, he supposed—although she had scarcely paused long enough for him to be certain. Pity, he had always found knowing the color of a woman's eyes to be most useful for spontaneous flattery.

Win suspected Lady Garret would not be susceptible to spontaneous flattery. In truth, there was a practical, no-nonsense air about her, vaguely reminiscent of a governess that said, far louder than words, that this was a woman not to be trifled with. "No, I most certainly was not."

She stopped to study the façade of the house and he nearly ran into her. It wasn't enough that she was a woman, but he would wager she was an annoying woman at that.

He cast her his most charming smile. It had served him well in the past. Indeed, he had been told it was very nearly irresistible. He doubted even the stalwart Lady Garret could long ignore it. "I assumed that Lord Garret—"

"I do apologize for the confusion, Lord Stillwell. I regret to say my husband died nearly three years ago." Her manner was brisk, her tone was matter of fact, as if her husband's death was something she had long ago accepted as part of her life. Which was, no doubt, an eminently practical, no-nonsense way of looking at it.

Now that he thought about it, he vaguely remembered having heard of the death of Viscount Garret some three or four years ago and the subsequent death—in an accident if he recalled correctly—of his younger brother and heir only a few months later. But he hadn't known either of the men. He assumed Lady Garret was the widow of the younger brother, but then he had also assumed she would be a man.

"My condolences, Lady Garret, and my apologies." He did so hate awkward moments like this, but when the architect one thought one was hiring turned out to be dead, well, awkward was probably to be expected. "I should have realized—"

"Nonsense. You have nothing to apologize for, my lord." She directed her words toward him, but her gaze stayed fixed on the house. He could almost see the gears and wheels of her mind spinning like the workings of a fine Swiss clock. He brushed the absurd idea from his head. She was only a woman after all. "But I do thank you nonetheless."

Apparently, Lady Garret was not about to freely offer an explanation as to why she was here representing her late husband's business instead of, oh, Mr. Tempest, who—one would assume, given the name of the firm—was Lord Garret's partner. Indeed, from the woman's calm demeanor, one might think she didn't feel an explanation was necessary. She was wrong.

"Forgive me, Lady Garret, for being blunt—"

"I am indeed the representative from Garret and Tempest. That is what you were about to ask, is it not?"

"Well, yes, but—"

"And, as I am quite alone, you needn't continue to look hopefully at the carriage."

"I wasn't," he lied. How could she possibly know that? She hadn't looked at him once since she'd stopped to consider the manor.

"Perhaps, as you are so obviously still confused, I should explain." Her tone remained pleasant enough, but her resemblance to a governess reasserted itself. Perhaps that was why he felt not unlike a small, chastised child. And a stupid child at that.

This was not the ideal way to begin a business arrangement if, indeed, he decided to hire Garret and Tempest. Although in truth, he had little choice. "That would be most appreciated."

"My husband founded Garret and Tempest shortly after we married. He was not expected to inherit the title, you see, although he did so a scant three months before his death. I then became the majority owner of the firm. I feel an obligation to my late husband's employees to ensure the continuation of the company . . ." She slanted him a pointed look. "In the same manner in which you, no doubt, feel a responsibility to your tenants and others who work for you."

He nodded.

"When the need arises, I do what I must to make certain the firm does not fail. This is one of those times." There was a note of resignation in her voice that one would expect from a well-bred lady who found herself involved in business. It didn't quite seem to ring true, although surely he was mistaken. He was, no doubt, still stunned that she hadn't fallen prey to his smile. "Our Mr. Clarke usually meets with clients and oversees construction. However, due to matters of a personal nature, he cannot assume that position at the moment. And that, Lord Stillwell, is why I am here." She cast him a polite smile, then returned to her perusal of the house. "You're quite fortunate that the façade is still intact."

The debris from the fire had, for the most part, been cleared away and indeed, from the outside, Fairborough Hall did not look substantially different from how it always had. A bit blackened here and there perhaps, but all in all not bad. He sent yet another silent prayer of thanks heavenward for the skills of the original builders and architects.

"The interior did not fare as well."

"Then perhaps I should see that." She started for the door and again he trailed after her. "It was wise of you to send along drawings, plans and photographs with your inquiries to the firm. How on earth did you manage to salvage them?"

"Only the center section of the house suffered serious damage," he said. "I believe I mentioned that in my letters. Neither of the wings burned although there was considerable damage from smoke. The items I sent you were in the library, which, fortunately, needs little more than cleaning. We have been doing nothing but cleaning for the last few weeks." He smiled in a wry manner. "We don't seem to be progressing very quickly."

"When you say 'we' I assume you mean servants and workers you have hired?"

"Yes and no. We have hired a great number of people to assist our servants in the cleaning. But this is my home, Lady Garret, the home of my parents and my cousin. My father will allow only a select few to work in the library—by his side, I might add. His books and his collection of rare manuscripts are entirely too dear for him to turn them over to someone else. My mother feels the same about the artwork, furniture and family heirlooms that survived. We are not averse to physical labor in this family under circumstances such as these. Throughout its long history, the Elliott family has done what was necessary in times of trouble." He wasn't sure why he felt it necessary to explain, but, for whatever reason, he did.

"Sometimes when we lose something of importance what we have left becomes even more precious."

"So it would seem."

They reached the front entry and the temporary door that had been erected to keep out unwanted intruders—human or otherwise. "I should warn you, while we have accomplished a great deal, it's still something of a mess inside. We had a carpenter from the village inspect the floor and he pronounced it sound, but you should watch your step." He opened the door.

"If you would be so kind as to hold these." She thrust the tube and her satchel at him and he had no choice but to take them. She picked up her skirts to step over the threshold. She wore the sturdiest, and possibly ugliest, shoes he had ever seen. "Are you staring at my ankles, Lord Stillwell?"

"I am scarcely in the habit of staring at the ankles of a woman I have only just met, Lady Garret," he said with all the indignation he could muster, even though he had long thought a nicely turned ankle to be most provocative. And he had never hesitated to consider an ankle when the opportunity arose, whether he knew the lady or not.

"Ah, but your reputation precedes you, my lord," she said mildly.

"One cannot believe everything one hears." He resisted the urge to snap.

Certainly, in his younger days he had been prone to misbehavior and even now, he did enjoy a rousing good time in the companionship of like-minded gentlemen and indeed, whenever possible, he availed himself of the charms of a beautiful and willing woman, but he wasn't the rogue he once had been. He simply didn't have the time.

And it was somewhat irritating to be considered so. He was thirty-three years of age, managed his family's business interests and property, and did so in a most successful manner. The Elliott family fortunes had more than prospered under his hand. Why, even his father was pleased with the man Win had become. That this overly sensible woman with her sturdy shoes had—

"One never can, my lord." She started into the house, paying him no attention whatsoever. It was most annoying.

"As much as it pains me to admit it . . ." He stepped to her side. "I was not looking at your ankles as one can barely see them being blinded by the sight of the most horrendous shoes I have ever seen."

"I am not going to a ball," she said absently, her gaze scanning what was once the center part of the house. She turned toward him, opened the satchel—which required a bit of juggling on his part as she made no effort to take it from him— dug around in what looked to be a bottomless pit of a bag and withdrew a notebook and pencil. "And these are eminently practical for the task at hand."

"God save us all from practical shoes on the feet of a lovely woman," he said under his breath.

"I daresay God has more to worry about." She stepped farther into the house, then stopped and wrote something in her notebook. He tried to get a glimpse of what she'd written, but she shifted and hid the notebook from his sight. He wasn't sure if her movement was deliberate or not. Regardless, that too was annoying.

"This was the entry hall. The main stairway was immediately in front of us." He glanced upward. "As you can see the fire burned through the first and second floors, the attic and the roof. The roof was—"

"Do forgive me, Lord Stillwell, but I can indeed see the extent of the damage. In addition, your correspondence was quite specific on that score. Beyond that, the plans and drawings you sent give me an excellent picture as to what was lost. This center portion of the manor housed the ballroom and various parlors on the first floor, mostly servants' quarters on the upper floors and an assortment of offices for your staff on the ground floor."

"Well, yes, but—"

"So if you would be so good as to refrain from comment for a few moments, perhaps I can get on with my work." She smiled in a polite yet distinctly dismissive manner.

"Are you telling me to shut up?"

"Of course not, my lord." Again, her attention turned away from him. "That would be rude."

He stared at her. This would not do. This would not do at all. "Perhaps I should speak with Mr. Tempest directly."

"Who?" she said absently, scribbling something.

"Mr. Tempest? Your late husband's partner? The man I assume will be designing the house."

"Oh" She hesitated. "*That* Mr. Tempest."

He huffed. "Who did you think I meant?"

"Well, I suspect he has a father."

"Why on earth—"

"And possibly a brother as well, no doubt."

"Why would I want to speak with his father or his brother?" he said sharply.

She shrugged. "I have no idea."

"They why would you—"

"Clarification, my lord. I don't wish either of us to be confused as to precisely what you want." She glanced at him as if there were no doubt in her mind as to exactly who would be confused.

"What about Mr. Tempest?"

"What about him?"

He clenched his teeth and resisted the urge—no, the need—to raise his voice. Or perhaps to scream. He was not, under ordinary circumstances, given to displays of temper. Indeed, he considered himself rather a jovial sort. The type of man much more inclined toward laughter than fits of anger. But then he had never come up against Lady Garret before. She would try the patience of even the saintliest of men. "I think I should speak to him about the rebuilding."

"I'm afraid that's not possible." She gazed

upward at the missing floors and roof, then jotted down another notation.

He forced himself to take a calming breath. "Why not?"

"Mr. Tempest is quite brilliant and considers himself an artist. He never meets with clients. Indeed, he's extremely reclusive and scarcely ever makes an appearance in public. Why, I myself have only dealt with him through notes and, of course, his drawings and plans. Oh, how does he put it?" She thought for a moment. "He feels it hinders his creativity, interferes with his muse he says, to deal with the more mundane aspects of a project. Or the world for that matter."

"Mundane?" he sputtered. He never sputtered. This blasted woman had him sputtering. "I would not call the reconstruction of Fairborough Hall mundane."

"Nor would I. So you needn't give it another thought as you won't be dealing with Mr. Tempest but with me or perhaps Mr. Clarke." She paused to take another note, then looked at him. "Is that a problem?"

"Well, I—"

"You were sent references and our reputation is excellent. I should think that would be enough." Lady Garret nodded and continued her inspection of the damaged building.

She had him there. He and Gray had both made inquiries and had found nothing but glowing recommendations as to the work of Garret and Tempest. It was a small firm but well respected.

He trailed after her, not unlike a dog on a leash, and managed to keep his mouth shut for a good minute or two. Admittedly, it was not in his nature to silently follow after a woman. "You do understand, I wish Fairborough Hall to be returned to its original state?"

"You mentioned that in your correspondence."

"And rebuilding must proceed as quickly as possible?"

"You mentioned that as well."

"Time is of the essence," he said firmly. "Every year in late June, Fairborough plays host to a Midsummer Ball. It's rather difficult to have a ball without a ballroom."

"One would think."

"It's to be exceptionally important this year as it will celebrate the Queen's Jubilee." He lowered his voice in a confidential manner. "In addition, I have it on very good authority that Queen Victoria herself might wish to attend."

"She would not find this at all amusing," Lady Garret murmured.

"So you can see why haste is of the utmost importance. The other firms . . ." The moment the words left his mouth he realized his mistake.

Lady Garret stopped and turned toward him. "The other firms?"

There was nothing to be done for it then but to

confess. "Yes, well, we did inquire as to the availability of other firms."

"Oh?"

He chose his words with care although, at this point, it would make no difference. "Most were not able to even begin work until late in the summer."

"I see."

"Those that could were unwilling to take on a project of this nature, given the urgency we require." So much for having the upper hand. It was never wise in business to let whomever one negotiated with know they were one's only valid option. Obviously, his sense of discretion evaporated in the face of a sensible woman in sturdy shoes. "They could not guarantee the project would be completed—"

"Nor can I, Lord Stillwell," she said firmly. "This is an enormous undertaking and the time in which you wish to have it accomplished is insufficient." She snapped her notebook shut and stepped closer to him. He held out the satchel obediently. Good Lord, she had him trained! "We would certainly bring all our resources to bear, and do everything humanly possible, but I cannot—I will not—guarantee completion by late June." She slipped the notebook and her pencil into the bag, took it and the tube from him and nodded. "Good day, my lord." She started toward the door.

"Where are you going?"

"Back to London, of course," she said over her

shoulder. "It seems pointless to linger as we cannot accomplish what you require."

"Wait." The woman had him as surely as if she had reached between his legs and grabbed him firmly by his privates.

She paused in mid-step. He really didn't have a choice and she knew it. "I shall double whatever you intend to charge for your services."

"Not including the actual cost of construction, of course."

He winced. "Of course."

"Even without a guarantee?"

He could practically feel her hand tighten and he had the most ridiculous desire to shift his weight from foot to foot. He couldn't see her face, but he was certain there was an all-too-smug smile curving her lips. He heaved a resigned sigh. "Yes, yes. Some progress is better than nothing, I suppose."

She turned back to him, amusement twinkling in her eyes. "Are you quite certain, my lord?"

"At the moment, I'm not quite certain of my own name." He stepped closer and once again relieved her of her bag and tube. "You're very good at this sort of thing, aren't you?"

"Am I?" She opened the satchel and retrieved her pencil and notebook. "I really can't say. I've never done this sort of thing before."

"You may rest assured, Lady Garret, you're very good at it." His voice was a bit sharper than he had intended, but there was nothing he liked less than losing. And while he wasn't sure what game they had just played there was no doubt in his mind he had lost it. "I've agreed to pay you twice your usual commission without any guarantee as to completion, you have me carrying your things and . . ."

"And?"

"And . . . and I will not say another word unless you require it of me."

"Excellent, then let us return to the task at hand." She cast him the first genuine smile of the day. Her eyes were definitely brown with little specks of gold. Really quite lovely. She started off again, then looked back at him. "Oh, and I do thank you for the compliment."

He shrugged. "As I said, you're very good at this."

"That too, but a few minutes ago you referred to either me or my feet as lovely."

"Oh." Damnation, he had forgotten about that. "Yes, of course."

"Goodness, my lord." She shook her head. "A compliment does tend to lose its effectiveness if it's just something one says."

"I shall keep that in mind."

"My, you are a rogue, aren't you?" she added under her breath.

Win stifled a frustrated sigh and resigned himself to following behind her and keeping his mouth shut. She had already made up her mind about him based on nothing more than gossip, a reputation he had very nearly grown out of and an insincere compliment. Even if, in that one moment when she'd been more amused than efficient, she had been far lovelier than he had first thought and he suspected her feet were lovely as well. Not that he planned to find out for himself. Not that he cared. Not about her smile or the color of her eyes and certainly not about her feet. Still, it did appear that this woman was about to become part of his life for the foreseeable future. He was putting his heritage in the hands of her Mr. Tempest after all.

For the next hour or so, he followed her like a well-trained puppy, answering her questions without additional comment. It was a pity, really; he was quite good at witty conversation. He considered it something of an art. Yet another of his charms that would be wasted on Lady Garret.

He did have to admit, she was much more intelligent than he would have expected. Not that he didn't generally appreciate intelligence in a woman. Why, there was nothing he enjoyed more than verbal dueling with a clever woman. But that was different. Lady Garret's questions were to the point and displayed knowledge of architecture and construction he would have found impressive even in a man. The woman might well know what she was doing, which made her all the more annoying and surprisingly a matter of some curiosity. There was obviously more to Lady Garret than first appeared.

At last he escorted her back to the carriage for the return ride to the train station. He handed her the satchel and tube—she never did reveal what was in the blasted thing. He assumed it contained the drawings and plans he had originally sent to her, but for all he knew she had simply lugged it along to appear more efficient. Not that she needed help in that respect.

"I have all I need for the moment, Lord Stillwell," she said, accompanied again by her polite smile. "Tomorrow, there will be men here to take accurate measurements."

"I sent you measurements and I assure you they are quite accurate."

She raised a brow.

He forced a weak smile. "But of course you will want your own. What is it they say? Measure twice, cut once?"

"Quite right." She nodded. "Once those are in hand, I daresay I will have detailed plans ready for your approval by next week."

"You mean Mr. Tempest will have the plans ready?"

"Isn't that what I said?"

He started to correct her, then thought better of it. "Yes, of course."

She paused before climbing into the carriage

and glanced past him for a final look at the manor. "You were right, my lord."

"Was I?" He brightened. It would be nice to be right about something in this woman's eyes. "About what?"

"You were extremely fortunate, all things considered." Her voice softened. "It's a grand house and it will be my—*our*—honor to bring it back to its former glory."

"Thank you, Lady Garret," he said simply, surprised at the pleasure her comment brought him. "We have a house in the city, of course, but Fairborough Hall is—well, it's been my family's true home for generations. I hope it will be home for those generations yet to come."

"We shall make certain of it." Her brisk manner had returned. She climbed into the carriage and he closed the door after her. "Oh." She leaned slightly out the window. "There was one other thing you were right about."

"Twice in one day?" he said wryly. "Whoever would have imagined?"

"Not I." For the second time today, a genuine smile curved her lips. Amusement glittered in her eyes and the most charming dimple appeared at the corner of her mouth. "But, practical though they may be, my shoes are indeed the most horrendous ever created." She leaned back in the carriage seat and signaled to the driver. "Good day, my lord."

"Good day, Lady Garret."

The carriage rolled off and Win stared after it thoughtfully.

He did like to know who he was dealing with. After all, this woman—and her elusive Mr. Tempest—had the future of Fairborough Hall in their hands. He was not about to put the fate of his family's home in the keeping of a woman about whom he had more questions than answers.

While he considered himself an excellent judge of character, he had long ago faced the fact that that particular skill was only accurate in regard to men. He had no idea how to correctly assess the character of women, a lesson painfully learned through the course of three failed engagements. But even he could see there was definitely much more to the prim, efficient Lady Garret than one might at first suspect. Some of her comments simply did not ring true. This was a woman who was hiding more than she revealed.

Which only raised the question of what did she have to hide?

And what would it take to find out?

Chapter 3

"I want to know everything there is to know about Lady Garret." Win paced the floor of the library at Millworth Manor.

"I thought you wished to know everything

there is to know about Garret and Tempest?" Gray's mild tone did nothing to disguise the pointed nature of his question.

"That's what I said," Win snapped, then caught himself. He was not normally a surly sort. Even in the days immediately following the fire, when even the best natured of men might well be surly, he had managed to regain his usual good humor. But a blazing inferno was a flickering match when compared to that woman. He could lay the blame for his current mood squarely at the sturdily shod feet of Lady Garret.

"What you said was that you wish to know everything about Lady Garret, not Garret and Tempest."

"You must have misheard me." Win waved off the comment.

"My hearing is excellent."

"Then I misspoke. You can't blame me. The woman lingers in one's mind. Lurking. Ready to pounce at the first opportunity."

"Like an unrepentant melody?"

"More like the taste of a new dish that one isn't certain one likes because it's so obviously good for the digestion."

Gray laughed.

Win paused in mid-step and glared at him. "This is not amusing. We are trusting this woman, and her eccentric Mr. Tempest, with the future of Fairborough Hall. If we muck it up, generations yet to come will look back at this very moment. They will say, 'There, that's when it happened.' " He shook a pointed finger at his cousin. " 'That's when that idiot viscount handed the rebuilding of Fairborough Hall off to that overbearing female.' I shall be known throughout all eternity as the man who allowed a woman to destroy his family's heritage."

Gray choked back yet another laugh. "You're being absurd."

"Am I?" Win said darkly. "We shall see. One never does give due credence to a prophet in his own time, you know."

"You're blowing this out of all proportion. I thought you would get over it by now. If anything you're more overwrought today than after you met with her yesterday."

"I've had time to think. Mark my words, Gray, that woman is —well, I don't know what she is exactly beyond annoying and superior and con-descending and far too intelligent—for a woman, that is." Win narrowed his eyes. "Do you know she has surveyors and men taking measurements at the hall even as we speak?"

Gray gasped. "Oh no, not that. Do you mean to tell me the vile woman is . . ." He paused for dramatic emphasis. "Efficient? Competent? Even, dare I say it, organized?"

Win glared at the other man. For a moment he wished they were boys again and he could take his cousin outside and thrash him thoroughly. Or rather attempt to thrash him, as they had always been evenly matched.

"You're just irritated because she got the upper hand with you yesterday."

"I allowed her to have the upper hand." Win sniffed. "It was part of my plan."

Gray grinned. "You don't have a plan."

"No, but if I did this would be part of it." He resumed pacing, but it didn't quite help his concentration as it usually did. No doubt because the library at Millworth Manor was not where he usually paced.

His family had arranged to lease the manor through the summer as it was no more than a half hour ride from Fairborough Hall. The owners, Lord and Lady Bristow, had decided to travel the Continent together in an effort to reacquaint themselves with one another after a lengthy separation. A separation in which most of the world believed Lord Bristow to be dead and, apparently, Lady Bristow simply wished he was.

"I am not used to dealing with women in matters of a business nature. Women should not be involved in business."

"I thought she explained that to you."

"She did, but . . ." Win shook his head. "Something about her explanation struck me as being . . . not a lie exactly, more like a half-truth. The woman is definitely hiding something."

"You said that yesterday."

"It cannot be said often enough."

"And you know this because you are so very good at recognizing when a woman is hiding something?"

"Well, I should be, shouldn't I?"

"One would think," Gray said under his breath in a not too subtle allusion to Win's three engagements.

Gray had been out of the country for years and had not witnessed firsthand his cousin's previous failures to wed. Although they corresponded regularly, Win had never written in detail about his ill-fated betrothals. He had made no mention of the third at all. Since Gray's return to England a few months ago, the cousins had spent long hours, with the appropriate libation in hand, discussing the various incidents, as well as all else that had happened in their respective lives. Win was able now to see the humor inherent in each engagement: the lady who had decided she would much rather marry a man with better prospects, the female who had considered him entirely too lighthearted to be a suitable husband and the very sweet young woman who was unfortunately in love with someone else.

"I did think you liked intelligent women."

"I do, under most circumstances." Win paused. He much preferred women who were clever and witty. Who could match him barb for barb.

Although he had long considered the idea that that might have been where he had made his mistakes in the past. A less intelligent woman was far more likely to agree with him, to see things his way. Still, in his experience, women who weren't clever weren't especially interesting either. Did he really wish to spend the rest of his life bored out of his mind? "What I dislike is a woman who makes me feel stupid. Who looks at me in a pitiful manner as if I were a child who can barely understand two words."

"I see." Gray was obviously once again holding back laughter. At least one of them was amused by all this. "Then you found her annoying because she is more intelligent than you and took no pains to hide it?"

"She is most certainly not *more* intelligent. Possibly *as* intelligent but definitely not *more*. It's ridiculous to even think such a thing. She is a woman after all." As much as Win liked women in general the very idea of a woman being more intelligent than a man was absurd.

"I wouldn't let Aunt Margaret hear you say that." Gray shuddered.

"Because I am indeed an intelligent man, I would never allow her to do so," Win said in a lofty manner, then thought for a moment. "It was the surprise, I think. Lady Garret caught me unawares. I simply wasn't prepared for a woman —for her. I shall be better prepared for our next meeting."

"Then you wish to continue with Garret and Tempest?" Gray studied him closely. "In spite of the indomitable Lady Garret?"

Win blew a resigned breath and sank into the chair that matched Gray's. "I don't see any other option."

"We could hire someone else, you know."

"No one else can take this on in as timely a manner." Win shook his head. "I don't want Fairborough Hall moldering in disrepair for the next six months. I want rebuilding to begin as soon as possible." He aimed an accusing look at his cousin. "Pity you won't be here to keep an eye on the work with me."

"I am sorry, Win, but I do have to return to America. There are matters I need to settle before I can again make England my home."

Gray had left some eleven years ago to make his fortune, and make it he had. His varied investments in shipping and railroads and imports had made him almost obscenely wealthy. Win had followed his lead and had vastly increased the Elliott family fortunes as well.

"I will make every effort to conclude my business as quickly as possible. I plan to be gone no longer than a month and less if all goes well."

"Hopefully, we should be nearing completion by your return and you will have missed it all."

"With any luck at all." Gray grinned. "But Lady

Garret did say she could not guarantee completion by late June and I intend to be back by then."

"Their references were excellent," Win said under his breath. He wasn't sure if he was trying to convince Gray or himself.

"Then it seems to me dealing with Lady Garret is a small enough price to pay," Gray said slowly.

"Yes, I suppose."

Gray leaned forward and met his cousin's gaze firmly. "What is it about this woman, Win? You've always been very good at handling women. In spite of any number of misdeeds I can name, there wasn't a single governess who came through this house that didn't vow you were the most delightful charge she had ever had. Growing up, you managed to avoid consequences of questionable behavior by dint of little more than your charming nature and your irresistibly wicked smile. It drove me quite mad, I can tell you."

"My apologies," Win said wryly.

"Why, I can recall seeing you wrap even the most formidable mothers of fresh-faced virgins around your little finger. And that despite an already somewhat wicked reputation."

"Well . . ." Win smiled modestly. What could he say? His cousin was right.

"The fine art of managing women has been a skill, no, a talent, even a natural gift of yours since you were a boy. Women of any age have always been putty in your hands. As long as you don't ask them to marry you, that is." Laughter gleamed in Gray's eyes.

Win snorted back a laugh. "That does seem to be my undoing." He thought for a moment. "I don't know why I found Lady Garret so annoying. I did make every attempt to be most charming and even, perhaps, a bit flirtatious. She would have none of it."

"No doubt that is precisely why you found her annoying." Lady Lydingham, Camille, swept into the library and the cousins rose to their feet at once.

Camille's parents owned Millworth Manor, and while they had invited the Elliott family to stay as their guests in their absence, Win's father had insisted they lease the manor instead. He was well aware of the costs of maintaining a country house. Camille and Gray had been engaged since Christmas. Win was fairly confident this was one wedding that would indeed take place, although why they were waiting until autumn to wed made no sense to him. The more time one gave a woman to ponder anything—especially marriage—the more time she had to reconsider. Still, in hindsight, in his experience, that had ultimately been for the best.

"Are you helping Winfield reach a rational, intelligent conclusion?" Camille moved to Gray's side and Win suspected would have kissed him in a most improper manner had Win not been present. From the look in Gray's eyes, he thought the same. "Or has his absurd and unreasonable dislike of Lady Garret vanquished all possibility of rational, intelligent behavior?"

"You know me so well, Camille." Win flashed her a smile.

"You are a dashing devil, one does have to give you that," Camille said in a reluctant manner although, until recently, Camille had barely spoken to him at all. "I can't imagine any woman not falling prey to your dubious charms."

"And what of me?" Gray cast her an offended look. "Am I not a dashing devil with dubious charms?"

"You always have been, Grayson," she said in an overly prim manner as if now, having decided to marry him, she should observe certain rules of society. But there was a subtle gleam in her eye when she looked at Gray that hinted that her thoughts were anything but proper.

"I do wish you would stop looking at him like that." Win glared at his cousin's intended.

"Like what?" Innocence rang in Camille's voice belying the wicked look in her eyes.

"Like he was a cake and you had a passion for sweets!" Win huffed.

"I like it." Gray cast his fiancée a wicked smile of his own.

"Oh, but I do have a passion for sweets," Camille said with a pleasant smile.

Win stifled a groan. Not that he wasn't happy for his cousin; he was delighted that Gray and Camille had found one another again after years apart. And delighted as well that Gray was so annoyingly happy. Admittedly he might be a touch envious that Gray had found what Win had not, but now was not the time to dwell on what he didn't have.

"She's a Hadley-Attwater, you know," Camille said abruptly.

Gray frowned in confusion. "Who?"

"Lady Garret, of course. She's the youngest of the Hadley-Attwater brood." She glanced at Win. "Weren't you friends with one of the sons?"

"Sebastian." He nodded. "Sir Sebastian now. We had some grand times together before he went off to explore the world. I haven't seen him in years." Perhaps it was time to renew that acquaintance. "What else do you know about his sister?"

"Nothing really." Camille shrugged. "I don't know her at all save to nod a greeting to in passing. Beryl would know more."

"And isn't that surprising?" Gray murmured.

Win bit back a grin. Beryl was Camille's twin and she was not at all fond of Gray. If there was one thing Win didn't envy his cousin about it was his future sister-in-law. Not that Win and Beryl hadn't always gotten on well together. Indeed, Beryl might well have been his first fiancée had things worked out in a different manner. But though he did enjoy sparring with the lady even now, they never would have suited. That was a marriage that would have been disastrous for them both. One would surely have killed the other.

"Beryl makes it a point to know whatever there is to know. It can be most beneficial. And what she doesn't know, she knows how to find out." She studied Win curiously. "Do you really want to know everything there is to know about Lady Garret?"

"About Garret and Tempest," Gray said.

Camille raised a disbelieving brow.

"Indeed I do. About both the firm and the lady."

"If that is the case . . ." Camille smiled as if she and Win were now somehow coconspirators. "Beryl has hired an excellent investigator in the past. I should be happy to give you his name."

Gray's gaze shifted between his fiancée and his cousin. "I must confess, there is something about the two of you in agreement that is not in the natural order of things."

"Nonsense. I am most appreciative of your assistance, Camille." Win's jaw tightened. "Only a fool fails to know precisely with whom he is dealing. And, while I may be many things, I am not a fool."

Even if Lady Garret disagreed.

62

Chapter 4

"What do you think?" Miranda's gaze scanned the drawing she had clipped to the mechanical drafting table John had purchased when he started the firm.

"Well . . ." Clara studied the rendering for Fairborough Hall thoughtfully. "If Lord Stillwell does indeed want his house returned to its original state, I would say you have come fairly close. However . . ." She leaned closer and narrowed her eyes. "There are differences, aren't there?"

"One can't possibly duplicate a three hundred-year-old structure exactly. One has to make allowances for progress." Miranda tried and failed to hide a note of pride in her voice. While in some ways reconstruction of an old building was easier than building anew, in many others it was more of a challenge. Especially when your charge was to recreate the past. "We are nearing the twentieth century after all."

"And is Lord Stillwell a progressive sort?"

"Lord Stillwell is a twit."

"Be that as it may . . ." Clara choked back a laugh. "He is a twit with a great deal of money."

"Which makes him a valued client although no less of a twit."

"I do so appreciate the manner in which you speak your mind." Clara chuckled.

"I do so appreciate that you allow me to do so." Miranda returned the other woman's grin. She did tend to keep her thoughts to herself when around others, especially her family. Life was so much easier that way.

But the blatant honesty she and Clara shared was a mark of their friendship. A friendship that neither woman could have foreseen. Indeed, they would never have met at all, and certainly never have become friends, had it not been for the deaths of Miranda's husband and Clara's brother. Her brother's demise, combined with her recent discovery that her fiancé was not the man she'd thought he was, had left Clara wanting a change in her life. It was she who had approached Miranda about employment with Garret and Tempest. Now, she was the only person completely in Miranda's confidence.

"Other than that unfortunate business about his being a twit, how did you find Lord Stillwell?" Clara's eyes shone with curiosity. "Aside from a brief conversation when you returned from Fairborough, you've not stepped foot in the office. And even then you were preoccupied. We've had no time to talk since your meeting with him."

"Admittedly, I've been consumed with this." Miranda's gaze returned to her drawing. It had long seemed wise to do what work she could in the privacy of her own home. While her employees certainly knew the truth about who the firm's true architect was—and had probably known even before John's death—by unspoken agreement, her position was not flaunted. In the four days since her initial meeting with Lord Stillwell, she'd only spoken to Clara once and that had been brief. "Lord Stillwell wishes to have Fairborough rebuilt as quickly as possible. And, as he is paying us twice our usual fees, I should like to accommodate him as much as is possible." She slanted a look at the other woman. "His glowing recommendation would serve us well in the future."

"Nor do I have the least doubt we shall earn that. Now . . ." An impatient note sounded in Clara's voice. "Tell me about the man himself. I am dying to know what he is really like. He's rumored to be quite handsome and charming."

"And it would appear he knows it," Miranda said in a wry manner. She skirted between her desk and Emmett's and settled in her usual chair.

The room was entirely too small for both desks and the mechanical table, but it was private. The remainder of the Garret and Tempest offices consisted of a small reception room, with a desk for Clara, and a much larger room with wall-to-wall windows along one side, providing excellent light for the draftsmen. It was on the top floor of a commercial building on a quiet street in

Holborn, an area neither fashionable nor disreputable.

"He actually attempted to flirt with me. Some nonsense about the sin of ugly shoes on a lovely woman."

"My God, not that!" Clara crossed her arms over her chest in mock indignation. "The fiend."

"It's not amusing, Clara."

"Oh, but I suspect it was."

Miranda stared for a moment, then grinned. "Well, perhaps it was a little amusing. He is obviously the type of man who expects women to fall at his feet when he directs that wicked smile of his toward them."

"Oh?" Clara's brow rose. "He has a wicked smile, does he?"

"A very well-rehearsed wicked smile. I would wager the man practices in the mirror."

Clara laughed. "I assume you put him in his place."

"Not in so many words, but I had work to accomplish." Miranda shrugged. "And he was being bothersome. Annoying, really." Even so, she might have been a bit harsh toward him, but she had wanted to appear serious and professional. It would not have done at all to respond to his flirtation, for him to think her frivolous. Not that she had flirted at all in recent years and, upon reflection, his flirtation had been minimal. The oddest thought struck her that he certainly could have made more of an effort. Not that she cared. "Although, to give the man his due, he was not expecting a woman. He was obviously taken aback by my arrival."

Clara's brow furrowed. "Will that be a problem?"

"Not for me." A satisfied smile curved her lips. "He was nonplussed, but I quite enjoyed it. I think the key to handling Lord Stillwell might well be to keep him off balance and somewhat confused."

"Do we really want to confuse a client?"

"This one we do."

"Still—"

"It's not as if we are going to recreate the Taj Mahal in place of Fairborough Hall." Miranda waved off Clara's concern. "We're going to give him exactly what he wants for the most part, with a few improvements that will ultimately make his house and his life better." Miranda thought for a moment. "It's all a matter of, oh, bringing the horse to water as it were."

"And then what? Holding his head under?"

"If necessary." Miranda grinned, then sobered. "But this is a great opportunity for us, Clara. The largest project we have undertaken thus far. It might well be a model for everything we do in the future. A model of . . . modernization."

"Which brings me back to my original question." Clara studied her closely. "Is Lord Stillwell a progressive sort?"

"Lord Stillwell is—"

"Don't say a twit," Clara warned. "We have already established that."

"I wasn't, although it does bear repeating. I was going to say Lord Stillwell is—or rather appears to be—a bit old-fashioned. Although, admittedly, my opinion is based on little more than his desire to recreate the manor precisely as it once was and his reaction to my presence. I could certainly be mistaken. However . . ." Miranda grimaced. "I am fairly certain he would withdraw his commission at once were he to learn that a woman was behind the designs for the building." She met the other woman's gaze. "He could well ruin us."

"Then we shall have to take every precaution to ensure that does not happen," Clara said staunchly.

"Indeed we shall, and Lord Stillwell has handed us the way to do exactly that."

"He has?"

"He has indeed." Excitement bubbled up inside Miranda. "He has given me a brilliant idea."

"Oh, I do love your brilliant ideas." Clara leaned closer and lowered her voice. "Don't keep me in suspense. What is it?"

"When I told him that John had passed on, Lord Stillwell wanted to speak to Mr. Tempest, who he assumed would be designing the hall."

"Because of the name of the firm?"

"Exactly." Miranda nodded. "I couldn't very

well tell him there is no Mr. Tempest. Or at least not one anyone here has ever seen."

"What did you tell him?"

"I told him Mr. Tempest never meets with clients as he is a bit eccentric, considers himself an artist and lives in fear of alienating his muse or some such nonsense. In fact, I said I've never even met the man, which is entirely true."

"And he believed you?" Doubt sounded in Clara's voice.

"Every word." Miranda couldn't resist a smug smile. "So I propose we continue to allow him to believe his architect is the elusive Mr. Tempest and . . ."

"And?"

"And this is the brilliant part." Miranda leaned forward in her chair and met her friend's gaze firmly.

"Go on then."

"And we allow clients in the future to believe that as well." Miranda finished with a flourish.

"We do?" Clara said slowly.

"Of course we do." Miranda's words came faster with the rush of her thoughts. "When I wasn't occupied with the plans themselves, this idea that Lord Stillwell set in motion has been fermenting, as it were, in the back of my mind. It makes perfect, and dare I say, brilliant sense."

"Then be so good as to explain it to me."

"We have never had anyone specifically ask

the name of our architect. Indeed, Mr. Clarke has dissembled on that point, on more than one occasion attributing our work—"

"*Your* work."

"The work of the firm to, oh, a joint effort, as it were. But if we allow people to believe Mr. Tempest is the chief architect, a man who never appears in public—"

"My God, that is brilliant." Clara's eyes widened. "We should have thought of it years ago."

"I can't believe we didn't." Miranda grinned with triumph. "If we lead people to believe Mr. Tempest is the architect no one will ever suspect the truth."

"And the danger of—wait." Clara stared. "But what of the real Mr. Tempest?"

Miranda shrugged. "What of him?"

"I daresay he would not approve of this."

"I daresay he will never know." Miranda ticked the points off on her fingers. "The man has never stepped foot in this office. John never met him. I have never met him. Whoever he is, he's not known in society. Why, we have no idea who the man really is. His name might not even be Tempest for all we know. He is, and always has been, a silent investor."

"There is that," Clara murmured.

"As long as we continue to meet our monthly financial obligation to him, I see no reason why he would object or interfere. Besides, and I do think this is the most important point, the only caveat to his investment—aside from repayment—was that Tempest be included in the firm's name. Which leads me to believe he would not be at all averse to allowing the world to think he is the archi-tectural talent at the heart of Garret and Tempest. Well?" Miranda held her breath. "Do you agree?"

"It does solve a lot of problems. It would certainly make life less difficult if we could defer to Mr. Tempest rather than avoid specifics as much as we have had to," Clara said thoughtfully.

"Exactly."

"All in all, I have to agree." Clara grinned. "It is brilliant."

"I thought so." Miranda stood, stepped up to the drawings, dipped a pen in ink and signed the drawings *Tempest* with a flourish and a satisfied smile. "And we have Lord Stillwell to thank."

"From what you have said, I can't imagine he would want our thanks."

"Oh, I suspect Lord Stillwell wants any number of things he doesn't know he wants yet."

Clara glanced at the drawings. "Are you talking about the hall?"

"For the most part."

"Need I remind you that no matter what you are in private, in public you remain the very respectable widowed Lady Garret?"

"Of course not." Miranda scoffed. "I could never forget that."

"Then what—"

"A man like Lord Stillwell is used to being in charge or thinking he is. He is also obviously used to being on the winning end of a proposition."

"And?" Caution sounded in Clara's voice.

"And I was not amenable at all to his attempts to be charming. I daresay it was most disconcerting for him."

Clara's eyes narrowed. "Go on."

"Therefore, when next we meet, I am going to be more, oh, shall we say willing in my dealings with him from now on."

Clara gasped. "You're going to allow him to seduce you?"

"Don't be absurd." Miranda brushed away Clara's comment. "I am simply going to allow him to think he is making progress in that direction. Allow him to think his flirtation might well bear fruit. It has been my observation that there is nothing easier to manage than a man who thinks he is moments away from getting you into his bed. A man who is confident of his own success thinks he is in control."

"You can't possibly—"

"Oh, but I can. Or at least I think I can. I never have, but I fully intend to." Miranda nodded firmly. "You must admit this is almost as brilliant an idea as that of giving substance to Mr. Tempest."

"I suspect its brilliance is yet to be determined." She thought for a moment. "It doesn't seem quite fair to use his arrogance as a weapon against him."

"Perhaps not, but one could say if he was not overly arrogant to begin with, there would be no weapon to use."

"Regardless, do take care with him. Overly charming men with wicked smiles are not to be trusted." Clara's fiancé had been charming with a wicked, irresistible smile. Unfortunately, Clara was not the only one he had cast his dubious charms upon. As it happened, the man had two other fiancées as well as a marriage of questionable legality.

"Oh, I would never trust him." Miranda's gaze strayed back to her rendering of Fairborough Hall. "But I do hope to gain a modicum of his trust. And convince him to accept—no, embrace —progress, the way of the future."

"As long as progress is all he embraces."

"Believe me, Clara, I have no interest in Lord Stillwell as anything other than as a client." Although Miranda did concede, if only to herself, the man was indeed quite dashing with all that dark hair and those blue eyes that flashed with annoyance or amusement. And what woman didn't appreciate a man who was tall and broad-shouldered and spoke of his family home with affection and pride. Then, of course, there was that wicked smile of his, which Miranda could see, under the right circumstances, might well be lethal. Even to a woman of business. "But I am determined to prepare Fairborough Hall for the future and bring Lord Stillwell along with it."

"Kicking and screaming, no doubt."

"If necessary." Miranda paused. "If I do it correctly, he'll think it was his idea."

"Perhaps." Clara studied the drawing. "I daresay he'll go along with the improvements in plumbing and heating, but this . . ." She tapped the drawing with her finger. "This might be rather more difficult."

"Admittedly, convincing him will be a challenge, but I have no doubt even an old-fashioned sort of man will ultimately see that if one does not move forward, one will surely be left behind. A grand old lady like Fairborough Hall does need to keep up with the times, and this is the perfect opportunity. I intend to help her do just that, even if it means allowing Lord Stillwell to think he has me in the palm of his hand, figuratively of course. When we are finished, Fairborough Hall will be restored to her original grandeur and prepared for the future with modern improvements including plumbing and heating and, best of all . . ." Miranda grinned. "Electricity."

Chapter 5

"Electricity?" Win couldn't recall ever having stared at a woman as if she was insane before, but then he had never before met a woman one could truly call insane. Until now. "Electricity?"

"Yes, my lord, electricity," Lady Garret said as calmly as if she were discussing something of no more significance than whether to paint the entry hall green or blue. She glanced at the drawings and plans she had laid out on the large burled walnut table in the Millworth Manor library. "You have heard of it, haven't you?"

"Of course I have heard of it," he said sharply. "It's a natural phenomenon. A force of nature."

"My apologies, of course you have. I simply meant that perhaps you were not aware of its practical applications." She smiled pleasantly as if she hadn't just questioned his intelligence.

"I am not uninformed about such things. Indeed, I consider myself quite up-to-date on innovation and invention and the like. But because I am amused by a parlor trick, and indeed I have seen several employing the powers of electricity, does not make me wish to run out and have it in my house."

"How very interesting," Gray murmured, studying the plans. Win's parents had gathered around the table to peruse the designs Lady Garret had presented.

"One must look toward the future, Lord Stillwell," she said primly, her resemblance to a governess apparent once again. "One cannot be mired in the past. One must either move forward or . . ." Again she smiled that pleasant smile, as if she were smiling at one who understood neither the topic nor the language. "Step aside."

"I have no intention of stepping aside," he snapped.

Someone—either his father or his cousin—snorted with amusement.

"I didn't mean it the way it sounded." Win shot a scathing look at his relations. "Indeed, I consider myself extremely progressive."

"My mistake, my lord." Lady's Garret's eyes widened innocently. "And I do apologize once again. But surely you can see how I might think you were not especially concerned with modern amenities as you wanted the house rebuilt exactly as it was originally, some three hundred years ago. I simply assumed you were happy with the building and all that goes along with it."

"I am happy," he said in a firm tone. "I am exceptionally fond of this house and I want it put back the way it was. I don't think that is too much to ask."

"Not at all and we shall do our best although that may be something of a challenge." She shrugged. "It is not easy to replicate antiquated plumbing and insufficient heating."

"Oh dear," Mother murmured.

"Blasted plumbing," his father muttered. "Never does work right."

"I don't want antiquated plumbing and insufficient heat! My God, I am not an idiot." Although he certainly felt like one at the moment. It was entirely her fault. She made him feel this way and he didn't like it one bit. "Certainly, the mechanical systems of the house should be modernized."

"Excellent." She beamed at him. "Electricity it is then."

He stared at her in disbelief. "I didn't say that."

"It does seem to me that this is an opportunity we should consider carefully," his father said. "One can embrace tradition without being trapped by the past."

Win's gaze snapped to his father. "You are the most traditional man I have ever known."

"Indeed, I do value tradition and Fairborough Hall embodies the heritage of this family. I don't see that improvements and bringing it up-to-date would be detrimental to that tradition. We do have to live here, after all, as do generations to come. However . . ." His father met his gaze directly. "I am leaving this in your hands. You are the next caretaker of Fairborough and it should be your decision."

"Lord Salisbury has installed electricity at Hatfield House," his mother said helpfully.

"Lord Salisbury is an idiot!"

"And yet he is prime minister," Gray said in a casual manner.

"I believe you have made my point." Win snorted. "I hear he has trained his family—even his children—to throw cushions at the sparks his electricity creates to stifle potential fires. If I recall correctly, I heard as well about an unfortunate incident regarding the electrocution of his gardener."

"Oh, I should hate to lose the gardener." His mother's brow furrowed. "He has such an excellent way with the roses."

"I do not wish to rebuild only to have the house burn down again." Win met Lady Garret's gaze directly. "Am I clear on this?"

"Most certainly." She bit her bottom lip in a nervous manner. "I shall relay your concerns to Mr. Tempest. He will, of course, have to make some changes to the plans. It might take him some time . . ."

"Oh, but, Lady Garret, there really is no time to waste. The work must begin as soon as possible. We have a ball to arrange, you know. And the queen might possibly attend, which would be lovely. One always hopes for a visit from the queen, even if it is usually a great deal of trouble." Mother smiled at the other woman in a companionable manner as if they both belonged to some sort of secret, female club, then turned to her son and straightened her shoulders. "I, for one, quite like the idea of being at the forefront of progress. Therefore, I vote for electricity."

"I did not call for a vote!" It was hard to believe the woman who had given him birth had now turned against him. "This is my decision. There is no voting about it."

"I vote for electricity as well," Gray added.

"*Et tu, Brute?*" Win glared at his cousin.

"I just think she's right." Gray shrugged. "I think it's the way of the future."

Win snorted. "Or it could be a passing fad."

"Parts of London as well as New York are already lit with electricity," Gray said mildly.

"Father?" Win turned to the earl. "Do you intend to vote against me as well? Not that we are voting," he added.

His father shook his head. "I have no intention of voting. I said this was your decision and I meant it."

"Well, that's something, at any rate." Win looked from his father to Gray to his mother and finally to Lady Garret. "As much as I think it's wiser to bide our time and see where electricity may lead us . . ." His jaw clenched. "I will consider this and make my decision by tomorrow."

"Good." His father glanced at Lady Garret. "I,

for one, quite approve of what your Mr. Tempest has done here. I look forward to seeing these plans come to fruition. Now, I have other matters to attend to. Good day." He turned and strode from the room. In the back of his mind, Win noted with more than a little relief how much more vigorous his father now appeared than he had in the days after the fire.

"Uncle Roland." Gray started after him. "Might I have a word?" He paused and smiled at Lady Garret. "It was my pleasure, Lady Garret. I daresay we will meet again before the last nail is driven."

"No doubt, Mr. Elliott. It was a pleasure to make your acquaintance." She smiled what appeared to be a genuine smile. Good God, he was beginning to recognize the termagant's smiles.

"Lady Garret." Gray nodded, cast Win a chastising look, then hurried after his uncle.

"Electricity, how very exciting." Mother beamed. "I must say, I can't wait." She inclined her head toward the younger woman in a confidential manner. "I know my son claims to be a progressive sort, but in truth he does have a tendency to be something of a stick-in-the-mud."

"Mother!"

"Don't take that tone with me. You know full well it's true." Mother sniffed. "Not that I'm not pleased that you value our heritage, but, Winfield, dear, you do need to move with the times."

Win's jaw tightened. "I do move with the times."

It was obviously all Lady Garret could do to keep from laughing.

"Well, we shall see." Mother cast him an affectionate smile that did little to take the sting out of her assessment of his character. One could certainly value tradition without being a stick-in-the-mud. "Lady Garret, I know you and Winfield have matters to discuss, but would you join me for tea before you take the train back to London? I know your mother, but it's been a very long time since I've seen her."

The younger woman hesitated, then nodded in a gracious manner. "I should like nothing better."

"Excellent. When you are finished here then." She glanced at her son. "Do try to be pleasant."

"I am being pleasant!"

"My mistake then. I thought you were being rather stiff and stodgy and annoyed and just the tiniest bit outraged. I'm sure no one else noticed." His mother traded amused glances with the younger woman and took her leave.

He turned his attention to Lady Garret. "Wasn't I being pleasant?"

"I am sorry, my lord," she said at precisely the same time.

"What?" He stared at her.

"I was offering you my apology."

He narrowed his gaze. "For what?"

"I put you in an untenable position with your family even if that was not my intention." She shook her head and sighed. "I had no idea you would be so averse to the idea of modern—"

"I am not averse to the idea of modern anything! I wish all of you would stop saying that!" he snapped, then caught himself. What was this woman doing to him? She had him ranting like a lunatic. He inhaled deeply and mustered his composure. "It is I who owe you an apology. You simply caught me off-guard, that's all. I had never considered the idea of electricity at Fairborough Hall."

"And are you considering it now?"

"Yes, I suppose I am." He shook his head. "But I have any number of concerns about this."

She nodded. "To be expected of course."

"There is the danger of fire to consider." Good God, did he really sound that pompous? It was a logical concern and yet his tone was decidedly, well, pompous. "I mean, we must think about safety." Oh yes, that was better.

"I cannot guarantee nothing will go wrong in the future, but I can tell you there are strides being made almost daily to improve the safety of wiring in a house."

"That's something, I suppose."

"Admittedly, there is always a great deal that will be unknown about a new endeavor."

"Indeed there is." It struck him that she was

82

very much a new endeavor and there was entirely too much unknown about her. "I am not the sort of man to blindly plunge ahead into the unknown."

"I never imagined that you were."

"I admit, there was a time when I perhaps made decisions in a particularly hasty manner when I should have given matters greater thought. When I plunged ahead when I should have considered said plunging rationally. But I have learned any number of lessons on the foolishness of rash decisions."

She nodded. "And a wise man learns from his mistakes."

"One can only hope."

Her gaze met his. He could have sworn her eyes were brown. Today they were definitely that elusive hazel color. It was the lighting in the library, no doubt. "But isn't something new, something unknown, even something that one fears might be a tiny bit dangerous, isn't that worth the risk? Why, one could say that is what makes life exciting."

"One could say that." He smiled, albeit reluctantly. "I fear I am leaning—no, I have decided—in favor of electrification. God help us all."

She laughed. It was surprisingly delightful. "I daresay—"

He held up his hand to stop her. "If you were going to say God has more to worry about than electricity coursing through the walls of my ancestral home, I would most heartily disagree. I would hope God could spare a moment or two to keep us safe from the ravages of progress."

"I should think God would be amenable to that, especially as electricity is one of God's creations and man is simply harnessing it."

"That does sound simple," he said wryly.

"But I didn't finish my apology. I am sorry that I pitted you against the rest of your family. It wasn't at all fair and certainly not what I envisioned."

She sounded sincere enough and yet . . . "I don't believe you."

Her eyes widened. "Why on earth not?"

"Because you strike me as the kind of woman who gets what she wants and will use whatever means necessary to achieve it. Who will not back down from a position when she believes she is right."

Surprise shone in her eyes. "I do?"

"The very fact that you are here, representing your late husband's firm, is a testament to that."

"Is it?"

"Indeed it is." He crossed his arms over his chest. "It is most unbecoming in a female."

"Oh?" Her brow rose. "Which part? Getting what I want? Using whatever means necessary? Or refusing to retreat when I know I am right?"

"All of it!"

"And what do you think is becoming in a female?"

"A female who knows her place in the world is most becoming," he said in a lofty manner. Even as he said the words he knew they were a mistake. But something inside him—something quite irrational and probably extremely stupid—made him want to annoy her as much as she annoyed him.

"Her place in the world?" she repeated as if she couldn't quite believe his words.

Win had a difficult time believing them himself. Indeed, he had always preferred women with a bit of independence and intelligence to them, women who made up their own minds and forged their own paths even if that had proved his undoing on more than one occasion.

"And what would that place be?"

"At home. With her family. Not out and about espousing *electricity*."

Her brows drew together. "Do forgive me, my lord, for not meeting your standards of feminine behavior."

"You manipulated me, Lady Garret. I do not like being manipulated. I particularly dislike that you used my family to do it."

"And for that I have apologized. I shall not do so again."

"What? Apologize or manipulate?"

"I certainly won't apologize again." She turned

in a dismissive manner and considered the plans spread on the desk. "Is there anything else we should discuss today?"

Ha! Obviously she thought better of continuing a debate she could not possibly win. Good. If there was a score being kept—not that there was—he would have won a point. He moved closer and studied the drawings. "I quite like the way Mr. Tempest has expanded the dressing rooms and added additional water closets and bathing rooms, even in the wings. Especially those in the family quarters."

"Even if they are not original to the house?" she said under her breath.

"Even then."

"It did seem to make sense, while much of the building was under construction, to include and expand amenities."

"Very clever of Mr. Tempest." As much as he hated to admit it.

She glanced at him. "Dare I take that as a measure of satisfaction on your part?"

"You may. I confess I did not consider things like plumbing and water closets and certainly not electricity, but all in all, yes, I do find this more than acceptable."

"Excellent." She straightened and met his gaze firmly. "Our next step then is to hire workers, locally if possible. If you could arrange for your estate manager to meet with Mr. Clarke tomorrow,

I suspect he would be most helpful in that regard."

"Excellent idea." He nodded. "Dare I hope Mr. Clarke's personal difficulties have been resolved satisfactorily?"

She looked at him sharply. "You remember that?"

"I am not a cad, Lady Garret. Most would say I am both thoughtful and considerate. As well as sincere."

She smiled as if she had doubts on that score. Obviously she was going to need some convincing.

"I can also be charming and amusing."

"That really isn't—"

"I never mistreat the servants or those less fortunate. I support any number of worthy charities. And I am unfailingly kind to . . . to animals and children. Why, I can bring in several children from the village who will attest to that. I usually carry sweets in my pocket to hand out when I happen upon them."

"Oh, yes, that is good for them."

"And dogs. I'm very fond of dogs." He glanced around. "Even that nasty little worthless beast of my aunt's has been known to curl up at my feet."

"No doubt, but—"

"And should you ever meet that embarrassment to the canine world you will certainly understand why it takes the kindest of men to—"

"Lord Stillwell!"

"My apologies. There is something about that dog. . . ." He grimaced. "Neither here nor there, of course. Do go on."

"Very well. The Mr. Clarke, Emmett Clarke, you graciously inquired after is still unavailable to oversee construction. That task will be taken up by his brother, Mr. Edwin Clarke."

"Edwin and Emmett? Twins?"

"Not to my knowledge. They have a sister named Eloise as well."

"Their parents were exceptionally fond of the letter E then?" He chuckled.

"I have no idea." She looked at him as if he had grown two heads. So much for his effort at amusing conversation. "As I was saying, we have engaged this Mr. Clarke's services in the past. He is quite knowledgeable and does an excellent job. He will be here every day during the course of the project. Is there a cottage at Fairborough or on the grounds of Millworth or perhaps something available in the village where he can reside? It would be much more convenient if he could live in the area during construction."

Win nodded. "We can arrange something suitable."

"Excellent. As you have agreed to the plans, work can begin next week." She hesitated. "Oh, and I will be here as well, of course."

Win stared. "You?"

"Yes."

He narrowed his eyes. "Every day?"

"I should hate to see anything go wrong and it will certainly slow progress considerably if Mr. Clarke is forced to stop work to scurry into London to clarify a point. I assure you, I am well versed on Mr. Tempest's designs." She studied him coolly. "So yes, I would think I shall be here very nearly every day from the first day of construction until the last."

"I see." If she was to be here nearly every day from next week into the foreseeable future he had best try to get on better with her. Again. He forced his most charming smile. "We have not started out on the right foot, you and I."

"Do you think so?" Her eyes widened in feigned surprise. He didn't believe her for an instant. "I really hadn't noticed. I thought things were going quite well."

He studied her for a long moment. This woman was an enigma and an annoying one at that. More so now in her refusal to admit that they were barely cordial to one another.

"Obviously I was mistaken then." Regardless of whether she admitted it or not, they had clashed from the moment she had stepped into his life. "Do not think you have won any sort of battle here today, Lady Garret."

"Why, my lord, I would never think such a thing." Her voice was overly sweet and her lashes fluttered in a flirtatious manner. He ignored it.

"Good. As long as we understand one another I believe we can survive the next few months."

"I have no doubt of it."

"Because you haven't, you know," he said firmly.

Confusion crossed her face. "Won a battle, you mean?"

"Exactly."

"No, of course not." She paused. "Unless we are engaged in a war that I was unaware of ?"

"Not to my knowledge." Ha! There had been no outright declaration and it may not be all-out war, but there was certainly an ongoing skirmish between them, whether she wished to acknowledge it aloud or not.

"That is a relief as you don't strike me as the kind of man used to losing. Battles or wars, that is," she added.

"I'm not."

"Then we do understand one another." She cast him an unexpectedly brilliant smile and in that moment he realized he was wrong. She was far more than pretty in an ordinary way.

"Excellent." This was much better. Satisfaction washed through him. She was at last seeing things his way.

"And you have decided upon electrification?"

"Yes, I have," he said staunchly.

"I shall see you next week then. Good day, my lord." She smiled, nodded and left the library. But not before he saw the distinct touch of triumph and more than a little amusement in her eyes. Her definitely brown eyes.

"Good day," he murmured. The tiny morsel of satisfaction he had tasted a moment ago vanished with the swish of her skirts and the close of the library door.

Damnation, he hated losing a battle, a skirmish or a war—whether it was officially declared or not.

Chapter 6

"Life changes us all, doesn't it, Lady Garret?" Lady Fairborough sipped her tea and studied the younger woman.

"My apologies." Miranda cast her a polite smile. She had wanted to return to London as quickly as possible, but instead found herself sitting in a parlor with Lord Stillwell's mother making small talk, although she had the oddest feeling it was anything but small. Still, it would have been rude to turn down Lady Fairborough's request to join her for tea. It was still early in the day and Lady Fairborough might well be her strongest ally if she ultimately needed one. "I don't quite understand exactly what you mean."

"Really? And I would have imagined you understood far better than most of us given the way you have stepped forward to take the reins of your husband's business. To insure the livelihood of his employees." Lady Fairborough nodded approvingly. "I find it quite admirable. It's so very modern of you."

Miranda chuckled. "I suspect your son disagrees with you."

"He often does." A casual note sounded in her voice. "Does it matter? What my son thinks of you, that is?"

"No, but it does matter what he thinks of Garret and Tempest. My intention is to improve our reputation, not destroy it." Although, admittedly, it was bothersome that the blasted viscount, who was well known for his exploits with women, seemed to find her more annoying than appealing. Not that she cared. "As we will probably spend a great deal of time together, I should prefer not to waste that time arguing."

"Oh, but there is much to be said for arguing with the right man. Especially when you can make him see the error of his ways." She smiled in a completely wicked manner and Miranda could see the family resemblance between mother and son. "Don't you agree?"

"I really couldn't say."

The older woman's eyes widened in surprise. "Didn't you argue with your late husband?"

"My late husband and I were usually in agreement." Indeed, as she looked back on her years with John she could scarcely remember fighting with him at all although surely they must have on occasion. No, life with John seemed rather perfect in hindsight.

"How very interesting," Lady Fairborough murmured.

But then Miranda scarcely ever argued with anyone about anything. Until, of course, she had crossed paths with the annoying Lord Stillwell. She did have to admit, their clashes had left her somewhat invigorated. Not that he was the right man or anything near that.

"You must forgive Winfield, Lady Garret. He is not usually so . . . so . . ."

"Stiff and stodgy and annoyed and outraged?"

"Oh, I did say that, didn't I?" Lady Fairborough winced.

Miranda laughed. "Indeed you did. And you called him a stick-in-the-mud as well."

"Oh dear." She sighed. "The problem with having sons is that eventually they become men. One day they are sweet and adorable little boys and the next day they are men with all those annoying qualities men, particularly men of responsibility, tend to have." She met Miranda's gaze directly. "Winfield has a great deal of responsibility."

"Does he?"

"He does indeed." Lady Fairborough nodded firmly. "You see the plan was always to divide the family responsibilities between Grayson and Winfield, but Grayson instead went off to make his fortune in America. After a while, it was obvious to all of us that Winfield would have to carry on alone. Lord Fairborough has made a concerted effort through the years to ease him into the duties that will one day fall entirely on his shoulders. To that end, he has completely taken over the management of the family's properties and business investments. He takes his responsibilities quite seriously."

"So I see."

"He has done an excellent job of it. His father is quite proud of him. And for very nearly the first time in his life, my husband is free to do the things he enjoys. He has an outstanding collection of rare manuscripts and he can now spend a great deal of his time doing whatever it is he does with them." She leaned forward in a confidential manner. "I suspect he does little more than engage in correspondence with other collectors, either trying to purchase something new or boasting about what he has. Although there are a few manuscripts in Latin he has been trying to translate for years." She wrinkled her nose. "Pointless, really, as he was never good at Latin. Still, one does try to support one's husband's pursuits, futile though they may be."

"It is fortunate they were saved from the fire."

"Oh my, yes." She shuddered. "I don't even

want to think how devastated he would have been had they been destroyed. The things that we did lose were bad enough." She paused for a long moment and Miranda wondered if she was thinking about all those family treasures that were lost. "You must understand, Lady Garret, Winfield has not been the same since the fire."

"I suspect none of you are the same," Miranda said slowly. "I can't imagine how horrible it would be to lose those things that are irreplaceable."

"Life goes on though, doesn't it? And we must carry on to the best of our abilities."

"Of course."

"I never dreamed I would call Winfield stodgy or stiff." Lady Fairborough heaved a heartfelt sigh. "But his responsibilities seem to weigh heavier on him now than they did before the fire. It's to be expected, I suppose, but he's always been so lighthearted and amusing and witty. Women in particular have always found him charming. Extremely so."

"So I have heard," Miranda said dryly.

"Are you speaking of his reputation?"

"It's nothing more than gossip, mind you. There have been stories . . . here and there. . . ." Miranda's voice trailed off helplessly. It was one thing to discuss a man's amorous reputation with a friend and quite another to talk about it with his mother.

"I am well aware of them. Most of them, any-way. Although I daresay there could be those I have yet to hear of, which is probably for the best." Lady Fairborough chuckled. "He did have a bit of a misspent youth, but then what spirited young man doesn't?"

Miranda smiled weakly.

"However, he never acted dishonorably, he never ruined a young woman's life and he was never involved in any sort of unforgivable scandals. As far as I know, that is, and I daresay I would know." She shook her head. "You would be surprised at the delight some people take in telling you the most dreadful stories about your offspring. However, most of his dubious misdeeds are long behind him." She narrowed her eyes slightly. "Unless you are referring to his engage-ments, which admittedly have not cast him in the best light."

Miranda drew a deep breath. "One does wonder . . ."

"As is only natural." Lady Fairborough pressed her lips together in a firm line. "But things are not always as they appear, my dear."

"It's been my experience that they rarely are."

"How very wise of you to understand that." She refilled Miranda's cup. "The earl and I haven't been abroad in years. We intend to travel when all is settled here." She handed her back her cup. "Including our son."

"What do you mean by settled?"

"Oh, I don't know. Nothing in particular." She shrugged. "Grayson is home now and will soon be wed. I simply wish to see both of my boys settled and happy."

"As any mother would," Miranda said cautiously.

"Have you ever considered that there is something to be said for a wicked man?"

Miranda started. "Well, I—"

"Lord Fairborough was quite wicked when we first met." The countess stirred sugar into her cup. "I must tell you there is nothing more fun than having a wicked man."

Miranda choked on her tea.

"And then"—Lady Fairborough flashed a smug smile—"reforming him."

Miranda cleared her throat. "Forgive me for being blunt, but why are you telling me all this?"

"Why?" Lady Fairborough's eyes widened innocently. "No reason in particular, I suppose. I was simply making idle chatter. The mention of Winfield's engagements did lead me to think about wicked reputations in general and well, there you have it." She shrugged. "It does seem like forever since I had tea with a friend." She reached over and patted Miranda's hand. "And I do hope we will be friends."

Miranda smiled with relief. "I would like that."

"Now." The countess straightened and picked

up a biscuit. "You should try the biscuits, they are excellent."

Miranda selected a biscuit and took a bite. It was indeed very good.

"Do tell me the latest news about your family. I can't remember the last time I saw your mother. I read your brother's last book. I must say . . ."

The older lady chatted on and Miranda responded as needed. It was, all in all, the kind of chat she might have had with any friend or female relation although she couldn't quite dismiss the growing conviction that Lady Fairborough wanted nothing more than for her son to find fiancée number four and for whatever reason, she considered Miranda a suitable candidate. That was certainly not going to happen.

For one thing, he didn't especially seem to like her. Admittedly, every time he had made an attempt to be witty or charming she had cut him off. She wasn't entirely sure why. Although there were any number of reasons. Even though she had told Clara she intended to be more amenable to his lordship's charms she hadn't been able to bring herself to do so. Not that he had made any particular effort to charm her. Which was most annoying. But she did wish to appear professional and certainly Lord Stillwell would not flirt with her if she were a man.

Then there was that whole business about the appeal of a wicked man. She would never admit to Lady Fairborough that she had always rather wanted a man who was a bit wicked. Not that she would ever have one. She was not the type of woman to seek out a man of that nature, and they certainly didn't fall into her lap. She was not unattractive but considered herself more ordinary in appearance than truly pretty. Rakes and rogues did not attempt the seduction of women of ordinary appearance and reserved demeanor. Which was for the best, really. She wasn't nearly strong enough to handle such a creature and he would surely break her heart. She would much prefer to avoid that, thank you very much.

Still, his lordship had said she was the kind of woman who got what she wanted and would use whatever means necessary to do so. She'd never thought of herself that way. Indeed, she'd always thought she was rather weak-willed and acquiescent. His assessment had been surprising and most flattering, even if he obviously didn't mean it as a compliment. Perhaps she was changing, evolving as it were. Or perhaps she already had. It was a shocking idea and oddly satisfying.

Finally, Miranda gently but firmly insisted it was time for her to take her leave if she was to return to London at a reasonable hour.

"I quite enjoyed our little chat, Lady Garret. We shall have to do it again." Lady Fairborough accompanied her to the parlor door. "And do give my best to your mother."

"Lady Fairborough." Miranda chose her words with care. "Might I say something to you in the strictest confidence?"

"A secret?"

"More or less."

Lady Fairborough shook her head in a mournful manner. "Oh, I'm afraid I'm not very good at keeping secrets. Especially if it is a particularly juicy, scandalous secret. They simply beg to be passed on. Is it? Especially juicy and scandalous, that is?"

"No, not really." Perhaps if she underestimated the extent of the secret the older woman would be less inclined to share it. And in truth, as secrets went, this one was relatively minor. At least when compared with the pursuit of a divorce. Not that it mattered really. This particular secret's days were already numbered. "It's no more than mildly interesting."

"Oh." Lady Fairborough's face fell. "Well, I daresay I can keep that. Please, go on."

"My mother, and the rest of my family, have no idea of the extent of my involvement with Garret and Tempest. That I am here representing the firm."

"I see." Her eyes narrowed thoughtfully. "And you're afraid they will disapprove?"

"To my knowledge, there has never been a woman in my family engaged in business. I am unique in that regard. To be honest, I have no idea what my family's reaction might be." Without thinking, she squared her shoulders. "Not that it matters, really. Of course, now that I have taken Mr. Clarke's place on this project they will, no doubt, learn of this eventually, but I would prefer to tell them myself."

"Very courageous of you, my dear." Lady Fairborough nodded approvingly. "It's not easy to stand up to one's family. But, of course, you haven't done that yet, have you?"

The woman's pleasant smile took the bite out of her words.

Miranda smiled. "Apparently I'm not as courageous as you thought."

"Or you let your head lead your heart. It's very sensible of you." Her gaze locked with Miranda's. "Or very foolish."

"Excellent timing, Chapman." Win closed the library door behind him and waved his visitor to the chair positioned in front of the desk in the library. "Lady Garret left a good half an hour ago." He took his seat behind the desk and drew a deep breath. "Have you found out anything?"

"I have," Phineas Chapman said in a mild manner that seemed at odds with the man's reputation as a tenacious investigator. But then Win wasn't sure what he had expected. "However, it seems there are more questions than answers at this point."

Chapman was the stepbrother of Viscount Billingsworth. He had been raised alongside the large Billingsworth brood and was the youngest of the lot. Chapman was considered quite brilliant and had started out in scholarly endeavors. Apparently that life did not prove especially interesting and Chapman had turned his inquisitive mind to the ferreting out of secrets and locating that which had gone missing, be it an object of value or a person. He was both successful and discreet, which made him highly sought after by those in society who needed his services. Services which were, as well, not inexpensive. Win had learned all this before their first meeting from Camille, whose information as always came from Beryl. Win did like to know exactly who he was dealing with. Camille had also informed him that Chapman was quite dashing with dark hair and piercing green eyes, which was neither here nor there to Win but probably did come in handy in Chapman's line of work.

"Go on."

"Much of what I have found out is common knowledge and you probably already know it."

"Let's pretend I don't."

"Very well." Chapman pulled out a small notebook from an inner pocket of his coat and glanced at it. "Garret and Tempest was founded by Lady Garret's late husband. His brother, then Viscount Garret, was either unable or unwilling to provide the funding necessary for his younger brother's endeavor. A private investor, one Mr. Tempest, came forward with a sizable investment, thus funding the business."

Win stared. "Mr. Tempest is a financier then and not the architect?"

"My lord." Chapman met Win's gaze firmly. "I prefer to reveal my findings in a chronological manner, much as I prefer to consider them in progression. I find it much more conducive to reaching a logical conclusion. Therefore, may I continue?"

"Yes, well, I suppose. Go on then."

"Thank you. As I was saying, Mr. Tempest funded the company some nine years ago with the provision that the firm carry his name and, naturally, that he be repaid over time."

"Has the debt been repaid?"

Chapman raised a chastising brow.

"Yes, of course, you'll get to that."

"Now, as they say, the plot thickens. According to the original agreement between Mr. Tempest and Lord Garret—Mr. Garret at the time— repayment was to be made out of the firm's profits. According to what I have been able to discover, there were years when, after expenses and debts and salaries were met, there were no particular profits to speak of and no payments made to Mr. Tempest. In addition, it appears Lord Garret continued to borrow from Mr. Tempest and while the debt is no greater than the original sum, at the time of his lordship's death it was not considerably smaller. As far as I can determine, Lady Garret has no knowledge of this financial discrepancy."

Win started to ask why Mr. Tempest didn't demand payment but thought better of it and kept his mouth shut.

"It wasn't until a year after Lord Garret's death, when Lady Garret began to take an active role in the company, that regular monthly payments were made." He paused. "Even in those months when there were no profits to be had, she took money from her private funds, an inheritance from her family, some sort of trust, I believe, to make good on the debt. When there are profits, she not only makes that payment but she pays into an account she has set aside for her employees in the event the business fails and they lose their livelihood. Aside from Lady Garret, the firm has seven full-time employees, including a very attractive young woman, a Miss Clara West, who oversees the office and manages the accounts. She is the sister of the man who was killed with Lord Garret."

"And Mr. Tempest?"

"He is not an employee."

"I see," Win said slowly, then frowned. "No, I don't. Who is this Mr. Tempest?"

"At this point"—Chapman shrugged—"I have no idea."

"But he's the architect." Win got to his feet, strode across the library to the table, where the plans for Fairborough Hall were still spread out. "Right here." He tapped the drawing. "This is his signature. Admittedly, he has done an excellent job even if he is an advocate of electricity, for God's sakes. Surely there must be some record of him?"

"Not insofar as I have been able to determine. The man has covered his tracks exceptionally well. If his purpose is to remain anonymous, he has done a brilliant job of it. Payments from Lady Garret go through a series of solicitors and bank accounts." Chapman shook his head in an admiring manner. "I have not yet been able to get to the truth of it."

"But Lady Garret *said* he is the architect. At least I think she did." Win returned to his chair and sank into it. "It could be she simply implied it." He thought back over their conversations. "Nonetheless she did lead me to believe that. And I distinctly remember her saying that Mr. Tempest never meets with clients because it hinders his artistic creativity or something equally ridiculous."

"Regardless of what she might have said, I can find no evidence to support that. And, as far as I have been able to determine, no one at Garret and Tempest has ever met the man, including Lady Garret. Lord Stillwell." Chapman leaned forward and met Win's gaze directly. "I am fairly certain that not only is Mr. Tempest not your architect, but I am beginning to suspect as well that he does not exist at all."

Win stared. "How is that possible? He invested in Garret and Tempest."

"Someone invested in Garret and Tempest. Someone who has gone to a great deal of trouble to make certain his identity remains unknown." Chapman paused. "I'm not certain this information is pertinent to what you specifically wanted to know. Do you wish me to pursue this line of inquiry?"

Win waved off the question. "I don't particularly care about who funded Garret and Tempest one way or the other, but I do want to know in whose hands I have placed the future of Fairborough Hall. And I want to know if and why Lady Garret found it necessary to deceive me."

"Then you wish me to uncover the name of the architect?"

Win nodded. "I do indeed and as quickly as possible."

Chapman studied him. "Might I ask why? I have found nothing to indicate Garret and Tempest's references are not legitimate. The firm has a good reputation. If you are happy with the work, does it matter?"

"Perhaps not, but I do like to know exactly who I am dealing with. I hate to be taken for a fool, and frankly, at this point, I am feeling extremely foolish." He had been right all along. Lady Garret was hiding something. "What can you tell me about Lady Garret?"

"Unless one considers the question of Mr. Tempest, Lady Garret appears to be something of an open book." He thought for a moment. "She is the youngest sister of the Earl of Waterston. She married John Garret, the brother of Viscount Garret, at the age of nineteen. They met at a lecture and shared a mutual interest in architecture. He inherited his title a few months before his death. His death was due to the collapse of scaffolding during the construction of a house his firm had designed just outside of London.

"Lady Garret has never been the subject of gossip, nor has she ever been implicated in scandal of any sort. While she has been involved in charitable work, she is not known to support more liberal causes, suffrage for women and that sort of thing. Indeed, among people who know her family she is considered the quietest and most reserved of the lot."

"Ha!" Win snorted.

"Ha?"

"Then she has changed, Chapman." He shook his head. "The Lady Garret you describe is not the woman I have been dealing with."

"Oh?"

"The Lady Garret of my acquaintance is

determined and stubborn and entirely more outspoken than is seemly in a properly bred female." He drummed his fingers on the desk. "She's not the least bit quiet, and reserved is the last thing I would call her. She is one of those women who charges ahead, mowing over anyone foolish enough to stand in her way. And she regards me as an idiot."

"Not that, my lord."

Win ignored the tone in Chapman's voice that did seem to imply, at this particular moment, that the other man agreed with Lady Garret. "This is not a personal matter, Mr. Chapman, it's a matter of business. I have entrusted my family's home to her firm, and I want to make certain it is in good hands. Lady Garret is hiding something, and I want to know what it is." He rose to his feet. "Do I make myself clear?"

"Perfectly, my lord." Chapman stood. "I shall do my utmost to find the answers you seek." He considered Win thoughtfully. "If I might make a suggestion?"

"Go on."

"From what you have said, I gather you and Lady Garret do not see eye to eye."

"You gathered that, did you?"

"One does not need a great deal of investigative insight to reach that conclusion. However, you have a certain reputation for being most charming with the ladies." A look flashed through the man's eyes as if he wondered what on earth they saw in Win. "It has been my experience that women tend to respond more readily to pleasantries and charm than direct confrontation."

"Not this one," Win said under his breath.

"Perhaps you have not given that direction the proper amount of effort. Honey as opposed to vinegar, as it were."

Win stared at the other man. Chapman was right, of course. It was obvious and yet . . .

What on earth had gotten into him? Now that he thought about it, he hadn't felt quite up to snuff since the fire. As if something of himself, something of his soul, had gone up in flames with his home. Perhaps he had been mourning and hadn't realized it. Silly, of course. The house could be—would be—rebuilt. But he had, as well, been burdened with any number of concerns as a result of the fire. He had been worried about his father's health, about finding places for those servants temporarily displaced, about rebuilding and about an endless array of unforeseen problems that piled up one on top of the other when one's house had burned. But his father was fine and all else had been resolved. Even with the questions that remained about Lady Garret, Chapman had confirmed her company's reliability. No, Win had matters—he had life—well in hand at this point. A familiar sense of confidence, the feeling that he could handle anything life had in store, surged through him. By God, he felt good.

Chapman was right on another score as well. Win had rarely met a woman he couldn't charm. He had forgotten that. One curt word from Lady Garret and he had practically rolled over and surrendered, like a dog hoping to be scratched. Well, that was at an end. He was Winfield Elliott, Viscount Stillwell and heir to the Earl of Fairborough. He was a dashing figure of a man and well known for his wit as well as his charm. Men liked him and women usually adored him. And aside from three fiancées who had decided for various reasons that he did not suit, he could name any number of other women who thought he was an engaging companion and quite a catch. Why, he had spent very nearly as much of his life being pursued as he had in pursuit.

"You're absolutely right, Chapman." He cast the other man a confident grin. "Honey it is then. You look for the answers I need in your way, and I shall endeavor to find them in mine."

"Excellent, my lord." Chapman nodded. "Then if that is all?"

"I am curious though." He glanced at the notebook in Chapman's hand. "Aside from when you opened your notebook, you never looked at it. Tell me." Win flashed him his most engaging smile. "There's nothing written in that book, is there?"

Chapman hesitated, then grinned. "No, my lord, there isn't."

"Then why have it?"

"My clients seem to expect that I would rely on something beyond my mind although I have no need to. The notebook seems to reassure them."

"Very clever, Mr. Chapman." Win chuckled.

"I know, my lord."

A few minutes later Chapman took his leave with assurances that he would contact Win as soon as he had something to report. He had already given Win a great deal to consider.

The fact that Lady Garret was providing for the future well-being of her employees spoke well of her. No matter what secrets she might be hiding, that alone eased Win's concerns.

In a few days construction would begin, Lady Garret would return and Win would put every effort into winning her over. He had absolutely no doubt the tide of this war had turned.

He had never met a woman yet who wasn't extremely fond of honey.

Chapter 7

There was something to be said for being at the center of a storm.

Miranda stood on the front lawn of Fairborough Hall and braced her hands on a rough, temporary table, no more than boards positioned on saw-horses, with a copy of the working plans tacked to it. She gazed around with satisfaction, a certain amount of excitement and more than a little pride. No matter that Mr. Clarke—Edwin—was in charge of construction or that the fictional Mr. Tempest had the credit for the design, this was her venture. Certainly, it was not the first project she had designed nor was it the first time she had been on the site of the construction—she had on occasion accompanied John—but somehow this was different.

Everywhere she looked, men hurried to and fro unloading wagons of freshly cut timber, carrying buckets of tools, nails and other supplies. Edwin directed them with the skill of an accomplished orchestra conductor.

They were fortunate to have engaged the services of Edwin. His presence was a practical necessity. Even if her employees were willing to work for a woman it would be unseemly for her to manage the construction site herself. Aside from the fact that she was smart enough to know she did not have that particular skill, men who worked in the construction trades would never have taken direction from a woman, no matter how well they were paid. She and Clara had agreed with Emmett that hiring his brother to oversee construction was the best course of action. Besides, it left Emmett free to remain at the

London office without having to worry about what might be happening here.

Edwin Clarke was a large man, skilled in construction and adept at handling the myriad details of a job like this. The man knew what he was doing. He was friendly and jovial as well, and even on this first day she could see he already had the loyalty and trust of the dozen or so men he had hired thus far.

"It's a good day to begin, don't you think?" a voice said behind her.

She straightened and turned. "Good day, Lord Stillwell."

"Lady Garret." He pulled a deep breath as if savoring the crisp, fresh air. "It is indeed a good day—no, a glorious day. There is nothing better than spring in England and no more appropriate time to start something new than this season of new beginnings. Don't you agree?"

"I do." She nodded, then paused. "Although, as I have never experienced spring anywhere else, I have nothing to compare it with."

"What? No travels through Europe? No grand tour?"

"I'm afraid not."

"I thought these days every well-bred young lady of good family made a grand tour. I have long suspected it was a requirement. A rite of passage, as it were."

"Unfortunately, not for me." She thought for a

minute. "I recall there were plans, but my father died and life was unsettled for a while. I then married my husband and, well, travel somehow eluded me."

"Would you like to travel?"

She shrugged. "Someday perhaps."

"Where?" He studied her closely, as if he really wanted to know. "What in the vast world do you long to see, Lady Garret?"

"Oh, there really isn't . . . Greece," she said without thinking. "I should like to see the ruins of ancient Greece." Her voice rang with unexpected determination. "I should like to see for myself what remains of those magnificent edifices built when the rest of the world was not yet civilized. I should like to stand in the Acropolis and gaze upon the Parthenon and imagine what it must have looked like when it was new and not ravaged by man and the ages. Oh, I have seen the marbles at the British Museum, but it's not . . . not enough."

"How very interesting," he murmured.

"Utter nonsense, really." Her face warmed and she pulled her gaze from his to study the house. She couldn't recall ever having told anyone that before and it was a bit embarrassing that she had told him. That she had revealed something so personal, something that had only ever been a dream. But, until now, no one had ever thought to ask. Even John, who had shared her love of architecture, had never asked if she wished to see the fabled ruins in person. She had no idea why she had told this man. The words had simply come of their own accord. "Well, however appealing the thought of Greece might be, here and now, there is work to be done." She adopted a firm tone. "The sun is shining and the skies are clear. We should make a good day of it."

"I like your optimism, Lady Garret." He grinned, a surprisingly infectious grin. Odd that she hadn't noticed before.

"I see no need not to be optimistic today, my lord." She returned his grin and a startled look crossed his face. But then he wasn't expecting her to be anything other than guarded, polite and somewhat curt.

In the week since she'd last been here, she had done a great deal of thinking. Not merely about the deception she was perpetrating on Lord Stillwell. That was done of necessity and would ultimately serve him well as he would get exactly what he wanted. And while she did not consider herself the type of person prone to deception, it did seem, even before John's death, that she'd been engaging in relatively innocent deceptions more and more. She had allowed John to take credit for her work and now she was allowing Mr. Tempest to do so. Certainly no one was harmed by her deceptions, but they were dishonest nonetheless.

Nor had she been especially honest with her family either. It had been remarkably easy to escape undue notice in the Hadley-Attwater household if one was the youngest, was discreet and kept one's mouth shut. She had learned that at an early age. It was John who had allowed her to do—no, *to be*—exactly who she was. Not that she was especially evasive with her family. She simply kept her affairs to herself. It was time— past time, really—to tell them of her work although the courage Lady Fairborough had thought she had did seem to falter when it came to her family. Still, she was resolved to make a clean breast of it with them. Sooner rather than later. Not today and probably not tomorrow, but definitely soon.

She wondered now, if it had been so easy to be herself with John, why wasn't it easy with others? Perhaps it came from being the only ordinary member of a family in which everyone else was far more than ordinary. Perhaps that was why the courage Lady Fairborough had spoken of was lacking. And perhaps, just possibly, it was time to turn over a new leaf. To stop being concerned as to what other people might think. To stop being afraid. Even if she was the family's most ordinary member, Hadley-Attwaters were never afraid. Past time as well to accept that heritage.

And perhaps the place to start was with the reputedly wicked Lord Stillwell. Even if, oddly enough, he didn't scare her at all.

"I didn't expect to see you here today."

"This is my home, Lady Garret and I am intensely interested in everything concerning it. Although my other responsibilities preclude my being here every day." He smiled down at her. His eyes were a deep shade of blue and twinkled with amusement. She hadn't noticed that before either. "I do hope I can count on you to keep me informed of the progress."

"I consider that part of my responsibilities. As the representative of Garret and Tempest," she added.

"It looks like your Mr. Clarke—Edwin?"

She nodded.

"It appears he has things well in hand." Lord Stillwell's gaze wandered over the activity. "It's really quite impressive."

"It's only the first day, but indeed all is going well." Satisfaction sounded in her voice.

"How long have you been here?"

"I took the first train this morning." As Fairborough was only an hour by train from London, there were several trains during the day. "You're fortunate to have such frequent service available."

He nodded. "It makes residing in the country much more convenient. While we do have a house in town I much prefer it here." He studied her in a casual manner. "Have you eaten?"

"Not since this morning," she said absently, watching workers lay out framing.

"It's well past noon, you know."

"Is it?" She'd been entirely too busy to note the passage of time. "I hadn't realized."

"You should have something to eat," he said sternly. "I would not want you to faint dead away from hunger."

She laughed. "I daresay that won't happen."

"One never knows." He shook his head. "Can you imagine what it might do to my reputation should it become known that women were fainting away at my feet?"

"I daresay it would only enhance it."

He laughed. "It could do with some enhancing. I haven't enhanced it for years."

She glanced at him. "Haven't you?"

"I'm afraid not." He shook his head in a mournful manner. "I fear I have been otherwise occupied."

"So your mother says."

"Good Lord." He groaned. "I dare not ask you what else my mother has said about me."

"That's probably best."

"Lady Garret." A formal note sounded in his voice that belied the smile in his eyes. "In an effort to keep you from utter starvation and collapsing at my feet, as much as it would invigorate a reputation that is sorely in need of it, would you do me the honor of joining me for luncheon?"

"Oh, I couldn't possibly join you." She looked

around. "It would take entirely too much time to go to Millworth Manor and back."

"I have no intention of taking you to the manor, and you have my word you'll be gone no more than an hour."

"Oh, but I—"

"Lady Garret," he said firmly. "Am I or am I not a valued client of Garret and Tempest?"

"Of course, but—"

"And do you not wish to keep your clients happy?"

"Certainly, but—"

"It would make me extremely happy if you were to join me for lunch." Again he smiled and it struck her that if indeed it was wicked, it was also natural and nearly impossible to resist. "I promise to be on my best behavior. I know going off unescorted with a man of my dubious reputation—"

She laughed.

"—might seem unwise but I assure you I do not ravish women who are weak from hunger."

Pity. Where on earth did that thought come from?

"Well . . ." She studied him for a moment. She could certainly be wrong, but while there might be a certain wickedness about him, she suspected he was a good man as well. After all, he did give candy to children. "I admit I am hungry."

"Excellent."

"And as I have your word."

"You do."

"But I should tell Edwin that I am leaving." She took a step away, then looked back at him. Well, why not? Hadn't she told Clara she intended to be more flirtatious? It wasn't as if anything would come of it after all. "Don't you want my promise?"

"Your promise?"

"That *I* will not ravish *you*."

"Why, Lady Garret, I'm shocked." He gasped and clapped his hand over his heart. "I would never hold you to such a promise."

He flashed his wicked grin again and her stomach did something unexpected and the oddest feeling of anticipation washed through her. As if this was the beginning of something quite wonderful. It was absurd, of course, but no less delightful for the absurdity of it.

She laughed and set off to find Edwin. She had never been especially flirtatious as a girl. Her sisters, Bianca in particular, had flirted enough for all of them. She couldn't remember flirting with John at all. They had been kindred spirits very nearly from the first moment they'd met and flirtation hadn't been necessary. If pressed she would say she couldn't remember how to flirt if indeed she'd ever known.

But this was a different Miranda Hadley-Attwater Garret. Why, hadn't she decided to turn over a new leaf ? Besides, flirting with the man was almost as much fun as arguing with him.

Lord Stillwell was right.

It was indeed a glorious day on which to begin something new.

Chapter 8

"Dare I ask where you are taking me?"

"If I told you it wouldn't be a surprise." Win smiled at Lady Garret, who was seated beside him in the gig he had driven from Millworth. The idea to spirit her away for lunch had been brewing since his last talk with Chapman. It was innocent enough; even the stalwart Lady Garret could scarcely view it as a seductive overture, although admittedly there had been occasions when he had intended a picnic to be exactly that. No, this was the first step toward conquering Lady Garret's resistance, carning her trust, even her friendship and learning her secrets. "And I think it would be best if this was a surprise."

"Oh dear. That sounds somewhat daunting."

"It's not, not at all." He paused. "In truth, it's always been one of my favorite places on the estate."

"Now I am intrigued."

"And I think, with your love of architecture, you'll appreciate it."

"My love of architecture?" Caution edged her voice. "Why would you say that?"

"It's obvious. At least to me." He glanced at her. Her smile remained, but her shoulders had tensed. How very odd. "You are conversant enough with Mr. Tempest's plans not only to understand them but to explain them to the rest of us. No one is that well versed in a subject they don't enjoy. Especially a subject that complicated. Believe me, Lady Garret, when I say that while I consider myself an intelligent man and I am competent in any number of areas, when I look at those drawings I cannot make head nor tail out of them."

She relaxed beside him. "Admittedly, plans can be confusing. I can explain them more thoroughly if you like."

"No, no, you have done an excellent job. Besides, I think it's part of your charge as the representative of Garret and Tempest to take me by the hand and lead me along the path to the new, modernized Fairborough Hall."

She chuckled. "You are adapting surprisingly well to that path."

"Who would have imagined?" He grinned at her.

"Not I. Especially as you think I should not be here at all."

"I never said that."

"Not in those precise words. How did you say

it?" She thought for a moment. "Ah, yes. You said my representation of Garret and Tempest was unbecoming. That my place was at home."

He winced. "I said that, did I?"

"And with a great deal of conviction."

"I hope you won't hold that against me."

"Oh, but I will."

"And if I apologize?"

"If your apology is sincere."

"I'll have you know I rarely make insincere apologies," he said staunchly. "If I have reached the conclusion that I was wrong, then I am more than willing to admit it."

"I see. And were you wrong?"

"I was certainly wrong to be so adamant, so pompous."

"But you do believe a woman has no place in business and should remain at home."

"I think . . ." He chose his words carefully. "All of us— male or female—have our own reasons for deciding to do what we feel we must. Or perhaps what we want. We must be content with our choices, with choosing the course of action we feel is right, whether or not other people agree."

Her eyes narrowed slightly. "What an excellent answer, my lord. It certainly wasn't the answer to my question but a good answer nonetheless."

"Thank you." He grinned. "Oh, my mother asked that I give you this." He pulled a note from his waistcoat pocket and handed it to her.

"And you have quite deftly changed the subject." She accepted the note and unfolded it.

"Clever of me, wasn't it?"

"But then you are a very clever man," she said under her breath. It did not sound like a compliment.

"Well?"

"Well, this is interesting."

"Has she invited you for tea again?" He pulled the carriage to a halt, hopped out and circled around to help her down.

"In a manner of speaking." She refolded the note, reached out to accept the offer of his hand and allowed him to help her out of the gig. Her attire today was far more casual than at their previous meetings. With the exception of her dreadful shoes—which seemed to be permanently attached to her feet—her apparel had always been moderately fashionable, if reserved, and perfectly proper, as it was today. It was simply more practical in style, almost as if she intended to pick up a hammer herself. He wouldn't put it past her. Her gloved hand fit nicely in his and the vaguest hint of loss washed through him when she pulled her hand away. She looked around. "I'm afraid I don't see much in terms of architectural interest. Although the trees and road appear structurally sound."

"We're not there yet." He pulled a basket from the back of the gig.

She raised a brow. "A picnic, my lord?"

"It did seem a shame to waste a fine spring day on nothing but work."

She stared at him for a moment, then nodded, and he had the distinct impression she had made some sort of decision. She smiled. "It does indeed."

He returned her smile. Thus far, this was going better than he had hoped, but then Lady Garret's manner was somehow different today. And most delightful.

"It's just down this path."

She eyed the narrow path warily. "Why don't you go first?"

"Excellent idea." He started down the path and looked back at her over his shoulder. "I never thought I would admit to this, but those shoes of yours should serve you well today."

"They are sensible."

"That's not all they are." He chuckled. "I do apologize that the path is not smoother, but it's scarcely used. Indeed there wasn't a path here at all until a few years ago. The only way to get to where we are going was on horseback or by foot. But I decided a path to the road would be convenient."

"Convenient to what?"

"You shall see." They walked on for a few more minutes until the path opened up. He stepped aside and allowed her to precede him. Then held his breath.

"Oh my." Lady Garret stared at the small structure centered in the clearing.

"Do you like it?"

"It's lovely." Her eyes widened and she stepped closer. "It looks like a Grecian temple."

Six stone columns on a six-sided base supported a domed roof. Stone benches curved between two pairs of columns. The building nestled amidst flowering spring blossoms and a neatly manicured lawn. A ray of sunlight peeked through the trees and cast the small structure in a radiant glow. He bit back a satisfied grin. Perfect.

"I daresay it's more someone's idea of a Greek temple and probably not at all accurate. It's a folly, really."

"I've always loved follies." She ran her hand up one of the columns. "It's marble, isn't it?"

"I believe so." He had loved this building and this spot from the time he had first found it as a boy. "It was built some two hundred years ago."

"The columns are ionic," she murmured. "It's really quite . . ." She glanced at him. "Magical, isn't it?"

"I've always thought so." He smiled. "If one is here at night, depending on the time of year, one might see fireflies flitting about like dancing fairies."

"How very whimsical of you, my lord."

"I can be very whimsical." He paused. "When I was a boy I thought this surely was where Titania and Oberon and all of the fairies lived. I was convinced they came out at night to frolic in the clearing."

She nodded. "Because of the Grecian style of the folly and the fact that *A Midsummer Night's Dream* is set outside Athens?"

"Not really. More because I hoped to catch one and I believed this was the best place to do that." He lowered his voice in a confidential manner. "They're supposed to grant wishes, you see."

"Ah, yes. Well, of course." She nodded solemnly. "I can see where that might be useful."

He heaved a theatrical sigh. "I never did catch a fairy."

"And you never got your wish." Sympathy sounded in her voice, but her eyes twinkled with amusement.

"However, I have not given up."

"On catching a fairy?"

"On getting a wish." His gaze caught hers and they laughed in unison. He liked her laugh. Better yet, he liked making her laugh.

"And what would you wish for?"

"It changes from day to day, I suppose." Win waved her into the folly. "When I was a little boy I wanted to fly."

"In a balloon, you mean." She stepped into the folly and settled on one of the benches.

"No." He scoffed and moved to the opposite bench. "I wanted wings. I thought flying would be

127

a most convenient way to get about. And, of course, as my cousin wouldn't have wings, I could lord my wings over him."

"I see. And now what do you wish for?"

"Well, I would still like wings, however I do now understand the impracticality of such appendages."

"So your wishes have become more practical?"

"We all grow up, Lady Garret." He set the basket down and opened it. "For one thing, I wish my tailor would be more accurate with my measurements."

She laughed.

"I assure you, ill-fitting trousers are not the least bit amusing."

He peered into the basket. He had no idea what Cook might have prepared, but he was confident it would be excellent even if she was unused to the kitchen at Millworth. Win wasn't alone in trying to adjust to the changes in life wrought by the fire. But Cook had always enjoyed preparing a special basket for him and whatever guest he might have. This was not his first picnic.

"No doubt. Anything else?"

"A month ago, I would have said I wished Fairborough had not burned."

"And now?"

"Now . . ." He shrugged. "I still wish that, but there's nothing to be done about it so it's a wish wasted."

"It does seem a shame to waste a wish."

He glanced at her. "I'll have you know, I am not the sort of man to waste a wish."

"I never imagined you were." She trailed her fingers over the stone bench. "This is really a lovely surprise. Thank you for bringing me here."

"In truth, I was going to bring you to the lake. But then you mentioned Greece and this seemed especially appropriate."

"I'm not sure why I mentioned Greece except that you asked and, well, I've never told anyone else. It's a silly dream, really."

"Then I am honored that you confided in me." He met her gaze and smiled into her eyes. Today, in the sunlight, they had a distinct green cast to them as if she were a nymph of ancient Greece transported to England, or a creature of the forest who danced with fairies. "Dreams, Lady Garret, are never utter nonsense."

For a long moment they stared at one another. He couldn't pull his gaze from hers. Nor did he wish to. For one brief instant he wanted nothing more than to lose himself in those eyes of hers.

At last she cleared her throat and smiled politely. "So, do you bring a lot of ladies here?"

"No." He cast her a sharp look and the moment vanished. "This is not the sort of place I bring women for purposes of seduction."

"I didn't mean to imply . . ."

He arched a skeptical brow.

"My apologies," she murmured.

"And the last time I did bring a lady here, well, let us just say she did not share your appreciation. Some people look at a folly and see no more than an error in judgment, a frivolity. I do not share this with everyone."

"I see," she said in a weak voice that was nonetheless gratifying.

"The folly was in an awful state of disrepair until about five or six years ago. I'm afraid we had neglected it dreadfully." He pulled out a large, cloth-wrapped bundle. Sliced ham probably, and entirely more than was needed. He set it aside. "I decided then it was too, well, special to be allowed to fall to pieces."

"Where would the fairies frolic if it was gone?"

"Exactly." There was as well bread and cheese, cake and—he noted with satisfaction—a jar of honeyed fruit. "So I had it repaired and I had the path made to make it easier for the gardeners." He gazed between the columns and surveyed the clearing. In spite of the distraction of the fire this year, Win was delighted to note the gardeners had not forgotten the folly. "This is the first time I've been here this season. They've done an excellent job."

"It is really quite beautiful."

"Aha. I thought as much." He pulled out a heavy, wrapped bottle, still cold from the cellar. "Champagne."

"For luncheon?"

"Why not?"

"Because it goes straight to my head and I would much prefer to have my head clear for the remainder of the day."

"You have my solemn promise, Lady Garret, that should I notice you becoming the least bit tipsy, I shall wrench the cup from your hand and dispose of it." He raised his chin bravely. "Even if that means I shall drink it myself."

"You are too kind, my lord." She studied him for a moment. "Why not indeed?"

She stood and crossed the folly to the basket. Plates, utensils and glasses were strapped to the inner sides of the wicker container. She unfastened the glasses while he opened the champagne.

He filled their glasses, then raised his in a toast. "To the successful rebuilding of Fairborough Hall and all that goes with it."

She raised her cup. "Including electrification."

"Including electrification." He sighed. "God help us all."

She took a sip of the wine. "You do not capitulate easily, do you, my lord?"

"In that I suspect we have much in common," he said wryly. "Now then, if we do not eat nearly every morsel that Cook has prepared, I warn you there will be hell to pay. And it will take the form of tough roast beef and undercooked potatoes."

"We can't have that."

They filled their plates and settled on opposite benches to partake of Cook's offerings. Lady Garret ate with enthusiasm; she had indeed been hungry. The food was excellent and he would have to remember to commend Cook.

When she had nearly finished she sat back and sighed with satisfaction. "Excellent, my lord. Really very good."

"I shall give your compliments to Cook."

"Please do." She looked around. "How did this folly come to be here? It's a rather inconvenient location, isn't it?"

"Deliberately so." He wiped his hands with a serviette and tossed it into the basket. "There's one exactly like it on the grounds of Millworth Park. That one was built by the owner for his wife, a testament to their love. This one was built as a surprise by his son, Thomas, for the daughter of the owner of Fairborough. Her name was Anne. They were very much in love, you see."

"What a romantic tale."

"Unfortunately, all did not end well." He shook his head. "He was reported to be lost at sea but she never believed it. She pined away for him and died just days before he returned."

"Oh my." Sympathy shone in her eyes. "How very sad."

"He died right here shortly after his return. Some say by his own hand, others suspected foul play. They're buried here near the folly although exactly where is unknown. Ironic as this is where they were supposed to be married." He paused for a moment. He had always enjoyed telling this story, but today it seemed entirely too tragic. "It is said the lovers were reunited in death and . . ." He braced himself. The last time he had told a woman this she had thought he was a lunatic. "There have been reports of their presence here and in the folly at Millworth."

Her eyes widened. "Ghosts?"

He nodded.

"How intriguing." She stared in fascination. "Have you ever seen them?"

He hesitated, then nodded.

"Did you really?"

"It was years ago." He shrugged as if it was of no importance, as if this sort of thing happened every day. "My cousin and I both saw them."

"How fascinating." She leaned forward eagerly. "Tell me, what did they look like?"

"They looked like . . . ghosts."

"Could you see through them?"

"They weren't entirely transparent, but they weren't completely solid either."

She nodded. "Understandable, of course."

"Anne was a beautiful young woman. One of the portraits Mother saved from the fire was of her."

"I should love to see it." Her eyes narrowed thoughtfully. "Do you think we could get them back?"

He started. "What do you mean 'get them back'?"

"I mean have you ever thought of having a séance?"

"Here?" Now who was the lunatic?

"This would be the perfect spot for it. This is where Thomas died and where he and Anne were supposed to be married. No wonder they returned. I mean, I certainly would."

He stared in disbelief. "I thought you of all people would think this was absurd."

She straightened with surprise. "Why?"

"Well, you're so very rational and sensible."

"Yes, I suppose."

"No-nonsense, really. Even if you don't say a word, one can see that from the way you dress."

"Are you talking about my shoes again?"

"Aside from your shoes . . ." He shuddered. "Your clothing is eminently practical. Why, one can see you're a woman who values function over silly things like fashion."

"Am I?"

"Efficient and competent as well."

"I do try," she said slowly.

"And assertive." He nodded. "Unyielding, really. Forceful even."

"Assertive?" Her eyes narrowed. "Unyielding?"

"Why until today, I have felt that I was in the company of a governess." The words were out before he could stop them.

She sucked in a shocked breath. "A governess?"

"I always quite liked my governesses," he said quickly, not that it made matters any better.

She rose to her feet. "Aside from a few rather terse conversations, you know nothing about me, my lord."

"I know you like architecture." He stood.

"Oh, and that was difficult to determine, wasn't it?" She downed the remaining champagne in her glass, collected the plates and other items they had scattered around, and fairly threw them into the basket.

"Lady Garret —"

She slammed the lid of the basket closed. He didn't think it was possible to slam wicker, but she managed it.

"I didn't mean to offend you."

"And yet you have."

"I don't know why you're so upset. It's not as if I said you were dull or ordinary."

"Oh, and I do thank you for that. Sensible, rational, assertive and unyielding are so very much better. For a governess!"

"Miranda—"

She whirled to face him. "Don't you dare use my given name!"

"I thought perhaps we were becoming friends," he said hopefully, although obviously he was mistaken.

"Friends? Ha!" Her eyes narrowed. "Are you always friends with your governesses?"

"I always got on well with my governesses. I was quite likeable as a lad. They very nearly always adored me."

"Well, I do not!" She stepped off the folly and started across the clearing.

He grabbed the basket and hurried after her. "Lady Garret—"

She turned on her heel and he nearly ran her over.

"Do you want to know what I thought of you until today?" Fire flashed in her eyes and by all that's holy, he could swear they were green. Bright, angry green.

He shook his head. "Absolutely not."

She cast him a scathing glare. "Then you are infinitely smarter than you appear." She turned and started down the path.

"Fortunately for me," he called after her, then cringed. Was he trying to make her think he was an idiot?

"That is fortunate!"

Apparently. And doing a grand job of it.

She made it to the gig a few feet ahead of him and climbed in before he could reach her. He suspected if he had been more than a handful of steps behind, she would have left him.

They rode in silence for a few minutes. "Lady Garret—"

She gave him a look of such vile disgust he thought better of trying to make amends for now.

At last they reached Fairborough and he reined the horse to a stop. "Lady Garret—"

She smiled in an overly pleasant manner that didn't fool him for a moment. Nor, he suspected, did she wish to. "Lord Stillwell, it is difficult enough for a female to be accepted on a building site without workers seeing her in a dispute with the owner of the property. To that end, I suggest we appear as cordial as possible."

He nodded. "My point exactly."

She shook her head in confusion. "Your point?"

"About the place of women," he said firmly, even as he knew it was not the best thing to say. Still, it was the truth.

She choked and he was fairly certain, had they not been in public, she would have had to have been forcibly restrained from wrapping her hands around his throat.

"Nothing to say?"

"Nothing you would not consider *unbecoming*."

"Well then, nothing is perhaps best." He hopped out of the carriage and circled it to assist her. She allowed him to do so in a perfunctory manner, that annoying pleasant smile still on her face.

"It was a pleasure, Lady Garret," he said with a pleasant smile of his own and the absolute conviction that he had won this particular skirmish. Even if that hadn't been his intention. Even if it gave him no particular satisfaction and, indeed, he felt rather bad about the whole thing. Not, he amended, about making his point about the role of women but about offending her by referring to her as a governess, although he still wasn't entirely sure why that had so angered her. "Perhaps we can do it again another time?"

"I would not wager on that if I were you. However . . ." She flashed him a brilliant smile, but her green—*green*—eyes sparked with anger. "I should love to join you for dinner."

His mouth dropped open. "Dinner?"

She leaned close and lowered her voice in a seductive manner. "And breakfast as well."

He swallowed hard. "Breakfast?"

"I do enjoy a good breakfast, especially after a long, long sleepless night. Why, I find I am usually famished."

His breath caught. "Lady Garret!"

"Shocked, my lord?" A cool note sounded in her voice. "Not expecting comments about long, sleepless nights from a *governess?*"

He stared at her for a long moment, then smiled his most wicked smile. "No, but I find it delightful. Why it's every little boy's dream come true."

If anything her smile brightened. "I should like nothing better than to crack my hand across your face."

He leaned forward slightly. "*Most* delightful."

"Or perhaps strangle you with my bare hands."

"I should like nothing better than to feel your bare hands around my neck." He paused. "Or elsewhere."

Her smile didn't so much as flicker. "One should be careful what one wishes for, my lord."

"Oh, I am always careful about wishes, Lady Garret."

Her gaze locked with his. Challenge simmered in her emerald eyes. And he realized she was much more than he had expected. More, perhaps, than he was prepared for. Still, he always had liked a challenge.

"Breakfast it is then, my lord. At a suitable interval after dinner, of course."

"And how shall we fill those hours between dinner and breakfast?" Had this been any other woman—oh, say, a woman who actually liked him—the answer would have been obvious. But he was beginning to realize, in spite of anything she might say, he could take absolutely nothing for granted with Lady Garret.

"Why, I expect we shall fill them in the same manner most men and women do. Until then, Lord Stillwell." She nodded, turned and strode off toward her makeshift command post.

And what manner is that? It was on the tip of his tongue, but for the first time today, he didn't say the wrong thing. Besides, he would have had to call out after her and she was right: that would have been most unseemly. He had no more desire to let the workmen know what they had been discussing than she did. Instead, he plastered a pleasant expression on his face, nodded to a few of the workers, climbed back into the carriage and started for Millworth Manor.

All had not gone exactly according to plan today. In some ways it had gone better. He had learned she longed to visit Greece and there was a decidedly whimsical touch to her nature. She did not discount his assertion that he had seen Thomas and Anne and did not think him an idiot. Well, not for that.

He still wasn't entirely sure why calling her a governess had annoyed her so, but it obviously did. He had thought his comments were rather complimentary. Besides, he had always liked his governesses. And Lady Garret did strike him as the kind of woman . . .

Realization smacked into him as hard as if she actually had slapped him across the face. What woman wanted to be complimented for her efficiency, competence and assertiveness? Even if the woman in question did indeed embody all those qualities. No, in his experience women wanted to be told their skin was like alabaster and their voices rivaled that of the angels and the glories of even the finest spring day paled in comparison to their loveliness. That was certainly an opportunity he had missed.

It had started out well enough today. He had

indeed thought they were becoming friends. There had been an ease between them at the folly he couldn't recall having with a woman before. Still, that was no excuse for idiocy.

What was wrong with him? He had always handled women extremely well. Why, charming a woman was almost a natural skill for him. A gift. Or at least it had once been. Had three failed engagements crippled him? No, that was absurd. He certainly hadn't been celibate in the three years since the end of his last engagement. But he'd had no relationship with a woman that had endured longer than a few weeks, which was, in truth, exactly how he wanted it. When the right woman at last came along, surely this time he would know.

Not that Lady Garret was the right woman. Indeed, she was the farthest thing he could imagine from the right woman. That the thought occurred to him at all was absurd.

No, he was interested in Lady Garret only insofar as she was involved in the rebuilding of his house. That and that alone was the only reason why he wanted to uncover her secrets. And she certainly had no interest whatsoever in him. That was clear enough.

Still, he couldn't quite put out of his mind her comments about breakfast and dinner.

And the long hours in between.

Chapter 9

"I'm not sure why you're so upset." Caution sounded in Clara's voice. "There are worse things to be called than a governess."

"Really?" Miranda glared at her friend. She had come straight to the office after arriving back in London and was still furious with the annoying Lord Stillwell. Governess, indeed! "Name two."

"Tart, strumpet, termagant, shrew, harlot, trollop—"

"I said two."

"And I said there are worse things to be called." Clara shrugged. "I believe I have made my point."

"Yes, well, no one ever called a tart boring and dull."

Clara gasped. "He called you dull and boring?"

"And ordinary!"

"How rude. Did you slap him?"

"I considered it." Miranda had regretted not smacking Lord Stillwell the moment she had decided against it. It would have served him right. She heaved a frustrated sigh. "He didn't actually say that I was dull and boring and ordinary. Indeed, he made a point of saying he hadn't said that. But it was implied," she added quickly. "He did say I was sensible and efficient and assertive."

"The beast."

"As well as unyielding, which is no more than another word for stubborn. And the man thought he was complimenting me." She shook her head in disbelief. "Can you imagine?"

"Miranda." Clara hesitated, then continued. "Have you considered at all that, well, you are sensible and efficient and unyielding?"

"That's not the point," she said in a lofty manner.

"What is the point?"

"I'm not sure." She grimaced. "All I know is that when he called me efficient and competent and assertive, it was most annoying."

"Odd, isn't it, as that assessment is not merely accurate but precisely how you wish to appear to others as well."

"Yes, I suppose." Miranda paced as best she could in the small confines of the office. "It's just not what one wishes to hear from . . ."

Clara's brow rose. "From?"

"From a man of his reputation." Miranda shrugged in an offhand manner as if it was of no significance.

"I see." Clara studied her for a moment. "Then it wasn't so much what he said, which we have agreed was accurate, but rather who said it that you found so annoying?"

"Well, I suppose . . . one could say . . ."

"If the same assessment had come from someone else . . ." Clara studied her closely. "Someone who was not well known for his charming manner and flirtatious nature, for his conquests and his wicked reputation, one does have to wonder if you would be as upset."

"I daresay I . . ." Realization widened in Miranda's eyes. "No, I don't suppose I would. I didn't realize I was quite that shallow." She thought for a moment. "It's humiliating, really, for a man with a reputation like Lord Stillwell's, a reputation in which he certainly does not appear to be the least bit discriminatory, to see you as . . ."

"As a governess?"

"As someone not worthy of flirtation."

Clara's brow rose. "And you wanted him to flirt with you?"

"Don't be silly." Miranda scoffed. "I simply expected it, that's all."

Clara nodded. "Given his reputation."

"Well, yes."

"It would only be natural, for a man like that."

"One would think so. That he did not deem me worthy of flirtation was insulting."

"And you were disappointed."

"I did think . . ." She nodded. "Yes, I believe I was."

"Especially as you had planned to allow him to think his flirtation might possibly be successful."

"There was that." She thought for a moment. "Actually, we were having quite a lovely day together. Almost as if we were friends and had known each other for a very long time. It might even have been most romantic under other circumstances. Not that I am interested in romance," she added quickly.

"Why not?"

"Why not?" She stared at her friend. "I don't know. I simply haven't thought about it, I suppose."

"But you do want to remarry someday?"

"I haven't thought about that either, really."

"Then perhaps you should," Clara said firmly.

"Perhaps." She'd been entirely too busy to give remarrying anything other than a passing thought. Of course, it had been three years since John's death and while she did miss him—and always would, no doubt—she had gone on with her life.

It never failed to amaze her how the very act of living eased one's loss. When John died, she had wondered if she would survive the pain of losing him. And day by day she had. Until now the thought of him brought no more than a touch of sadness at what was lost and what would never be. The plans and hopes and dreams they'd shared that would now never happen.

Certainly she had reached a point where her mother would soon begin nudging prospective husbands in her general direction. Mother had a list of which of her children should be married next and Miranda's unmarried siblings lived in fear of moving to the top of that list. But three years was, in her mother's mind, long enough for a young woman to grieve. She hadn't done anything overt yet, but Miranda knew it was only a matter of time.

"But that's really neither here nor there at the moment."

"Lord Stillwell is eminently eligible."

"Good Lord, Clara, Lord Stillwell is not at all the type of man I would want to marry."

"Why not?"

Miranda stared at the other woman. "Any number of reasons." She counted them off on her fingers. "First—he is entirely too traditional in his thinking. He firmly believes women have no place outside the home."

"Most men believe that," Clara said mildly.

"Yes, but in most men, it's not that annoying. Secondly, I don't know that I would want a man who has quite as much experience with women as he has."

"According to gossip, that is."

"While one cannot believe everything one hears, gossip usually has some basis in truth. The man has been engaged three times, remember." Miranda paused. "Although, it might not be fair to judge him on that. At least according to his mother's comments."

"One never really knows what goes on between two people in the privacy of a marriage or an engagement," Clara said. Was she speaking now of Lord Stillwell or herself ?

Clara had never given Miranda more than the barest details of her own broken engagement. Other than the fact that the man had apparently had a wife as well as two other fiancées, each of whom were as financially well off as Clara. Clara's father had been a successful merchant and had left each of his children a sizeable inheritance. As her brother had had no heirs, upon his death, Clara had ended up with his portion as well. She had no real need for the small salary she earned at Garret and Tempest; she had made that clear to Miranda when she had applied for the position. And she had no intention of sitting around waiting for the next man who wanted her for her money to come along. As Clara was quite pretty Miranda was fairly certain money was not the only attraction. But Clara had said she wanted to do something with her life—something different and interesting—and she was very good with numbers.

"And third I don't like him. Why, it's all I can do to keep from slapping him, verbally or otherwise, after more than a few minutes in his company." Although admittedly Miranda had enjoyed his company today. Much more so than she had expected.

"That's right, I had nearly forgotten." Clara nodded. "The man is a twit."

"Indeed he is." Miranda brushed aside a twinge of guilt that perhaps Lord Stillwell was not quite as much of a twit as she had originally thought. "And fourth, the man doesn't especially like me."

"Because he doesn't flirt with you?"

"I should think that's a rather good indication, as a man like that flirts with every woman who passes by. But beyond that . . ." She waved off the question. "He doesn't like anything about me. He doesn't like that I'm not sitting at home like a proper little widow, he doesn't like my ideas and he doesn't like the way I dress."

"Those shoes are dreadful."

"It's not just the shoes, I agree with him about the shoes. But he said I was a woman who values function over fashion which, to me, doesn't seem like a bad quality. But believe me, it was not a compliment." She glanced down at the dress she had worn to Fairborough. Light gray in color, it was a simple walking dress with a jacket bodice and most suitable to today's activities. "I quite like this dress."

"It does look . . ." Clara winced. "Comfortable. Even practical."

"Out of necessity," Miranda said staunchly. "And it's quite fashionable."

"A few years ago perhaps."

"Oh, but it's still . . ."

Clara's brow rose.

"Oh dear." Miranda wrinkled her nose. "I

suppose I did have it before John died. Good Lord, aside from the clothes I had made for mourning John, I haven't had a new gown in over three years."

"Perhaps it's time for that as well."

"I do not intend to purchase new clothes simply to impress Lord Stillwell." Miranda sniffed.

"I would never suggest such a thing," Clara protested. "But, might I remind you, it was your idea to allow him to think you might possibly welcome his attentions. You wish to keep him confused, remember? Unless you have changed your mind on that score?"

"No, confusion still seems best."

"And you are the one who is miffed because he has not directed his attentions toward you—"

"Which is of no importance whatsoever."

"No, of course not."

"Certainly it does make me wonder why a man, who will apparently pursue any female who walks upright, considers me not worth the effort. As if there was something wrong with me." She met her friend's gaze. "Is there?"

"Don't be absurd," Clara said a little too quickly.

Miranda narrowed her eyes. "Is there?"

"My dear Lady Garret." Clara paused, obviously to choose her words carefully.

While the two women had become fast friends —indeed Clara was her closest friend outside of her family—and usually dispensed with formality and called one another by their given names, on occasion, when the subject was of a delicate nature, Clara would address Miranda as Lady Garret and Miranda would call Clara Miss West. Apparently, this was one of those times. Miranda braced herself. "Go on."

"Are you sure you want to hear this?"

"Oh, I definitely want to hear this, Miss West." She crossed her arms over her chest. "Out with it."

"Very well." Clara squared her shoulders and met her employer's gaze firmly. "Your hair is a rich and very pretty shade of brown and if not arranged in such a stiff and stern manner would be an asset and most flattering to your face. Your features are nicely regular—"

"Regular?" Miranda stared. "You mean ordinary?"

"No, and stop being so determined to take this in entirely the wrong way." Clara huffed. "I mean when one looks at you they don't say 'My God, look at that enormous nose!' or 'Her lips are askew and her chin is off center and dear Lord, is that only one eyebrow?' "

Miranda bit back a laugh. "Well, I do have two eyebrows."

"Some women don't, you know," Clara said firmly. "What I am trying to say is that there is absolutely no reason why, with a little effort, you can't be quite lovely, even striking."

"Oh, I don't think—"

"And add to all that, your eyes." Clara shook her head. "You have the most remarkable eyes I have ever seen. You do realize they change colors depending on your mood?"

"I always thought that was rather odd."

"It's unique, and I daresay most men would consider them nothing less than fascinating."

"I doubt that." She thought for a moment. "No man—besides John, that is—has ever even mentioned them before."

"No man has ever had the chance, has he?"

"I suppose not." Looking back on the days before her marriage, she had attended any number of balls and parties but had always tended to hover on the edges of the festivities.

"As for your clothes . . ." Clara drew a deep breath. "Quite frankly, you dress as if you are trying to hide from the world. Your clothes are not merely out of date, but they are indeed somewhat dull and boring. The colors are drab and the fit is entirely too loose. They are not the least bit flattering."

"I dress like a governess then."

"Goodness, I suspect even a governess would dress with a mind toward looking her best."

"That bad?"

Clara nodded. "I'm afraid so."

Miranda shook her head. "I really hadn't noticed."

"And therein lays the problem, my friend."

"Yes, I suppose." She smiled reluctantly. "I do appreciate your honesty."

Clara returned her smile. "We have always had honesty between us."

"You should have said something sooner."

Clara laughed. "Goodness, I wouldn't have said something now if the subject hadn't come up."

And who better to tell her than Clara? With her blond hair and striking blue eyes, and the simple yet fashionable clothes she wore, even in the sedate atmosphere of the office, she was a picture of understated elegance. Besides, if Miranda was trying to hide from the world, in very many ways wasn't her friend as well?

Until her father's death, Clara had managed his household, served as his hostess and even helped with his accounts. After his passing she had met that worthless, scheming fiancé and had barely escaped unscathed. Then, of course, her brother had died and Clara had come to work at Garret and Tempest.

In spite of the differences in their stations in life, they were very much kindred spirits. Although admittedly Clara did seem to have a clearer understanding of their circumstances.

But hadn't Miranda changed? Certainly she wasn't the same quiet, reserved wallflower she had once been. Why, she had absolutely no difficulty standing her ground with the wicked

Lord Stillwell. Perhaps her appearance should reflect her newly acknowledged confidence and strength of purpose.

"You're right, Clara." Miranda nodded. "Even if I am practical and efficient and all those other dull if necessary attributes, there's no need for my appearance to scream them. After all, one can catch more flies with honey."

"Absolutely."

"I cannot see my dressmaker today; I am to meet my sister in less than an hour. I shall see her tomorrow then although she cannot possibly have anything ready for me before I leave for Millworth Manor on Monday as it's already Thursday."

"Millworth Manor?"

"Apparently I was too annoyed at Lord Stillwell to mention this." Miranda shrugged. "He delivered a note from his mother inviting me to stay at Millworth during construction. She pointed out, if I was going to be at Fairborough most days, it would be more convenient to reside at Millworth and travel into London as needed rather than the other way around."

"How very clever of her," Clara said thoughtfully. "Did you tell Lord Stillwell of his mother's invitation?"

Miranda shook her head. "I intended to, but I didn't have the opportunity. Still, I'm certain he's aware of it."

"One would think." Clara studied Miranda. "Can you perhaps borrow some things from your sister?"

"Bianca?" Miranda nodded. "She is a little shorter than I am, but I'm certain she has some things that will do. I am still trying to determine what to tell her about my absence from the city."

"It has always seemed to me, when one is trying to concoct a story that sounds truthful, that it's beneficial to stay as close to the truth as possible."

"That makes sense."

"So you will be staying in the same house as Lord Stillwell," Clara said thoughtfully.

"Yes."

"That should be interesting."

"Oh, I can scarcely wait to see what we battle about next."

"Perhaps it's your turn to insult him."

"I would never do that deliberately." She raised a shoulder in a casual shrug. "But accidents do happen on occasion."

"And one can't help an accident."

"No." Miranda smiled slowly. "One certainly can't."

Chapter 10

". . . and Lady Fairborough mentioned how pleasant it was in the country. She's a friend of Mother's, you know." Miranda knew full well she was talking entirely too fast, but she couldn't seem to help herself. As if, somehow, the faster she talked the more likely Bianca was to believe her story. Or perhaps, the more likely she was to simply miss any confusing points. "She and her family are residing at the moment at Millworth Manor. Did you know that Fairborough Hall burned?"

Bianca sat across from her at their usual table at the Ladies Tearoom and nodded slowly. "I had heard that, yes."

"Well, I'm still not entirely sure how it happened, but the next thing I knew, she was inviting me—and several others, I believe, although that wasn't entirely clear—to come stay with her in the country for the spring. And summer. Possibly into the fall." It wasn't a complete fabrication. For all Miranda knew Lady Fairborough was welcoming half of London to Millworth Manor for the entire rest of the year. Yet another deceit to pile on with the rest of them. "And I accepted."

Bianca's eyes widened. "Why on earth would

you do that? You scarcely know the woman."

"I suspect I shall get to know her much better. She is very nice and I really do want to spend some peaceful time in the country."

"But you could always go to Waterston Abbey. Adrian and Evelyn would love to have you. I daresay Sebastian and Veronica would enjoy your company as well at their country house."

Miranda cast her sister a wry smile. "Perhaps you missed the word peaceful."

"Ah, yes. Well, our family is rarely peaceful, is it?"

"Rarely if ever."

"You do realize there is a family dinner—at Mother's, I believe—next month?"

"And I have no intention of missing it." Miranda nodded. "Besides, Millworth is scarcely an hour by train so I do plan to come into London fairly often."

"And when do you intend to go?"

"Monday," Miranda said blithely and sipped her tea.

"But we are right in the middle of the season."

"Goodness, Bianca, you know I don't care about such things, although . . ." She paused for dramatic effect. This was either going to work beautifully or not at all. "I do think it's perhaps time that I . . . well . . ."

Bianca gasped. "You are going to rejoin the living!"

Miranda chuckled. "I suppose you could put it that way although I didn't realize I was not among the living."

"Oh, you know what I mean." Bianca waved away her sister's comment. "I was wondering when you would come around. I don't mind saying I was beginning to be concerned. I understand how much you loved John and what a devastating blow his death was, but it is time to go on with your life."

"I have gone on with my life," Miranda said firmly. "For the most part. But I could use your help."

"Anything."

"I think it's time I did something about my wardrobe."

"Thank God." Bianca breathed a sigh of relief. "You never really paid much attention to fashion, even before your marriage. And I suppose it wasn't all that necessary afterwards, but now that you are returning to society you do want to look your best. Well, better than your best, really."

She stared at her sister. "I sound dreadful."

"Oh no, not at all." Bianca paused. "Yet dreadful is not entirely inaccurate."

"I had no idea," Miranda murmured.

"I know. That's why we found it so awkward to bring it up."

"We?"

"Oh, yes. Mother, Portia, Diana and I have

talked about this. Even before John died, we thought you needed to do something. You have always had a great deal of potential, but you have never taken advantage of it."

"Why didn't you say anything?"

"We didn't want to hurt your feelings. Although, if you hadn't found a husband as quickly as you did I'm certain we would have forced ourselves to say something."

"I must say I'm shocked, as none of you have ever been good at keeping your opinions to yourself."

"We also assumed at some point, you would come to see what we did and then would ask for our help."

It was one thing to hear this from Clara, who had only known her for a few years, and quite another to hear it from a member of her own family. Miranda bit back a sharp retort and instead forced a smile. "What would you suggest I do?"

"Well." Bianca studied her with an assessing eye. "Everything, I should think."

"Everything?" Miranda choked. "Surely there is something acceptable?"

"Your eyes are lovely."

"That's all?"

"Your hair is a nice color," Bianca said thoughtfully. "Although you should wear it in a less severe fashion. Less like, oh, I don't know, a governess—"

"Governess?" Miranda's voice rose.

"Don't look at me like that. We had some lovely governesses." Bianca's brow furrowed. "Do you remember Miss Jenkins? She was quite beautiful as I recall."

"Miss Jenkins?"

"You might have been too young. She wasn't with us for very long at any rate." She thought for a moment. "She had been governess for the widowed Earl of Dentwick but resigned that position rather abruptly and came to work for us. She was with us no more than a few months—"

"Of course, now I remember. Lord Dentwick came and made quite a scene in the front hall. We all watched from the upper stairs." Even after all these years Miranda smiled at the sheer romance of it. "He made a grand impassioned speech about love and not caring what the rest of the world thought and swept her off and married her. How could I possibly forget that? Why, it fueled all of our hopes and dreams for years."

Bianca nodded. "And *she* was a governess."

"*She* was a *beautiful* governess even as *she* would have been a beautiful scullery maid. Even when she first came to us, we all agreed she was entirely too lovely to be a governess but must surely have been a lost princess under a magic spell of some sort. However . . ." A firm note sounded in Miranda's voice. "She was the exception. Most governesses do not look like lost princesses. Nor do I."

Bianca stared in surprise. "My dear sister, you have a quiet sort of loveliness that the rest of us envy and it quite suits you. You simply do not take advantage of it."

"I'm not sure—"

"Your complexion is perfect although you could use a touch of color." Bianca studied her. "I don't suppose you'd be amenable to the barest hint of rouge?"

"Absolutely not!" Miranda huffed. "Mother would have some sort of fit if she knew you had suggested such a thing."

"Then we won't tell Mother," Bianca said sharply. "However, might I remind you that we are adults and can certainly do as we wish without the threat of being sent to our rooms without supper."

"I know that, but—"

"Very well then, we shall have to make do." Without warning, Bianca reached across the table and gave her sister a sharp smack on each cheek so quickly Miranda had no time to protest.

"Ouch!" Miranda clapped her hands over her stinging cheeks. "Why did you do that?"

"To give you a bit of color."

"Feels like more than a bit," Miranda muttered rubbing her face.

"One must sacrifice for beauty, you know."

Bianca tilted her head and studied Miranda. "Oh, that is much better. Why the red in your cheeks fairly makes your eyes glow."

"Lucky, lucky me."

Bianca refilled her cup, then took a sip. "Your figure is very nearly as nice as mine as well." Bianca's eyes narrowed and her gaze drifted over her sister. "Your bosoms might even be a tad larger than mine, but then you're a few inches taller so that works out nicely."

"I am so glad something meets with your approval," Miranda said under her breath.

"Now, if you would simply dress in a more flattering manner—"

"My point exactly."

"Your point?" Bianca frowned. "How is that your point?"

"Well, that's the point I was getting to. Now that I have decided to begin anew, as it were, I should like to start immediately. I have already arranged for an appointment with my dressmaker for tomorrow."

"Absolutely not," Bianca objected. "You shall see my dressmaker. I shall make the appointment myself. I don't trust yours."

"Very well. However, as I am joining Lady Fairborough in the country on Monday—"

"You don't have anything to wear, do you?"

"Not really." Miranda grimaced. "Oddly enough, the clothes that I thought were perfectly suitable this morning now seem drab and dull."

"It's so awkward when a veil has been lifted."

"You have no idea."

"Well, I have more than enough clothes to spare and you are welcome to anything you need. We shall go straightaway to my house when we're finished here and explore my wardrobe. Let's see . . ." She thought for a moment. "You shall need gowns and tea dresses and walking ensembles and—oh yes—if you're going to be in the country you will need a riding habit." Bianca beamed. "This will be great fun. Almost as if we were girls again, dressing up in clothes found in trunks in the attic. I must confess, I could certainly use some fun at the moment."

Miranda searched her sister's gaze. "You're speaking of that matter of divorce, aren't you?"

Bianca nodded. "I have spoken with a solicitor."

Miranda's eyes widened with surprise. "Not Hugh?"

"No, not yet." Bianca shook her head. "It's going to be long and complicated and unpleasant, but worth it, I think. I want to know exactly what I am getting myself into before I involve Hugh. Besides, if I confide in our brother I would also have to ask him to keep this confidential. It doesn't seem fair to expect him to keep a secret of this magnitude from the rest of the family, but I'm not quite ready to tell the others yet."

"Perfectly understandable."

"I will be—ready, that is," Bianca said quickly. "As soon as I have everything in order."

"If there is anything I can do to help . . ."

"I wish you could, but no." Her jaw clenched. "Apparently my first step is to find my missing husband. He's vanished like a fox gone to ground."

"What are you going to do?"

"I do have an idea," Bianca said slowly.

"That sounds promising." Bianca's ideas were usually brilliant or disastrous and on occasion, both.

"We shall see," Bianca murmured.

Miranda studied her sister thoughtfully. It was not at all like her to keep things to herself. Although, Bianca would probably say the same thing about Miranda. Miranda wondered what everyone else in the family might be hiding. Regardless, both their secrets would be revealed soon enough.

"Are you finished?" Bianca asked although it did seem there was little left to eat or drink on the table.

Miranda popped the last bite of her biscuit in her mouth and nodded.

"Then let us be off." Bianca rose and gathered her things, Miranda a beat behind her. "This will be such fun. I can't remember the last time—"

"Mrs. Roberts," a voice called from halfway across the room.

Both sisters turned to see a beautiful, dark-haired woman crossing the tea room toward them. Even from here, Miranda could see the radiant blue color of her eyes. Now this was a woman no one would ever confuse for a governess.

"Mrs. Hedges-Smythe." Bianca greeted the newcomer.

"I thought that was you." Mrs. Hedges-Smythe cast Bianca a brilliant, and shockingly perfect, smile. "And I just wanted to say hello. It has been quite some time."

"Indeed it has." Bianca smiled a fairly perfect smile of her own. "I don't think you know one another. Allow me to introduce my sister, Lady Garret. Miranda, this is Mrs. Hedges-Smythe."

"How lovely to meet you." Mrs. Hedges-Smythe aimed that perfect smile at Miranda.

"Mrs. Hedges-Smythe and I were on a committee for one of Mother's charities, I forget which one, several years ago now," Bianca said to her sister, then addressed Mrs. Hedges-Smythe. "I believe you two have an acquaintance in common."

"Oh?" Miranda's brow rose.

"Do we?" Mrs. Hedges-Smythe beamed. "How delightful. Who?"

"Miranda was invited to spend some time this summer in the country with Lady Fairborough."

"Lady Fairborough, I see." A number of emotions flitted across the woman's face: curiosity, regret, even the oddest touch of something that might possibly be jealousy. "You shall have a lovely time. The gardens at Fairborough Hall are exquisite. Oh . . ." Her brows drew together. "But didn't I hear something about a dreadful fire at Fairborough?"

"I'm afraid so." Miranda nodded. "But they are rebuilding."

"That is good to hear. It's a grand house." Mrs. Hedges-Smythe studied Miranda curiously. "I do hope you enjoy your stay with Lady Fairborough. I must confess, I don't think she ever especially liked me. Ah, well. Not surprising, as it turned out." She and Bianca exchanged a few more comments about nothing of any significance; then Mrs. Hedges-Smythe took her leave to join a small table of ladies on the other side of the room.

Bianca's gaze followed the woman. "You have no idea who she is, do you?"

"No, but she is beautiful."

"Indeed she is." Bianca paused. "She was a fiancée of Lady Fairborough's son. The first, I believe."

Miranda started. "She was engaged to Lord Stillwell?"

"Oh my, yes." The gazes of both women settled on Mrs. Hedges-Smythe and her friends.

"Do you know what happened?"

"Well, according to what I've heard, and my sources are always most reliable, she threw him over for a man with greater prospects."

Miranda gasped. "She didn't!"

"Oh, but she did." Bianca took her sister's arm and they started for the door. She leaned closer and lowered her voice. "She was engaged to Mr. Hedges-Smythe within weeks of calling off her wedding to Lord Stillwell. You see, Mr. Hedges-Smythe was the only heir of the elderly Duke of Monmount until the duke married a much younger woman and had twin sons."

Miranda choked back a laugh. "Good Lord."

"Yes, well, one does like to think a higher power had a hand in that somewhere." Bianca grinned.

"Why didn't I hear about this?" Miranda frowned.

"I have no idea, except that you never pay attention to interesting things like this."

"Gossip, you mean."

Bianca sniffed. "I prefer to think of it as news."

"How dreadful for him," Miranda said. "Lord Stillwell, that is. To be abandoned by the woman he was to marry because someone better came along. He must have been devastated."

"I daresay he recovered."

"No doubt," Miranda murmured. "It all depends, I suppose, on whether or not he was in love with her."

"Not everyone marries for love, you know."

"Of course not." Miranda cast a last look at Mrs. Hedges-Smythe chatting with her friends. She didn't look quite as lovely as she had a moment ago but looked rather hard instead. Almost like a glass bauble one originally thought was a diamond. One sparkled with a richness and depth that bespoke rarity and value. The other simply glittered.

"Now then, we shall find all sorts of wonderful things for you to wear during your sojourn in the country," Bianca said while they waited for her carriage. "You'll no doubt meet Lord Stillwell during your visit."

"I would imagine."

"I've never actually met him, but I've certainly heard about him. I understand he's quite dashing and handsome and extremely charming."

Miranda smiled in a noncommittal manner. "So I have heard."

"I believe he and Sebastian were friends once."

"How nice."

"You do realize it's entirely possible Lady Fairborough has invited you with an eye toward her son finding fiancée number four."

Miranda laughed. "That's absurd."

"If she is a friend of Mother's, all things are possible."

Bianca's carriage approached and Miranda turned to her sister. "You know when I told you I was invited to stay with Lady Fairborough, you never said a word about Lord Stillwell."

"No, darling sister, I didn't. But then . . ." She studied Miranda closely, as if she could see all her secrets. "Neither did you."

May

Chapter 11

Win strode down the main stairs leading to the entry hall. It was fast becoming a habit to ride over to Fairborough once a day to assess the progress and perhaps annoy Lady Garret as well. Although she hadn't been annoyed as she hadn't been back since the day of their picnic, which in itself was most annoying. If she was going to take on the role of the Garret and Tempest representative, she had damn well better be here to do so. Admittedly, her Mr. Clarke had things well in hand. Why, the woman didn't really need to come back at all. The oddest thought struck him that he might well miss her, if, indeed, he didn't already.

He reached the ground floor and started for the already open door, nodding at the footman stationed beside it. It was fortunate that most of Lord and Lady Bristow's servants had relocated to the family's house in London while the older couple was out of the country and the servants from Fairborough Hall could smoothly take up their positions. Win would much prefer not to have to pay two full staffs when one was more than sufficient.

He was a scant step or two from the door when another footman, balancing several valises and a few hatboxes, staggered into the house, followed almost immediately by two more servants each holding one end of a small trunk, with more hatboxes stacked on the trunk. It appeared someone had arrived for a visit and intended to stay for quite some time. A step behind them, yet another footman struggled to juggle at least a half dozen paperboard tubes and what looked to be an artist's case. His eyes narrowed. He only knew one person who had paperboard tubes.

The distinct voice of feminine laughter sounded from beyond the door. Win stepped over the threshold and squinted, momentarily blinded by the bright spring sunlight.

"Oh, there you are, Winfield." His mother waved from the bottom of the steps. "Do come greet Lady Garret."

He blinked hard to adjust to the sunlight, then caught sight of the younger woman beside his mother. What had she done to herself? Her striped skirt in shades of blue and solid blue jacket were not merely fashionable but fit her like a second skin. A beribboned and feathered hat sat upon soft, brown curls at a jaunty angle. *Jaunty? Lady Garret?*

"Good day," he murmured and walked down the steps.

"Good day, Lord Stillwell." Lady Garret cast him a knowing smile. "You look surprised."

"Shocked is a better word."

"Oh?" A warning sounded in her voice and he was not stupid enough to ignore it.

"I did not expect to see you here," he said quickly. He moved closer, took her hand and raised it to his lips. "Might I say you look lovely today."

"Oh." Surprise crossed her face. "Why, thank you." She tilted her head in a manner that could only be called flirtatious and lowered her voice. "Not like a governess then? Like every little boy's dream?"

"My dear Lady Garret." He met her gaze in a flirtatious manner of his own. "Exactly like every little boy's dream."

"Why, my lord, you will quite turn my head with comments like that." There was the tiniest breathless note in her voice that did something odd to the pit of his stomach.

"Will I?" He brushed his lips across her hand. "What an intriguing idea."

"Is it?"

"Indeed it is." For an endless moment he stared into her eyes, more brown than green today. The strangest sensation washed through him. As if this was the beginning of something quite remarkable. Absurd, of course. Still . . .

She tried to pull her hand from his, but he held firm. "Allow me to apologize again. I never meant to offend you."

"I know that and I'm not entirely sure why I was

offended." She shrugged. "Just one of those silly female things, I suppose."

"I suspect you are many things, Lady Garret." He chuckled and reluctantly released her hand. "But silly is not one of them."

"You're being charming now, aren't you?"

"I am trying, but . . ." Odd, he was really making no particular effort to charm her. "I meant every word I said. You're not the least bit silly and you are indeed quite lovely today. Not that you weren't lovely before," he added quickly. "You are simply lovelier today, if indeed that is even possible."

"Oh, but, my lord—" She smiled and that charming dimple appeared at the corner of her mouth. He had the most outrageous desire to lean forward and kiss it. She would most certainly slap him then. Still, it might well be worth it. "You haven't yet seen my shoes."

He winced. "Are they the ugly, horrendous shoes?"

She laughed. "No." She raised the satchel she held in her other hand, the same one she had carried on their first meeting. "But I did bring them. It is certainly silly to wear nice shoes to a site of construction."

"How very sensible of you." He nodded. "Or perhaps I should say wise."

"Sensible will do."

"Winfield," his mother said. Odd, he had nearly

174

forgotten she was there. "I had the most brilliant idea."

"Did you?" He pulled his gaze from Lady Garret and turned it toward his mother. Speculation gleamed in her eyes for no more than an instant although possibly it was simply the sunlight. "And what brilliant idea was that?"

"I invited Lady Garret to stay here during the rebuilding of Fairborough." A smug note sounded in his mother's voice. "It seemed to me if she was going to be here nearly every day anyway, it made far more sense for her to reside here and go into London when she needed to rather than the other way around. Don't you agree?"

"I do." He nodded. "I should have thought of it myself."

"You don't mind then?" Lady Garret studied him closely.

"I think it's an excellent idea. This way you can keep us apprised of the progress without undue effort. And while the trip into London is not a difficult one, making it every day would be terribly wearing especially for—"

Her brow rose. "For a woman?"

"I was going to say for someone whose time is as valuable as yours is," he said smoothly although it had been on the tip of his tongue to say "a woman."

"Excellent." Mother nodded. "I shall instruct Prescott to have appropriate rooms prepared and your bags unpacked." She turned to Lady Garret. "I shall send for a carriage to take you to Fairborough."

Lady Garret nodded. "I am eager to see what has been accomplished in the last few days."

"I'll take you," Win said abruptly. "I was about to go to Fairborough myself."

She hesitated, then smiled. "That would be most appreciated."

"Then I shall see you both later." Mother beamed at the couple, and Win was certain there was more than a little triumph in that look. He wasn't entirely sure what she was thinking, although he did have his suspicions, but he was certain it was best not to know. "It will be such fun having another woman in the house. Aside from Camille, that is."

A few moments later he helped Lady Garret into the gig and they started off toward Fairborough. Now that they were alone, he wasn't entirely sure what to say to her. They had had such a convivial time of it on their picnic until, of course, he had mucked it up.

"If you look through the trees, toward the top of that hill, you might be able to catch a glimpse of the Millworth Manor folly," he said at last, trying not to sound like a tour guide. "Its location is not nearly as remote as the Fairborough folly."

"But then it wasn't built as a surprise either, was it?"

"I don't think so, but it could have been, I suppose."

"It would have been quite a lovely surprise for a man to build for his wife."

"A nice piece of jewelry would have been easier," Win murmured.

She stared at him for a moment, then laughed. "You don't mean that. I suspect you are quite a romantic sort."

"Me?" He raised a brow. "Why would you think that?"

"A man cannot have as many conquests as you have had without being something of a romantic. I can't imagine women simply fall into your lap."

"Oh, you would be surprised," he said in an overly somber manner. "I scarcely have to do more than bid a woman good day and she is falling at my feet. It can be quite awkward, you know, if there is a group of them." He shuddered. "I recall one incident when there were a dozen or so ladies walking in Hyde Park. Young, old, all shapes and sizes, some were even there to chaperone the others. All I did was tip my hat and smile . . ." He flashed her his smile. "And the ground was fairly littered with fallen bodies. Why, it was all I could do to step around them and make my escape. I tell you, I feared for my life."

She stared at him. "You're making that up."

He grinned. "Not all of it."

"Most of it then."

"Possibly."

She laughed. Every time she laughed it was as if he had won some sort of prize. He quite liked making her laugh.

"Why did you change?" he said abruptly.

"Change?"

"Your hair is different and your clothes . . ."

"What about my clothes?"

"Shall I be honest?"

"Absolutely." She nodded. "I am a firm believer in honesty."

"You're not going to get annoyed and take it out on perfectly innocent eating utensils?"

"I shall try to restrain myself," she said wryly.

"I don't know." He shook his head in a mournful manner. "I fear I will be taking my life in my hands."

"What fun is life without risk?"

"You are an enigma, Lady Garret." He glanced at her. "That's the second time you've said something like that. On the one hand you are here, assuming a position few women would attempt. Even if you are doing it out of a sense of responsibility toward your employees."

"And on the other hand?"

"On the other hand, I get the distinct feeling you are not the kind of woman who takes risks."

"Imagine that," she said under her breath.

"Are you?"

"That's not a simple question, my lord. And I fear my answer is equally complicated." She thought for a moment. "I suppose it all depends on how one defines risk. It was indeed something of a risk to assume Mr. Clarke's—Mr. Emmett Clarke's—usual duties at the site of a project. To assume a position not usually taken by a woman. And yes, I find taking that risk most exhilarating." She paused. "One could say adopting a new manner of dress to be something of a risk as well."

"And your hair."

"What?"

"You've changed your hair as well." He smiled. "It's most becoming."

"And before?"

"We are back to that, are we?"

"I am nothing if not tenacious, my lord." She chuckled. "You should have added that to unyielding and assertive."

He winced. "You are going to hold that against me forever, aren't you?"

"I wouldn't be at all surprised."

"It was meant as a compliment, you know."

"It didn't feel like one, which is probably as much my fault as it is yours." She sighed. "Now then, Lord Stillwell, tell me about my hair."

"I am probably going to regret this." He drew a deep breath. "It was entirely too severe. Even under your hat one could see it was entirely too . . . restrained. As if it was being punished for some vile crime. As for your clothing . . ."

"Yes?"

"What you have worn up until today was not entirely out of fashion—"

"And you are conversant with the latest fashion?"

"I know women who are conversant with the latest fashion," he said in an offhand manner. "As I was saying, while not exactly unfashionable it was also sensible, practical, somewhat drab, a bit too big—"

"I haven't really had—"

"Nondescript." He nodded. "That's the word for it. As if the woman wearing that clothing wished to blend into the background and escape notice. Like a chameleon. Your manner of dress was completely at odds with your nature." He met her gaze firmly. "You are entirely too clever and sharp and vibrant to ever escape notice."

Her eyes widened. "Am I?"

"I find it most interesting that you don't seem to know this."

"I am the youngest of six siblings." She shook her head. "It was usually easier to keep one's mouth shut and avoid confrontation."

He chuckled. "You seem to have grown out of it."

She grinned.

"Now it's your turn. I gave you my honest

assessment of your clothes. Now tell me why you have made such a dramatic change."

"I suppose I am tired of hiding." She shrugged. "Besides, I have been a widow for three years and perhaps it's time to make certain changes in my life."

"I see." He nodded. "You are looking for a husband then." He cast her a stern look. "I do hope you've not set your cap for me."

She gasped. "Good Lord, no!"

"You needn't be so vehement about it."

"I didn't mean to be. I do apologize. But you and I would never suit." She shook her head.

"Probably not," he said under his breath, ignoring the tiniest sense of disappointment.

"And I'm not particularly looking for a husband, but my family—that is to say, my mother . . ." She blew a resigned breath. "My mother firmly believes that no one unwed can possibly be happy. She also thinks three years is long enough to mourn."

"Is it?" He held his breath.

For a long moment she didn't say anything; then she nodded. "I think it is, yes."

"But you are not actually looking for a husband?"

"Absolutely not."

"However, you are amenable to the possibility. Should the right man come along, that is."

"Yes, I suppose I am. The idea of spending the

rest of my days alone is not a pleasant thought. It's not how I planned my life." She fell silent and he wasn't sure what to say. "My life continues even if my husband's did not. I thought I had moved on, but I now see it wasn't enough. I only took half steps, I think. It's time now to go forward and probably has been for a while. I cannot live in the past, nor do I wish to. Furthermore I believe I'm ready, even perhaps excited, about what the future may hold." She cast him a wry glance. "Admittedly, I hadn't given remarrying or the future a second thought until the last few days when it was pointed out to me how dreadful my appearance was."

He laughed. "It wasn't entirely dreadful. For a governess."

She laughed, then studied him. "And what of you? You obviously wish to marry."

"You've heard about my past engagements then?"

"I suspect there is no one in England who has not heard." She paused. "I assume then that you do wish to marry."

"It's part and parcel of my responsibilities to my family, really. My parents, in particular my mother, wish me to marry and are disappointed that I have as of yet failed to do so. Believe me, I have tried."

"Have you?"

"Is that a note of doubt ringing in your voice?"

"Well, yes, I suppose it is. I mean one failed engagement is awkward, but these things happen. But three engagements—well, three is a habit."

"A habit?"

She nodded. "A bad habit."

"I confess I have any number of bad habits, but this is not one of them," he said in a sharper tone than he had intended. "I'll have you know I am not in the habit of randomly proposing to women only to have that promise of marriage end in . . . nothing."

She grimaced. "Now I have offended you."

"Not at all." His jaw tightened. "I shall make you a bargain. If you do not ask me about my engagements, I will not ask you about your marriage."

"Very well, but my marriage was quite satis-factory. One might even say perfect."

"And yet after a mere three years you are willing to move on."

"There was nothing mere about the last three years," she said in a hard tone. "You have no idea how difficult they have been."

"You're right. My apologies."

They drove on in silence.

"Could you stop the carriage please?"

"Why?" he snapped.

"I need to change my shoes and I don't want to do it in front of the workers."

"Very well." He reined in the horse.

She stared at him. "Well."

"Well?"

"I would appreciate it if you would turn away." She fluttered her hand at him. "Go on."

"Good Lord." He groaned, shifted in his seat and stared out into the countryside. "I can promise you, Lady Garret, the sight of your bare feet would not inflame my passions."

"Are you sure?" He could hear her opening her bag. "I've been told I have very nice feet."

"While I am certain your feet are exquisite, I am equally certain the sight of them would not tempt me to seduce you."

"Oh." The sounds of her changing shoes continued. "Then what would?"

He started. "What?"

"What sort of temptation would you not be able to resist? In terms of seducing me, that is."

"Lady Garret!" He was as shocked at her comment as he was his reaction.

"I thought I should know. Just in case . . ."

"I assure you, I have no intention of seducing you."

"Excellent, as I have no intention of allowing you to do so." She sniffed. "There. I have my shoes on, you may turn around."

"Thank God because in another minute I don't know if I would have been able to control myself!"

"Imagine my surprise," she murmured.

184

Lady Garret was fast passing annoying and heading firmly into infuriating. Seduce her, indeed. He pushed the surprisingly tempting idea out of his head.

They started on their way again and were nearly at Fairborough when he heard her sigh.

"There is something about you," she said. "I can't quite put my finger on it."

"I suspect there are any number of things you can't quite put your finger on."

"No doubt, but I find myself saying things to you I had no intention of saying, telling you things I have never told anyone." She shook her head. "It's most disconcerting."

"I find your candor enchanting," he muttered.

"You do not."

He pulled the horse to a stop and heaved an exasperated sigh. "Oh, but I do. Women are not usually honest in their dealings with me."

"And you are always honest with them?"

"Don't be absurd." He scoffed. "Women don't expect honesty from me and I do hate to disappoint. But I do know where a line should be drawn. You should know I have never asked a woman to marry me that I did not fully intend to wed." He paused to pull his thoughts together. "Unfortunately, women usually see me as two distinctly different creatures. One is an admittedly dashing—"

"And modest as well."

"—and charming rogue with any number of amorous conquests to his credit."

"Credit?" Her brow rose.

He ignored her. "Somewhat lighthearted, prone to amusing conversation, even perhaps frivolous. He likes nothing better than telling a good story that will make his listeners laugh unless it's having a good laugh himself. No one expects anything of a serious or especially honest nature from him. And he plays his role with the skill of a practiced actor."

"Go on."

"Or they see me as a man of property and wealth. The current Viscount Stillwell and the next Earl of Fairborough. I tell you, Lady Garret, there is nothing more demeaning to a man's soul to be wanted for what he has rather than who he is."

She stared. "I had never thought of it before, but I can well imagine."

"It's neither here nor there at the moment, I suppose." He quickly got out of the carriage, in part to hide his embarrassment. He had never revealed that much of himself to any woman. Not even those he had planned to marry. He circled around to help her down. "I'm rather surprised to admit that you and I may be more similar than dissimilar as I too have revealed things to you I have never said to anyone else. I do hope you will keep my confidence."

"Of course." She studied him. "And may I ask the same courtesy?"

"Absolutely." He nodded. "I shall have a carriage sent back for you this afternoon."

"You're not going to stay and check on the progress?"

"I shall leave that in your capable hands," he said in a curt manner.

She stared at him for a moment, then nodded, her manner every bit as curt as his. "Very well then." She turned and walked off and he tried not to watch the way that striped skirt swayed with every step.

Win was on his way back to Millworth before he could change his mind. He would have liked nothing better than to have spent the rest of the day in her company. That in itself was surprising. It wasn't her change in appearance. Indeed, he had already acknowledged to himself that he considered her most attractive. But it was the ease with which they had talked to each other that was nothing short of frightening.

More similar than dissimilar indeed. He couldn't believe he had said that. Why hadn't he just called them kindred spirits? Or worse—soul mates. What utter nonsense. He didn't believe in soul mates. Perhaps he had once, but that was long ago and well before he'd had three fiancées, each of whom he had planned to love but none of whom he did at the time. Which was the only reason he'd survived humiliation and embarrassment and, in one case, the slight cracking of his heart.

He had liked each of his prospective brides, of course. After all, he had planned to spend the rest of his life with them. But he'd chosen them as much for their suitability as a wife, as the next Countess of Fairborough, as anything else. Which he now realized was fairly stupid. Now, he wanted more.

Now he wanted a woman he could share his hopes and dreams and fears and innermost thoughts with. A woman who was at once intelligent and flirtatious. A woman who would be as much friend as lover. That was a woman he could happily spend the rest of his life with.

Not that said woman was Lady Garret. For one thing, they didn't particularly like one another, although that did appear to be changing, at least on his part. But she did seem to spend a great deal of her time deliberately annoying him. Beyond that the woman was, well, unexpected. Yes, that was it. He didn't know from moment to moment what she might say or do next. It was at once disconcerting and exciting. Certainly life with her would never be dull although she would more than likely drive any sane man mad. Under other circumstances she might well be a woman he could . . .

Ha! The very idea was absurd and no doubt only

occurred to him because of their discussion of her marriage and his engagements. She was absolutely right: they would never suit one another.

No, Lady Garret was not the right woman for him. For one thing she obviously believed she was smarter than he was. The thought crossed his mind that perhaps she was. He ignored it. For another, regardless of what she might have said, she was still hiding something significant about Mr. Tempest and Garret and Tempest. And that he was determined to find out. Indeed, it was most frustrating that he hadn't done so as of yet. But then very nearly every encounter with Lady Garret left him frustrated and annoyed.

More so when he realized he hadn't come any closer to finding out her secrets today, but he had certainly revealed some of his.

Chapter 12

Miranda studied herself in the mirror in the rooms she had been given at Millworth although she wasn't really sure who she was looking at. The woman who stared back at her wearing one of Bianca's gowns was really rather pretty. She wasn't at all used to thinking of herself as pretty, but, unless this was some kind of magical mirror from a fairy story, the woman in the mirror was definitely pretty. The bodice was a bit snugger than she was used to and molded to her figure, making her bosom seem, well, inviting. She wasn't used to that either. She grinned at her reflection. She rather liked it.

Would Lord Stillwell like it as well? Not that it mattered, of course.

She patted her hair one last time, soft brown curls framing her face, something else she wasn't accustomed to, and started for the dining room. The man had the oddest effect on her. When she didn't want to smack him, she wanted . . . What did she want?

She had no idea and it was disconcerting. It had been most satisfying today when she had arrived and had seen the look on his face. It was definitely not the look one gave to a governess. Her cheeks heated at the thought of "every little boy's dream." The man was incorrigible as well as annoying.

He was also somewhat more than she had expected. For one thing, he was, well, nice. She'd already known he was amusing. And known as well she enjoyed his company. But in his company she found herself saying the most improper things, as well as revealing far more than was probably wise. Even with John she'd been fairly reserved until they had known each other for a significant amount of time. But with Lord Stillwell, she found herself sharing all sorts of intimate details about her life and her thoughts. That it seemed so natural to do so made it no less confusing.

"Lady Garret." Lady Fairborough descended upon her the moment Miranda stepped into the parlor. "I'm so delighted you could join us."

Miranda smiled. "I don't know if I have properly thanked you for inviting me to stay."

"It was strictly selfish on my part. I must confess, I was exhausted just thinking about you going back and forth to London nearly every day. It simply didn't make sense. And I do pride myself on my sensible nature."

Across the room, Mr. Elliott and Lord Fairborough traded amused glances. A lovely blond woman stood beside them. Lord Stillwell was nowhere in sight.

"You are looking exceptionally lovely tonight, my dear." Lady Fairborough's gaze flicked over Miranda and she nodded in approval. "Oh my, yes, you'll do quite nicely."

"Do for what?" Miranda said slowly.

The older lady's eyes widened innocently. "Why, do for dinner, of course. Now then, I don't believe you know everyone." She took Miranda's arm and led her toward the others. "You've met Lord Fairborough, of course, and my nephew, Grayson."

"Good evening, Lady Garret." Mr. Elliott smiled a greeting. "How nice to see you again."

"Mr. Elliott." Miranda smiled.

"Grayson, if you please." He cast an affectionate look at the woman by his side. "Allow me to introduce my fiancée, Lady Lydingham."

Taller than Miranda and very blond, Lady Lydingham was the epitome of classic English beauty. The kind of beauty that made everyone else pale in comparison. For a moment, Miranda felt extremely pale. She ignored the thought and smiled at the other woman. "Good evening, Lady Lydingham."

"Oh, please, do call me Camille." She returned Miranda's smile. "It would be too dreadfully awkward to live under the same roof and continue such formality. And in spite of its appearance, Millworth has never been overly formal."

"I would be honored, and you must call me Miranda," she said. "This is your family's home, isn't it?"

Camille nodded. "My great-grandfather acquired Millworth, oh, a hundred years or so ago. Unfortunately, the property is entailed and my parents weren't clever enough to have sons so I'm not sure what will happen to it in the future." She glanced around the parlor. "My sisters and I all have our own homes of course, so we certainly don't need Millworth. Still, it will be rather sad when the day comes that it passes to some distant, unknown relative. Probably some annoying twit of a creature who will see it only for the value of its property and not the richness of its heritage. I have no idea who that might be, but I am certain we have one somewhere." She heaved a resigned sigh. "Every family does, you know."

Miranda bit back a smile. "It is a grand house."

"It is indeed," Lord Fairborough said firmly. "This house and Fairborough Hall were originally built by members of the same family around the same time. But Fairborough Hall has stayed in our family from the time the first stone was laid, nearly three hundred years, whereas Millworth has changed hands any number of times."

"And it seems each new owner left his mark on the manor with additions or remodeling or whatever suited the fancy of the new occupants," Grayson added. "Which is why the façades of Millworth and Fairborough don't resemble each other."

"I see," Miranda said. She had noticed the various styles incorporated in Millworth in a surprisingly harmonious manner on her first visit. "How interesting."

"But that was a very long time ago," Camille said firmly. "What I think is much more interesting is what is happening now with the rebuilding of Fairborough Hall." She cast Miranda an admiring look. "I can't believe you managed to convince Winfield to install electricity."

"Where is Winfield?" Lady Fairborough

frowned. "He should have been down by now."

"Some sort of business matter to attend to, Aunt Margaret," Grayson said to his aunt.

"I'm afraid I can't take credit for Lord Stillwell's change of heart," Miranda said. "It was more the influence of his family, rather than anything I said, that led to his decision to allow electrification."

"And improved plumbing," Lord Fairborough said.

"Nonetheless, I find what you're doing quite admirable," Camille said.

"What I am doing?"

"Being here to oversee the construction. It's not at all the sort of thing most women would so much as attempt, although I daresay most of us would be quite good at it." Camille nodded. "It's quite . . . oh, progressive of you."

"I'm not really overseeing the work," Miranda said quickly. "We have a gentleman who does that. My responsibility is more in the manner of a liaison, as it were, between the architect and the actual construction."

"Regardless, I think it's most impressive," Lady Fairborough said firmly. "And quite courageous. It's not easy to be progressive and look toward the future rather than the past. But we are nearing the twentieth century and there is no doubt in my mind that the world is going to change and we must change along with it."

"Well, we are getting electricity," Lord Fairborough said under his breath.

Lady Fairborough cast her husband an unyielding glance. "And that, Roland, is only the beginning."

"God help us all," the older gentleman muttered and took a sip from the glass he held in his hand. Whisky, judging from the color.

Grayson chuckled. "What do you have in mind, Aunt Margaret?"

"I'm not entirely sure yet." Her eyes narrowed in a thoughtful manner. "I would think next . . ." She aimed a triumphant smile at the rest of the group. "Telephones!"

Camille's eyes widened. "Oh, that does sound like fun."

"Doesn't it? They already have them in parts of London, you know." Eagerness rang in Lady Fairborough's voice. "I believe there's a problem with wires and such here in the country, but once the hall was finished, I was going to propose installing them in the Mayfair house."

"While we're at it, why don't we build a stable for the horseless carriage and a dock to tether the flying machine to as well?" Lord Stillwell strode into the parlor.

"I should quite like a horseless carriage." Lady Fairborough grinned at her son. "And a flying machine."

"I might have to draw the line at a flying

machine," Lord Fairborough said. "Man was not meant to fly."

"At last we agree on the limits of progress, Father." Lord Stillwell addressed the older man, but managed to slant Miranda a smug look.

"Perhaps *men* weren't meant to fly, but I am one woman who thinks it sounds quite exciting," Camille said in a mild manner.

"If one finds the threat of imminent death from plunging to the earth exciting." Lord Stillwell scoffed. "I, for one, intend to keep my feet firmly on the ground."

"Perhaps it's the mechanism of flight that concerns you, my lord." Miranda adopted her most pleasant expression. "Perhaps you would not be as amenable to a flying machine as you would be to, oh, say, wings."

Grayson choked.

Lord Stillwell's eyes narrowed. "Birds have wings."

"As do insects." She favored him with her sweetest smile. "Annoying pests and the like."

"Lady Garret—"

"Lady Garret?" Camille snorted. "Good Lord, Winfield, you needn't be so stuffy. You never have been before and I can't imagine why you are now."

He glared at her. "I have a great deal of responsibility."

"It's not quite as easy as it once was to be

Winfield Elliott." Grayson bit back a grin.

"And yet, I bravely carry on." The corners of Lord Stillwell's mouth twitched as if he too was resisting a smile.

"We have agreed to dispense with formality and call each other by our given names." Camille pinned him with a firm look. "Now then, Winfield, might I present Miranda? Miranda, this is Winfield."

"How delightful to meet you, Winfield." Her gaze met his and she smiled. This was silly but more than a little fun. It struck her that this group had much in common with her own family.

"The pleasure, Miranda . . ." He stepped closer, took her hand and raised it to his lips. His gaze never left hers. This was the second time he had kissed her hand and while the first had triggered a fluttering in the pit of her stomach, now warmth spread from the touch of his lips through to her very toes. "The pleasure is entirely mine." He lowered his voice, his words for her ears alone. "You are a vision tonight, Miranda."

"Every little boy's dream?" she teased.

"No." His gaze bored into hers. "Every man's." Her breath caught, her gaze locked with his and for an endless moment there was no one in the room, no one in the world save the two of them. The wicked lord and the governess. And something that might well have been desire washed through her.

"After all," Camille's voice sounded from somewhere very far away, "we are all living in the same house. And you and Miranda will be together for a very long time."

"A very long time?" Miranda and Winfield said in unison. She snatched her hand from his and stared at Camille, and his gaze followed hers.

Grayson laughed or coughed, one couldn't be quite sure as his hand covered his mouth.

"Well, yes." Camille's gaze slid between Miranda and Winfield. "It was my understanding that construction will go on for months. Which to me does seem like a very long time." Her eyes narrowed thoughtfully. "I was not referring to the rest of your lives."

Winfield scoffed. "The thought never crossed my mind."

"Of course not." Miranda forced a short laugh. "How absurd."

"Grayson said Fairborough wouldn't be completed until well after we return," Camille continued.

"Until who returns?" Lady Fairborough frowned.

"We shall explain it all to you." Camille blithely waved off the question and nodded toward the door. "And I believe Prescott has come to call us into dinner."

"Very well then." Lady Fairborough took her husband's arm, then glanced at her son. "Winfield, do escort Miranda, if you please."

"I would be honored." He smiled politely and offered his arm.

It would have been unacceptable not to take his arm; still, she knew the briefest instant of hesitation, then braced herself. She slipped her hand onto his arm and again that strange sensation of warmth washed through her. At once terrifying and exciting.

He held back until the rest of the group was nearly at the dining room, then walked slowly after them, speaking in a low tone out of the side of his mouth. "That was odd."

She knew at once what he was talking about and nodded. "Extremely odd."

"You do realize what they are all thinking?"

"Oh, surely not."

"Perhaps you have not met my mother."

"I have met mine . . ." She winced. "We shall just have to set them straight then."

"How?" He stopped in mid-step and looked at her. "Denying that . . . that . . . *moment,* for lack of a better word, that we shared in front of them would only give legitimacy to it."

"Legitimacy?" She stared at him.

"Well, yes, acknowledging it gives it credence. If we ignore it, it will go away."

"Do you really believe that?"

He nodded. "I do."

Disappointment mixed with relief and something else she couldn't quite define. Anger perhaps? "Excellent idea. We shall pretend it never happened."

"That does seem for the best."

They took another few steps and she paused. Definitely anger. "Although . . ."

"Although?"

"If we really want to convince the others of the insignificance of the *moment* . . ."

"And we do."

"Without question," she agreed. "But it seems to me we might want to do more than just ignore it."

"More?"

"You and I seem to be exceptionally good at annoying one another." She smiled in as pleasant a manner as she could muster. "Perhaps we should just let that natural tendency of ours take its course."

He studied her for a moment, then nodded. "That will do, I suppose."

"Yes, it will." She clenched her teeth. It was obvious the man had no interest in her whatsoever, even interest of a prurient nature, which was unreasonably upsetting. Infuriating, really, although it made no sense. Why, she didn't even like him. Even if, for less than an instant, it had seemed there might be something quite remarkable between them. It was an aberration, no doubt. Not the least bit significant. It would be best to ignore it completely and pretend it never happened. Because if it was not important to him, she would absolutely not allow it to be important to her.

"Very well then, Winfield." She cast him her brightest smile. "Shall we join the others?"

It was going to be an interesting evening.

". . . and therefore I have decided to go with him." Camille's gaze circled the table. "I have never been to America and who knows when I might have another opportunity. Delilah"—she glanced at Miranda—"my younger sister, has agreed to join us so it won't be the least bit improper."

"I don't know why you have to go at all." Lady Fairborough aimed a pointed look at her nephew. "You just returned to England in December after eleven years of being away. Eleven years, Grayson, is a very long time."

"I am well aware of that." Grayson smiled at his aunt.

"And now you are leaving again." She huffed.

"I am leaving, Aunt Margaret, to settle my business affairs and make the necessary arrangements so that I can return to England for good," he said in the kind of firm but gentle tone one uses when one has explained something more than once. "But I shall always have to travel to America on occasion."

"Business, my dear"—a firm note sounded in Lord Fairborough's voice—"is business."

"Besides, we won't be gone long," Camille said.

"Grayson says it will be less than a month and probably only three weeks. Why, we shall spend more time in travel than actually in New York. Which does seem a pity, really. But we do want to be back before the Midsummer Ball."

"The queen might yet come," Lady Fairborough murmured.

"The last thing I want is a visit from the queen," her husband muttered. "Problems enough without a royal visit complicating life."

"Nonetheless, it is a pity Fairborough won't be completed by then." Camille sighed. "I haven't been to the Fairborough Midsummer Ball in years and I was quite looking forward to it."

"I am sorry, but . . ." Miranda shook her head. "The project is huge. There was a great deal of damage and rebuilding to Lord—to Winfield's—specifications is not an easy task. We have really just started and it is already the beginning of May. Completion by late June is next to impossible."

"Next to?" Winfield raised a brow. "I thought you said it was impossible? Next to impossible implies that there is an iota of a chance that makes it indeed possible."

"I am sorry, I misspoke." Irritation clenched her teeth. "It is indeed impossible. It simply cannot be done."

He leaned forward slightly, his gaze meeting hers over the dinner table. "Why not?"

"I just said it was an enormous project."

"One wonders if another firm could accomplish it."

"And yet other firms were not willing to so much as attempt it." Was he doing this deliberately or was he just being his usual annoying self?

"Perhaps this could be accomplished if a man was in charge," he said in a deceptively casual manner.

"Or a promise would simply be made that would not be kept as men are prone to do." She shrugged. "Promises not kept, engagements broken, that sort of thing."

His eyes narrowed. "It seems to me anything can be done if one puts enough effort and resources into it."

"And money," she snapped. "This is already costing a small fortune. Are you willing to spend even more?"

"How much more?"

"I have no idea. We would have to vastly increase the number of workers." She thought for a moment. "Construction costs would be at least twice what we have allocated. Perhaps even three times as much."

"And could you then guarantee completion by late June?"

"No! Absolutely not!" What part of this did the blasted man not understand? "I simply cannot promise you the house will be finished. For one thing, I will not have men working on Sunday. That is not negotiable."

He nodded. "I understand."

"Nor will I allow Mr. Clarke to sacrifice safety for speed," she said sharply. "And I will not permit shoddy workmanship."

"Nor do I expect you to."

"Even if we could get the floors, walls and roof in place by late June, the finishes could never be done. Keep in mind, you want Fairborough put back precisely the way it was. That means replicating carved woodwork and molded plasters. I have craftsmen in London working on some of that already, but it is going to take a considerable amount of time to be done correctly."

"I shall make a bargain with you." His gaze locked on to hers. "If the Midsummer Ball can be held at Fairborough, as it has been for well over a hundred years—"

"One hundred and twenty-seven, to be exact," someone murmured.

"There is a bonus in it for you."

She stared at him. "What kind of bonus?"

"Substantial." He paused. "I am already paying you twice your usual commission. I will give you a bonus equal to your original commission."

"On the condition that your Midsummer Ball is held at Fairborough?" She studied him closely. Surely he wasn't that stupid?

"Exactly." He nodded. Apparently he was.

"And you are willing to pay the extra construction costs incurred?"

"I am."

"I see." A bonus of that size, above and beyond the original contracted agreement, was pure profit and could be put in its entirety into her employee fund, thus ensuring their security. And that was especially important now.

Her presence at Fairborough would not go entirely unnoticed. She might well be able to get away with the same excuse she had originally given Winfield—that she was simply taking Emmett's place out of necessity—but she was realistic enough to understand that that would not hold up for long. Even if the elusive Mr. Tempest was given credit for the architectural work, one thing would surely lead to another and the truth would come out. That was the dreadful thing about truth: it very nearly always came out eventually. The house of cards she and Clara had so cleverly built would tumble and Garret and Tempest would tumble with it.

"I am more than willing to spend your money, Winfield."

"Ah, spoken like a true woman."

"I accept. I shall make certain the ball is held at Fairborough." She nodded. "On my next trip into London, I shall have an addendum to the contract drawn up."

"Oh, I don't think that's necessary." He

shrugged. "I should think a simple agreement between the two of us should suffice. I am a man of my word after all. Especially when it comes to an agreement with a beautiful woman."

"As evidenced by your history with giving your word to women."

Someone at the table choked and abruptly Miranda realized she had quite forgotten that they were not alone. She looked around the table to find four pairs of eyes staring at her and Winfield in either horror or amusement or shock or disbelief.

"My apologies," she murmured and grabbed her glass of wine and drained it.

"I think we . . . well . . ." Winfield began. "Sorry." Then he too tossed back his wine.

"Ah yes, well . . ." Lord Fairborough cleared his throat. "Have you made your travel arrangements yet, Grayson? Might I suggest . . ."

The discussion around the table turned to the less volatile topics of travel and ships and what Camille looked forward to seeing in America and who knew what else. Miranda's mind was anywhere but on the conversation, and she counted the minutes until she could gracefully make her escape. If Winfield's intention had been to show his family that their *moment* was not indicative of some sort of feelings between them—as indeed it wasn't—he'd succeeded admirably. No one at this table could possibly think there was anything between them that was not of a business nature. Indeed, if she was trying to convince anyone they did not so much as like one another, this would have been an excellent way to go about it. Not that it wasn't the truth.

At long last dinner dragged to a merciful close. The ladies were to retire to the parlor; the gentlemen were headed to the billiards room. Miranda excused herself, pointing out she had a great deal to do in the morning. She headed toward her rooms and started up the stairs.

"Lady Garret. Miranda." Winfield hurried toward her. "Well, what did you think?"

"What did I think?" She paused on the second step and studied him. "What do you mean?"

"I mean the opportunity presented itself and I took advantage of it." He grinned with what looked like pride.

"What are you talking about?"

"I am talking about seizing the moment. Carpe diem, if you will."

"What moment?" She stared with growing horror.

"When Camille asked about completing the house before the ball and, of course, I know how determined you are. Even ambitious."

"Go on," she said slowly.

"And I knew the mention of another firm would infuriate you as well as my inference that a woman should not be here at all."

"Inference?" Her voice rose. "Inference?"

"I didn't actually say it, you know. I simply implied."

She tried to scream, but the oddest squeaking, croaking sound came out instead. Was the man truly mad?

"Although I did think your comment about broken engagements was a bit too much," he said in a chastising manner.

"Did you?"

"It didn't seem quite in the spirit of our plan."

"What plan?"

"It was your idea." He studied her for a long moment; then his eyes widened with realization. "You weren't acting, were you? You meant everything you said."

"I had no idea you didn't!"

"Well, I didn't!"

"I didn't know that!"

"Now you do!"

"And?"

"And?" His eyes widened with horror. "You do realize this whole bonus nonsense was no more than part of an act. Given that, I assume you will not hold me to it."

She stared at him for a long moment. The man was not merely mad but stupid as well. "Oh, but I will."

His eyes narrowed. "It scarcely matters. You can't complete the work by the ball; therefore you will not earn the bonus."

"Oh, I will earn the bonus, Winfield." She started up the stairs. "You may count on it."

"Excellent, as that means the house will be finished," he called after her.

"It only means the ball will be held at Fairborough," she said in a tone too low for him to hear. He'd realize his mistake soon enough. She was wrong about Winfield Elliott. He was indeed a twit after all.

And for that he'd have to pay.

Chapter 13

"Well, dinner was certainly interesting." Gray leaned over the billiards table and positioned his shot.

Win had hoped his cousin and his father were going to do the decent thing and pretend nothing out of the ordinary had occurred at dinner. Of course he was wrong. Gray had only been waiting for Win's father to retire for the night. Win suspected his cousin and father had agreed between them to let Gray deal with this.

Gray took his shot, then nodded with satisfaction. "It was like watching a play performed during dinner. Although, admittedly, one did tend to forget about one's food."

"I'm glad you were entertained."

"I'm not sure anyone was entertained exactly.

In spite of a few excellent lines on her part, it wasn't that good of a play." He thought for a moment. "Actually, it was more like watching a collision that you know is coming, that you know as well you should try to prevent, and yet you can do nothing but stare."

"Thank you for your assistance."

"I assumed you could handle it." Gray shrugged. "Apparently not."

"I did handle it." Now was not the time to confess he didn't mean anything he had said but was acting a part designed to show his family he and Miranda had no interest in one another. In hindsight, it had not been his best idea. It had certainly not been well thought out but rather evolved with every word out of his mouth. Nor did it turn out as he had expected. He still wasn't entirely certain what happened, but once again it was as though he had lost a game he didn't know he was playing.

"Ah, yes, well, if you define handling it as agreeing to give the woman a great deal of money . . ."

"A bonus, Gray," Win said firmly. "On the condition that Fairborough is completed by the day of the ball. She has said from the beginning it can't be done, so it's really a moot point."

"I see." Gray chalked the tip of his cue. "I have never seen you quite so befuddled by a woman before."

"What utter nonsense." He leaned over the

table and took his shot. The ball refused to cooperate, but then wasn't that to be expected given the rest of the evening? "I am not the least bit befuddled."

"You have no idea what you have agreed to, do you?"

"Of course I do. I just said—"

"The exact wording of your agreement, an agreement upon which you gave your word, as was witnessed by the rest of us, was that she would receive a substantial bonus if the ball could be held at Fairborough."

"And?"

"And, it seems to me, and probably to her as well, that the ball can indeed be held at Fairborough without construction being completed."

"Don't be absurd." Win scoffed. "Completion was implied. Part and parcel of the agreement."

"And yet as it was not stated . . ." Gray shrugged.

Win stared at his cousin. "You're telling me if the ball is held in an unfinished ballroom, or even on the front lawns, then she has earned her bonus?"

"I would think so," Gray said in a mild tone as if his cousin hadn't just thrown away a significant amount of money. "I would wager she thinks so as well."

"Bloody hell." Win blew a long breath. "I didn't see that."

"No, you were too busy doing battle with the fair Lady Garret." He paused. "Who, I might add, was looking exceptionally fair tonight."

"She always looks exceptionally fair," Win said absently. How could he have made such a stupid mistake? Of course, he hadn't realized that his words would be taken seriously. He'd had no idea she wasn't playing the same game he was. Now that he knew the truth of it, her comments carried a bit more sting than they had initially. He had thought they were becoming at the very least friends. Was it at all possible that she really didn't like him? That she thought his ill-fated engagements were an indication of his lack of honor? That he was not a man of his word?

"So what are you going to do now?"

Was there a chance that the odd sensations that had swept through him when he had gazed into her eyes tonight, feelings of inevitability and completion and, yes, even fate had not been shared? Feelings that were at once terrifying and yet hopeful and exuberant. Regardless, it was entirely too soon to place credence in such moments. Why, it could have been nothing more than an aberration. He barely knew the woman after all. If he had learned nothing else in regard to women, he had learned restraint.

"I said, what are you going to do now?"

Besides, in spite of what she had said about not being opposed to remarrying, was she indeed ready to give up ties to her late husband? She was, after all, engaged in keeping his company solvent. It was not unreasonable to think that was one way of keeping him or the memory of him alive. He wasn't sure he could compete with a dead man. Not that he intended to.

"Win?"

Win's gaze snapped to his cousin's. "What?"

"I asked what you were going to do now." Gray's eyes narrowed. "Although it was apparent you were paying no attention whatsoever."

"I was distracted."

"Obviously."

"I don't know what I am going to do now." Win shrugged. "Nothing, I suppose." He thought for a moment. "I don't mind the extra costs of construction if it speeds the work along. I don't even mind paying her the bonus. But . . . she's done it again, you know. Manipulated me to suit her own purposes."

"She manipulated *you?"* Gray's brow rose. "That wasn't my observation."

"She's very clever about it." He shuddered. "She's very clever about everything. She may well be the cleverest woman I have ever met."

"Apparently." Gray studied him closely. "You don't seem very upset about it."

"I'm getting used to it," he said under his breath. And it really was his own fault. Maybe she did have him befuddled after all. His life had certainly become much more complicated and confusing since the moment her sturdily clad feet had walked into it.

"You are preoccupied tonight, cousin."

"Am I?"

"You've barely noticed that I am about to claim victory."

"Are you, indeed?" He glanced at the table. "Apparently you are."

Gray shook his head in disbelief, put his cue in the rack on the wall and picked up his half-empty glass of brandy. "Well?" He sat down on the well-worn leather sofa positioned so as to enable the watching of a game or simply idle conversation. "Do you wish to talk about it?"

"Talk about what?"

"Tonight? Everything? The look you and Miranda exchanged before dinner? The fact that the two of you can scarcely go ten minutes without sparks of some sort flying between you? The deal you struck with her?"

"I don't know what happened." Win shook his head. "I am usually not that—"

"Stupid?"

"For lack of a better word, yes."

"Then what were you?"

"It's going to sound, well . . ." He winced. "Stupid."

"All the better." Gray nodded. "Go on then."

"It seemed the best way to convince the rest of

you that there was nothing between Miranda and myself . . ." Without thinking, he paced the length of the table. "Which there isn't, of course."

"Of course not."

"In spite of that . . . that moment."

"The one in which neither of you seemed to notice the rest of us were present?"

Win nodded. "That's the one. In order to prove that it meant nothing—"

"Which you wished to do because?"

"Because, for one thing, you know how Mother is when she suspects there is the possibility of an appropriate match so much as passing by." He grimaced. "I wouldn't want to wish Mother's determination on anyone, let alone Miranda."

Gray nodded. "Go on."

"It simply seemed like a good idea to allow free rein to our natural tendencies to clash. And, in doing so, show all of you there is certainly no possibility of anything between Miranda and myself."

"I see." Gray sipped his brandy thoughtfully. "You do know it didn't work."

"It didn't?"

"Absolutely not." He paused. "If anything it convinced us all there was something extremely interesting occurring between the two of you."

"That's absurd."

Gray leaned forward. "What's absurd is the fact that after choosing the wrong woman three times, you are unable to see when the right one comes along."

Win stared. "Miranda Garret is absolutely not the right one. That is the most ridiculous thing I have ever heard."

"Why?"

"For one thing, she doesn't like me. She certainly doesn't trust me. She thinks I am hopelessly behind the times. She disagrees with me about what women should and should not do. And I suspect she is not entirely over the death of her late husband."

"And yet she has changed her manner of dress and the way she wears her hair. It seems to me that is indicative of a woman who is moving on with her life."

"I daresay you're—"

"As well as being an indication of a woman who wants a man to notice her."

"I have noticed her," he snapped. "I have noticed any number of things about her. Most of them extremely annoying."

"But not all?"

"Of course not all." He'd noticed that a dimple appeared at the corner of her mouth when she smiled. And he'd noticed the delightful sound of her laughter. And he'd noticed the way she seemed to smell vaguely of the promise of spring and how the color of her eyes changed with her mood.

"It seems to me," Gray said slowly, "that Miranda has presented you with quite a challenge."

Win narrowed his eyes. "A challenge?"

"You have always enjoyed a good challenge."

"What do you mean by a challenge? What kind of challenge?"

"Why, winning the heart and hand of the fair Lady Garret."

Win stared. "I don't want her hand or her heart." He shook his head. "She has already pointed out that she and I would not suit one another."

"And therein lies the challenge." Gray shrugged. "Change her mind."

"I don't want to change her mind. I have no interest in Miranda Garret, nor does she have the tiniest bit of interest in me."

"Very well."

"Very well what?"

"It's no business of mine."

"No, it isn't."

"I'll be off to America in a few weeks anyway."

"Yes, you will."

"For the best, really. Although I was looking forward to watching your demise at the hands of yet another female."

"There will be no demise."

Gray cast him a look of what could only be called pity.

"There won't." He huffed. "I assure you there is

nothing between Miranda and myself, nor is there the slightest possibility that will change."

"Very well."

"Stop saying that!"

"As you wish." Gray bit back a smile and sipped his brandy.

"I do wish," he snapped.

Admittedly though, Gray might well have a valid point. Even if Win was confused and befuddled, his cousin was not. And if Gray saw something that Win didn't, wouldn't it be wiser to find that out rather than miss it entirely? This was the rest of his life after all. If he had learned nothing else from being engaged to the wrong woman three times it was caution. There was no need to rush into anything. Although, it was entirely possible that he was too worried about making yet another mistake to be able to recognize the right woman when she came along. Nonetheless, didn't he owe it to himself to find out?

The worst part was while she might possibly be the right woman for him, not merely every man's dream but his, it was more than obvious he was not the right man for her.

"Lord Stillwell—Winfield." Miranda paused on the top step of the short flight leading to the drive. Winfield stood beside two saddled horses, their reins held by a groom. She couldn't help but notice how dashing and handsome he looked in his riding clothes. She could certainly see what all those other women saw in him. Not that she cared. Even if he had invaded her dreams last night in a most improper and all too exciting manner. But she certainly couldn't help what happened in her sleep. "I didn't expect to see you so early."

"I was told you intended to ride to Fairborough today and I thought I would accompany you." He smiled in a pleasant manner. Given the way they had left things between them last night, she wasn't sure she trusted that smile.

"I am more than capable of getting to the hall by myself."

"I have no doubt of that, Miranda, as long as you stay to the road. However, there is a shorter way through the fields that trims a good ten minutes off the time. It's much more . . . efficient."

"Oh well, as long as it's *efficient*." She wasn't at all sure why his reference to efficiency annoyed her and yet it did. She allowed him to help her into the saddle, ignoring the unwelcome sensation of the warmth of his hands.

He mounted his own horse and they started off. Within a few minutes she was glad she had decided to ride rather than take a carriage. Riding beside one another negated the necessity for conversation. But sitting together in a carriage they'd be forced to speak to one another or endure long stretches of awkward silence. Admittedly, she did rather enjoy conversing with him, aside from that irritating tendency she had to say whatever crossed her mind. She did need to do something about that.

"Do you think it can be done?" he said at last.

"Do I think what can be done?"

He slanted her a skeptical look, as if he knew that she knew precisely what he meant. "Can Fairborough be completed by the ball?"

"I believe I have made myself clear on that question," she said in a cool tone.

"Then the answer is no?"

"The answer has always been no."

"And yet you do intend to take my bonus despite the fact that completion of Fairborough was implied?"

"Indeed I do."

"You are going to claim victory because of an error in semantics?"

"Absolutely."

"In spite of the fact that I thought we were just putting on an act for the others?"

"In spite of that, yes." She nodded. "Or perhaps because you didn't make certain that I understood what you were doing."

"Well, then it is my fault entirely."

"Indeed it is."

"And I should be made to pay for my mistakes."

"And you shall."

He sighed. "It does seem a high price to pay."

"You can afford it."

"Thank God." He paused. "You know, for a woman I am not engaged to, you certainly are expensive."

She choked back a laugh. "Have all your fiancées been expensive?"

"Only one, really. Women do not tend to return expensive baubles when an engagement has ended." He shrugged. "The first had very expensive tastes."

Mrs. Hedges-Smythe, of course. Not the least bit surprising. She had the look of a woman with expensive tastes. "And the rest?"

"The second was really quite sensible and rational." He chuckled. "As it turned out, she considered me entirely too amusing for her."

"You're making that up."

"I wish I was."

She reined in her horse and stared at him. "You're serious, aren't you?"

"I'm afraid I am."

"And the third?"

"I thought we had agreed not to discuss my engagements or your marriage."

"Yes, I suppose we did." She thought for a moment. "It doesn't seem at all fair that I have asked about your engagements when we agreed not to discuss them. Even though you brought up the subject."

"Then I deserve what I get," he said in a somber manner that didn't seem the tiniest bit genuine.

"Indeed you do; however, to be fair, as I asked you three questions about your engagements you may ask me three about my marriage."

"I believe you asked four questions."

"Perhaps." She shrugged. "But I only recall three and as I didn't need to offer you any at all it's three questions or nothing."

"Three it is then." He nudged his horse and started off.

She pulled her horse up alongside his. "Well?"

"Well, I'm thinking." He glanced at her. "I only get three questions and I don't want to waste any of them."

"Goodness, it's not as if they were wishes, you know," she said under her breath.

He smiled in an annoyingly knowing manner. "No, but they might be much more valuable."

"I doubt that." She shrugged. "You may ask anything you like."

His brow rose.

"Within reason," she said quickly.

"Very well then."

They rode on in silence for a few more minutes. "Surely there is something you want to know?"

"Oh, there are any number of things that have piqued my curiosity."

"This is your opportunity."

"I am aware of that." He thought for a moment.

"Where did your husband kiss you for the first time?"

"The Egyptian Saloon at the British Museum," she said promptly. "It was nearly closing and there was no one else around."

"Not the Elgin Saloon?" He glanced at her curiously.

"John was not as interested in Greek antiquity as I was," she said in an offhand manner as if it didn't matter. And at the time, it hadn't. Now, however, she was surprised to realize, it might. "He preferred the relics of the ancient Egyptians."

"Therefore, that is what you saw when you accompanied him to the museum."

"It's not all we saw." Although in hindsight it did seem that way. They did tend to see what held John's interest rather than hers. She wondered why she'd never thought of that before.

"I see."

What, exactly, did he see? Or think he saw? "Your next question?"

"I shall save that for another time." He slid off his horse and she realized they had arrived.

"I may not be willing to answer another time." She looked down at him. He reached up to help her dismount and for a moment she was in his arms. Then he quite properly stepped back.

"That's a chance I shall have to take then." He smiled. "I shall return to collect you for afternoon tea. I assume you'll be done for the day by then."

"I would think so, but there's no need for you to have to come all this way. No doubt I can find my way back without any problem."

"Nonetheless, my mother would never forgive me if anything happened to you. Nor would I forgive myself."

"I understand, but—"

"Miranda." He leaned close and lowered his voice. "I could certainly ask that you allow Mr. Clarke to see you back to the manor every time you are here and I have no doubt that you would accede to my request until the day it became inconvenient for you or him."

"Don't be absurd," she said in a weak voice, knowing full well he was right.

"You know neither the roads nor the country-side, nor are you familiar with whatever mount you might be given. Therefore, I shall escort you here every day and back to the manor every night. And this . . ." His gaze met hers directly. "Is not subject to negotiation."

As much as she hated to admit it, he really did make perfect sense.

She favored him with a bright smile. "As you wish."

He studied her suspiciously for a long moment. "You do realize you're frightening when you're agreeable."

She laughed. "Then I shall have to be agreeable more often."

"I'm not sure I could bear up under that."

"Surely you're stronger than you think."

"I would have to be."

They exchanged a few more comments; then he remounted his horse and started back toward Millworth. She watched him for a moment, admiring how he sat in the saddle and the ease with which he controlled the animal. She wondered what else he might ask about her marriage and why he wanted to know. She had nothing to hide on that score. How very interesting that his first question had been where she first kissed John.

She turned, spotted Edwin and started toward him. They needed to discuss just how much of Fairborough could indeed be finished by the ball. Not that she wouldn't get the bonus regardless. Still, it did seem like an excellent idea to at least make an effort.

She was immersed in the details of speeding up construction, possible costs and labor questions within minutes. Still the oddest thought lingered in the back of her mind and refused to go away. It was completely absurd and not at all what she wanted. Nonetheless . . .

Where might she be the first time Winfield kissed her?

And, more to the point, why hadn't he done so already?

Chapter 14

"Excellent cake, Mother," Diana said with a look of sheer bliss on her face. "Your cook has outdone herself."

"She always does, dear." A satisfied smile curved the older woman's lips. "It's why I pay her so well."

There was nothing Mother liked better than having her cook's offerings praised. Unless, of course, it was having her daughters together under one roof, if only for a meal.

Miranda had received the note from Mother asking that her youngest child join her and her sisters for luncheon last week during her brief return to London. And while their presence was requested in the form of an invitation, it was really more of a command performance. One did not turn down the queen and one never refused Mother. She was far more lenient with Evelyn and Veronica, as they were only daughters by marriage and they did seem to have exceptionally busy lives. But then wasn't Miranda's exceptionally busy as well?

It had been three weeks since she had taken up residence at Millworth Manor and this was only the third time she had managed to come into the city. Rebuilding was progressing nicely at

Fairborough although not quickly enough for completion by the Midsummer Ball. The question of Winfield's bonus was one she and Clara discussed each time Miranda visited the office. While both women agreed the extra fee should go directly into the employee fund, as they could both clearly see the writing on the wall, on any given day one or both of them had a few moral qualms about taking money on what really was a technicality. After all, was it right to take money from a man who was too dim to realize what he had said? However, as Winfield had a great deal of money it did not seem as great a sin. The man could well afford it, whereas the employees of Garret and Tempest could not afford to lose their jobs without any kind of compensation.

"I shall soon need a new cook." Portia sighed as if losing her cook was a disaster of unmitigated proportions. "Mine has apparently agreed to wed the man who provides the butcher with chickens so she will be off to the country soon. She did promise to stay until I hire someone new, but I fear her patience is growing thin."

"Marriage does seem to be in the air," Bianca said in an innocent manner, as if she didn't know exactly what she was starting. "But then it is spring after all."

"Portia," Mother said thoughtfully. "I happened to cross paths with Lord Plumstead the other day. What a pleasant gentleman he is."

"Is he?" Portia cast Bianca a scathing look and sipped her tea. Portia was currently at the top of Mother's list.

"As pleasant as he might be, Mother, there is always a most distinct aroma around him." Diana shook her head. "I suspect it comes from whatever he uses to plaster his remaining hairs on the top of his head in a futile effort to make it appear that he has more hair than he does. It's extremely pungent, although I can't quite put my finger on what it is."

"Well, yes, I did notice that," Mother said. "Still, perhaps all he needs is the right woman to point out the error. . . ."

As much as Miranda considered London the greatest city in the world—although admittedly she had never seen those other cities considered great, Paris, Vienna and the rest—at the moment she would have given nearly anything to be back in the country. Indeed, each and every time she left Millworth for London it grew a little harder to do so. And the blame for that could be laid squarely at the feet of Winfield Elliott.

While she had originally thought it would be both confining and annoying to be escorted to and from Fairborough each and every day, it had quickly become a habit and as natural a part of her life now as breathing. In no time at all she had found she looked forward to their daily trips either by carriage or horseback. He rode quite well, as did she. She enjoyed their discussions of matters serious or silly. Indeed, she enjoyed his company. The man was amusing and entertaining and thoughtful and far more intelligent and complicated than she had expected. In truth, he was a man of many unsuspected facets.

And as annoying as it was to admit it, every time she left him, she missed him. Indeed, she seemed to miss him more and more. Which only brought to mind the question of whether or not he missed her. They had certainly become friends, but Miranda suspected mere friends did not think about the other rather more than was necessary. Friends certainly didn't wonder when another friend might kiss them. And she'd never before had a friend who visited her in her dreams and left her longing for something that might not be proper or acceptable or even right, but something she wanted nonetheless. Something wonderful and altogether wicked.

"Miranda?"

Miranda's gaze jerked to her mother's. "Yes?"

Mother frowned. "Where were you just now?"

Miranda widened her eyes. "Why, here of course."

"You most certainly were not. I can tell when one of my girls is wool gathering."

"She has been more than a little preoccupied of late." Suspicion was in Bianca's voice.

229

"Indeed, I have noticed that for some time now. A year or more, I think."

"Mourning." Diana nodded knowingly.

"That's not it." Bianca considered her sister closely. "If I didn't know better, as Miranda has always confided anything of importance to me, I would think she had some sort of secret."

"A secret?" Miranda widened her eyes. "Me?"

"That does seem rather farfetched," Mother murmured.

Miranda forced a light laugh. "What utter nonsense."

"You're being absurd, Bianca. Miranda has never had secrets. But she does look exceptionally nice today." Portia studied her with a critical eye. "Her hair is different and the dress she's wearing is positively stylish."

"Thank you," Bianca said with a smirk.

Mother raised a brow.

"Well, they are my clothes." Bianca sniffed. "I simply loaned them to her."

"And very kind of you to do so too." Mother reached over and patted Bianca's hand. "She looks lovely. That color is extremely flattering on her."

"Thank you, Mother." Miranda did think the salmon sort of color of the dress she wore today was indeed most flattering.

"Dare I ask why you have adopted such a dramatic change?" Diana said. "You've never been especially interested in clothes."

"Then isn't it past time I was?"

If she told any of them, especially her mother, half of what she had told Bianca about making changes in her life, her mother would immediately assume it was for only one reason: attracting a new husband. Before Miranda would be able to so much as open her mouth to protest, she would be at the top of Mother's list. And every eligible bachelor who could stand upright would be aimed in her direction. There was nothing that gave Mother greater joy than when one of her children ran toward her matchmaking efforts rather than fleeing in terror. Miranda and her sisters had agreed among themselves that if Mother was a bit more selective—if only in regard to superficial things like appearance, age and hair—in the suitors she threw at them, perhaps she would be more successful. Although none of them would ever tell Mother that. It would only increase her efforts.

"Good Lord, yes," Portia said with a bit more enthusiasm than was necessary. "We thought you'd never notice that you looked like—"

"A governess?" Miranda raised a brow.

"Nonsense." Mother smiled at her youngest child. "You've always been quite lovely in a sweet, quiet, reserved sort of way." Mother flashed a sharp look at the other women. "Don't we think so? Each and every one of us?"

"Of course," Bianca said weakly.

"Without question." Diana smiled in a supportive manner.

"I don't remember thinking any such thing. I thought we had all agreed . . ."

"Portia." Mother's eyes narrowed.

Portia paused, then smiled at Miranda. "We had all agreed that you were quite lovely in a quiet sort of way."

"It's always so good to hear what your sisters truly think of you," Miranda said wryly. "I said this to Bianca and I shall say it to the rest of you—I do wish you had said something."

"Why on earth would we do that?" Mother met her gaze firmly. "You were quite happy with your appearance and your life. It scarcely mattered what we thought." She smiled and picked up her teacup. "Now, tell me how my dear friend Lady Fairborough is."

"I didn't realize you knew Lady Fairborough until Miranda mentioned it to me, Mother." Suspicion sounded in Bianca's voice.

"My dear girl, I know everyone." Mother cast her a condescending smile. "I have been a part of London society for longer than I care to admit. There is no one that I do not have at least a passing acquaintance with."

"Which is a far cry from dear friend," Diana said under her breath.

Portia and Bianca exchanged glances. Portia smiled in an overly innocent manner. "Then do tell, Aunt Helena, what is Lady Fairborough's given name?"

"Margaret." Mother's smile matched her niece's. "Her husband, the Earl of Fairborough's given name is Roland. Their family name is Elliott. Lady Fairborough's maiden name was Shaw. Their son is Winfield, Lord Stillwell. Their nephew, who was raised by the family much as Portia was raised by us, is Grayson. He has made a significant fortune in ventures in America and was recently betrothed to Lady Lydingham." She took a sip of her tea. "Lady Fairborough was considered quite a beauty in her youth, as was I. Lord Fairborough had a rather disreputable reputation, but then they all did, including your father. It does appear that his son has followed in his footsteps although I must say I have heard nothing of any significance about him in some time. Even his last engagement, one of three if I recall correctly, was several years ago."

"Oh well, if it was several years ago," Bianca said under her breath.

The other women stared.

"Now then, Miranda." Mother turned her attention to her youngest. "How is my dear friend Lady Fairborough?"

"Quite well," Miranda said. "She sends her regards."

"And have you met that charming son of hers yet?"

Miranda shrugged. "In passing."

"He is not engaged again, is he?"

"Not as far as I know," Miranda said slowly.

"Not at all surprising, really." Mother considered her thoughtfully. "I do think the peace and fresh air of the country have done you a world of good," she said abruptly. "There is certainly more color in your cheeks than usual. Or perhaps it is the color of that dress. You should definitely wear that color much more often." She nodded. "Do give Lady Fairborough my best." Mother turned her attention to the others. "Diana, it has occurred to me that your . . ."

Miranda stared at her mother in disbelief. It was not at all like her to overlook anything. Why, the moment Winfield's name came up in the conversation, Miranda had expected Mother to pounce on the possibility of a match like a cat on a mouse. It did seem farfetched that, for once, her mother had either not seen an opportunity or had chosen to ignore it. Perhaps it was Winfield's reputation or, more likely, his failed engagements. There was nothing Mother saw as a greater sin than an engagement that failed to produce a marriage.

Still, as much as Miranda loved the woman, she didn't trust her. Not when it came to the possibility of a suitable match for one of her children. No one knew better than the Dowager Countess of Waterston that the rules of fair play did not apply in love and war and apparently in making an excellent match as well.

No, one would be foolish to let one's guard down with Lady Waterston. With her mother, anything could happen and, more often than not, did.

Miranda would have liked nothing better than to spend a quiet night alone in the cozy house she had shared with John. Even if her thoughts would have been about another man entirely. But late in the afternoon she and Bianca had joined Veronica at the Ladies Tearoom, where they had unfortunately been talked into accompanying her to a lecture given by Sebastian at the Explorers Club.

"I am so pleased the two of you decided to join me," Veronica said as they took their seats in the very last row in the crowded lecture hall. "Sebastian is always happy when anyone from the family can make one of his lectures. Although, really, the man should understand that, unless he's speaking on an entirely new topic, we have all heard what he has to say over and over and over again."

"Do you go to all his lectures?" Miranda asked.

Veronica nodded. "Unless, of course, I can think of some clever reason why I cannot attend."

"He does tend to fill a room." Bianca looked around. "There are scarcely any seats left."

"His books are selling quite nicely too,"

Veronica said with a satisfied smile. "I do hope you don't mind my giving up the seats Sebastian had reserved for us in the front row."

"I thought it was very gracious of you to give them to those dear elderly ladies." Miranda smiled.

"Yes, well, we shall see." Veronica sighed. "They are friends of my aunt, who is a firm believer in membership for women in the Explorers Club. As she is not here tonight, I am assuming they will be well behaved, but one never knows."

Miranda stared. "I can't imagine that they wouldn't be well behaved. They appeared docile enough."

"Appearances, my dear Miranda, can be quite misleading. Especially when it comes to elderly women with a cause." Veronica shook her head. "Why, every time my aunt comes here she inevitably gets into a dispute with the club director. And my aunt appears as meek and unassuming as her friends."

Miranda and Bianca traded glances. They had met Veronica's aunt. Meek and unassuming is not how they would describe her.

"Admittedly, that impression only lasts until she opens her mouth," Veronica murmured.

A minute later, Sebastian took his place behind the podium and cast for his audience what his family privately referred to as his professional smile. Warm, welcoming and just intimate enough to create the impression among each and every listener that he was speaking to them and them alone.

"Good evening, ladies and gentlemen. Tonight we shall go on a journey . . ."

It wasn't that her brother wasn't an excellent storyteller, but it was difficult to keep one's attention on a story one had heard any number of times before. Especially if one's mind was grappling with all sorts of questions that had nothing to do with navigating the Amazon or locating an oasis in the Sahara or whatever Sebastian was talking about tonight.

She didn't know how she felt about Winfield, although admittedly her reluctance to acknowledge or accept that there might be something quite remarkable happening between them could certainly be fear on her part. Fear that she was making a mistake or that he wouldn't share her feelings. It had been so easy with John. But Winfield was completely different from her late husband. Then again, wasn't she a completely different woman now?

". . . when considering such an expedition, one should always keep in mind . . ."

Perhaps it was time to take a risk that went beyond business or how she dressed or wore her hair. And if she wanted the man, perhaps she needed to do something about it. If, of course, he was indeed what she wanted, which did seem to be the question.

"Good Lord," Bianca said under her breath and leaned closer to her sister. "There's another one."

"Another one what?"

"Another one of Lord Stillwell's fiancées."

"Where?" Miranda craned her neck to look around.

"Right there." Bianca nodded in the general direction of most of the rest of the crowd. "To the far right, two rows in front of us. The blond woman with the boring blue hat. Three seats in from the end."

Miranda caught sight of a woman wearing an intense expression, as though what Sebastian was going on and on about was actually quite interesting, although it probably was if one was hearing it for the first time. She wore a sensible blue ensemble that struck Miranda as something she might have worn a few weeks ago. "She's very pretty."

"And very proper," Bianca said. "I can't imagine the two of them together."

"Who is she?"

"Lady Eustice—Lucille, I believe."

On Miranda's other side, Veronica leaned closer. "Who are we talking about?"

A woman seated in front of them turned and glared.

"Sorry," Miranda said weakly.

"It's my husband speaking, you know," Veronica said under her breath. "I have earned the right to interrupt him if I wish." She glanced at Miranda. "We shall talk more later."

Miranda pushed all thoughts of Winfield and his assorted fiancées out of her head and tried to focus on what her brother was saying. For the next few minutes she was carried away by Sebastian's tales of lost cities and lost treasures and the adventurous pursuits of both. He did tell a good story, even if she had heard it before.

"Now then, I must confess, I am simply beside myself with curiosity," Veronica said as soon as the applause had faded and the crowd had begun to mill and move toward the foyer lured by the promise of tepid lemonade and perhaps a personal word with tonight's lecturer. "Who were you talking about?"

"Lady Eustice." Bianca nodded toward where the lady in question was engaged in an animated conversation with a gentleman who did not appear the least bit amused.

"Really?" Veronica's gaze followed her sister-in-law's. "Why?"

"No particular reason," Miranda said quickly.

"Wasn't she engaged to Lord Stillwell?" Bianca asked.

Veronica nodded. "She was fiancée number

two. The man has been engaged three times, you know."

"Which does make one wonder what is wrong with him," Bianca said in an offhand manner. Miranda shot her a sharp look.

"I don't think there's anything wrong with him aside from a tendency to choose the wrong woman. But men often do stupid things, especially when it involves women. And one must admit, she is lovely." Veronica's gaze lingered on Lady Eustice. "No, I don't think the problem lies with Lord Stillwell. Indeed, the fact that the man has had several fiancées and has never married actually speaks well for him."

Miranda drew her brows together. "Do you really think so?"

"Without question. It's much wiser, and far more courageous, to escape from an engagement than to be forced into a lifetime with the wrong person," Veronica said.

"She certainly has a point there," Bianca muttered.

"That is one way to look at it, I suppose." Miranda nodded.

"It's the only way to look at it," Veronica said firmly. "Besides, as I have met both Lady Eustice and Lord Stillwell, I can say without question he had a narrow escape."

"Oh?" Miranda's gaze drifted back to the other woman. "Why?"

"For one thing Lady Eustice is one of the most annoyingly proper women I have ever met."

"Even including Portia?"

"Believe me, Portia is a leader of free-thinking and liberal causes when compared to Lady Eustice." Veronica shook her head. "The woman's corset is obviously laced entirely too tight."

Miranda choked back a laugh.

"Lord Stillwell deserved far better." Veronica nodded. "He has always struck me as . . . as a very nice man. I have no idea what he ever saw in her."

"You know him then?" Miranda adopted an innocent tone. "Lord Stillwell, that is."

"Oh my, yes, I've known him for years. Not well, of course. It's not as if he was a confidant or close friend or anything of that nature. But we exchange pleasantries when we happen upon one another and we have chatted now and again. I find him flirtatious and charming and really quite delightful. I might add he is also an excellent dancer." She thought for a moment. "He and Lady Eustice were a mismatch if ever I saw one. She is the type of woman who takes life entirely too seriously, but then her first husband, Sir Charles, was entirely too serious as well. Although I suppose Lord Stillwell was going through a serious period of his own at the time."

"What do you mean?"

"First of all, you must realize this is all based on things I have heard and my own observations.

But it is my understanding that between his first engagement to a woman who was much more interested in what he had than who he was—"

"We know Mrs. Hedges-Smythe." Bianca nodded.

"Ah well, then I needn't say more on that score." Veronica sniffed in disdain. "Men can be such idiots. As I was saying, after the fortuitous failure of his first engagement, Lord Stillwell became adept at handling his family's financial interests, investments and property and the like. He gained a name for being most astute and quite successful. I heard somewhere that when Lady Eustice realized there was more to him than the somber man of business he had apparently seemed to her, she wanted nothing more to do with him."

"Too frivolous, no doubt," Miranda murmured.

"Something like that, I think." Veronica grimaced. "Lord Stillwell is most amusing and I daresay she didn't want a husband whose company might be amusing. Or a husband with a past, for that matter."

"Well, he does have a certain reputation," Miranda said.

"Oh, indeed he does. And a decidedly wicked one at that." Veronica smiled in a wicked way of her own. "But then I wouldn't want a man who didn't."

"You wouldn't?" Miranda stared. "Why not?"

"Well, I would think he'd be rather boring, for one thing. For another, a man who has already tasted of what the women of the world have to offer is not a man likely to, oh, how shall I put this?" She thought for a moment. "Ah yes, not as likely to want to continue to order off the menu, as it were. He has selected his dish and is quite content with it because he knows, from experience, that all the other dishes pale in comparison."

Miranda stared.

"In addition, that same experience makes him . . . again, I can't quite think of the right word although I suppose 'skilled' will do."

"You're speaking of Sebastian now, I assume," Miranda said cautiously.

"Of course." Veronica's eyes widened in surprise. "Your brother is quite—"

"Oh, I think it's best if we don't know too much on that score." Bianca winced. "He is our brother after all."

"Yes, of course, I hadn't thought of that." Veronica nodded. "That might indeed be awkward. Suffice it to say, a man with experience, with a wicked reputation, as long as he is a decent and honorable sort otherwise, is a man who can keep a woman happy for the rest of her life. A wicked man is very nearly always too tempting to resist." Veronica's gaze drifted to the doorway, where Sebastian could be seen speaking with a group of admirers. Again, a wicked sort of smile creased her lips. "Very happy indeed."

June

Chapter 15

"And are there other ghosts as well?" Miranda said to Win, beside her in the gig. They were returning from Fairborough to Millworth for the day and the conversation had turned once again to the two estates' matching follies.

"Oh, both Millworth and Fairborough are filled with the spirits of those who have gone before and now refuse to leave," Winfield said in a mock serious tone.

It struck him that Miranda by his side might well be how life was supposed to be. It certainly seemed both natural and, well, right. Quite simply, he missed her when she wasn't there. He wasn't at all pleased that she was going to London again tomorrow. Not that he could protest. She did have business to attend to and family and friends as well, no doubt. Still, he didn't like it. Didn't like the hole she left in his world. Didn't like wondering what she was doing or who she was with. Didn't like seeing her only in his dreams.

She had been at Millworth for a full month now and had gone to London at least once a week since her arrival at the manor, although it did seem like more. The first week, when she'd been in London, he had missed her company but did not consider her absence significant. The second week, he dismissed his sense of loss as the natural feelings of anyone whose daily companion had vanished for a bit. The third week, he had been impatient and out of sorts until she had returned and he could see her smile and hear her laugh. Certainly, she was every bit as annoying now as she had been on their initial acquaintance, but he missed that as well. Missed the banter and the battle and all else that went with it. What would he do when she returned to London for good? Or perhaps the real question was: What was he willing to do to prevent that?

"One can scarcely walk through the halls of either house late at night without tripping over one or more ghosts."

"I haven't." She shrugged. "Tripped, that is."

"Just wait," he said in an ominous tone.

"I've been here a month. One would think I would have seen at least one by now. How long do I have to wait?"

"I have no idea." He shook his head. "But I suspect when one is dead, one does not follow a schedule."

"I don't believe you, you know."

He cast her a skeptical glance. "You think ghosts have schedules to keep?"

She laughed. "That's not what I meant and you know it."

He chuckled. "You believed me when I told you I had seen Thomas and Anne."

"That was different," she said in an offhand manner. "That was an excellent story. Not merely random ghosts littering the corridors."

"Then you would believe me if I had a story for every ghost?"

"Possibly, but they would have to be good stories."

"I have been known to tell very good stories."

"Yes, I have noticed that." She thought for a moment. "But Anne and Thomas were, oh, star-crossed if you will. It made perfect sense that if they could not be together in this life, they would certainly remedy that failure in the next."

"I see." He pulled up to the front entry of the manor, hopped out of the carriage and came around to help her down. "So the only reason one would return from the dead would be if one was seeking a long lost love?"

"Now you're being silly. It's not the only reason certainly, but a most powerful one, I would say."

He reached to assist her and he steeled himself against the immediate desire to pull her into his arms. It wasn't easy. He was not the sort of man used to denying desire and caution had never been his strong suit. Still, with Miranda, continued caution seemed best for both of them. He did not want to make another mistake.

"And I thought haunting by ghosts was due to unfinished business of some sort. Or to avenge a wrong or something of that nature. Or perhaps simply because they aren't entirely sure they're dead."

"Or to be reunited with the love of their lives," she said firmly.

"Soul mates then?"

"For all eternity." She nodded. "It's really quite romantic when you think about it. The idea that a great love defeats even death itself." They started up the steps to the door.

"I don't think defeat is the right word." He shook his head. "After all, they did not end up happily living their lives together. They ended up dead. Indeed, of all of the truly great love matches of history or literature, I can't think of one that ended well."

She stopped and stared at him. "Don't be absurd."

"And I daresay you can't name more than, oh, five famous couples whose romance ended well. If that many. Usually, they end up . . . dead."

"Nonsense." She scoffed. "There are dozens."

"All I'm asking for is five." He'd wager she was hard-pressed to think of one.

"Give me a moment."

"I'm waiting."

"I'm thinking," she snapped.

"However, I can think of any number that did not end well. Let's see." He counted them off on his fingers. "There was the most famous of all,

Romeo and Juliet. Dead by their own hands after the demise of numerous relatives."

"They are fictional." She shrugged. "They shouldn't count."

"Oh, but they do. And, as fiction is often truth in the eyes of the author, I'd say it is reflective of the way of the world. Next we have Heloise and Abelard. She became a nun, he became a eunuch and a monk."

"Well, yes, in that—"

"Antony and Cleopatra. He fell on his sword, she was bit by a snake. And then there was Lancelot and Guinevere, the very epitome of soul mates, who nearly destroyed a country although admittedly they might not have existed. I believe he became a hermit and she—yes, once more we have a nun. And, oh, she was married to another man."

"Very well, but—" She searched her mind. "Elizabeth Barrett Browning and Robert Browning!" Triumph sounded in her voice. "Their romance ended quite well. They were together until the day she died in his arms."

"Nonetheless, she did die."

"It's not the same and you know it. You are simply too stubborn to admit it." She thought for a moment. "Aha! Miss Bennett and Mr. Darcy! Surely you've heard of them?"

"Do you really think I would not be familiar with Miss Austen's work," he said mildly. "Do you think I am that much of an idiot?"

"Not always."

"Oh well, as long as it's 'not always.' " He shrugged. "Personally, I never really thought they suited. It seems to me she was swayed more by circumstances than affection in the end." He smiled in a smug manner. "Regardless, that's only two, you know."

"I'm thinking." She sucked in a sharp breath. "How could I possibly have forgotten Queen Victoria and Prince Albert?"

"How indeed? Although Albert is, oh, what is the word? Dead."

"But you must admit theirs is a great love story."

"I will admit great love stories that end well, real or the stuff of legend, are few and far between." He studied her for a thoughtful moment. "Love, my dear Miranda, is a fragile and elusive thing. This I know from reading overly sentimental poetry written by the likes of Mrs. Browning."

"And not from experience?"

"I'm afraid not."

Her eyes narrowed. "Even with three—"

"No," he said firmly.

"And to think I thought you were a romantic sort."

"Then this is where the reality of life conflicts with that wicked reputation of mine." He shook his head in a mournful manner. "I do so hate to disappoint."

"And I am dreadfully disappointed." She heaved an overly dramatic sigh. "I have always rather fancied a wicked man myself."

And wasn't that interesting. "Have you now?"

"Indeed, I have." She fluttered her lashes at him. "But he would have to be truly wicked."

"I'm truly wicked," he said staunchly. "And I have the reputation as well as three broken engagements to prove it."

"Well, there is that." She shook her head regretfully. "Although you have spent a great deal of time telling me—how did you put it?" She thought for a moment. "Oh yes, you did say your reputation could stand enhancing as you had not enhanced it for years."

"Pity, isn't it?"

"I'm not sure pity is the right word." She turned to go into the house.

"Miranda?"

She looked at him. "Yes?"

"You do realize you only gave me three examples, therefore I believe I have made my point."

"You do know how to win an argument, I'll grant you that." She huffed. "I find it most annoying."

He laughed.

"Still, it's all rather sad though, isn't it?"

"Sad?" He stared at her, the victory of a moment ago fading.

"All those star-crossed lovers."

"Well, yes, I suppose. . . ."

"Destined to be together and yet never able to do so." She heaved a heartfelt sigh and continued toward the door.

He watched her for a moment, then huffed. How on earth had she managed to turn the tables? Why, as he had clearly won, did he feel as though he had somehow lost?

"I know exactly what you just did, you know," he called after her.

"Good."

Miranda was still smiling with satisfaction when a footman opened the door. There was nothing more amusing than snatching the thrill of victory from Winfield.

Prescott greeted her. "Lady Fairborough requests you join her in the parlor, Lady Garret."

"Thank you, Prescott." Lady Fairborough often invited Miranda for tea when she arrived back at Millworth. That too would be something she would miss. It was usually most enjoyable and quite informative. Who knew a lady in the country could get that much gossip? One did wonder what would happen when Lady Fairborough had a telephone at her disposal.

Miranda headed for the parlor. Each and every time Miranda had tea with Lady Fairborough, she held her breath waiting for some comment about the, well, friendship, for lack of a better word, between Miranda and her son. Either the woman didn't see her as a potential daughter-in-law or she was very, very crafty.

Miranda would have wagered on the latter. Lady Fairborough could have been her mother's long lost twin.

She stepped into the parlor. Lady Fairborough sat on the sofa facing the door. "There you are, Miranda. We were wondering when you would arrive."

A woman was seated in the chair facing the older lady. Miranda couldn't see her face from the door.

"Am I late?" She crossed the room.

"Oh no, not at all." The other woman turned and grinned.

Miranda's breath caught, but she smiled nonetheless. "Why, Bianca, whatever are you doing here?"

"I was simply curious as to what you have been up to. We haven't spoken in a very long time."

"Nonsense, it hasn't been long at all. I saw you just last week in London." Miranda pinned her sister with a hard look.

"Seems much longer." Bianca sipped her tea.

"And I planned to come into London tomorrow, as I believe I did mention to you," Miranda continued. "Surely whatever you wish to talk about could have waited until then."

"Ah well, I must have forgotten. So." She shrugged. "Here I am."

Miranda narrowed her gaze. "Indeed you are."

Lady Fairborough patted the sofa beside her. "Do sit down, my dear."

Miranda took the suggested seat and reached to pour a cup of tea from the tea service on the table beside the sofa. What on earth was Bianca doing here? And, more to the point, what did she know?

"Lady Fairborough has been telling me all about the work you've been doing here," Bianca said, and Miranda's heart sank. "She's quite impressed."

"I am indeed." Lady Fairborough nodded firmly. "I so admire any woman with courage enough to see what needs to be done and does it." She frowned. "Oh dear, I do hope I was not speaking out of turn. I assumed, as your sister was here, she knew all about it."

"Of course I do. *All* about it." Bianca aimed a pointed glance at her sister. "Miranda tells me everything."

"As sisters should." The older woman smiled at Miranda. "I must confess, you have been an inspiration for me, my dear."

"I'm very flattered, but I can't imagine how."

"Even though I have always been a progressive sort, most of the gentlemen in this household are not."

"True enough." Miranda braced herself. "And?"

"Why, I have begun to think that it's all very well and good to have electricity and telephones and call it progress, but . . ."

Bianca stared as if she were mesmerized. Obviously she too realized something of significance was approaching. Miranda did hope it wasn't a speeding train.

"But?"

"But when life returns to a semblance of normalcy, when Fairborough is completed and we have again taken up residence in our own home, I think I shall join one of those societies for women's suffrage. I have come to the conclusion . . ." The older woman's resolute gaze slid from one sister to the next. "That I should like to vote."

Bianca choked on her tea.

Miranda stared. It was only a small train but a train nonetheless. Winfield was going to love this. She wasn't sure if she was terrified of the moment when Lady Fairborough announced her desire for suffrage to her son or if she was looking forward to it.

"Then vote you should." Bianca dabbed at her mouth with a serviette. "We should all vote. Indeed, we should all join one of those societies. If not two or three." Bianca inclined her head toward Lady Fairborough and lowered her voice in a confidential manner. "I daresay my mother would join us as well."

"Oh, that is good news. Perhaps I should write to her and share our thoughts."

"No," the sisters said in unison.

"We mean, not yet," Miranda said quickly.

"We should really decide at least on which society we intend to join before we involve Mother," Bianca added.

"Excellent idea." Lady Fairborough nodded. "Now then, I shall leave the two of you alone so that you may have a proper chat. I know what it's like when sisters haven't seen each other in some time." She sighed. "I quite miss my sister. I don't see her nearly as often as I should. Although she never goes anywhere without that nasty little dog of hers. That dog hates every man who comes near it but does seem to especially dislike Winfield." She thought for a moment, then shook her head. "Ah well, then." She looked at Bianca. "Mrs. Roberts, will you be staying the night? I daresay it may already be too late to catch the last train."

"Do call me Bianca, please," Bianca said. "And yes, that would be lovely."

"No," Miranda said sharply. "I mean Bianca does have to get back."

"Not really." Bianca cast her sister her sweetest smile. "And if I stay here the two of us can return to London together in the morning."

"Excellent." Lady Fairborough beamed, expressed a few more sentiments on the special nature of sisters, notwithstanding their adoration of terrorizing pets, and left the parlor.

At once Miranda turned to her sister. "What are you doing here?"

"I think the real question is what are *you* doing here?" Bianca's eyes narrowed. "Well?"

"Well," she hedged.

"That's how you're going to do this?" Bianca's brow rose. "Very well then. What I know thus far is that you are here managing—"

"I wouldn't say managing. I'm really more of an . . . adviser."

"Whatever you wish to call it scarcely matters. You've been doing it for weeks and weeks. Indeed, I suspect you are back to your old tricks."

"What old tricks?" Caution edged Miranda's voice.

"I thought John's death had put an end to that. Obviously I was wrong. You're designing buildings or whatever it is you do, and letting someone else take the credit again, aren't you?"

Miranda stared. "How did you know?"

"You told me once in passing—oh, years and years ago—that you were behind John's designs."

Miranda narrowed her eyes. "I don't remember that."

"It was an offhand comment, in the middle of some festivity if I recall, and I believe we had both had more than our share of wine. It didn't

259

seem important then, and I only remember it now because I finally put two and two together. Your continuing absence from London, the fire at Fairborough Hall and hearing it was being rebuilt." She shrugged. "Also I paid someone to ask a few questions, I visited with your servants in London and I spoke with Miss West."

"Clara?"

"Oh my, yes. Lovely woman. And very loyal to you. She was reticent to say anything at all. Miss West would have held up well under medieval torture. The rack and the like. I'll have you know I was quite tempted by the thought of those methods, but I restrained myself." Bianca shook her head. "Fortunately, by the time I spoke with her, I had all but a few details."

"And?"

"And I know that you are running Garret and Tempest. I am certain as well that you are the architect for Fairborough Hall and every other project your husband's—or I should say your— firm undertakes."

"Is that all?"

"Is there more?" Bianca's brows drew together. "Have I missed something?"

"Not really. You're quite good at this. Very thorough, I might add. Now that you know . . ." She paused. "Will you tell the rest of the family?"

"Do you really think I would?"

"Well . . ."

"Why on earth would I tell the family?" Bianca scoffed. "One never knows how anyone might react. Honesty is certainly not worth the risk."

Miranda nodded. "My thoughts exactly."

"Furthermore, I, for one, agree with Lady Fairborough. It's quite courageous of you. You've always liked drawing buildings and that sort of thing. I never thought it was at all fair that John took the credit for your work even if you didn't seem to mind."

"I didn't at the time."

"Why should you be kept from doing what you enjoy, what you are apparently quite good at, because you are female? The only reason that you are doing it in a clandestine manner is because men have driven you to it. Men rule the world and men make the rules. Fortunately for us, the vast majority of them are idiots. And while one shouldn't usually take advantage of those less fortunate, men are the exception. So I say bravo, Miranda, and what can I do to help?"

Miranda stared. "Nothing, but thank you."

Bianca considered her sister. "You do realize, if I found out, it's only a matter of time before—"

"Yes, yes, I know." Miranda waved off the comment. "I am going to tell them."

"When?"

"Well, that's the question, isn't it?" She shook her head. "Definitely not tomorrow but probably soon."

"Apparently you're not as courageous as Lady Fairborough thinks."

"No one is." Miranda leaned forward and met her sister's gaze. "Might I ask when you intend to tell them of your pursuit of a divorce?"

"Ouch." Bianca winced. "That was not at all kind of you."

"My apologies," Miranda said wryly.

"That is a topic for another conversation. We are discussing you at the moment," Bianca said firmly. "And might I point out news of your activities will be much better coming from you than if it becomes gossip."

"I really can't imagine it's all that interesting," Miranda said under her breath. "As scandal goes, that is."

"You're not serious." Bianca stared at her with disbelief. "You're competing in a man's field and you are not only doing it as well, you're doing it better. I think it's mad and brilliant. As scandal goes, this has everything but a virginal governess and a wicked scoundrel."

"How absurd." Miranda laughed. "It's not nearly as interesting as a virginal governess and a wicked scoundrel."

"Pardon me, ladies." Win lounged in the open doorway. "I thought I heard somebody call for a wicked scoundrel."

Chapter 16

"Eavesdropping, Winfield?" Miranda shot him an exasperated look.

"Winfield, is it?" Bianca murmured with a knowing look at her sister.

"I was trying." He sauntered into the room.

"How much did you hear?"

"Not nearly enough. I would apologize, but when one is innocently passing by an open door and hears talk of 'virginal governesses' and 'wicked scoundrels' bandied about, well . . ." He glanced at Bianca. "What was I to do?"

Bianca stared. "Eavesdrop?"

"Exactly." Winfield's eyes narrowed. "Are you exchanging secrets?"

"Deep, dark secrets." Miranda nodded. "Secrets that come perilously close to gossip."

"About virginal governesses and wicked scoundrels?"

"Those are the best kind of secrets as well as the best gossip." There was nothing Bianca liked better than a juicy bit of gossip.

He laughed and relief washed through Miranda. He couldn't have heard anything of importance or he wouldn't be so lighthearted.

"Although, I don't know," Bianca said thoughtfully. "Now that I think about it, there have been entirely too many secrets about virginal governesses and wicked scoundrels. Why, that's all you ever hear about. It may well be time for new secrets."

Win flashed his wicked smile at her sister. "My sentiments exactly. Shall we ferret out one of our own, or shall we simply make it up?"

"I wouldn't think it's necessary to make anything up as there are so many—"

"Winfield, I don't believe you've met my sister, Mrs. Roberts," Miranda cut in smoothly. She had no idea what Bianca might say and no desire to find out. "Bianca, this is Lord Stillwell."

Bianca's brow rose. "Ah yes, the notorious Lord Stillwell."

"Good Lord, I hope not." He grinned.

"I have heard a great deal about you." Bianca studied him curiously.

"Nothing good, I suspect." Winfield glanced at Miranda. "I should warn you, anything your sister says is not true."

"Really?" She shot a speculative glance at Miranda. "You needn't worry on that score. She hasn't mentioned you at all."

He winced. "That is even worse."

"Bianca is staying the night and then I am accompanying her back to London tomorrow," Miranda said lightly. "I have some matters to attend to. But Mr. Clarke has things well in hand."

"I have no doubt of it." He paused. "How long will you be gone?"

"A few days, I think."

"Ah well, we shall have to carry on without you then." His gaze met Miranda's and her heart leapt. Nonsense, of course. "I have matters of my own that are calling me. Very nice to meet you, Mrs. Roberts. Until dinner then." He nodded and left the room.

Miranda's gaze followed him. What was the man doing to her?

"He doesn't know, does he?" Miranda's gaze jerked to her sister's. "No, he thinks the architect is Mr. Tempest."

Bianca studied her. "Are you going to tell him?"

"Not unless I have to." She shook her head. "He has some very definite ideas on what women should and should not be doing in this world. He would never understand and might well discharge me on the spot."

"But surely you have some sort of written contract."

"Of course, but I wouldn't put it past him to pay our agreed-upon fees and discharge me anyway. He certainly has the money to do so and the truth would no doubt infuriate him." Miranda blew a long breath. "He would see this as a massive deception."

"Forgive me for pointing this out, but isn't it?"

"Well, yes, I suppose, but it isn't, oh, personal."

"And he would take it as a personal affront?" Bianca said slowly.

"It certainly didn't start out that way, but now . . ."

"Now?"

"Now we have become, oh, friends of a sort, I would say."

"Friends?" A skeptical note sounded in Bianca's voice.

"Yes," Miranda said firmly. "Friends."

"I see."

"I know that tone, Bianca." Miranda stared at her sister. "What exactly do you think you see?"

"Not a thing. Absolutely nothing." She shook her head. "However, you did not answer my question."

Miranda stared in confusion. "Which question was that?"

"When I asked if he knew, I was not referring to your work."

"No?"

"No indeed." She met Miranda's gaze directly. "I was asking if he knew how you felt about him."

"I don't feel anything about him."

"Oddly enough, I don't believe you."

"Well, you should." Miranda absently picked at the threads on the arm of the sofa. "Although admittedly there are indeed any number of things I feel about him. He is one of the most annoying men I have ever met. Worse, he seems to enjoy annoying me."

"He is quite handsome," Bianca murmured.

"He is also dreadfully old-fashioned and can be extremely stiff and stodgy."

"He certainly didn't look either stiff or stodgy."

"Looks are deceiving. Why, the man isn't nearly as wicked as his reputation would make you think."

"Pity. Wicked men can be most amusing." Bianca grimaced. "As long as they are decent, honorable sorts as well."

"In addition, even his mother says he's something of a stick-in-the-mud."

"He seemed rather charming to me."

"You don't know him," Miranda snapped. "Certainly on the surface he seems all charming and dashing. But he likes nothing better than a rousing argument about something inconsequential like famous love matches. We argue endlessly, although it does tend to be rather, well, fun."

"Fun?"

"Yes, fun." She sighed in surrender. "There is nothing in the world like a verbal battle with Lord Stillwell. And nothing better than winning that debate."

"I can imagine," Bianca said under her breath.

"And yes, he can be most amusing. And indeed he makes me laugh rather more than I have in years. And admittedly, he is surprisingly intelligent. Why, he has taken over complete control of his family's business concerns and properties. And done quite well with them I might add. And he—"

"Has he kissed you?"

Heat washed up Miranda's face. "Don't be absurd. Why would you ask such a thing?"

"Oh, I don't know." Bianca considered her closely. "Perhaps it's the way he looks at you. As if it's all he can do to keep his hands to himself."

"That's ridiculous." Miranda scoffed. "I haven't noticed—"

"Or perhaps it's the way you look at him."

"That too is absurd. I don't look at him—"

"As if he were a gift you cannot wait to unwrap."

"That is the silliest—"

"I have never seen you look at a man like that." She leaned forward and met her sister's gaze firmly. "Not even John."

"I loved John," she said staunchly.

"Of course you did."

"John and I never argued."

"And why would you? You were too busy doing exactly what he wanted."

The fact that they had never argued had never seemed a bad thing. Until now. "We were simply in accord on everything."

"You simply acquiesced to him on everything."

"I wouldn't put it that way. But I was his wife, after all."

"And an excellent—dare I say, perfect—wife you were too."

"I certainly wasn't perfect." Although thinking back on it, perhaps they had never argued not merely because she never disagreed with him but because she had always tended to retreat rather than stand fast on her positions. Indeed, she had never really argued with anyone. Until recently. Until Winfield Elliott, that is. "I don't see why that is the least bit significant."

"What?"

"The fact that I never argued with John and yet I seem to argue with Lord Stillwell all the time."

Bianca studied her for a long, thoughtful moment, then nodded. "I agree. It's not the least bit significant."

"Now, I don't believe you."

"Miranda," Bianca began, "John was a good man."

"Absolutely."

"And you loved one another."

"Of course we did." She nodded firmly.

"But . . ." Bianca drew a deep breath. "You are not the same woman you were when you married him nine years ago, nor are you the same woman you were when he died. You have changed. I can't quite put my finger on how, but you have. There is somehow, I don't know, *more* of you than there used to be."

And hadn't Miranda come to the same conclusion herself? "Do you think so?"

"Without a doubt." Bianca nodded. "I was remiss in not noticing it before now. But then you have been elusive and I can be so very self-centered on occasion. . . ."

"On occasion?" Miranda smiled. "My dear sister, if you are expecting me to disagree now, I shall have to disappoint you."

"That is disappointing." She paused for a moment. "Might I give you some advice?"

"Can I stop you?"

"Probably not."

"Go on then."

"I don't believe in things like soul mates. The idea that we are destined to be with one person and one person only in this life, that there are no other possibilities for happiness." She shook her head. "I simply don't believe it, that's all."

Miranda nodded. "I can understand that."

"Loving once, Miranda, does not preclude you from loving again."

Was Bianca speaking of Miranda's life or her own? As dreadful a mistake as her sister now knew marriage to her husband was, she had loved him once. Or thought she had.

"Was that the advice?"

"Wait, there's more." She thought for a moment. "You have, oh, I suppose 'blossomed' is the right word, since John's death."

"Good Lord. That sounds dreadful."

"Rightly or wrongly, Miranda, it is indeed what happened. I should have recognized it sooner. The secrecy, the preoccupation—all the signs were there, but I was too busy with my own concerns to notice and for that you have my apologies. But there is something between you and Lord Stillwell that I never saw between you and John." She shook her head. "Even if you don't see it, it scarcely took me more than a moment to recognize that there is something quite remarkable happening between the two of you. I suspect Lady Fairborough and everyone else here have noted it as well."

"Lady Fairborough hasn't said a word."

"Clever of her, isn't it?" Bianca chuckled. "Exactly what Mother would do if she was encouraging a match."

"She's certainly not . . ."

Bianca's brow rose.

"I will admit . . ." Miranda chose her words with care. "There does seem to be something between us, although I am not entirely sure what it is. I don't know that we suit one another. He is so dreadfully annoying. And I daresay he feels exactly the same way about me."

Bianca laughed.

"What do you find so amusing?"

"Your indecision." She grinned. "You weren't the least bit indecisive about John."

"I never had any doubts about John." She sniffed. "We were perfectly suited from the first moment we met. There was never a disagreeable word or discordant note between us."

"Pity."

"What?"

Bianca shrugged. "There's a great deal to be said for the passion of argument as well as the passion inherent in setting things right."

"It scarcely matters." Miranda shook her head. "Once Lord Stillwell knows that I have deceived him, he will never forgive me. He values honesty, especially in women, which I suspect has to do with his former fiancées."

"Then don't tell him."

"You said it yourself. This is bound to come out soon. And then . . ." She shuddered.

Winfield wasn't anything like John. But then she had begun to realize, neither was she. She had always thought John had given her the freedom to be herself, and in many ways he had. But she had never disagreed with him and surely there were any number of times when she should have. Rather, she avoided confrontation, anger, raising her voice. Life was so much easier that way.

But not nearly as exciting. The thought popped into her head unbidden. And wasn't doing battle with Winfield exciting? Wasn't it—wasn't *he*— challenging and exhilarating? And hadn't she indeed been having a great deal of fun?

And when they gazed into one another's eyes, wasn't there something that snapped between them like the sparks from Lord Salisbury's electricity? Something compelling and rare and eternal? Something that might never come her way again?

But what if she was wrong? What if everything she was coming to feel was only because he was so good at what he did? In spite of his claims that his reputation was not being actively *enhanced,* he was reportedly an expert in seduction. What if she was just another conquest? What if he broke her heart?

"The only thing you can do at the moment, however, is try to figure out what it is you want." Bianca's gaze met hers. "Or possibly who."

Miranda stood on the terrace, gazing out over the Millworth gardens, silhouetted by the deepening twilight. She looked not unlike the figurehead on a grand sailing ship of a century ago. Brave and strong and determined. A fanciful notion, of course, but no less accurate for the whimsy of it.

Win moved to stand beside her at the stone balustrade. "May I join you, or are you plotting your next assault on all I hold dear?"

She smiled but continued to gaze out over the grounds. "I would never admit to that. Surprise, you know, is everything in an assault."

"Oh, well then." He leaned back against the

273

balustrade and studied her profile. "I must say, you are shockingly pensive tonight."

"Shockingly?"

"It's rather disconcerting. You are generally not the least bit pensive. At least not to my knowledge."

"I daresay there are all sorts of things you don't know about me."

"Perhaps." He chuckled. "Although I thought I was coming to know you quite well."

"Have you really never been in love?" she said abruptly and turned toward him.

He stared. "Why would you ask that?"

"This afternoon you said that you knew love was a fragile and elusive thing from poetry and not from experience." She studied him carefully. "I took that to mean you had never been in love."

"Well, then you know my secret."

"Are you sure?"

"Fairly sure."

"But if you have never been in love how would you recognize when you weren't?"

He drew his brows together. "I have no idea. I just assumed I would know when I was."

"How?"

"I don't know." He huffed. "Birds and butterflies would be flitting about. The sun would be shining. A choir of angels would be singing in the heavens. You know, the usual sort of thing."

"Now you are being sarcastic, whereas I was being quite serious," she said in a lofty manner.

"It's a ridiculous question. How does anyone know when they're in love?"

"I would still like an answer."

"I don't have an answer."

"How can you have had three fiancées and never have been in love?"

"I don't know," he snapped. "Luck? Fate? Timing?"

"Even so—"

"How did you know when you were in love with your husband? I assume you were in love with him."

"Of course I was and . . ." Her eyes narrowed. "Is that your second question? About my marriage, that is?"

"Yes, yes, it's not the question I had intended, but yes."

"Oh." She paused. "What question did you intend?"

"I don't know, I haven't thought of it yet, but I suppose this one will do. How did you know when you were in love with your husband?"

She shook her head. "I don't know. I just did."

"Aha!"

"Aha?"

"When I said the very same thing, when I said I just assumed I would know, you would not accept that answer." He crossed his arms over his chest. "Therefore I cannot accept yours."

"Now you're being childish."

"I am not," he said, though he did feel rather like a child at that.

"Well, that's the only answer I have." She shrugged.

"Nonetheless, you shall have to do better."

"I'm not sure I can."

"Come now, Miranda. While I have never known love myself, I am not completely ignorant of what is supposed to occur when love is involved."

"The birds, the sun and the choir of angels, you mean?"

"Among other things." He slipped off the balustrade and straightened. "First." He took her hand. "Your heart should flutter oh so slightly when he takes your hand."

"Oh?"

"Then, as he raises your hand to his lips, and you gaze into his eyes"—he matched his actions to his words—"your breath should catch as you wait for the first touch of his lips upon your hand."

"I see." Her voice had the faintest breathless quality. His stomach tightened.

"You feel the tiniest stab of loss when he releases your hand."

"Do I?"

"But then he steps near to you." He moved

closer. "So close you can sense the heat of his body next to yours."

"Can I?"

"Indeed you can." He wrapped his arms around her waist. "His hands slip around you and he gently pulls you closer. And the beat of your heart speeds up."

"Does it?" She swallowed hard.

"And then he gazes into your eyes, his lips moving inevitably closer. And you can't look away because in his eyes you see a reflection of your own feelings. And that, I suspect, is the final piece. That, I suspect, is when you know." His lips met hers and he murmured against them. "And you know, when he kisses you, as he will, that it's not just a kiss, it's an acknowledgement of what he holds in his heart. And a promise that this is only the beginning."

"Is it?" she whispered.

"If I am very, very lucky." He gathered her closer and pressed his lips to hers. She hesitated, and then her mouth opened to his and she tasted of spring and promises and everything he'd ever wanted. Everything he'd ever longed for. He deepened his kiss and she responded in kind. And for an endless moment there was nothing in the world beyond her and him and the two of them together. At last he raised his head and gazed down at her.

She stared up at him. "Why did you do that?"

"Because I've wanted to do that for a very long time."

"But what does it mean?"

He smiled. "It means, my dear Miranda, that I wanted to kiss you and judging from your response, that you wanted to kiss me back."

"Are you in love with me?"

"Love?" He hadn't really considered love. He stared down at her. "That was not the reaction I was expecting."

"What were you expecting?"

He released her and stepped back. "I'm not sure, but that was not it."

"I haven't done this for a very long time, you know." She turned and paced the terrace.

"I assumed as much."

"Therefore you must forgive me if I am out of practice."

"I thought it was a most excellent kiss."

"Oh yes, well, that." She waved off his comment. "That was indeed excellent. It might well be the most excellent kiss I have ever had."

Ever? "Well, then I don't understand what—"

"Goodness, Winfield, it was obviously an excellent kiss because you have had so much practice at it."

"You did say you rather fancied a wicked man."

"Indeed I did, which was why I was prepared for your kiss." She stopped mid-pace and looked at him. "And it was an outstanding kiss."

He crossed his arms over his chest. "How outstanding?"

"Why, my toes curled inside my shoes." She nodded. "That outstanding."

"Good."

"Which is why I am so confused."

"No more so than I," he muttered. "Go on."

She resumed pacing. "How am I to know if, when my toes curled and before that, as you so expertly described, when my heart raced and I forgot to breathe, that it truly meant something of significance. If you are kissing me because it is indeed love, all those things are to be expected, even welcomed. Or did I only experience all that—"

"The toes, the heart, the breath?"

She nodded. "Was that significant, or did that only happen because you are so good at what you do?"

The woman made no sense whatsoever. "What I do?"

"Seduction," she said with a dramatic flourish in her voice.

Damn it all. Didn't she know him better by now? "Do you really think I would seduce you right here, Miranda? On the terrace—"

"All sorts of things could happen on a terrace," she said darkly.

"When I have the perfect opportunity every day on the way to or from Fairborough—"

"I have often wondered if you had thought of that."

He stared at her. "Of course I have thought of that, which is neither here nor there at the moment, and as inappropriate as that might be, it is surely not as inappropriate as seducing you here on the terrace when we are about to be called into dinner. With my family!"

"It did seem rather dangerous. Still, you are a dangerous sort, aren't you?"

He closed his eyes and prayed for strength. "I was not seducing you. I kissed you. It was one simple kiss."

"I'd scarcely call it simple," she pointed out. "It was a very good kiss."

"Indeed it was. On both sides, I might add." He narrowed his gaze. "Given that, one might well think you have had a great deal of practice as well."

She gasped. "I cannot believe—"

"Ahem."

Win didn't have to look to know that was Prescott's way of discreetly announcing his presence. He wasn't sure if he was grateful or annoyed. Probably both.

"I assume you're here to call us to dinner."

"Yes, my lord," Prescott's voice sounded from the shadows near the door.

"Very well then. We shall be right in."

"I beg your pardon, my lord."

"What is it now?"

"I was told to wait for you."

Win's jaw tightened. "Why?"

"I was instructed to do so by Mrs. Roberts."

"Ha!" Miranda leaned closer to him and lowered her voice. "She too is obviously concerned about seduction."

"As well as by Lady Fairborough and Lady Lydingham."

"My, my." She swept past him on her way to the door. "It seems that again your reputation has preceded you."

"My reputation is greatly exaggerated!"

She snorted in disbelief.

He stalked after her, well aware that once again he had no idea of what had just happened. Once again he had the distinct feeling that he had lost some unknown game and once again he wasn't sure if she was mad or he was.

Even worse, he didn't know the answer to her question.

And worst of all, he was afraid to find out.

Chapter 17

Win leaned back in the chair behind the desk in the Millworth library and stared at nothing in particular. But then, he had found himself doing a lot of that lately. Miranda and her sister had left for London this morning. Already he missed her, even if the woman seemed determined to drive him mad.

Was he in love with her? What kind of question was that to ask after a kiss? One, single kiss. Extraordinary or not, that was not the thing to ask after one kiss, particularly not a first kiss. Why, there was a time in his life when a kiss meant nothing at all. It certainly wasn't a commitment for the rest of his days.

The truth of the matter was, he didn't know how he felt about her. And, as he had never told a woman he loved her before, that did seem a rather significant declaration to make without serious thought.

He had certainly grown accustomed to her presence. To talking with her, teasing, debating about nothing of significance as well as about matters of importance.

It was as if they had agreed to an unspoken truce on those trips to and from Fairborough. Neither brought up a topic guaranteed to infuriate the other. Not that they didn't frequently disagree. There were books she liked that he didn't. Artists he enjoyed that she considered dabblers. And their disagreement was as stimulating as when they stumbled onto common ground and found they both shared an appreciation of something unexpected.

Evenings with his family were enjoyable as well. They proved to be quite a convivial group. And if his mother had originally intended to nudge Miranda in his general direction she had either thought better of it or someone had urged discretion.

Two months ago he hadn't even met the woman. Now, he suspected he knew Miranda Garret better than he had ever known any woman, indeed any person male or female except possibly Gray. Now, he could scarcely bear a day without seeing her. And now, he wasn't at all sure what he would do without her. As much as it would be convenient to have the rebuilding completed by the Mid-summer Ball, he was beginning to wish it would never be finished. Silly of him, of course.

There had as well been a few additional *moments* when their gazes had met unexpectedly and the very air between them was charged with desire so palpable he could almost touch it. Time itself stopped and the world vanished save for the two of them. That's when he had found a sheer strength of will he hadn't known he had and wasn't especially delighted to discover as it was the only thing that had kept him from grabbing her and pulling her into his arms and never letting go. Until last night, that is.

Of course he had thought of seducing her. On the route from Fairborough, in the newly framed ballroom, at the folly, in the gardens, under the stars, in the library and, yes, on the bloody terrace. With each day that passed he thought about seducing her. Why he hadn't so much as kissed her until today was as much a question to him as whether or not he loved her. Or perhaps one question answered the other.

He wanted the woman; that was obvious. But did he love her? How was he expected to know?

He certainly did not want to make another mistake. Nor did he want to fall in love with a woman who might well still be in love with her first husband. A first husband she had thought was perfect because she didn't know of his manipulations of the debt to Mr. Tempest. Whoever he was. Which brought to mind an entirely different problem.

Aside from all the other reasons for caution, she was still hiding something important from him. No matter how well he thought he had grown to know her, there was still something she refused to share. What that might be, he had no idea. But he would not fall in love with a woman he could not completely trust. Unfortunately, having never been in love before, he had no idea how to prevent it.

But he knew with every day and every minute in her presence, he came perilously close to falling over the edge of a precipice from which there would be no escape. At least, no escape that left him unscathed.

If, indeed, it wasn't already too late.

A knock sounded at the library door.

"Yes?"

The door opened and Gray sauntered in, Prescott a step behind him. "Mr. Chapman is here to see you, my lord."

Win glanced at his cousin. "How very interesting."

"My thoughts exactly." Gray settled in one of the two chairs positioned in front of the desk. "Which is why I've decided to join you."

Win had told Gray everything he had learned from Chapman so far, and his cousin was now as curious as he was. "Show him in, if you please, Prescott."

"Very good, sir." Prescott left the room, closing the door behind him.

"I wonder what he has uncovered," Win said.

"Hopefully enough to satisfy your curiosity." Gray studied him closely. "But does it really matter at this point? Who the architect is, I mean. Given your friendship with Miranda, that is."

"Probably not." Still, Win did want to know.

A knock sounded again, the door opened and Prescott stepped aside to allow Chapman to enter. Then he closed the door, leaving the three men alone.

Chapman strode across the room and extended his hand to Win. "Good day, my lord."

"Mr. Chapman." Win shook the other man's hand, then gestured for him to take a seat. Chapman shook Gray's hand, then sat down.

"I am assuming you have some information for me," Win said.

"Indeed I do." Chapman started to pull out his notebook, paused, grinned at Win and thought better of it. "It appears there are either two separate and distinct Mr. Tempests or he does not exist at all."

"Oh good, I do love complications," Gray murmured.

"I shall try to explain." Chapman thought for a moment. "There is indeed a Mr. Tempest, or someone using that name, who advanced money to John Garret for Garret and Tempest. I still have not been able to determine exactly who he is. However, he is definitely not the same Mr. Tempest being credited with the plans for your house."

Win drew his brows together. "Mr. Chapman, your attempt to explain is falling short."

"It is somewhat confusing."

"That much is clear," Gray said.

"No one at the offices has ever seen Mr. Tempest. No one speaks of him as if he is simply an absent member of the firm. Furthermore, before the rebuilding of Fairborough Hall, his name was not associated with designs produced by Garret and Tempest."

Win shook his head. "I don't understand."

"I said it was confusing. As I suspect it was intended to be."

Gray frowned. "What do you mean?"

"I am still trying to put all the pieces together. And while I have not learned anything about Tempest the architect . . ." Chapman leaned forward and met Win's gaze directly. "There were rumors in certain circles, no more than idle speculation really and quickly dismissed as improbable."

"Go on."

"Even before the death of her husband, there was talk—most discreet, I might add, and given no credence—that the true designer at Garret and Tempest was not John but Miranda Garret."

"Good God." Gray stared.

Win narrowed his eyes. "Are you sure?"

"The truth is a remarkably elusive thing in this case so, no, I am not completely sure. But I am certain that the style of the designer has not changed since Lord Garret's death."

"Of course, it wouldn't, would it?" Win said

under his breath. Oddly enough, Chapman's revelation was not nearly as startling as he would have expected. It had been obvious from the beginning that Miranda knew far more than she let on.

If indeed she was the architect, and he had very little doubt about that now, it made perfect sense that she would not want the world to know. After all, the design of buildings was not an accepted female activity. Nor was the running of a business although it was obvious she did that as well. And that business would vanish if word got out that the true architect at Garret and Tempest had never been Lord Garret but rather Lady Garret, no matter how skilled she was.

Certainly there would be some progressive sorts that would applaud her independent nature, mostly ladies of independent means, he suspected. Regardless, the fact of the matter was that, here and now, men ruled the world of business. No matter how excellent Miranda was at what she did, she would never be accepted.

He had never questioned that before. It was as it should be. He firmly believed in a woman's proper place in the world. But now it struck him as, well, stupid to disallow talent and intelligence because of one's gender.

Good Lord, the woman had *reformed* him or transformed him or something equally annoying. He'd never had any desire to change his way of thinking and yet—there was no getting around it—he had. She had changed him.

"What now, my lord?" Chapman asked.

"Now?"

"Yes, now," Gray said cautiously.

"What do you wish me to do now?" Chapman said. "I can continue to attempt to prove that Lady Garret is the architect you have hired, although it seems to me the most straightforward way to do that is to ask her outright." He shrugged. "And that, I think, would be best left to you."

Win nodded. "Quite right."

"Then will you do so?"

"No," Win said without thinking. "The quality of work is undeniable."

Gray nodded his approval.

"As such, it really doesn't matter whose work it is," Win continued. "My intent has always been to have the house rebuilt. And she has that well in hand. Her reasons for keeping her activities quiet are obvious." He met Chapman's gaze firmly. "I assume this information will remain confidential."

"Without question." Indignation sounded in Chapman's voice. "I never reveal what I have uncovered to anyone other than my client. Discretion is part and parcel of what I do. I would never have another job if I did not keep my findings confidential."

"Quite right." Gray nodded.

Win thought for a moment. "I know I said I didn't care as to the identity of her investor, of this Mr. Tempest, but I find I have changed my mind. I do now want to know who he is."

"Do you?" Gray studied his cousin.

Win shrugged. "It seems like a good idea."

"And isn't that interesting?" Gray said under his breath.

"I'll do what I can, sir." Chapman rose to his feet and Win stood as well. "But I cannot guarantee success. The man is both clever and elusive. However . . ." He cast Win a confident smile. "I do hate it when questions are too easily answered."

"That's where we differ, Chapman. I much prefer questions that are easily answered. And I am not at all fond of deception."

"Few men are." Chapman paused. "Might I ask why you do not intend to confront Lady Garret about this?"

"You may ask, but I'm not sure I have an answer."

"I know I am surprised." Gray smiled in an annoyingly knowing manner.

Win considered the question. "As I said, it doesn't matter in the scheme of things. Not really. As it is her secret, it seems it is not up to me to reveal it."

"I see." Chapman nodded. "But she deceived you."

"Not just me." He chuckled. "The entire world. Damnably clever of her, really."

"If the truth was revealed, her business would fail." Chapman shook his head. "No one would deliberately hire a female for work of this nature."

"Not deliberately, no." That too now struck Win as a pity.

"She is a woman concerned with the welfare of her employees. If her true position becomes known, they would be out of work." Chapman nodded thoughtfully. "Which explains why she set up a fund to assist them. She must realize her deception cannot go on forever."

"Especially now that she has taken a public role in the construction at Fairborough," Gray added.

Win met his cousin's gaze. "Exactly why she is holding me to my promise of a bonus. That is money above and beyond anything else that she could put directly into her employee fund. She must understand that time is no longer on her side."

"I'm afraid I'm still confused as to why you don't tell her you know," Chapman said.

"Because I wish for her to tell me herself." The moment Win said the words he knew they were true. "Lady Garret and I have forged a friendship of sorts and I would much prefer she trust me enough to tell me the truth."

"I see." Chapman chuckled. "That's the way of it then."

"The way of what?"

"Indeed it is, Mr. Chapman," Gray said abruptly and rose to his feet. "If that is all for today?"

"It is." Chapman nodded and stood, then addressed Win. "I shall do whatever is necessary to learn the truth about Mr. Tempest."

Win considered the other man thoughtfully. "I do hope this unanswered question isn't the one that defeats you."

"That, my lord," Chapman said firmly, "is not a possibility."

The men exchanged a few more words with Chapman promising to contact Win as soon as he learned anything new; then he took his leave.

"Interesting," Gray said, retaking his seat. "But not especially surprising, I would say."

"No, it's not at all surprising." Win shrugged and sat down. "I should have recognized the truth myself. There is a way she looks at the drawings and plans, a look in her eyes when she watches the progress at Fairborough that speaks of pride of ownership. And indeed she should be proud of her work."

"Yes, she should."

"She has done and is doing an excellent job."

"Indeed, she is. And it seems to me your questions have now been answered." Gray studied his cousin closely. "So explain to me why you have changed your mind. Why do you want to know about Tempest?"

"Because, whoever he is, he has a hold, if only financial, on Miranda's company and therefore on her life."

"And what will you do if you find out who he is?"

"I don't know." Win shook his head. "But it seems in Miranda's best interest to find out the truth of it."

"Oh, she'll certainly see it that way."

"I daresay she might see this as being none of my concern. Regardless, whether she likes it or not, she has become my concern."

"Oh?"

"We've become friends," Win said firmly, "good friends. This is no more than I would do for any friend."

"Yes, of course, exactly what I was thinking. And I suspect what Chapman was thinking as well."

"Why did you interrupt him?" Win studied the other man. "When he made his cryptic comment about the way of it?"

"I simply wanted to save you the effort of denial. Chapman was obviously about to charge you with having fallen in love with her."

"Don't be absurd. The man's powers of observation may well be acute when it comes to recognizing intrigue, but he knows nothing about matters of the heart."

"And yet I would say his observation in that quarter was quite accurate."

"Utter rubbish."

"Still, you are not going to confront her but rather wait for her to confide in you. Wait for her to, dare I say, trust you?"

Win nodded. "Exactly."

"As one friend would trust another."

"Precisely."

Gray fell silent, his gaze thoughtful and considering.

"What are you thinking now?" Win said sharply. He did not like the look on his cousin's face.

"I am simply wondering what has you so scared."

Win scoffed. "I am not the least bit scared."

"I have never seen you scared in matters involving a woman before."

"I am not scared." Win rolled his gaze toward the ceiling. "What on earth do I have to be frightened of?"

"If it was me, I would be afraid of making yet another mistake," Gray said in a casual manner. "I would be afraid that having at last fallen in love, if that feeling was not reciprocated then my heart would be crushed. I would be afraid that a woman who was continuing the work she had done with her late husband was not entirely willing to let him go. I would be afraid that she was still in love with a dead man."

"Then it's a good thing I am not you," Win said in a sharper tone than he had intended, but he could not dismiss Gray's comments, nor could he ignore the thoughts crowding his mind.

Was Miranda continuing with the work she and her husband had apparently done together because it was her desire to do so, or was it important to her because it had been important to him? Was allowing Mr. Tempest to take the credit for her work any different from when her husband had done so?

In spite of her claim that it was time to make changes in her life, that she was not opposed to remarriage, had she really moved on? As long as Garret and Tempest existed, wasn't her husband still present in her life, at least in spirit? Was she fighting for her company's survival for her employees? Or for a dead man?

He wasn't at all sure he wanted to know the answer because he wasn't at all sure why he wanted to know. Yet another question he didn't have an answer to.

"That is fortunate." Gray chuckled. "I would hate for you to be in that position."

Was Gray right? Was Win so concerned about making another mistake that he refused to see when the right woman was at last standing directly in his path? Even his soul mate, if one believed in such nonsense.

Of course, there was the distinct possibility that while he might have found his destiny in her, she might have already found it with her husband. It would be just his luck to have finally found his soul mate only to discover she had found hers in someone else.

"Have you ever considered the idea of soul mates?" he said abruptly.

"Well, yes, I suppose," Gray said slowly. "I feel very much that way about Camille. But then I have loved her for most of my life."

"What if she was dead?"

"That is not something I wish to think about." Gray stared at the other man. "And I can't believe you asked that."

"All right then, what if you were dead?"

"I'm not sure I like that any better."

"Humor me. If you were dead, do you think Camille would find another man so perfectly suited to her as you? Another soul mate?"

"This is a serious question, isn't it?"

Win nodded.

"Very well. If I were dead . . ." Gray grimaced. "I suppose it would depend on when I was dead. I mean if I were to die forty years from now, I'm not sure Camille could or would find someone to take my place. I'm not sure she would want to. There would be too much of life we had shared, I think. However, if I were to die tomorrow . . ." He winced and met Win's gaze. "This is a dreadful conversation, you know."

"I do." Win nodded. "Go on."

"I don't like this game," he muttered, then

sighed. "If I were to die when Camille was still a fairly young woman I would hope that she could find what we had shared with someone else. I would hope—because I am not the least bit selfish, mind you—that she could indeed find another soul mate, as it were."

"So you're saying there is a possibility, even if one has found and lost a soul mate, to find another?"

"Yes, I suppose. At least I would hope so." He glared. "I hope you are happy now, whereas I am very much feeling my own mortality and I don't like it one bit."

"Not happy exactly, although I do appreciate your effort. You see, I can't help but wonder . . ." Win blew a long breath. "If you're wrong. If one only has one soul mate per lifetime. And if one has already met and married one's soul mate, even if he has died . . ."

"And I think you are making up absurd excuses that are so esoteric in nature as to sound quite brilliant when, in truth, they are nothing more than a way for you to avoid admitting your feelings. And doing something about them."

"I am going to cling to the fact that you called it brilliant and ignore the rest," Win said.

"However, I can play as well as you do. Consider this, cousin." He leaned forward and met Win's gaze firmly. "Continuing the premise that one has only one soul mate, what if you did meet and marry someone you were convinced was your soul mate? You were well suited to one another and indeed had a lovely life together."

"Go on."

"Well, what if . . ." Gray paused in the manner of a storyteller reaching a climactic moment. "You were wrong?"

Chapter 18

"All in all, I think everything is going exceptionally well." Clara glanced at the notebook in her hand. "This month's payment to Mr. Tempest's account has been made and even better, you will be able to return to London for good in a few days."

Miranda stared at the other woman. "I will?"

Clara nodded. "Mrs. Clarke has given birth to a healthy baby boy. She is doing quite well, although Emmett still seems a bit dazed. He was in the office earlier and said as soon as she is back on her feet, he will take over your duties at Fairborough."

"I see." Miranda paused. This was not at all what she wanted. "There's no hurry, really. We wouldn't want to push the poor woman."

"Of course not, but—"

"I know when my sister Diana had her children, she had no difficulties whatsoever, yet it still took weeks for her to be able to get back to normal."

Clara's eyes narrowed. "Weeks?"

"In some cases, months," she said in a serious manner, ignoring the thought of how delighted Diana would be to discover she'd had all that time to recover.

"Well, then we can't ask him to leave London daily to travel to Fairborough," Clara said slowly.

"Absolutely not." Miranda nodded firmly.

"Unfortunately, this means you shall have to continue to reside at Millworth."

"That is unfortunate." Miranda heaved an overly dramatic sigh.

Clara stared at her for a moment, then grinned. "Dare I ask, Lady Garret, just whom do you think you're fooling?"

"I have no idea what you mean, Miss West."

"You know exactly what I mean." Clara rested her hip against the edge of one of the desks and studied Miranda. "You don't want to come back to London."

"Nonsense." Miranda scoffed. "I miss London terribly. It's simply that the fresh country air is so very stimulating."

"The country air, is it?"

"Absolutely." Miranda inhaled deeply and resisted the need to cough. "While there is nowhere in the world that can compare to London, English country air is the best in the world."

"Which explains why you look so delightfully

refreshed." Clara studied her for a moment. "And I must say that dress is most becoming."

"Another one of my sister's. I did stop at the dressmaker on my way here for a final fitting." Indeed, since she and Bianca had arrived in London this morning, she'd scarcely had a minute to think. Exactly as she wanted it. Thinking would serve no one well. Especially as there was only one thing—or rather, one person—on her mind. "My new wardrobe will be delivered tomorrow."

"There is nothing like a new wardrobe to make a woman feel invincible."

"I had never realized that before, but you are absolutely right."

"And how is the progress at Fairborough?"

"Coming along far faster than expected. Edwin is brilliant at managing the workers. And as we have doubled the number of men working, the bulk of it will be completed sooner than we thought. While all the work certainly won't be finished, I do have several ideas as to how we can hold the Midsummer Ball there."

Clara's brow rose. "We?"

"If it is going to be held at Fairborough, someone is going to have to arrange all the details. Oh, not the music and refreshments and such. That we shall leave in Lady Fairborough's capable hands. But rather exactly where in the unfinished building to actually place it."

Clara nodded. "I see."

"I brought some drawings with me. I thought it might help." Miranda selected one of the paperboard tubes and pulled out a rolled drawing, a bird's-eye view rendering of the building and the gardens. Clara took it and clipped it to the mechanical table. Both women considered it carefully. "It's rather a pity that Fairborough won't be completely done by the ball."

"Is it always held in the ballroom?"

Miranda nodded. "As far as I know."

"Why not have it outside this year?"

"My thoughts exactly."

Clara's eyes narrowed thoughtfully. "This terrace overlooks a lawn bounded by—what are those?"

"Hedges. Huge beech hedges. It's really quite interesting. They form six open-air rooms, three on either side of the wide lawn." Miranda pointed out the rooms on the drawing. "Each one is different. There's a rose garden in one, a pool and fountain in another, tennis and croquet courts in two more and then the last two are filled with plants and statuary and all sorts of things that one might think are confusing but are really very lovely. They are arranged and planted at Lady Fairborough's direction."

"If you place tables and chairs and refreshments here—" Clara tapped the drawing. "And musicians here . . ."

"And constructed a temporary floor for

dancing . . ." Miranda smiled slowly. "This will do beautifully. And what better place to have a Midsummer Ball than under the stars?"

"And what better way to earn a bonus?"

Miranda laughed and the two women continued with ideas and thoughts on the arrangements until she and Clara were confident that this too was well in hand.

"This will work out nicely," Clara said. "Lord Stillwell will have his ball at Fairborough, even if not exactly as he had intended. And Fairborough itself will be completed a few months later."

"With any luck at all."

"And then, as there will be nothing further to keep you in the country, you will at last return to London," Clara said in a most casual manner. "Won't you?"

Miranda hesitated no more than a fraction of a second, but it was enough.

"Aha!" Clara's eyes shone with triumph.

"Aha what?"

"I thought there was more than construction keeping you in the country." She smiled in a decidedly smug manner. "It's Lord Stillwell, isn't it?"

"Oh, I wouldn't say—"

"Has he kissed you?"

Miranda gasped. "That is an entirely inappropriate question to ask."

"You're right, of course. Especially as you have just given me the answer." Clara smirked. "A more pertinent question to ask is did you kiss him back?"

"Miss West!"

Clara's brow arched upward.

Miranda stared at the other woman, then sighed. "Yes, I kissed him back."

"And?"

"And it was . . . very nice."

"Oh?"

"Well, perhaps extraordinary is a better word." She grinned at her friend. "It may well have been the most extraordinary kiss I have ever experienced. Although, John was the only man I have ever kissed before," she added quickly.

"And I would never ask you to compare Lord Garret's kiss with Lord Stillwell's."

"Nor would I do so." Miranda sniffed. Still, she couldn't help comparing them herself.

John's kisses had been quite lovely even if she couldn't quite recall specifically how they had made her feel. Which did seem horribly disloyal. When Winfield kissed her, her breath stopped and her toes curled and her heart had skipped a beat. And she'd known the most incredible longing for much, much more.

"But I will say . . ." Miranda smiled slowly. "I'm not sure I have ever experienced a kiss like that before."

"How delightful." Clara laughed. "One can't ask for more than that."

"Oh, I'm afraid one can." She shook her head. "One does have to wonder if it was extraordinary because it meant more than a mere kiss. Because it was special. Or because he is so very skilled at it. The man has a great deal of experience, you know."

"Yes, well . . ." Clara considered her for a moment. "Men of experience can be exceptionally dangerous not merely to a woman's reputation but to her heart."

"I am beginning to see that," Miranda said under her breath.

"The man I was engaged to . . ." Clara began slowly. "He was a man of vast experience. And he kissed in an excellent manner, I might add."

Miranda smiled weakly.

"But what he wasn't was a man of honor." She chose her words with obvious care. "It seems to me that isn't the case with your Lord Stillwell."

"He isn't my Lord Stillwell."

"Of course not." Clara paused. "I suppose there is really only one way to find out exactly what his kiss meant."

"And what would that be?"

Clara grinned. "Kiss him again."

This was obviously the price one paid for a sojourn in the country.

Miranda blew a long breath and stared at the papers laid out before her on the desk. For the last hour, she had been awash in correspondence, receipts, accounts and all the other various and sundry bits of work that did tend to pile up when not attended to every day or so. Certainly, there was much that Clara could and did do, but there was equally as much that demanded Miranda's particular attention.

Which did nothing to ease her mood. She'd scarcely had a wink of sleep last night. She was tired, she was confused, and even when she was engrossed in the work before her, she couldn't get Winfield out of her head. And, blast it all, she did want to be kissed again.

"My, my, my, aren't you the very picture of professional efficiency," a voice sounded from the door.

"Why is it that you keep appearing where I least expect you to be?" Miranda put her papers aside and looked up at her sister. "Where I least want you to be?"

"Oh, just luck, I should think." Bianca cast her a brilliant smile. "I have never been to my sister's place of work before and I do want to see it."

"You do not. Besides, I do as much of my work as possible at my home and you have indeed been here before."

"Not when you were here."

"Then my initial assumption was correct."

Miranda rose to her feet. "You are only here to annoy me."

Bianca gasped. "You wound me deeply, sister dear." She moved to the mechanical table and studied the drawing of Fairborough. "Is this Fairborough then?"

Miranda nodded.

"It's very large, isn't it?"

"And very old and quite grand. Once." A firm note sounded in Miranda's voice. "And it will be again."

"I have no doubt of that," Bianca murmured.

Miranda circled the desk. "If you have seen enough . . ."

"Oh, but I haven't, and don't think you can be rid of me that easily." Bianca huffed. "I am really quite offended that you think I have nothing more to do with my time than annoy you. I am curious, and I do wish to lend you my support, that's all. Besides, it seems to me if I am to keep a secret of this magnitude for you, I should know all the details."

"I would think the less you know, the less you are likely to reveal."

Bianca ignored her and glanced around. "It's very small, isn't it?"

"Yes." Miranda crossed her arms over her chest. "Now, what particular details do you want to know?"

"I have no idea." Bianca's curious gaze

wandered over the room. Not that there was much to see. It struck Miranda that perhaps they should do something to improve the look of the office. It had never crossed her mind before, but then she had never seen it through the eyes of her sister. "I would think you would know what sort of details I should know."

"I think you know entirely too much already."

"Perhaps." Bianca glanced at her sister. "Is there more to Garret and Tempest than this?"

"You saw the reception room. There is another large room with desks and tables and files for draftsmen and clerks. Including Miss West and Mr. Clarke we have seven employees."

"How very interesting," Bianca said in a tone that indicated she wasn't the least bit interested. "Although it's not, is it?"

"It's not what?"

"Interesting."

Miranda blew a long breath. "It's a business, Bianca. It may not look espccially interesting, but I find it all fascinating. The designing, of course, is something I have always loved, but the rest of it—managing employees, overseeing accounts, balancing finances . . . it's really the most interesting thing I have ever been involved in." She sighed. "I shall hate to give it up."

Bianca's brows drew together in confusion. "Why would you have to give it up?"

"When my role here is revealed . . ."

"Of course. That slipped my mind for a moment." Bianca studied her thoughtfully. "Will you really give it all up then?"

"If I have no clients, no new business, I'll have no choice. I shall hang on as long as I can, but . . ." Miranda shrugged. "Who would knowingly hire a woman?"

A sharp knock sounded at the door and it opened at once. Clara poked her head in. "Lady Garret, there is a gentleman asking to see you."

"Why would a gentleman be asking to see me here?" she said slowly. In truth, she was rarely at the office. Indeed, aside from her employees, no one really knew of her continued affiliation with Garret and Tempest. Other than Lord Stillwell, of course. She narrowed her eyes. "Is he somewhat handsome?"

"He is undeniably attractive," a voice called from behind Clara.

Clara cast her an apologetic smile and opened the door wider. Winfield stepped into the already crowded office.

"Good afternoon, Mrs. Roberts, Lady Garret." A devilish grin curved his lips. "And might I say, you are looking especially delightful today."

"I was going to say that," Bianca murmured and looked at her sister. "You are, you know. Amazing what a change of wardrobe can do."

"Thank you both." Miranda narrowed her eyes. "What, may I ask, are you doing here?"

"Perhaps you have forgotten, but my cousin, his fiancée and her sister left for America today. Grayson asked me to take care of some things here in London while he was gone."

"Yes, of course. I had forgotten." She paused. "Which explains why you are in London, but not why you are here."

"I had planned to attend a play tonight and I wondered if you would like to join me." He smiled down at her and her heart fluttered.

"That would be most—"

"Oh, but she can't," Bianca said with an innocent smile.

Winfield frowned. "She can't?"

Miranda stared. "Why can't I?"

"It is fortunate I came by to remind you as it is so obvious you have forgotten," Bianca said.

"Forgotten . . ." Miranda shook her head, then sucked in a hard breath. "Good Lord, I had forgotten. Dinner, tonight, with the family at my mother's house." She glanced at Winfield with more than a little regret. "I am dreadfully sorry. One cannot fail to attend one of my family's dinners without an exceptionally good reason."

"Death and the like." Bianca nodded.

"I would like nothing better than to accompany you to the theater, but it appears I have other plans."

"Ah, well, it is probably one of those plays that I would have liked and you would have hated." His blue eyes twinkled with amusement.

"Unless, of course, it was one of those that you would have hated and I would have adored." She studied him for a moment. "Dare I ask which play you had in mind?"

He grinned. "Absolutely not."

They stared at each other for a long moment, and she wondered if he was thinking about what might have happened after the play. Here, in London, where they were, for all intents and purposes, quite alone. God knew she was. The oddest sense of what might have been desire rippled through her.

"I say, I have an excellent idea," Bianca said abruptly, and the moment between them vanished.

"Do you?" Winfield smiled.

"I doubt that," Miranda said under her breath.

"Why don't you join us for dinner?" Bianca cast Winfield her brightest smile.

Miranda stared in horror.

"It's just our family," Bianca continued, "but I believe you do know our sister-in-law Veronica."

"I am acquainted with her husband as well, although it has been a long time," Winfield said slowly.

"But you were intending to see that play tonight," Miranda said quickly. "So we will understand entirely why you won't be able to join us. Another time perhaps?"

"On the contrary, my dear Lady Garret, I

should like nothing better than to meet the rest of your family." His gaze met hers and he smiled. "Indeed, I wouldn't miss this dinner for anything in the world."

Chapter 19

Win stepped out of the door opened by the footman at his family's Mayfair house and came face to face with Miranda. "What are you doing here?" He studied her suspiciously. "If you have come to dissuade me from joining your family for dinner, I warn you, I consider it rude to fail to appear when I have accepted an invitation. And I am never rude."

Her brows drew together over her enchanting brown eyes. *Brown?* She was obviously concerned about something. "I don't want you to be rude. Indeed, I want you to be at your most charming."

"You needn't have come here to tell me that."

"I didn't." She wrung her hands together. He wasn't sure he'd ever seen her quite so distraught. Or distraught at all. Angry perhaps, but not worried. "But there are things that you should be aware of before you meet the others."

"What sorts of things?" Was she going to take him into her confidence? Was she going to confess all? Since he'd learned the truth yesterday, he'd thought of a dozen different things he might say and another dozen various reactions he might have, but at the moment he couldn't think of one. It all depended on exactly what she had to say.

"I can't tell you here, on the street, where anyone might eavesdrop."

"Excellent point." He took her arm and steered her toward a parked carriage. "I have a cab waiting. I suggest you confess all to me on the way to your mother's."

"Are you mad?" She stopped and stared up at him. "We can't possibly arrive together."

"We can't?"

"Absolutely not!"

"Why not?"

"Because if we *came* together they would assume we *were* together."

He had given a great deal of thought to that as well since yesterday. It was not an unpleasant idea.

"Here's a suggestion. It's not far to your mother's house and one could reasonably walk if one were not already running behind," he added under his breath. "Why don't we take the cab together and I shall get out a block before we reach our destination. Therefore I shall arrive on foot. You will arrive by cab and no one will be the wiser."

"That's very good." Her brows pulled together. "You're very good at deception, aren't you?"

As are you, my dear Miranda. "It's one of my many charms."

She nodded. "I like it."

"The idea or my charms?"

She grinned. "Both."

He helped her into the cab, gave the driver the address, then took his seat beside Miranda.

"You are quite clever, you know." She studied him curiously. "But then you've probably had a great deal of practice at it."

"At what? At arriving separately at a dinner so that a lady's family would not know I was— what? Having an affair with the lady?"

She nodded. "Yes, indeed, let's go with that."

"You're mad, aren't you? Your family would never think such a thing."

"You would be surprised." She leaned slightly closer to him and he caught the faintest whiff of her scent. He had missed that as well. "We seem, on the surface, like an extraordinarily proper family, but there are all sorts of secrets flitting about. Why, I daresay if one did little more than scratch the surface, any number of scandals would pop out and run amok."

"About virginal governesses and wicked scoundrels?"

She scoffed. "At the very least."

"I don't believe you. You're making that up."

"Not all of it," she said under her breath and he bit back a laugh.

"I don't want to hurry you, but if you still intend to tell me whatever it is that brought you to my door, perhaps it would be wise to—"

"Yes, yes, of course. We are nearly there." She drew a deep breath. "You see . . . that is to say . . ."

"Go on."

"I am going on, I'm simply trying to find the right words."

"Straightforward and forthright is always best. Go on then, say it."

"Very well." She paused, obviously to summon her courage. Pride in her surged through him. She was a remarkable woman. It was never easy to confess one's sins. "My family doesn't know that I have taken an active role in the rebuilding of Fairborough Hall. Nor do they know that I have any involvement in Garret and Tempest whatsoever—aside from owning the firm, that is."

He stared at her. "That's it?"

"Isn't it enough?"

No! "I suppose."

"So I would be most grateful if you would restrain from mentioning my involvement in the rebuilding."

"But Mrs. Roberts knows, doesn't she?"

"Bianca did uncover the truth." She sighed. "She can bear the most uncanny resemblance to a ferret when she sets her mind to it. Which is why she should have no trouble at all finding—"

"Finding what?"

"Finding . . . her lost earbobs. Yes, that's it." Miranda nodded. It was amazing that she had managed to deceive him for so long. She was not an accomplished liar. Which did tend to ease the sting of her deceit. Her sister was definitely not looking for lost earbobs. Perhaps Miranda was right about her family.

"So . . ." He chose his words with care. "What exactly am I supposed to say about, well, anything?"

"I have given that a great deal of thought. Now, do pay attention, Winfield, because I am not going to have time to say this more than once."

"You're sounding like a governess again."

"Enjoy it. Now then." She drew a deep breath, obviously for strength. "Your mother and I met at a society meeting, we became friends, I complained of the air in London, she said it would only get worse as spring and summer wore on, I agreed, she invited me to come stay in the country, Fairborough is being rebuilt but I have nothing to do with it, and if pressed, you will say that while it is on the tip of your tongue, you cannot for the life of you remember the name of the firm that is managing the construction, but you are certain it will come to you at any minute. Well?"

He stared in stunned disbelief.

"Well?" she said again. "Say something."

He narrowed his gaze in suspicion. "What kind of society?"

"That's your question? Out of all that, that's what you chose to ask about?"

"It is indeed. My mother has been acting very oddly ever since she met you. Electricity and telephone and horseless carriages. The next thing you know she'll be demanding to vote."

Miranda uttered a decidedly weak laugh. "Don't be absurd." She rapped on the ceiling and the cab pulled to a halt. "Besides, it doesn't matter as we are just making it up. You need to get out now."

He huffed and got out of the cab, then turned to her. "I shall see you in a few minutes then."

"I shall linger in the entry and arrange an accidental meeting. And thank you for keeping my confidence."

"Of course." He nodded. "But I must confess, I thought what you wished to keep from your family was, well, us."

"I didn't know there was an us."

"Yes, you did."

"Yes." She sighed. "I did."

"Perhaps it's time we did something about that."

"Perhaps."

"Possibly decide what exactly 'us' entails?"

"Possibly." She paused. "You do realize, once we speak aloud of this, *of us,* there can be no going back."

He nodded. "No one is more aware of that than I am."

"We stand to risk what we have. And I must confess, I value the time we spend together and the friendship we have forged."

"As do I, but it's not enough, is it?"

She stared at him. "No, it isn't."

"We can't continue on this way. Or rather I don't wish to. I would hope that you don't wish to either." His voice softened. "I want more. Do you?"

She nodded slowly. "Yes, I do."

"Isn't it said, the greater the risk the greater the reward?"

"Yes."

His gaze locked with hers. "And didn't you once say 'one must either move forward or step aside'?"

"That was in reference to progress, but . . ." She raised her chin, determination and something new and intriguing and quite remarkable in her eyes. He swallowed hard. "I have no desire to step aside."

"Nor do I, Miranda. Nor do I."

He signaled to the cab driver and the carriage started off. Win briskly strode after it.

He was not entirely sure what they had just agreed to. Nonetheless, he smiled, he couldn't wait to find out.

". . . and to prove his claim . . ." Mr. Hadley-Attwater, Hugh, paused in the manner of an expert storyteller and allowed his gaze to circle the table, no doubt to ensure the attention of each and every listener. "He brought the pig."

Laughter erupted around the table.

"Not into the magistrate's chambers surely?" Miranda's oldest sister, Lady Cressfield, Diana, stared at her brother.

"How else to make his point?" Hugh grinned. "I'm not sure who was more surprised, but by my observation, it was the pig."

Once again, laughter circled the table, but then it was that kind of convivial group. All in all, dinner with the Hadley-Attwater family was comparable to a play and perhaps much better acted. If, of course, Win could get all the players straight.

There was the head of the family, the Earl of Waterston, Adrian Hadley-Attwater and his wife, the lovely Evelyn. There was Hugh Hadley-Attwater, barrister and expert storyteller, which obviously ran in the family. He already knew Sir Sebastian and his wife, Veronica, who had been seated beside Win. Sir Sebastian had made a name for himself as an explorer and adventurer and now wrote works of fiction about explorers and adventurers. Then there was Miranda's oldest sister, Diana, and her husband James, Lord and Lady Cressfield; her cousin, Portia, Lady Redwell, a widow; and of course Bianca, Mrs. Roberts, who was apparently estranged from her husband as far as Win could tell. The man's name was never mentioned, and when he was referred to in passing there were fleeting expressions of dismay, or even perhaps mild disgust, on the faces of those around the tables, so quick he couldn't be sure he had seen anything at all. And then, of course, there was the matriarch of the family, the dowager countess, Lady Waterston, Miranda's mother. She reminded him very much of his own mother and he caught her studying him with a speculative look in her eyes on more than one occasion during the course of the meal.

Upon Win's arrival Bianca had explained his presence by saying as Miranda had been spending so much time in the country with Lady Fairborough, and as Bianca had had a chance meeting with him today, she thought it would be lovely if they could reciprocate the hospitality. While the explanation did make a certain amount of sense, he suspected Lady Waterston was not completely taken in. If she was indeed anything like his mother, she was no doubt wondering what, if anything, his connection was with her youngest daughter.

Win was acquainted with all the gentlemen. As much as London was the greatest city in the world, it was in many ways a relatively small community. Indeed, he believed the earl, his brothers and brother-in-law belonged to some of the same clubs Win did, but Sebastian was the only one he had more than a nodding acquaintance with. And he really hadn't seen Sebastian in some time.

"As much as I do hate to turn the subject away from the fascinating topic of pigs," Portia began, "I was wondering if any of you . . ."

While there was a great deal of banter and teasing and laughter and the kind of comfortable conversation one experiences in the midst of a group of people who not only care for each other but like one another as well, there was one notable aberration that made no sense to him at all. The woman sitting across the table from him was not the Miranda he knew. This woman was fairly quiet, and while she did contribute to the discussion she was far more reserved than he would have thought possible. Indeed, there were several points made on various topics where he fully expected her to pick up the gauntlet that had been thrown down. Yet she refrained, although he was certain, given the same conversation at Millworth, she would have been right in the thick of it. Especially if Win had been the one to say whatever it was she disagreed with. Oddly enough, he was the only one at the table who seemed to have noticed her reserve.

"Lord Stillwell," Adrian said, "I understand you have undertaken the rebuilding of Fairborough Hall?"

"It was a fire, wasn't it?" Veronica asked. "Was there a lot of damage?"

"I hate the thought of fire in these grand old country houses." Miranda's mother shivered. "I live in fear of something like that happening at Waterston Abbey."

"Fortunately, as it turns out, a previous earl had a very similar fear," Win said. "He was a witness to the Great Fire of London in 1666."

"History is always full of surprises," Evelyn said with a smile.

"We had always thought that the house had never been altered since its initial construction," Win continued. "But we discovered after the fire, that changes had been made to thicken the walls, providing something of a firebreak between the main portion of the house and the wings. Both wings suffered no more than damage from smoke. As bad as the destruction was, I shudder to think how much worse it could have been."

"How very clever of him," Miranda's mother said. "Miranda has always been interested in the design of buildings. Indeed, her late husband was an architect."

Miranda smiled.

"Why, they first met at a lecture on something of architectural interest." The older woman looked at her daughter. "What was it, dear?"

"It was a lecture on Palladian influence on English architecture," Miranda said smoothly. "But I am sure Lord Stillwell isn't interested in that."

"Oh, but I am." Win smiled across the table at her. "I find I am interested in anything that captures Lady Garret's attention."

"That's right." Diana's gaze flicked between Win and her sister. "Miranda has been staying in the country with your mother. At Millworth Manor, isn't it?"

Miranda nodded.

"My family has leased the manor until the building at Fairborough is completed."

"Then the two of you obviously know one another, don't you?" Diana looked at Win. "Unless you spend most of your time in London?"

"I do try to get to Millworth whenever possible," Win said in a casual manner.

Miranda shrugged. "And our paths have crossed there."

"You have undoubtedly seen the construction for yourself then, haven't you?" Sebastian asked.

"Once or twice," Miranda said with a weak smile.

"I suspect, as rebuilding is already under way, that you have an architectural firm engaged," Adrian said. "Otherwise, I would strongly recommend the services of Garret and Tempest, Miranda's late husband's firm."

"Garret and Tempest?" Win forced an innocent note to his voice. "I'm not sure I've heard of them."

"The firm has an excellent reputation." Adrian smiled at his youngest sister. "In spite of the loss

of Lord Garret, it's my understanding that the business is continuing to do well."

"Imagine that." One did wonder what it would take to awaken the Miranda he knew. "I believe we did make inquiries, but . . ." He shrugged. "Their office is managed by a woman you know, a Miss West."

"She is most efficient," Miranda said firmly. "You may not be aware of this, but I hired the woman."

"Miranda now owns the firm," Adrian added.

"But Miranda has nothing to do with the day-to-day functioning of it," Portia pointed out. "That would be most inappropriate. I can't imagine what people might say."

"Nonsense, Portia," Veronica said. "There are any number of businesses run by women."

"Oh, certainly milliners and dress shops and the like." Portia shrugged. "But not professions and certainly not something where you would have to mingle with men in the construction trades." She shivered. "I can't imagine a lady doing any such thing."

"Nor can I." Win met Miranda's gaze over the table. "Can you, Lady Garret?"

"I suppose . . ." Her words were measured. "That one does what one must."

"What an interesting answer," Evelyn murmured.

"Do you really think a woman could do that sort of thing?" Win studied her. "Run a professional business, that is? Manage a site of construction? And do so as well as a man?"

Portia rolled her gaze toward the ceiling. "Now that is a ridiculous idea."

"I would imagine a woman could do anything she set her mind to." Miranda cast him a pleasant smile, but her green eyes flashed.

"Absolutely." Bianca nodded. "Indeed, I don't see why a woman couldn't be every bit as successful as a man in a professional enterprise."

"Still," Win said slowly, "it's been my experience, in doing any kind of business that one needs to trust whomever one is doing business with. There is a level of honesty that must be achieved in any business dealing. Don't you agree, Lady Garret?"

"I suspect honesty is relative," Miranda said in an offhand manner. "I would think if the service provided is as expected, one can't ask for more than that."

"Honesty is not a gray area," Hugh said firmly. "In the law it is very much a matter of black and white." He paused. "Unless, of course, one is dealing with pigs."

Laughter again washed through the gathering and the topic changed to discussion of a charity event Diana was involved in. Miranda cast Win a last scathing look, then turned her attention to the others.

Beside him, Veronica leaned close and spoke

softly out of the side of her mouth. "Winfield Elliott, whatever are you up to?"

"Nothing," he said quietly. "Nothing at all."

"I see. So apparently honesty is not something you aspire to?"

"If I said it was none of your concern, would you leave it be?"

"Goodness, Winfield. That's not at all in my nature." She laughed softly. "You might be interested to know Miranda, Bianca and I attended a lecture recently and we ran into one of your previous fiancées."

"Oh?" He resisted the urge to wince. "Which one?"

"Lady Eustice. Miranda was quite interested in what had transpired between the two of you."

"No one knows what transpired between the two of us," he said firmly.

"Nonsense. That sort of thing never stays completely private." She glanced at Miranda. "Nor will this."

"Nor will what?" he said cautiously.

"Whatever is going on between you and Miranda. The others may not see it, but then no one expects to see what they are not looking for." Her voice hardened. "I do hope this is not another dalliance on your part. I have not been a member of this family for very long, but I can tell you Miranda is the most vulnerable, even fragile, among them."

"She's nothing like that." He stared at her. "The woman sitting across the table from me at this very moment might well appear vulnerable and fragile, but that is not the woman I have come to know." Bloody hell, were these people all mad? Without thinking, he raised his voice. "The woman I have come to know is the most determined, outspoken, maddening creature I have ever met. In addition, she has perhaps the most intelligent and creative mind I have ever come across in any woman, or man for that matter. She is both resourceful and resilient. Indeed, this is a woman who could well do anything she set her mind to and could probably do as well or better than any man, which, I might add, was not an easy conclusion for me to reach or accept. Aside from everything else, she is truly lovely and there is nothing in the world as wonderful as hearing her laugh. Miranda Garret is the most remarkable woman I have ever met and I am eternally grateful for the day she stalked into my life in the ugliest shoes I have ever seen."

Veronica's eyes widened and it was only then he realized all talk at the table had ceased and stunned silence hung in the air. His gaze snapped to Miranda. She stared at him as if in shock and for a long moment no one said a word.

At last Bianca cleared her throat. "I do hope we have dessert."

"If you will excuse me." Miranda quickly rose to her feet and left the room.

"I'd go after her if I were you." A smug smile curved Veronica's lips.

"Of course." He got to his feet and glanced around the table. "This has been quite an enjoyable evening. Lady Waterston, my compliments to your cook and thank you so much for having me. Perhaps we can do it again another time." He nodded and hurried after Miranda.

"Bianca," her mother said behind him, "explain this if you will."

"Oh, but I won't, or rather, I can't," Bianca said. "In truth, I am as shocked as the rest of you. Shocked, I tell you. Whoever would have imagined Lord Stillwell and Miranda? Why I had no . . ."

He fairly flew down the steps to the ground floor and caught up with her in the front entry. "My apologies, Miranda, I never thought—"

"Did you mean what you said in there?"

He nodded. "I did."

"Do you really think all those things about me?"

"I'm afraid so."

"And that last part?"

"I won't apologize for that." He shook his head. "The shoes are ugly."

"Not that." Her gaze searched his. "The rest of it."

"Yes." He stepped closer to her and stared into

her eyes and for the life of him he could not determine their color. "The luckiest day of my life is the day my house burned because it brought you into my life."

"You're mad, aren't you?"

"Probably."

"Mad enough to kiss me?"

He narrowed his eyes. "If I kiss you here, mere steps away from where your family is still reeling from the revelations at dinner, will you accuse me of attempting to seduce you?"

"Of course not." She grabbed the lapels of his coat and pulled him close. "But I shall hope."

Without another word, his lips crushed hers. She tasted of wine and promises and forever. He wrapped his arms around her and pulled her tighter against him and he could not get enough of her. The faint scent of spring that she wore wafted around him and circled his heart and crept into his soul. And he was lost and it was wonderful.

"Ahem."

He groaned against her lips. Would there ever be a time when he could kiss her without interruption? Reluctantly he released her, gratified to note she was just as reluctant to release him.

"Lord Stillwell." Adrian stood at the top of the stairs flanked by Hugh on one side, Sebastian on the other and James a step behind. "A word, if you please."

"No." Miranda stared up at her brothers.

James choked.

"No?" Confusion crossed Hugh's face. "Did she say no?"

"I think that is exactly what she said." Sebastian stared.

"Miranda," Adrian began in his best I-am-the-earl voice. Win recognized it immediately as he had a similar voice. He did so enjoy using it. "This is none of your concern."

"No, Adrian, this is none of *your* concern."

"You are my sister, my youngest sister, and everything that affects you concerns me."

"Don't be absurd."

Win grinned. Now this was the Miranda he knew.

"I am twenty-eight years of age and more than capable of making my own decisions. I have been married and widowed. I have my own finances. And I . . ." She glanced at Win and he nodded. "I not only own Garret and Tempest, I run it. I am not merely the youngest Hadley-Attwater, *I* am a woman of business."

The men at the top of the steps stared in stunned silence. Apparently, this was the night for it. Win wondered if dinner with the Hadley-Attwater family was always this interesting. He wouldn't be at all surprised.

Her brows drew together and she looked at him. "Did you know that? That I run the firm, that is?"

"I have never been as stupid as you have thought I was."

"I never—well, perhaps I did . . ." She had the good grace to blush at that. He liked it.

"Miranda," Adrian said. "You barely know this man."

"On the contrary, I know him quite well. I know he is stubborn and can be stiff and stodgy on occasion. I know he is suspicious of progress. I know he has very firm ideas about the place of women in this world."

"Oh, I do sound delightful," Win said under his breath.

"I know as well that he values tradition and heritage. He treats his parents with affection and his servants with respect. He makes me laugh more than I can ever remember laughing in my entire life. He is kind to children and small animals, even his aunt's dog, who is not at all a pleasant beast. He is intelligent and not unattractive. And when he kisses me—"

One of the other men groaned.

"He makes my toes curl and my heart skip a beat."

Win flashed her brothers a smug smile. "Add to that my title and fortune, and I am quite a catch."

"A catch is not what I would call you," Adrian said sharply. "Are you aware of his reputation with women? Do you know he has had three fiancées? Three?"

"I can't imagine there is anyone alive who is not aware of that, but might I point out, dear brother, that while you may not have the trail of fiancées he does, your reputation was no better than his. Why, we had begun to think no decent woman would have you before you met Evelyn."

Adrian sputtered.

"As for Sebastian—"

"No, no that's quite all right," Sebastian said quickly. "I am well aware of my past reputation."

"I never had an especially scandalous reputation," Hugh said in a lofty manner.

"No, Hugh dear, you were too busy studying, although I do recall a few incidents."

Hugh's brow furrowed in thought; then he winced.

"See here, Miranda," Adrian began.

"And didn't you have this same discussion with Diana about James before they married?"

"I don't recall," Adrian muttered.

"I do." James shuddered. "Diana nearly killed you." He took a cautious step back. "However, it does strike me that this discussion would be best confined to blood relations so perhaps I should—"

"Oh no, James," Miranda said sharply. "You're not going anywhere. You're a part of this and it's not over, as there are a few more things I wish to say. And I would appreciate it if the four of you would come down to this level so that I don't feel like I'm talking to the gods on Mt. Olympus!"

The men exchanged glances, then reluctantly descended the stairs.

"You're absolutely right," Adrian declared in an obvious effort to regain control. "It's not over."

"She's yelling at us, you know," Sebastian said in an aside to Win when they reached the ground floor. "Bianca yells, Portia yells, Diana yells. Miranda never yells."

Win chuckled. "You'd be surprised."

"What have you done to her?"

"The real question, old man, is what has she done to me?"

Sebastian shook his head.

"Now then." Miranda's gaze shifted from one brother to the next. "I am going to leave with Lord Stillwell in a few minutes. He will escort me home. Tomorrow I am going to accompany him back to Millworth so that I may resume my work at Fairborough. I am not managing construction— I have a very capable gentleman who does that. But I am in something of an advisory capacity in regards to the plans and blueprints as well as a liaison between the office, the architect and the construction site."

Win stared. So she wasn't going to confess everything? Wasn't that interesting?

"And, of course, I report on the progress to Lord Stillwell and his family. Now, is there anything else?"

"Miranda." Adrian glared. "As head of this family, I absolutely forbid you to leave with this man."

"I give you my word she'll be perfectly safe. I promise not to sell her to a harem," Win said solemnly.

Hugh snorted back a laugh.

"Don't be a twit, Adrian. You have nothing to say about it. If I wish to leave with him, if I wish to embark on a torrid, scandalous affair—"

Win grinned.

"If I wish to tie him up and have my way with him—"

"Every little boy's dream," Win said under his breath.

"I shall do exactly that." She glared at her brothers. "Do you have anything else to say?"

Adrian stared at his sister for a long moment, then drew a deep breath. "What do you propose I tell Mother?"

"Tell her I shall see her soon and whatever else you wish. I love all of you, but it simply doesn't matter. It is my life, and I am very tired of hiding what I think and how I feel. However . . ." She thought for a moment. "I have people who depend for their livelihood on the continuation of Garret and Tempest. Obviously I therefore want it to be viable as long as possible. I am well aware that when the extent of my involvement becomes known publicly we will lose most of our commissions. And the fewer people who know about this the better. So. . . ." Her eyes narrowed in a menacing manner. It was most impressive. "I want your word that you will not tell Mother, Diana, Evelyn and especially not Portia."

"Bianca knows, of course." Sebastian scoffed.

Hugh stared. "And what would you have us tell them?"

"Well, it seems to me the truly juicy part of all this is when Lord Stillwell went on and on about what a remarkable woman I am." She flashed him a quick grin. "I should think that would provide more than enough topic for discussion and speculation. Good Lord, Portia and Mother could live off that little bit alone for weeks."

"Very well." Adrian nodded with what might have been the vaguest suggestion of a smile on his lips. "I suspect we have no choice."

"You don't." Miranda smiled. "But thank you. Thank you all."

Adrian's gaze locked on to Win's. "You and I still need to talk."

"And talk we shall. Eventually." Win cast him a pleasant smile. "But I believe I have another discussion I must have first."

"Yes, well." Adrian's gaze slid from Win to his sister and back. "I wish you good luck, Stillwell. I suspect you're going to need it."

"That is much appreciated, Waterston." He offered Miranda his arm. "But I think I already have it." A footman opened the door and they swept out into the night.

"Now that," he said with a grin, "was a grand exit."

She laughed. "I've always wanted to make a grand exit."

"What now, Miranda?"

"Well, in that direction is my house and you may escort me home. Or . . ." She nodded in the direction of his house. "Your house is that way. Much closer, wouldn't you say?"

"Well, yes, I would, but . . ."

"Winfield." She gazed into his eyes. "This is entirely your choice. You may still escort me home and the evening will be at an end."

"Good Lord, Miranda, I couldn't 'still escort you home' at this point if I was offered a million pounds to do so. I just want to make sure this is what you want."

"My darling Lord Stillwell." She smiled up at him. A smile filled with promises of tonight and forever. "There is nothing I want more."

Chapter 20

It was the damnedest thing.

If someone had told Winfield Elliott, Viscount Stillwell, heir to the Earl of Fairborough, a man who had once been known for his exploits with women and skating on the thin edge of scandal, that he would feel even so much as a hint of nerves at taking a woman to his bed he would have laughed and called him a liar. But there was definitely something very much like nerves that twisted in his stomach now.

He and Miranda said little on the brief ride to his house, but then what was there to say? Small talk didn't seem appropriate and even that he couldn't seem to manage. Miranda, however, did not appear the least bit apprehensive. Indeed, a serene smile had played on her lips in the carriage, in the foyer when he had dismissed the servants for the night and as he had escorted her to his rooms. Even now, as she stood near the fireplace discarding her evening wrap, the smile lingered.

He had no need to be anxious about this. He snapped the doors closed behind him. It was not as if he was about to seduce a virgin, not that he ever had. Although he suspected Miranda had never been with a man other than her husband. At least not before her marriage and probably not after she'd been widowed either. He couldn't be completely certain and it was not something he could ask. Besides, it would be most hypocritical of him to care one way or the other and he did hate to be hypocritical.

She tugged at one of her gloves and slowly pulled it off in a manner as mesmerizing as if it were her stocking. "You surprise me, Winfield."

"Oh?" He swallowed. "In what way?"

"From the look in your eye, one would think you'd never had a woman in this room before, which I find hard to believe." She glanced around the bedroom with its dark wood furnishings, deep claret-colored wallpaper and matching bed hangings and draperies. "Indeed, this is a room that fairly screams seduction."

He started to deny it, then thought better of it. "And I thought it was a room that fairly screams Winfield Elliott."

"Aren't they one and the same?" She pulled off her other glove, again in a slow and decidedly seductive manner.

"You give me entirely too much credit, Miranda."

"Do I?" She smiled and started toward him.

He had the strangest impulse to flee. "I believe I have mentioned that I have not . . . well . . ."

"Dallied with women recently?" She continued toward him. "Enhanced your reputation? That sort of thing?"

"Something like that." He resisted the urge to step back.

"But you've certainly not been celibate for any length of time."

"I suppose that depends on how you define length of time," he said cautiously. In spite of her comment about wanting a wicked man she was a respectable lady from a respectable family. There had never been so much as a breath of scandal about her. Indeed, he hadn't been especially aware of her existence until the day they met.

"What a clever answer, Winfield." She stopped less than a foot away and stared up at him. "It wouldn't be at all fair of me to condemn you for activities in the past. Would it?"

"And yet women often do."

She sighed, reached out and untied his necktie. "We are a confusing lot."

He stared down at her. What was wrong with him? He had done this any number of times before. "I would define length of time as being well before I met you."

"Oh?" She slowly pulled his necktie free and dropped it to the floor.

He shrugged in as offhand a manner as he could manage given that his heart was thudding in his chest and various other parts of his body were responding to her nearness. "I have been . . . busy."

"Ah well, that explains it then." She unfastened his collar.

"Explains what?"

"Why you haven't seemed nearly as wicked as I had expected." She started to pull off his collar.

He caught her hand and stared into her eyes. Her definitely green eyes. "Are you disappointed?"

"Not yet."

The moment between them stretched, lengthened, endless, eternal. At once he understood. This wasn't any woman. This wasn't another conquest. This was different. This was important. This was Miranda. He didn't know if it was love, wasn't sure he'd recognize love, but he had never felt this way about a woman before. And he'd never wanted any woman more.

His nerves vanished.

He pulled her into his arms. "I've never been with a woman of business before. Or for that matter"—he smiled—"a governess."

"What? You've never fulfilled that dream of every little boy?"

"Not yet." He bent closer and kissed the curve between her neck and shoulder. She shivered.

"Then we are well matched." A slight breathless note sounded in her voice. Her eyes were green and glazed with desire. "I have never before been with a wicked lord."

"You will tell me if it doesn't live up to your expectations," he murmured against her skin.

"You shall be the first to know." She pulled away, wrapped her arms around his neck and drew his face to hers.

Their lips met in a kiss, slow and deliberate. A kiss that said they had all the time in the world. A kiss to savor, to relish and enjoy.

It was not enough.

Restraint between them shattered. Desire he

had denied for too long rose up within him. He couldn't get enough of her. His hands, his mouth were everywhere at once. She responded in kind, touching him, tasting him. He wondered if he had ever felt such passion before and knew as well that it was not because she was lovely and enticing but because she was Miranda. He wanted her. He wanted more.

Within moments he had her clothes off and was removing his own.

"Good Lord, Winfield." She snatched the coverlet from the bed and held it up in front of her.

"What?" He froze and stared at her. His shirt hung open, his trousers were halfway down his legs.

"Well, I didn't expect, that is . . ."

"If you have thought better of this." His words were measured and she knew it took a great effort on his part. "If you have changed your mind . . ."

"No, no, of course not." She shook her head. "I want this. I want you. It's only that . . ."

"Yes?"

"Well." She winced. "You do seem to be shockingly efficient. Which is to be expected, of course. You had no difficulty whatsoever with my gown and my corset and . . . everything. I don't think my maid could have disrobed me better and certainly not faster."

He stared. "Thank you?"

"It's just that you are so . . . so . . . so very skilled."

"It's a gift?"

"Don't be absurd." She scoffed. "It's because you have had a great deal of practice."

"You knew that," he said slowly.

"Yes, and it doesn't concern me whatsoever." Her gaze flicked over him. "Would you mind either pulling up or taking off your trousers? I find it most disconcerting to see them hanging around your knees like that." Although, in many ways, it was rather charming.

"My apologies," he muttered and pulled up his trousers. "I had not intended for them to remain in that position."

"I know and I am sorry. In truth I find your vast experience exciting."

"Then why are we standing here?"

"Goodness, Winfield, I have only ever done this with one man. No other man has ever seen me without clothing before. And the lamps are still lit and . . ." She knew she sounded like an idiot, or worse, a frightened virgin.

"Oh, I see." He nodded. "Should I put the lights out?"

"That does seem rather cowardly." Besides, she wanted to see him although it did seem somewhat wanton to admit such a thing. "It's understandable that I would be a little apprehensive. Not that I don't want to continue," she added quickly.

"Forgive me, if I'm confused." His brow furrowed. "But not more than a few minutes ago, you were as eager to get my clothes off as I was to remove yours."

"Oh, I am eager." She nodded with enthusiasm. "Extremely eager. I can't recall feeling this sort of desire ever before."

"Ever?" His brow rose.

"I mean, that is to say . . ."

"Go on."

"Oh Lord, I shouldn't be saying this. But I do tend to say all sorts of things to you I shouldn't. Relations with my late husband . . . well, John and I were . . . oh, what is the right word?" She thought for a moment. "Civilized, I suppose."

"Civilized?"

"Always quite pleasant, but, yes, civilized. I suspect with you it will be anything but civilized."

"I'm not sure if I should be flattered or insulted."

"Definitely flattered. Civilized isn't nearly as exciting. And might I say this would be a moot point by now, given the way we were, oh, swept away by . . . by passion a few minutes ago, if you had not stopped the proceedings to disrobe."

He narrowed his eyes. "It's extremely awkward otherwise."

"Unfortunately, you gave me a moment to think. To come to my senses, as it were." She pinned him with a firm look. "I would think a man of your experience would know better."

"One always has something to learn," he said slowly.

"And then I became apprehensive, you understand, the enormity of it all. Not for you, of course, but for me. And, well, here we are," she added weakly.

"Indeed, we are." He studied her for a long moment. Good Lord, what if he'd changed his mind? "Apparently, there is only one thing to do."

"Oh?"

He moved to her and drew her into his arms. His lips brushed across hers. "We cannot allow you to think."

"No . . ." She sighed against his lips, warm and full and oh so wonderful. "Thinking is not at all a good thing."

He shifted his head and ran kisses along the line of her jaw.

"Oh my." Her eyes closed and her head dropped back. "That is not at all conducive to rational thought."

"Good."

His lips continued their exploration. Down the column of her neck to the base of her throat. She shivered beneath his touch, his glorious touch. Her back arched and his mouth drifted lower, to kiss between her breasts.

"Oh God, Winfield, yes . . ."

Slowly he pulled the coverlet from her hands

and let it drop to the floor. She scarcely noticed.

He held her with one arm, and cupped her breast with his free hand. Exquisite. She'd never noticed how large his hand was, how gentle, how exciting. His thumb lightly brushed her nipple and she gasped. He took her nipple in his mouth and sucked lightly. His tongue and his teeth teased and toyed until she grabbed at his shirt to steady herself. Pleasure spread from his touch to wash through her and desire pooled in her stomach.

She moaned softly and he shifted to lavish attention on the other breast. "Oh . . . yes . . ."

His hands skimmed over her sides and he slowly sank to his knees in front of her, his lips trailing light, teasing kisses lower to her stomach. His tongue traced slow circles on her midsection and she gripped his shoulders and reveled in the feel of his lips on her skin. His hands slid over her, around her and he caressed her derriere. And she wondered that her knees could still support her.

He slipped a hand between her legs and explored the inside of her thighs and moved higher. Slowly. Deliberately. Her muscles tensed with anticipa-tion, and she throbbed with needing him. At last his fingers brushed over her so lightly she wasn't sure she felt anything at all. Save her growing need for much, much more.

Without warning, he got to his feet, swept her into his arms and carried her to the bed.

"Winfield—"

"You're not thinking again, are you?" His voice was low and harsh with desire.

"No." She could barely get out the word. He laid her on the bed and opened her legs. "I can't . . . think."

"Good."

He climbed on the bed and lay between her legs. His head lowered and she felt his breath on her. His tongue flicked over her and she sucked in a hard breath at the sheer sensation that shot through her. A loud moan sounded in the room and she realized it was hers.

His tongue teased her with long slow strokes, every touch bringing a sensation of pleasure so intense it was nearly unbearable. Her hands fisted in the bedclothes and she writhed beneath the pleasure of his touch. He teased her, tasted her, drank of her. He reduced her existence to a creature of no more than pure sensation. She existed only in the touch of his mouth, the caress of his lips. Tension she had nearly forgotten spiraled within her, growing, gathering. Her past experience had not prepared her for the force, the power of the pleasure he gave her. His tongue, his teeth, his hands brought her inevitably closer and closer still until she was very nearly—

Abruptly, he stopped and slid off the bed.

Shock and disappointment coursed through her and she whimpered in frustration. Did the man have any idea what he had done to her? She struggled to prop herself up on her elbows and stared at him. "What are you doing?"

He shrugged off his shirt and pulled off his trousers faster than she could have thought possible. "Well, I'm not giving you time to think."

"You have robbed me of all coherent thought," she murmured.

Her gaze flicked over him. His shoulders seemed broader without clothes, his muscles tight and defined, his legs long and lean. And his erection, his *cock,* was most impressive. She'd never used the word before, even in her own mind. It was no doubt a measure of her arousal that she did so now and did not find it distressing but most exciting. The word and the appendage. "Indeed, there is only one thing on my mind." She reached out to him.

He flashed her his wicked grin, took her hand, then joined her on the bed. He took her in his arms and the long length of his naked body pressed against hers. His flesh was hot and hard against hers. His lips met hers and she opened her mouth to him, welcoming his tongue, his taste. Her hands explored the hard curves and planes of his back, his buttocks. Her legs entwined with his. His cock pressed against her, hot and demanding. Dear Lord, she wanted this. Wanted him. She hooked her leg over his and tried to pull him closer.

He shifted to cover her body with his and slipped his hand between them, sliding it between her legs. He caressed her, his hand slick with her own desires, and she throbbed against his fingers. And again tension, aching and intoxicating, built within her. She reached down and wrapped her hand around his cock and he groaned with a need that echoed her own. She stroked him, reveling in the feel of his hard heat pulsing in her hand. He moved her hand and guided himself into her. Slowly, he pushed into her and she held her breath, existing only in the feel of their joining. He filled her with a perfection she had not expected, not imagined, not even in her dreams of him. So full, so right, so complete. As if they were made one for the other.

He thrust into her, then withdrew almost entirely and thrust again. She wrapped her legs around his waist and urged him deeper. He stroked into her again and again, and she rolled her hips against him meeting his thrusts. She moved in rhythm with him, harder and faster, in a tempo as perfect as life itself. A cadence increasing with every movement of him within her, every rock of her hips. The room, the world filled with the sound of their passion. The bed rocked and creaked beneath them. She scarcely noticed and didn't care. She was lost in sensation and pleasure and the need for more. Faster and faster he drove into her. Her blood pounded in her ears. Her breath came short and fast. She wanted. . . . She needed. . . .She ached. . . .

She tightened around him and release exploded within her. Waves of sheer delight coursed through her and she arched upward and cried out with the joy of it. And she felt him thrust again, deep and hard, and he shuddered within her and groaned with the power of his own release. He buried his head in her shoulder and for a long moment, his body shook against hers, with hers.

And for a minute or an hour or forever, they lay together spent, content in each others arms.

"Good God, Winfield," she murmured against his neck.

He chuckled, raised his head and looked at her. "Dare I take that to mean you were not disappointed?"

"I have no doubt you can do better." She giggled at the startled look on his face. "But I can't imagine how." She grinned. "No, my dear darling Lord Stillwell. I thought this was quite remarkable."

He stared into her eyes. "As did I, Lady Garret, as did I."

He shifted off of her, then wrapped himself around her, pulling her back against him. She fit quite nicely. She could feel his cock, still shockingly hard, nestled against her. They might yet have to do something about that. . . . The thought brought her up short. Twice in one night? She grinned. Who would have thought?

As much as she tried not to, she couldn't help

but compare Winfield to John. It was unfair of her. John had not been nearly as experienced as Winfield. And he'd had very definite ideas about what was proper and what was not. John never would have buried his head between her legs or made love to her with the lights on. And while she had experienced release with John, it had never been quite this explosive. More like tumbling gently off a cliff than flinging oneself over the edge, with rapt abandon, completely out of control. No, it wasn't fair at all to compare the two; it was simply unavoidably accurate.

There was far more to be said for a wicked man than she had imagined.

And she would never be civilized again.

He lay on the bed beside her, propped his head on his elbow and studied her. At long last he had found the woman of his dreams. The woman he could spend the rest of his days with. "Did you know your eyes change colors depending on your mood?"

"I am aware of that, yes."

"They're brown with flecks of gold when you're happy or amused or concerned. Green when you're in the throes of anger or . . ." He leaned over and brushed his lips across hers. "Passion. And a blend of colors—hazel, I suppose—the rest of the time."

"And what color are they now?"

"More brown than green at the moment." Her eyes were glazed with the sort of somnolence seen in women who have been well satisfied. "And extremely smug."

She laughed.

"You should know," he said in a casual manner, as if it wasn't at all important. "I believe I have found my last, my final fiancée."

"Me?" She propped herself up on her elbows and stared at him. "You want to marry me?"

He chuckled. "It does seem like a logical next step."

"Does it?" She glanced around. At his clothes and hers strewn around the room and the disheveled sheets and coverlet that said more than words what had happened here. He resisted the impulse to grin like a fool. A happy fool. "Because of this?"

"Not entirely, although you must admit, this was well worth doing again and again until the day one of us breathes our last."

She grinned. "I am more than willing to admit that."

"Given that we agree on that crucial point, marriage seems most convenient." He shrugged as if it was of no importance. "Indeed, I think it's an excellent idea."

"Did you ask all of your fiancées to marry you after"—she waved at the crumpled bed sheets—"this?"

"I'll have you know I never did . . ." He repeated her gesture. "*This* with any of them."

"Why not?"

"I have no idea." He shook his head. "It didn't seem honorable, I suppose."

"Now, I'm not sure if I should be flattered or offended."

"Or perhaps I could simply wait for *this* until marriage with them. With you I could not wait another moment."

She nodded. "Flattered then."

"Perhaps if I had I would be married now."

"Then one does have to be grateful for your restraint."

He took her hand and raised it to his lips, his gaze never leaving hers. "And dreadfully unhappy because I would have missed you."

"That is a very sweet thing to say."

"And sincere, I hope. I am most sincere."

She smiled. "It did sound sincere."

"So." He turned her hand over and kissed her palm. "Will you agree to be my next fiancée?"

She studied him for a moment. Her hair was tousled and down around her shoulders. Her skin flushed and warm. He could indeed spend the rest of his life with this woman. "Absolutely not."

Shock coursed through him. "What do you mean 'absolutely not'?"

"I mean . . ." She sat up and drew the sheet up around her. "No."

"No?" He stared at her. "Why not?"

"You do not have exceptional luck with fiancées. The thought has occurred to me that you might possibly be cursed."

He drew his brows together. "Cursed?"

"Well, as you pointed out earlier tonight, you are an excellent catch."

"Cursed?" He shifted away from her and sat up.

"So one does have to wonder why you have never made it to the altar."

"I chose the wrong women," he said staunchly.

"Three times?"

"Apparently." He glared. "I'll have you know, I have never indiscriminately asked women to marry me. I selected each of them quite carefully as to her suitability as a wife and the next Countess of Fairborough." He paused. "Well, perhaps not the first but definitely the second and third."

"Surely this has occurred to you? The idea of a curse, that is. I mean, honestly, Winfield, three fiancées?" She grabbed the sheet and struggled to wrap it around her, then slid out of bed. "How many people have had three fiancées and yet have never been married?"

"We are a small but select group."

She plucked a stocking off the bedpost. "And you claim as well that you have never been in love." Her eyes narrowed. "Are you in love now?"

"I don't know," he snapped. "I'm not hearing choirs of angels if that's what you're asking."

"You needn't be snippy about it." She spotted her corset, crossed the room and retrieved it.

"Forgive me," he said in a dry manner. "I've never been in this position before. Snippy is the very least of what I'm feeling."

"You mean you've never had a woman who didn't jump at the prospect of marrying you?"

"They do tend to say yes—before today, that is," he said sharply, then drew a calming breath. "Allow me to ask you the same question. Are you in love? Do you love me?"

"I'll answer that only on the condition that you do not respond by saying aha." She grimaced. "That is beginning to be most annoying."

He nodded. "Agreed."

"Then, in answer to your question . . . I don't know."

It was all he could do to keep his mouth shut.

"It was so very easy with John." She circled the room collecting her clothing. "I had no doubts, no questions. Of course, I was much younger."

"And with me?" He held his breath.

"You, my dear Winfield, are nothing but doubts and questions."

"It seems to me not having all the answers is rather exciting." He studied her closely. "Aren't you the one who told me that something unknown, something new, even something

dangerous was worth the risk. Wasn't that what made life exciting?"

"You're going to have to help me with all this, you know." She scooped her chemise off the floor.

"Miranda." He slid out of bed, grabbed his trousers and attempted to pull them on. "Am I worth the risk?" He hopped across the floor, struggling with the trousers.

"Having difficulties?"

"Yes," he snapped and managed to finally get the blasted trousers on. He straightened and glared at her. "Are *we* worth the risk?"

"Probably." She smiled in a wry manner. "Do understand I'm not saying I won't marry you." She pulled her chemise on over her head and allowed the sheet to drop to the floor at the same moment. Nicely done and quite modest had it not been for the lamp behind her that turned the sheer fabric transparent.

"How very odd as that's exactly what I thought you said." He noted his shirt, slid halfway under the bed, snatched it up and put it on.

"Not at all." She settled into his comfortable reading chair by the fireplace, shook out a stocking and drew it up her shapely leg. He could certainly watch that for the rest of his life. "I don't want to be engaged to you. It's as simple as that."

He stared in confusion. "That's not simple."

"Of course it is. It's extremely simple." She tied her garter and met his gaze firmly. "You do not

do well with engagements." She shrugged and started pulling on the other stocking. It was most distracting. "It might be a curse or simply bad luck or more likely poor choices on your part."

"Thank you," he muttered.

She tied her garter and stood up. "But I do not think it's wise to become fiancée number four."

"I see," he said slowly. "So while you are not open to a betrothal you are not precluding the possibility of marriage?"

She beamed at him. "Exactly." She picked up her corset and wrapped it around herself, then turned her back to him and glanced over her shoulder. "Help me with this if you please."

"What are you doing?" He moved closer.

"I'm getting dressed, of course. I can't return to my house carrying my clothes instead of wearing them."

"Why don't you stay here?" He took the corset laces and started tightening the undergarment.

"Because if I am not there in the morning, my servants will certainly notice and think that something dreadful has happened to me. They will then contact my family and God knows what might happen next." She glanced back at him. "Do you want that?"

"You have a point there." There was nothing quite as erotic as a woman in little more than a corset. Pity, they tended to wear them *under* their clothes. "But didn't I hear someone say tonight that she was twenty-eight and able to make her own decisions?"

"One step at a time," she murmured.

He leaned close and kissed the nape of her neck. "When?"

"When what?"

He wrapped his arms around her and pulled her against his chest. "When will you marry me?"

"Do pay attention, Winfield. While I didn't say I wouldn't marry you I never said I would either. If we agreed to a specific *when* we would essentially be engaged." She hesitated. "Beyond that, I'm not sure your previous engagements didn't fail because you rushed into them. I think we should take our time and continue on as . . . friends."

"Friends?" He kissed the side of her neck.

She moaned softly. "Yes, indeed, friends. We've done quite well as friends."

"I don't really want to be your friend." His thumbs toyed with the undersides of her corseted breasts. "I have friends."

"Yes, well . . ." She swallowed. "I simply prefer to get my affairs in order before taking such an enormous step, that's all."

"We're talking about marriage, not death." He trailed kisses along her neck and her shoulder.

She shivered. "Marriage is permanent and should not be taken lightly. After all, there are only two ways to get out of a marriage, death and divorce. And frankly death is the easier of the two."

"Although so final . . ."

"You wouldn't want to make another mistake."

"This is no mistake, Miranda. Trust me on this."

"You do want to be certain."

"I am certain."

"When the time comes . . ." She leaned back against him and his hands drifted over her. She made the most delightful moaning sound in the back of her throat. "I might well marry you."

"But you won't say when that time might be."

"Fairborough should be completed first," she murmured.

"That appears to be a very long time from now."

"And who knows what might happen between now and then." She turned around to face him and stepped backward, to rest herself against the wall. Her eyes were green once again and desire gripped him. She hooked her fingers in his trousers and pulled him close. "We might discover the differences between us are entirely too great to overcome."

He pressed against her and directed his attention to the base of her throat. He could feel the beat of her heart against his lips. "I doubt that. I rather like the differences between us. I find them delightful."

She moaned and slid her arms around his neck. "There's so much we don't know about one another."

"And yet, I suspect there is no one who knows me as well as you." He wrapped one arm around her waist. "And I suspect no one who knows you as well as I." He slid his other hand down her leg. She hooked her leg around his.

"And do you know what I want now?" Her gaze met his, her green eyes simmering with desire.

"I have my suspicions." He unfastened his trousers and let them fall. "It wouldn't be at all civilized."

"Good."

He lifted her leg and wrapped it around his waist. Then slipped into her. She was slick and warm and ready.

"Oh, God, Winfield. This is . . ." She clutched at his shoulders.

"Yes?" He thrust into her and she shuddered.

"So good, so . . . oh . . ." She rocked her hips to meet him. "Oh yes . . . yes . . ."

"Not civilized then?" he growled against her ear.

"Not in the least." She sighed with pleasure. "Civilized is highly overrated."

"I believe, Lady Garret, you are insatiable."

"I believe, Lord Stillwell, you have made me that way. . . ." She arched into him and urged him on.

And in that last moment before he lost himself

once more in the feel and taste and touch of her, the thought occurred to him that if they didn't have trust between them, perhaps they didn't have anything at all.

Chapter 21

"You don't trust me, do you?" he said abruptly.

Miranda stared at Winfield seated beside her in the Elliott carriage. The driver had met them at the train and was returning them to Millworth. "Is this what has been bothering you?"

The man had been pensive and preoccupied all morning. Indeed, he had been unusually quiet when he had brought her home last night, and he'd scarcely said anything to her on the train. But then he'd had his nose buried in a newspaper nearly the entire time. Still, this was not at all like him. The last things she would call Winfield Elliott were pensive and preoccupied and reserved. An uneasy hand wrapped around her heart.

"Shouldn't it bother me?"

"No," she said firmly. "Because it's simply not true."

"Then you do trust me?"

"I haven't given it any thought one way or the other. But I suppose I do, so yes."

"Yet, you're not willing to trust me with your future."

She stared at him. "I never said that."

"You won't marry me."

"I never said that either. If you recall, what I said was—"

"Yes, yes, I know what you said," he snapped. "You said while you would not be engaged to me that did not preclude the possibility of marriage."

"Exactly and—"

"It seems to me if you do not trust me enough to agree to an engagement, which is nothing more than a promise of marriage, you do not trust me to keep my word."

"You're twisting what I said." She shook her head. "That's not at all what I meant."

"If we don't have trust between us, what do we have?"

"I never said I didn't trust you."

"Do you trust me to keep your secrets?"

"I don't have secrets." Well, there was that one. "Not really, nothing of significance. Why, I am very much an open-book sort of person."

"Not to me." He snorted. "Indeed, I find you one of the most complicated, confusing creatures I have ever met."

"Thank you!"

"In my experience, there are three reasons why a woman would refuse to marry. One, she has found someone better."

She scoffed. "That's absurd."

"Secondly, she has found you were not to her

liking. That you did not suit for whatever reason."

"Nonsense." She sniffed. "I can't imagine any woman thinking you were less than quite . . . wonderful."

"Last night you said the differences between us might be too great to overcome."

"And you said our differences were delightful. Although, admittedly, not at the moment," she muttered.

"And three, there really is someone else."

She stared. "And who might that be?"

"How would I know?" he said sharply. "You are not the open book you claim you are. I think you have any number of secrets whether you are willing to admit that or not."

For a long moment neither of them said a word; then he drew a deep breath. "You said it was time to make changes in your life."

"I did."

"Still, one wonders if you have truly put the past behind you." His gaze locked with hers. "If you have truly put your husband behind you."

"Of course I have."

His eyes narrowed. "And yet you continue to run his business. You continue his work."

"That's different." She shrugged off his charge.

"Is it?" His gaze pinned hers.

"Of course it is. He is dead. I accept that."

"So my third question about your marriage is do you still love him?"

"He will always have a piece of my heart. He was my husband after all."

"I don't think you're willing to let him go."

"That's absurd."

"Prove it." His eyes narrowed. "Give up Garret and Tempest. Close it or sell it."

"I will not," she said without thinking.

"I didn't think you would."

"I don't see—"

"You said you were tired of hiding. I think you're hiding behind your husband's name and your husband's work and everything you shared. Everything you refuse to give up."

She sucked in a hard breath. "I am not!"

"Prove it. If not to me, then to yourself."

"I see no need to prove anything to anyone. Not to myself and certainly not to you."

"Imagine my surprise." Sarcasm colored his words. "You said you were amenable to marriage should the right man come along."

"I do wish you would stop telling me what I have said! I know full well what I have said! And I resent having my words thrown back in my face!"

"I merely want to make certain you have not forgotten. I haven't. And it is apparent now that I am not the right man."

"Winfield—"

"I'm not willing to give my heart to a woman who does not trust me. A woman I therefore have difficulties trusting entirely. That, my dear Lady Garret, is one risk I am not willing to take."

Her breath caught. "Your heart? Are you—"

"If you're going to ask again if I am in love with you, again I will say that I don't know. But I have never felt about any woman the way I feel about you. If I were asked to wager on it, I would say yes, blast it all, I am in love with you. Either that or I am completely mad. I can't imagine it feels substantially different!"

"Winfield, I—"

"Let me tell you something about my previous fiancées. I quite liked every one of them and I assumed I would grow to love every one of them. There was no reason not to. I believed in every case we were right for one another. But in hindsight, I realized I chose them as much for what I needed in a wife, a perfect wife perhaps, and a future countess as for any feelings of affection. And that, aside from the ladies themselves, was my biggest mistake." He shook his head. "I did not let my heart rule my head then and frankly, I am afraid to do so now. I am afraid to trust my heart, my life and my future to a woman who does not trust me."

Shock held her tongue. There were a dozen things she knew she should say, a dozen more she wanted to say, but the words would not come.

"If we don't have trust, if we don't have honesty between us, I'm not sure we have anything at all."

Her heart twisted. "What are you saying?"

"I'm saying I accept your rejection of my suit."

"But I didn't—"

"Oh, but you did." Resolve sounded in his voice; his blue eyes were hard, cool. A shiver ran up her spine. What had she done?

The carriage pulled up in front of the manor. He got out and came around to help her down. His manner was again reserved, polite, cold. He held her hand no longer than was necessary and escorted her into the house. She didn't know what to say. A horrible weight settled in the pit of her stomach and a voice in the back of her head screamed she needed to say something, to do something, anything.

"Lord Stillwell." She stared up at him.

"I assume you will wish to go to Fairborough as soon as possible."

She nodded. At least that would give her some time to talk to him. To reason with him. To attempt to explain.

"Very well. I shall have Prescott arrange for someone from the stables to drive you. Mr. Clarke can escort you back."

"Why aren't you—"

"I have a number of pressing issues to attend to. Grayson has charged me with taking care of his business interests while he is out of the country and I have responsibilities of my own to see to." He nodded. "Do have a pleasant day,

Lady Garret." With that, he turned and strode toward the library.

Without warning, anger, irrational and unrelenting, swept through her and she called after him. "Tell me, Winfield, is it your heart I have wounded or is it your pride? Is number four the straw that breaks the camel's back?"

"Governess!" His faint response drifted back, punctuated by the slamming of the library door.

"Twit!"

"Ahem."

She jerked her attention to Prescott standing a short distance away.

"Yes?" she snapped.

"Do you wish me to call for a carriage now, Lady Garret?"

"In a half an hour, I think. I wish to change first." She drew a deep breath. "And my apologies, Prescott, for my ill temper. And for Lord Stillwell's also."

"Not at all, my lady," Prescott said smoothly. "We have been expecting it."

Expecting what?

Miranda had never thought the ride to Fairborough was either long or dull, but today it was both. Of course, there was no one to talk to save the man assigned to drive her and she had no desire to chat aimlessly. At the moment all she wanted was to get to Fairborough, confer with

365

Edwin, assess the progress, answer any questions that had arisen in her absence, then return as quickly as possible. Impatience gripped her. The sooner she returned to Millworth, the sooner she could confront Winfield.

But to what end?

Did she trust him? Of course she did; that was not in question. At least not to her. And while she wasn't a superstitious sort, she did think an engagement was tempting the forces of fate. Perhaps the man simply was not meant to be engaged. Which, of course, then led to the question of whether he was meant to marry at all. And the further question of whether she wished to marry him.

She'd not even seriously considered it before last night. She'd been entirely too busy enjoying his company, the stories he told, the way he made her laugh. She liked how everything with him was a battle—exhilarating and exciting. He never made her feel stupid or foolish. She loved the look in his eyes when he teased her or the way the corners of his eyes crinkled when he was considering something of importance. And she loved the way he looked at her, not just last night but on occasions before then, as if she were something precious and special and rare. And she loved . . .

And she loved him.

It was as simple as that. It was more than merely

having become accustomed to his company. Loving Winfield had crept up on her slowly with every touch of his hand, every shared laugh, every argument. He had slipped into her heart and captured her soul when she wasn't looking, wasn't aware it was so much as a possibility. Now, the thought that she had lost him, the idea of living her life without him brought with it a pain nearly too great to bear. She had to set things right, although she had no idea how to do so. At this point, agreeing to an engagement was obviously not enough.

But how could she tell him she too was afraid?

Afraid of loving him and afraid of losing what, in the years since her husband's death, she had found.

She had loved designing buildings and planning constructions and the like when John was alive and she loved it now. In many ways it had become part of her, part of who she was. Indeed, it made her who she was. Her confidence in her work had somehow become confidence in herself. And change, too, had crept upon her without notice.

But in spite of Winfield's words to her family, she was under no illusion about his attitude toward a woman's proper place. There was no conceivable way he would allow her to continue her work. Was she willing to give it up? The woman she had once been would have done so without hesitation. But she was a far cry from the woman she had once been.

She'd always thought she was completely herself with John. She could be the Miranda no one else knew with him. It was only after his death that she'd realized their life together had been so perfect because she'd made it so. She'd never questioned him. Never really felt her own thoughts were important. It was, after all, much easier, much safer.

It had, as well, always been much safer to keep her mouth closed with her family and avoid conflict and confrontation. And it was much safer to hide behind a man, real or fictional, to do the work she so enjoyed.

Winfield had called her courageous, as had his mother; even Bianca had commended her courage. They were wrong.

She didn't have the courage to admit publicly to her work and face ridicule and failure. She didn't have the courage to become fiancée number four, and become as well the subject of gossip and speculation. To risk the curse—real or imagined—that had plagued his fiancées and ultimately lose him. She didn't have the courage to tell him everything about herself and then be forced to choose between what she loved and who she loved.

The truth of the matter was that she was terrified.

Of being the woman she truly was.

And of losing the one man who might well love her for it.

It was obviously a tenet of life that the more impatient one was to complete the task at hand, the more obstacles were thrown in one's path. Nothing was especially wrong at Fairborough, but there were all sorts of minor difficulties that needed to be resolved ranging from supplies that had been misplaced to a dispute over the placement of a water closet. Miranda was embroiled in one problem after another and was unable to return to Millworth until it was nearly time for dinner.

She considered seeking Winfield out before dinner, but she barely had enough time to change. Besides, given the way they had left things today, it might be better to see him again at the dinner table in the presence of his parents. Surely he would be back to his usual self by now. Why, with any luck at all he would have realized how unreasonable he had been and would be ready, even willing, to discuss things in a calm and rational manner.

Lord and Lady Fairborough had already been seated when Miranda slipped into the dining room and took her chair, moments before her soup was served.

"Lady Garret." Lord Fairborough nodded.

"Good evening, Miranda," Lady Fairborough said in an overly bright manner.

"My apologies for my tardiness." Miranda glanced at Winfield's usual place. Empty.

"How are things at Fairborough today?" The older woman's smile matched her tone.

"There were a few difficulties. Minor, really, and easily resolved."

"I am certain you handled it with your usual efficiency." There was something not quite right about Lady Fairborough's manner tonight. Almost as if she was trying to be cheery when she was anything but.

"Isn't Lord Stillwell joining us for dinner?" Miranda said in as casual a manner as she could manage. It was not at all easy.

"I believe he went to London." A gruff note sounded in Lord Fairborough's voice. "Didn't he, Margaret?"

"Yes, dear." She nodded. "That's what he said."

He's gone? Miranda's throat tightened. "But we've just returned from London."

"Yes, well, it did seem a bit odd . . ."

Coward! Miranda toyed with her soup. "Did he say when he might be back?"

Lord and Lady Fairborough traded glances.

"I can't imagine he'll be gone for very long," Lady Fairborough said. "After all, the ball is in a mere three weeks."

"Three weeks?" Miranda stared. Surely he wouldn't be gone three full weeks?

"Oh, I can't imagine he would be gone that long," Lady Fairborough said quickly, "although he did seem rather out of sorts."

Lord Fairborough snorted.

"Still, it's not like him to be in a foul mood for long." His mother's brow furrowed thoughtfully. "He is usually such a cheerful sort."

"Unless, of course . . ." Lord Fairborough began. His wife shot him a hard look. "Never mind. I obviously have no idea what has occurred. Nor am I intelligent enough to comment on it even though I may well have a valid opinion and exceptionally helpful, even, dare I say, wise advice."

Lady Fairborough's eyes narrowed in a menacing manner. "Do you really think so, Roland?"

He stared at his wife for a moment, then blew a resigned breath. "No, of course not."

Miranda stared at her soup. Mock turtle and one of her favorites. But her appetite had vanished, swept away by the direst sense of disaster. She had to do something.

"If you will excuse me." She rose to her feet. "I find I am not hungry after all. And it has been a very long day. Indeed, I am really quite exhausted. So, if you will forgive me, I believe I shall retire for the evening."

"Yes, of course." Lord Fairborough nodded.

"You do look tired." Lady Fairborough studied

her sharply. "Rest is probably the best thing for you."

Miranda forced a smile and took her leave, trying very hard not to look as if she was fleeing. Although fleeing had a great deal of appeal. She had no idea what to do now, although she did have something of a plan. First, she would fling herself onto her bed and weep for a bit. She didn't think she had cried since the day John died, but she certainly wanted to cry now. Her throat ached and her eyes burned.

She reached her rooms, closed the door behind her and collapsed onto the bed. And waited. She sniffed. Nothing. She forced an odd sort of tentative sob. Still nothing. She certainly wanted to cry, certainly felt like she should. The very thought that she had lost the man who might possibly be everything she had ever wanted, the man who might well be her soul mate, was devastating.

The answer was obvious. She sat up. When John had died she could do nothing about it and so she had cried. But she could certainly do something about this. And she would. Good Lord, she really was a different woman. Well, then it was time to start acting like it.

She got to her feet and paced the room. She was not about to let Winfield Elliott stalk out of her life in a foolish, silly fit of, well, pride, really. She was certainly willing to compromise, if compromise was what it took. She could indeed close or sell Garret and Tempest, which would not mean she could not still continue to do her work. Oh, there would be a battle about it, of course, but they did battle so well. She would also have to tell him there was no Mr. Tempest, at least not in the position of architect. She would indeed have to confess everything and hope that he loved her enough to forgive that tiny little deceit. After all, it wasn't really personal. She'd been deceiving the entire world, not just him.

A knock sounded at the door.

"Yes?"

The door opened and Lady Fairborough poked her head in. "Miranda, my dear, I was wondering if I might have a word with you."

"Of course, do come in."

Lady Fairborough closed the door, crossed the room to one of the two slipper chairs positioned near the bay window. She sat down and smiled expectantly.

"What did you wish to talk about?" Miranda said slowly.

"I actually have nothing to say." The older woman paused. "I thought perhaps you might like to talk."

"Not really."

"Oh, well then, I suppose . . ." Lady Fairborough studied Miranda for a long moment.

"You should know I have never seen my son in this sort of state because of a woman."

"I'm afraid I have no idea what you're talking about." She wasn't at all sure she wanted to discuss the nature of her problems concerning Winfield with his mother.

His mother's brow rose.

Although apparently Miranda had no choice. "I don't mean to be blunt—"

"Don't be absurd," Lady Fairborough scoffed. "Under certain circumstances, blunt is called for. Indeed, blunt can be quite efficient."

"Very well then." Miranda sat down in the other slipper chair and studied Winfield's mother. "What do you think you know?"

"Very clever, my dear." The older woman chuckled. "I couldn't have played it better myself." She thought for a moment. "I don't know nearly as much as I surmise. I don't know exactly what happened between you and Winfield in London, but might there have been a proposal involved?"

Miranda nodded. "Something like that."

"And a rejection?"

"Apparently Winfield and I differ on that. One of us thought it was not so much a rejection as it was, oh, caution."

"And the other one got his nose all out of joint and went back to London in a huff?"

"That's fairly accurate."

"I see," Lady Fairborough said in a sage manner.
"I have no desire to be fiancée number four."

"Which does not mean you are not willing to marry him?" Hope sounded in the older woman's voice.

"Exactly." Miranda huffed. "But he certainly didn't see it that way."

"Frankly, my dear, what way could he see it?"

Miranda stared. "I thought you understood my side of this."

"There are no sides here. We all have entirely the same purpose." She cast Miranda a chastising look. "But you know as well as I do, Winfield is a traditional sort. And he expects that certain things are done in a certain manner. One becomes engaged before one marries."

"That hasn't worked out especially well for him thus far."

"Be that as it may, he still believes in the natural order of things. It is difficult for him to understand why a woman would not wish to be engaged." She shook her head. "Although when it comes to my son, I certainly can."

"Oh?"

"Don't mistake my words, I think Winfield has become a son to be proud of and will make a fine husband. But goodness, Miranda, fiancée number four will be the object of unrelenting gossip and speculation." She rolled her gaze toward the ceiling. "Will she come to her senses and end it with him? Will one of them do something unforgiveable and will yet another engagement come to an end? Will Lord Stillwell finally make it to the altar? Surely you've considered that?"

"Absolutely not," she lied. "Gossip is certainly not a concern."

"It should be. Whether we like it or not, it is a fact of the world in which we live. And you know full well, the attention would be squarely on him as it would be expected that he would be the one to create a problem. Why, a fourth fiancée would be a gift from heaven to gossips. Beyond that, I can't imagine this wouldn't be the subject of any number of wagers."

"You do have a point."

"Regardless of my son's feelings, I commend you for not being willing to subject Winfield to that." She paused. "Now what are you going to do?"

"Well, I had considered following him into London."

"Oh, I wouldn't do that." Lady Fairborough shook her head.

"Why not?"

"For one thing, I have never seen him like this. Who knows what stupid thing he may say or do under these circumstances. Such things are nearly impossible to forgive."

"Regardless, it does seem to me that the sooner all this is resolved the better."

"I'm not sure I agree with that either." She shook her head slowly. "In many ways, Winfield is exactly like his father. If you go after him, if you are the one to make the first overture, he will gain the upper hand and you will never have it back."

Miranda stared.

"It's not the way to begin a life together, my dear," Lady Fairborough said firmly. "Regardless of the world's view of women as somehow inferior, it has been my observation and my experience, that the most successful marriages, the ones in which both husband and wife are truly happy, are the ones in which they are indeed partners and equals. No man will ever admit that, of course, and yet it is the truest thing I know."

"I don't know what to say."

"And that is the mark of an intelligent woman. Few men will admit they don't know what to say and most of them will say something anyway, stupid though it may be."

"Then what do you suggest I do?"

Lady Fairborough smiled slowly and in that moment looked eerily like her son. "Nothing."

Chapter 22

Win paced to and fro in the parlor of the home of Lord Waterston. He'd come the minute Chapman had finished his report, although he really wasn't sure why he was here.

His first day in London had slid into the second, the second to the third and so on until an entire bloody week had passed. It might well have been the longest week of his life. Win fully expected to miss seeing Miranda less and less with each passing day. To be less and less, well, hurt really. With the kind of dreadful gnawing sort of pain that no amount of whisky could dull. Thank God, he had never known love before. He surely wouldn't have survived. Thus far he only missed her more.

It did seem ironic that three women he didn't love had agreed to marry him but the one woman he did love wouldn't. Oh, she didn't phrase it that way. No, she had some ridiculous aversion to an engagement, but she did not, in the strictest of definitions of the word, *refuse* to marry him. Still, the effect was the same.

He'd been down this road before, but this was different. He'd been infatuated with his first fiancée, selected his second because she was such a sensible choice and had come very close to falling in love with his third. And as different as all three women were, they did have one thing in common. He had trusted them, which was, for the most part, a mistake. It wasn't merely that he had made poor choices, but he had given them the gift of trust and been betrayed. How could he trust her if she didn't trust him?

Nor had he ever had to fight for a woman. Couldn't remember ever wanting to. No, the women in his life had come and gone with relative ease. Even those he had been engaged to. There was embarrassment and annoyance and even a touch of anger, but he had gotten over it quickly enough. He suspected he would never get over Miranda, which only raised the question of whether or not he wanted to. And if he did, why was he here?

She hadn't said she wouldn't marry him, but she certainly hadn't said she would. Regardless, he would not marry her until he was certain he had her trust. Until she trusted him enough to confide in him about her work. Until she trusted enough in a future with him to fully give up her past. Until she trusted him enough to agree to an engagement. Because, damnation, he wanted an engagement.

He wanted to announce to the world that this was the woman he intended to marry and then, blast it all, he wanted to do so. He wanted a wedding—his wedding—planned at Fairborough

Hall that would take place as expected. He wanted to say vows in front of God and their families and anyone else who might be interested.

Miranda had won far too many of the battles between them. Electrification, for God's sakes. This one she would not win. The Midsummer Ball was in two weeks and he would stay in London until then if necessary. Aside from all else, it was a practical matter. He had a great deal of business to deal with, as well as Grayson's affairs. And it would give her time to decide if he was what she wanted.

What he absolutely refused to do was go running back to Millworth with his tail between his legs just because he missed her. And wanted her. And loved her.

No, if she wanted him back she could, just this once, bow to his wishes. He was the man after all.

"Lord Stillwell." Adrian strode into the room, took his seat behind the desk and gestured for Win to take the chair in front of it. "I must say I was expecting to see you before now."

"Why?" Suspicion sounded in Win's voice.

"Our last encounter left me, and my entire family for that matter, with the impression that you intended to marry my sister as she is, as you announced, such a remarkable creature. I assume you are here to ask my permission."

"No, I'm not." He paused. "Would you give it? Your permission, that is?"

"If that is what Miranda wants, I would indeed. Not that it would make any difference to her, I suspect." Adrian chuckled. "She has certainly changed in recent years. Oddly enough, none of us seemed to notice until the other night. But then, I suppose, she didn't allow us to see it either. So . . ." He considered Win curiously. "If you are not here to ask for my sister's hand in marriage, why are you here?"

"I know."

Adrian shook his head in confusion. "What is it you know?"

"I know the identity of the elusive Mr. Tempest."

"I see," Adrian said slowly. "Does Miranda know?"

"Not to my knowledge."

"Do you intend to tell her?"

Win hesitated. "I haven't decided yet. I suppose it all depends on what you have to say."

"Ah, yes, well, I thought it might." He paused. "Might I ask how you uncovered this information?"

"I paid a gentleman a great deal of money to ferret it out."

Adrian nodded. "And the name of this gentleman?"

"You can't honestly expect me to tell you that?" Win scoffed.

"I had hoped."

"It seems entirely unwise of me to do so. After all, you went to a great deal of trouble to conceal the truth and you did so in an exceptionally clever and skillful manner."

"Ah, Chapman then." Adrian nodded knowingly.

"I should have figured it out myself. I know very few investors who are willing to allow anyone to continue to borrow without demanding complete repayment at some point over the course of nine years. Investors who are not related to the borrower's wife, that is."

Adrian chuckled. "I suppose that might have been something of a clue. If one had all the facts and a desire to know the truth. Fortunately, my sister had neither."

"Why would she? I suspect she had no idea of the size of the original loan and therefore no idea that the amount did not diminish but instead grew."

Adrian grimaced. "John was not at all good with money."

"Apparently." Win paused. "Why did you keep this a secret from your sister?"

"It wasn't my idea." Adrian thought for a moment. "John didn't want Miranda to know he had come to me after his own brother had refused his request for funding. Although that made sense after his brother's death as the Garret family fortune was surprisingly depleted. But John had no idea at the time. He was annoyed and more than a little embarrassed. He asked me not to say anything to Miranda and I agreed. It was business after all and none of her concern."

"And you decided to go by the name of Tempest?"

"Clever of me, wasn't it?" Adrian chuckled.

"Because *The Tempest* is the work of Shakespeare's in which Miranda is the heroine?"

"It was my little joke and it seemed right somehow to include a reference to Miranda in the name of the firm."

"More than you realize," Win said under his breath. "Are you aware that Miranda is the true architect at Garret and Tempest? And apparently was even before her husband died."

"Not in the beginning, but the idea had crossed my mind."

"She claims the architect is Mr. Tempest, which makes perfect sense given the name of the firm."

"Very clever of her." Adrian nodded. "John Garret was a good man, but I never thought he was especially gifted in that regard. Indeed, when the firm began doing moderately well, I had a few inquiries of my own made."

Win raised a brow. "Chapman?"

"No." Something in his tone said more than words could that Adrian would not reveal more on this particular subject.

"Why didn't you tell her the truth after Garret's death?"

"Why would I? If I told her then I'd have to tell her why the debt had continued to increase." He shook his head. "Garret was dead and it seemed pointless to tell her he was not quite as wonderful as she had thought. At least not when it came to finances."

"Are you aware that, since his death, in those months in which there was no profit generated, she made her payment to you out of her own funds? An inheritance or some sort of family trust, I believe."

Adrian stared. "I had no idea." A slow smile crossed his face. "Good for her."

"I said she was a remarkable woman."

"That's not all you said." Adrian studied him for a moment. "You do realize one doesn't murmur phrases about 'every little boy's dream' to the brothers of the woman he is about to—" A pained expression crossed Adrian's face.

"Escort home?"

"Yes." Relief sounded in Waterston's voice. "Let's go with that. So . . . do you intend to marry my sister?"

"Yes." The moment he said the words, Win knew he had not given up. She might not agree to an engagement, she might not trust him, but he would win her hand and her trust. She would bloody well marry him even if it took him the rest of his life to convince her. "However, she does not seem especially inclined to marry me."

Adrian stared. "She turned you down?"

"Yes and no." Win sighed. "She refused my offer of engagement, but she says that does not mean she won't marry me."

Adrian's brow pulled together. "That makes no sense."

"Exactly my reaction." Win shook his head. "She says she does not want to be my fourth fiancée."

"Oh, well, now I understand. I can see where that might be awkward for her," Adrian said mildly.

"Awkward for *her?*" Win scoffed.

"You do seem to have made a habit of breaking engagements."

"On the contrary, Waterston," Win said firmly. "I have never once reneged on my word. Each and every time I asked a woman to marry me, I fully intended that we would be wed. As much as it is difficult to admit it, I was never the one to change my mind."

Adrian winced. "That is awkward." He got to his feet, crossed the room and poured two glasses of whisky from a cut glass decanter. "You're telling me they ended the engagements? All three of them?"

"One found someone with better prospects. Another decided I was too frivolous for her. And the third . . ."

"The third?"

"She was the only one that I truly regretted losing." He shrugged. "I wasn't in love with her, but I could have been, quite easily. Indeed, with all three I assumed love would come."

"Very reasonable of you."

"But the third, well, with the third I came close. As it happened, she was in love with someone else and while she was entirely willing to marry me, I was no longer willing to allow her to do so. She was a lovely woman and she deserved to be happy."

"Quite noble of you."

"I have my moments."

"In truth," Adrian said slowly, "I have never heard anything really objectionable about you." He returned and handed a glass to Win. "You look like you could use this."

"It's not my first today," Win muttered and took a long swallow.

Adrian took his seat. "Indeed, aside from the string of broken engagements and somewhat wild reputation that appears to have lingered from your youth—as it does with all of us, I might add—you are well respected in business and finance. Your fortune is sound and your family connections excellent."

"I gather you've been asking a few questions of your own."

"She is my sister after all."

"The other night, you forbid her to leave with me."

"As I said, she is my sister. And it's not as if she listened to me." He nodded at the whisky. "Dare I presume you are having difficulties with the most remarkable woman in the world?"

"You have no idea."

"Probably not, although I have known Miranda all of her life. But I fear I have not been a very good brother." Adrian sipped his whisky thoughtfully. "Until the other night, I never imagined what it might be like to be the youngest girl in a family such as ours. We can be a bit . . . overwhelming."

Win snorted.

"We all feel rather protective toward Miranda, as the youngest, you see. She was always so quiet and reserved. I had no idea she was actually running her business. No idea really that she was capable of doing so. Apparently, there is quite a lot about my sister I don't know. Why, I don't think I have ever heard her raise her voice before."

"She seems to have no problems raising it with me."

"And isn't that interesting?" Adrian sipped his whisky. "But then one could say she started fresh when she met you. You had no expectations of who she was or who she appeared to be. She could be completely at ease with you. Completely herself."

"That's one way of looking at it."

"It speaks well of you." Adrian paused. "I

suppose it's too soon to welcome you to the family?"

"As that outcome remains a matter of some dispute, entirely too soon."

"Tell me, Stillwell, why did you wish to know about Tempest and the debt?"

He met the other man's gaze firmly. "I wanted to know about anything that could bring Miranda harm."

Adrian nodded. "Excellent answer. I would expect nothing less. As much as you don't need my permission to marry my sister, you have it."

"I appreciate that. Unfortunately, you're not the one I need to convince." He shook his head. "But she doesn't trust me enough to agree to an engagement and she certainly doesn't trust me enough to confide in me."

"That is a problem." Adrian thought for a moment. "Although you might wish to force her hand."

"And how would you suggest I do that?"

"I'm not sure." His brows drew together and he considered the question. "Perhaps it's time she met Mr. Tempest?"

"You?"

"No." Adrian smiled. "Her architect."

Nothing was far more difficult than it had sounded. At least when it came to what to do about Winfield. Now that she had realized she loved him, it did seem she should do something. She certainly wasn't sleeping, she had no appetite and she had the most absurd desire to simply gaze unseeing into the distance and sigh. She couldn't remember feeling this way about John, but then everything about John had been so very easy. Winfield was the very definition of difficult.

But Lady Fairborough did have a point. And at least Miranda had work to keep her busy. She immersed herself in the Fairborough construction during the day. She'd discovered the moment she wasn't busy, her thoughts would return to Winfield as surely as if they were a compass and he was true north. Good Lord, she missed the man. Missed talking to him and laughing with him and arguing with him. And wasn't it a shame they'd only had one night in his bed? Why, if the man had lived up to his wicked reputation, he would have seduced her long ago. And the unbidden thoughts and dreams of writhing bodies and skillful caresses that had filled her restless nights would have much more substance. Although admittedly, she wasn't sure how.

Still, she couldn't fill every waking moment. And she couldn't help but wonder if it would be so bad to let him have his way on this. After all, hadn't she spent her entire life acquiescing to other people's wishes? It would be so easy and it hadn't been so bad, really. What was one more?

No. She dashed the traitorous thought from her

mind. She would not live her life that way. Not anymore. But she was willing to compromise to a certain extent. And she did need to prove to him that she trusted him. She wasn't entirely sure how, but it seemed the only way to do that was to admit to her work. Perhaps if she could just talk to him . . .

"And I think there should be flowers in large urns here, here and here." Lady Fairborough tapped the point she referred to on the bird's-eye view drawing of Fairborough and its grounds, the one Miranda had shown Clara.

Even Miranda's evenings were busy, filled with plans for the ball. Lady Fairborough made certain of it. Tonight, as she had every night in the ten days since Winfield had been in London, Miranda joined Winfield's mother in the breakfast room the older woman had commandeered for purposes of planning the event. At least one of them was having a grand time.

Miranda had explained the idea to hold the ball itself out-of-doors on the terrace off the ballroom and construct a floor for dancing on the lawn below. Tables would be placed on the croquet and tennis courts. The musicians would be off to one side of the terrace, overlooking the lawns.

"Let me think." Lady Fairborough glanced at the notebook she held in her hand. "We have sent out the invitations, arranged for flowers and decided upon menus."

Miranda nodded. "It seems to me, aside from all those fine points that can't be attended to until the day before the ball, we have everything well in hand."

The older woman stared at her as if she had just said something blasphemous. "Don't be absurd. Why, there are any number of things still to be decided." She shook her notebook at Miranda. "We are not nearly prepared as of yet."

"Still, it does appear—"

"Nonsense, my dear girl." She pinned Miranda with a firm look. "I have learned from past mistakes that the only time one can truly relax is when the last guest has departed and not before they have arrived. As we have no actual ballroom in which to hold the ball this year, there are any number of additional details to attend to. You must trust me on this. I plan this ball at Fairborough every year and have since I first arrived there as a bride. In addition, I have planned three weddings at Fairborough." Her attention turned back to the drawing of the grounds. "Although only one actually did take place."

"Oh?"

"It was Winfield's last fiancée," she said absently. "A lovely young woman. As it turned out, she had already given her heart to someone else. When Winfield discovered that, well, what could he do?"

Miranda stared. "I have no idea."

"He was quite fond of Caroline, that was her name. So he arranged for her young man to take his place and the wedding did indeed occur as planned, even if it was not Winfield's wedding."

"How very kind of him."

"It was indeed." Lady Fairborough nodded. "He is a very kind man and something of a romantic too, I suspect."

And his kiss curls my toes. "I believe I should go into London tomorrow."

"Do you?"

"Well, I do have matters of business to attend to. . . ."

"And if you should happen to cross paths with Winfield?"

"I really hadn't thought about that. . . ."

Lady Fairborough slanted her a disbelieving look. "No? And here I suspected you have thought of nothing but that."

"Well, perhaps . . ."

"Absolutely not," Lady Fairborough said firmly. "I know my son. I have never seen him like this. He's being stubborn and he's being foolish. It's entirely out of character, which indicates to me he cares deeply for you. Of course, that comes as no surprise to me."

"It doesn't?"

"Oh my, no." She scoffed. "I knew it the moment he agreed to electrification. Furthermore, he has never had to expend any effort for a woman

392

before. Indeed, it has been my observation they have fairly fallen at his feet. If he wins this battle, you have lost the war. No, he needs to come to you and admit his mistake."

"What if it was my mistake?"

"Was it?"

"I don't know. Perhaps I was a bit unyielding about the idea of an engagement. And then there is the whole question of trust. . . ."

"He fears that you don't trust him enough to agree to an engagement?"

She nodded. "That's part of it."

"It seems to me the first step is to trust that he cares enough for you to come to his senses."

"What if he doesn't come back?"

"Oh, he'll come back," Lady Fairborough said with far more confidence than Miranda had. "One thing you can count on is Winfield's sense of tradition. The Midsummer Ball is as much a part of his heritage as Fairborough itself. It's only a scant week and a half away now. He's never missed one before and he will not miss this one."

"It's been nearly two weeks since he left."

"Nonsense, it's been barely over a week."

"It seems much longer," she murmured.

She couldn't deny Lady Fairborough's point. If she gave in now, it would set a precedent for the rest of their lives. No, she could be just as stubborn as he was. Annoying man.

Admittedly, compromise might well be in order.

And hadn't she already decided she could indeed give up Garret and Tempest? If only to prove to him she had put her past behind her and was ready to move ahead. And Winfield was the man she wanted to move ahead with.

Yes, she was willing to compromise.

But was he?

Chapter 23

"What, my dear boy, do you think you're doing?" Mother said the moment Win stepped into the parlor of the Mayfair house.

"And what do you intend to do about my daughter?" Lady Waterston stood at his mother's side.

Win's gaze shifted from one irate lady to the next. As Prescott was in the country, his duties at the house in London were being managed by an underbutler. A competent young man who nonetheless apparently did not understand that one could not simply announce there were ladies awaiting him in the parlor without a warning as to exactly who those ladies were. At least when those ladies were older women with a cause.

"Good day, Mother," he said cautiously. "Lady Waterston."

His mother surveyed him with a critical eye. "You look dreadful."

"I was not unaware of that, but thank you for noticing." He nodded. "Is Father with you?" Obviously, he could use an ally.

"We parted company a few hours ago. I believe he muttered something about going to his club." Mother huffed. "We did not see eye to eye on our purpose for coming to town."

"And what is that purpose?" Win braced himself for the answer.

"Why, I came to renew my acquaintance with my dear old friend, Lady Waterston."

"We have let entirely too much time pass since we have seen one another," the other lady added. He didn't believe them for a moment.

"Then I hope you both have a lovely visit." He edged toward the door. "I have matters that demand my attention, so if you will excuse me."

"Absolutely not." Mother fairly sprinted across the room and plastered herself against the door. He didn't know she could move that fast. He would have to physically remove her to escape. Tempting, but perhaps not a good idea. "You are not going anywhere."

"The only matter that should demand your attention at the moment is the question of Miranda." Lady Waterston glared. "What do you intend to do about her?"

He stared at one lady, then the next. "I had intended to marry her, but apparently her intentions and mine are not the same."

The ladies traded glances.

"It is my understanding," Lady Waterston began, "that the question is not so much one of marriage as it is one of engagement."

"That's part of it." He narrowed his eyes. "How much do the two of you know?"

"We know that, while she refused your offer of engagement," Mother said, "she did not say she wouldn't marry you."

"Might I point out she did not say she would?"

"A minor matter." Lady Waterston waved off his comment. "And you do not strike me as the sort of man who would take no for an answer."

His jaw tightened. "She did not say no. Nor did she say yes."

"Well then, there you have it." Mother smiled in triumph.

"Have what?" He stared in confusion.

"It's obvious to us," Lady Waterston said, "that you have not given this sufficient effort. Or any effort at all."

"What?"

"Goodness, Winfield, instead of staying at Millworth to convince her of the suitability of this match, you have fled to London like a frightened rabbit." Mother cast him a look of disgust.

"I have not fled to London like a frightened rabbit!"

"It's rather cowardly, if you ask me," Lady Waterston said under her breath.

"It is not!"

"You're behaving like a child," Mother said.

"I am not," he said although he did feel rather childish at the moment. "And frankly . . ." He cast a hard look at one woman, then the next. "This is none of your business."

"You are my business." Mother pinned him with a determined glare. "As is your future. I have never interfered in your difficulties with one of your fiancées before—"

"I do not have a fiancée, which, might I point out, is one of the problems."

"What happens to my daughter is most certainly my business." Lady Waterston huffed. "Surely, you don't think I wouldn't be concerned given all she revealed at dinner?"

He studied her closely. "She didn't say anything at dinner."

Lady Waterston rolled her gaze toward the ceiling. "Goodness, Lord Stillwell, do you honestly believe, after your announcement to the entire family as to the regard in which you hold my daughter, that I would not follow my sons to hear what you had to say?"

"Then you heard . . ."

"Every word. Of theirs and of yours, some of which was most improper I might add."

He winced.

"And every word of hers." She squared her shoulders. "Miranda has come into her own, quite unexpectedly, I might add. Indeed, I never imagined she had the strength she obviously has. I must admit I was both shocked and impressed with the revelation that she is running a business. And I was quite proud of the way she stood up to her brothers and put them in their place."

"As was I," he muttered.

"And I was as well struck by the two of you together." She studied him for a moment. "You seemed, well, right together. As if you were partners of some sort. Halves of the same whole, as it were. As I said, it was most impressive."

"Every day you stay away, Winfield," Mother said, "is another day for her to realize she might well be able to live without you."

Lady Waterston nodded. "Which brings up the question of whether you can live without her."

"And do you really want to?"

His gaze shifted from one woman to the other. They were obviously of one mind. One would think they had rehearsed their arguments as one lady's comments flowed without pause to the other's.

"After all, it's taken you this long to finally find the right woman."

"Three engagements?" Lady Waterston shook her head. "Really, my lord. How extravagant."

"Give her what she wants."

"It seems a small enough price to pay."

His gaze bounced from one mother to the other.

"Do not allow this one to get away, Winfield."

"Any fool can see you were meant for one another."

"You will resolve nothing as long as you keep your distance."

"Arrange a special license, ask her to marry you without an engagement, then whisk her off and do so."

"There's more to it than that." He shook his head. "She doesn't trust me. She doesn't trust me with her secrets."

"Nonsense. Miranda doesn't have secrets." Lady Waterston paused, obviously remembering the revelations of the other night. "Well, she can't possibly have any more."

"And she does not trust me with her future. She has not yet let go of the past." He paused. "And while I know the answer the two of you will give me, I will ask nonetheless. What about what I want? Shouldn't I have some say in all this?"

The looks the two women gave him were nothing short of pitying.

"If you want her, you will have to do something about it," Lady Waterston said.

"And, my dear boy, you need to do it . . ." Mother shook her head. "Before it's too late."

What did they mean: Before it's too late?

If the purpose of joining forces was to give him something further to think about, then his mother and hers had done their work all too well. *Before it's too late* reverberated in his head over and over again.

Certainly there was always the possibility she could meet someone else. Although at the moment she was safely ensconced in the country. And if she loved him . . . of course she hadn't said she loved him, had she? No, she had hedged about that the very same way he had until he was forced to face the truth. Had she faced it? He refused to consider the possibility that she did not share his feelings. Apparently, hope was the only way to survive heartbreak.

He had managed to get rid of the ladies by claiming a business meeting he could not avoid. Mother said she and Father had considered spending the night in London, but she had decided there was entirely too much to do in the country, what with the ball fast approaching. She was to meet Father in a few hours and return to Millworth. In the meantime, she and Lady Waterston planned to renew their friendship over tea or something of that nature. He hadn't paid a great deal of attention at that point; indeed, he could scarcely think with *before it's too late* echoing in his head. He suspected there would be continued plotting in regard to their children on the ladies' part although he could have sworn he heard the word "vote" from one of them on their way out. No, they were obviously not done with him yet and wouldn't be until the day he and Miranda were safely wed.

Which was exactly what he wanted. But it all came down to trust and he didn't have hers. That was a far bigger obstacle between them than the question of an engagement. And there didn't seem to be anything he could do about that. Adrian's idea to give Miranda no choice but to confess the truth by presenting her with a real live Mr. Tempest was tempting but entirely too dangerous to risk.

Of course, the ladies did have a point. Nothing whatsoever would happen as long as he stayed away from her. Perhaps he was being childish after all. Or simply stubborn. Which might well be the same thing.

"Have they gone?" a familiar voice said the moment he opened the door to the library.

Win sighed. "If you have come to tell me to return to Millworth and fight for Miranda's hand, I should warn you I have heard that lecture already today."

"Quite the contrary, my boy." Father sat in his favorite chair near the fireplace, a glass of whisky in his hand. "I have come to tell you to hold firm. Stand your ground and all that."

Win eyed his father with suspicion. "Have you?"

"I have indeed. Mark my words, if you start off on the wrong foot with this woman, you will be one step behind her for the rest of your days."

"Then your advice?"

"As I see it you have three choices. Go to her. Wait for her to come to you. Or come to some sort of a compromise. Meet her halfway as it were. Metaphorically, of course, not physically."

"I thought you said to stand my ground?"

"Is your ground that firm?"

"I think so." Perhaps not as firm on the matter of an engagement, which might well have more to do with pride on his part than anything else. But certainly when it came to issues of trust, his ground was exceptionally solid.

"Pour yourself a glass, then sit down, son, and let me explain to you how the dealings between men and women actually work."

"I know how the dealings between men and women work," Win said wryly. "I am not inexperienced after all."

His father's brow rose. "How many fiancées have you had?"

"I see your point," Win muttered. He filled a glass for himself, then settled in the chair nearest his father's.

"As I was saying, when compromise is your idea, you are standing your ground. You become a man of reason rather than emotion. Women are very emotional creatures, but they don't like to see themselves as such. Therefore, a reasonable approach is an excellent way to go about getting nearly everything you want. Better to make the best possible deal you can rather than lose altogether. And believe me, when it comes to a woman you love, you will lose. But compromise, Winfield." His father raised his glass. "Compromise is one of the keys to a sound marriage. It allows both parties a measure of victory and there is no actual loser."

"I'm not sure compromise is possible in this instance."

"Rubbish. Compromise is always possible." Father studied him for a moment. "I don't have all the details and I suspect there is more to the problems between you than this nonsense over an engagement."

"It's not nonsense."

"Pride then." He shrugged. "I can certainly understand why you might want the world to see you in an engagement that actually leads to marriage. You do have a lot to live down."

Win snorted.

"On the other hand, does it matter? Really? In the scheme of things? Isn't it more important that she marry you than you become engaged?"

"As that has proven so successful for me in the past?"

"I wasn't going to say that." Father chuckled.

"Your restraint is appreciated."

Father sipped his whisky thoughtfully. "Although I do think this is the kind of thing best worked out face to face."

"You think I should return to Millworth?"

"Is that what your mother said?"

He nodded.

"Then absolutely not." He shook his head. "But I do believe you should make some sort of an overture. Perhaps send her a note. I would be happy to take it to her."

"And what would I say?"

"I have no idea." Father thought for a moment. "First of all, you should make the point that it is business, and nothing else, keeping you in London, which I assume is not entirely inaccurate."

Win nodded. Indeed, in the two weeks he'd been here he'd accomplished far more regarding the family's finances and investments and properties than he would normally accomplish in two months. But then again, he had nothing else to do except imbibe vast quantities of spirits and consider the prospects of a bleak future without the woman he loved.

"That changes the tenor of all this dramatically. You are no longer a sulking child who has not gotten his own way but rather a man of responsibility and duty."

Win stared at his father. "That's brilliant."

"I've been married a long time." He smiled over his whisky. "Then tell her you will return as soon as is feasibly possible and you do hope she understands that it is your responsibilities that keep you away and not the argument you had."

"I like that."

"And I would say something about regretting your disagreement, point out your affections have not changed, mention that you are certain you can overcome your differences, that you're counting the minutes until you see her again, all you can think about is her and so on and so forth."

"I think I can manage the rest, Father." Win grinned, got to his feet and moved to the desk. He sat down, pulled a sheet of stationary with the Fairborough crest embossed at the top from the desk drawer, dipped his pen in the inkwell and began.

My dearest Miranda,

"So," he said in as casual a manner as he could muster. "How is she?"

"Well, she doesn't look as bad as you do, but then I can't imagine anyone could. Too little sleep and too much alcohol, I suspect."

"It seemed like a good idea at the time," Win murmured. "The alcohol, that is. There seems to be little I can do about the lack of sleep."

"From all appearances, I wouldn't say Lady Garret is sleeping well either."

"Well, well, imagine that." Win resisted the urge to smirk with satisfaction. So she wasn't sleeping. That alone would make him sleep better tonight.

"Of course, your mother is keeping her busy when she's not at Fairborough, with plans for the ball." He paused. "You do understand it will be held at Fairborough regardless of whether it's completed or not?"

He chuckled. "I realized that, Father, the same night I agreed to pay a bonus if the ball was held."

"It will be the most expensive ball we've ever had," his father muttered.

"But well worth it."

I regret that circumstances keep me from Millworth, from you. More than you can imagine, I suspect. . . .

Oh yes, that was good.

"I like this one, you know."

"You liked some of the others," Win said absently. "The first and third I believe."

"Not in the way in which I like Lady Garret." His father swirled the whisky in his glass. "There is something in the way you look at her. I've never seen you look at a woman like that before. How could I possibly not like a woman you look at like that?"

Win smiled.

"I should warn you, marrying a woman who is nearly as intelligent as you are is both challenging and infuriating. It won't be easy." He chuckled. "But it is a great deal of fun."

• • •

Miranda couldn't quite stop smiling.

She read and reread and read again the letter Winfield had had his father deliver to her. And every time she read it she could hear his voice, feel the touch of his hand and see his wonderfully wicked smile. And her heart melted.

He said he missed her. That he couldn't wait to see her again. Couldn't wait to talk to her. He was amusing and dear and romantic. But he didn't mention engagements or marriage or the questions of trust that had separated them. Which would have been somewhat disconcerting had not the rest of his letter been so wonderful.

Two days later a second letter arrived via a courier. Two days after that, a third arrived. The fourth letter was awaiting her the next day when she returned to Millworth after a morning spent at Fairborough and Miranda decided enough was enough.

This was the man she wanted, the man she wished to spend the rest of her life with, and she would not let his mother's advice or his own stubbornness stand in her way. Blasted, annoying, wicked twit of a man that he was. She'd never really gone after anything she had wanted. Past time that she did.

The ball was the day after tomorrow and that alone was excuse enough to go to London and haul him back to Millworth. As for what else she would tell him, well, that depended on whether or not he was glad to see her. Whether or not he missed her as she had missed him. In spite of his words, this was a man who was well used to charming women. And whether or not he had meant it when he had said he loved her—she thrust that thought from her mind. Miranda wasn't at all sure she could bear it if his reluctant admission of love was something he had simply said in the heat of the moment.

"Prescott." She glanced around the entry hall and pulled on her gloves. The butler hurried toward her. "Do be so good as to call for a carriage to take me to the train. And please hurry. I don't want to miss the next train into London."

Prescott's brow rose. "London, my lady?"

"I have had quite enough of Lord Stillwell's nonsense." She set her chin in a firm manner. "It's past time he stopped acting like a child."

"But, Lady Garret—"

She held up a hand to stop him. "I know what you're going to say, Prescott, and yes, it is a bit unorthodox and most improper, but then what about all this isn't?"

"Yes, Lady Garret, but—"

"You've known him far longer than I have, but even I realize he is entirely too stubborn to admit when he's wrong, especially when he wasn't entirely wrong."

"Of course, my lady, but—"

"The carriage, Prescott, if you please?" She tried and failed to keep a note of impatience from her voice. Now that she had decided on a course of action, she was eager to set it in motion.

"I should be happy to call for a carriage to take you to the train, Lady Garret." Prescott squared his shoulders. "But if your only purpose is to fetch Lord Stillwell, I would strongly advise against it."

She heaved a frustrated sigh. "Why is that, Prescott?"

"His lordship returned from London this morning, my lady. He is in the library."

Chapter 24

"He did what?" Win rose to his feet and stared.

"He hired me to be your Mr. Tempest." Chapman sat in the chair before the desk and smiled up at him.

Adrian had suggested this when Win had met with him and, as he did hope the man would be his brother-in-law in the near future, it had not seemed wise for Win to say he thought it was a stupid idea certain to have unexpected repercussions.

"Why?"

"He didn't confide the why to me, Lord Stillwell. He said you would understand."

"Indeed, I do," Win muttered. Adrian had

thought presenting Miranda with Tempest the architect would force her hand, as it were, and lead to her confessing about the true creative mind behind the reconstruction of Fairborough Hall as well as Tempest's real financial connection to Garret and Tempest. While Win didn't tell Adrian the idea was absurd, he really couldn't recall exactly what had been said on either side. Miranda's brother was exceptionally generous with his whisky and their meeting had extended well into late afternoon. Still, Win couldn't imagine he had agreed to this, although admittedly he couldn't be certain one way or the other. "But why you?"

"Lord Waterston said, as I already knew all the particulars and my discretion in this matter could be trusted, I was the perfect candidate, although it does seem to me there are all sorts of things that can go wrong with a scheme like this. Still . . ." He shrugged. "As there is nothing illegal about it, the whys of the matter are really not my concern."

Win eyed the other man ruefully. "I imagine Waterston has paid you handsomely for this."

"I certainly wouldn't do it otherwise. It does strike me as a bit, oh, dangerous. One never knows how a woman might react when confronted with a reality she thought was fictional. Indeed, while she does know her investor as Tempest, I am fairly certain she, and her cohort Miss West, decided it would suit their deception to credit Tempest as well with being the architect. Quite clever when you think about it."

"That's exactly it, Chapman." Win sat down and drummed his fingers on the desk. "One never knows how Lady Garret might react to anything, and while her brother obviously thinks this is a brilliant plan, I don't. The Lady Garret I know is not the same as the sister Lord Waterston knows. While he had a sample a few weeks ago as to the change in his sister in recent years, I don't think he truly realizes just how different she is from the woman she once was. That lady might well be forced into a confession by being confronted with a fiction come to life. This one probably would not. And should she ever discover the truth . . ." He shuddered. "I don't even want to think about the consequences, but murder is not farfetched."

Chapman nodded. "Of her brother."

"No," Win said sharply. "Of me. And then perhaps her brother. But I would be the one she would not be able to forgive. Therefore, I think we should abandon this particular endeavor before it goes any further. There's no harm done yet, I suppose. Lady Garret is still at Fairborough and probably won't be back until later today. You can be gone before she returns."

"As much as I appreciate your argument, my lord, I'm afraid that presents some difficulties."

"Because Waterston paid you?" Win scoffed. "I shall return his payment to him and you may keep his money."

"That's not the only problem." Chapman paused. "I have worked for Lord Waterston before. The man is not entirely as he appears. I cannot simply abandon a task he has charged me with because someone else thinks it might be a mistake."

"A mistake?" Win stared. "The fall of Rome was a mistake in comparison to this."

"Be that as it may—"

"This is my life, Chapman," Win said firmly. "My future. I shall deal with Lord Waterston. He is a reasonable man and I am certain, in the light of day without the undue influence of an excellent Scottish whisky, he will understand completely. But I cannot—I will not—risk the rest of—"

Without warning the door shot open and Miranda burst into the room. "Winfield!"

"Miranda!" Win rose to his feet; his heart thudded in the most absurd manner in his chest at the look in her eyes and the smile on her face. "What are you doing here?"

"I intended to go to London, but then I discovered you were here."

"You did?" he said cautiously.

"I decided one of us was being absurd and stubborn and it really didn't matter which one. And your letters, Winfield, your letters . . ." She shook her head and crossed the room toward him with the obvious intention of throwing herself into his arms. Thank God. She pulled up short at the sight of Chapman rising to his feet. "Oh my, I had no idea anyone else was here. I beg your pardon, I . . ."

"No apology is necessary, Lady Garret," Chapman said with a charming smile. "In truth, I am delighted to see you."

"Although he was just leaving," Win said quickly, circling around the desk. He knew full well Miranda would think it impolite of him not to offer an introduction, but if he introduced Chapman as Chapman it was entirely possible that someday she would hear the name of the investigator, put two and two together and there would be hell to pay. "As we have concluded our talk."

Miranda ignored him. "Are you?" She studied the other man curiously. "My apologies, sir, but I'm afraid you have—"

"He has to leave," Win said firmly and attempted to steer Chapman toward the door before it was too late. "Didn't you say you had an urgent appointment? In London?"

"Nothing that can't wait." Chapman neatly sidestepped Win and smiled at Miranda. "I have been remiss in my duties, Lady Garret, and for that I owe you my apologies."

"No, no, no apologies are necessary." Win snatched up Chapman's hat from the chair and thrust it at him. "You do need to be going. Wouldn't want to miss the train."

"Nonsense." Chapman shrugged, then took Miranda's hand. The man was much more attractive than Win had noticed up to now. "This is far more important."

"I'm afraid you have me at a disadvantage," Miranda said slowly. "I'm not entirely sure—"

"To be expected, of course." Chapman chuckled.

Miranda's brow furrowed in confusion. "To be expected?"

Win bit back a groan. It was fast approaching too late and there was nothing he could do about it.

"It's been years, really, since I've actually been in the offices." Chapman shook his head. "It was entirely selfish of me."

"Selfish?" Miranda's eyes narrowed. "I'm afraid I don't understand."

"Of course not, as we have never actually met. But you are as lovely as your late husband said you were." Chapman glanced at Win. "Lord Stillwell, would you be so good as to introduce us, as we have only met on paper?"

"No," Win snapped without thinking. "I mean, I wouldn't want to delay you any further."

Miranda stared at him as if he had lost his mind. Perhaps he had or would at any moment. "What on earth has gotten into you today?"

"Do forgive Lord Stillwell, Lady Garret," Chapman said smoothly. "His confusion is entirely my fault. You see, he did not expect to meet me here today, nor did I expect to see you. But I am delighted that circumstances have prompted our meeting at long last. Once again, an oversight that is my fault." He continued to hold her hand. It was most annoying. "Allow me to introduce myself."

Win stared in sheer horror, a voice in the back of his head noting this must be how one felt when one was about to plunge over a cliff and there was nothing that could be done to prevent the fall. Or slow the descent.

"My name . . ." Chapman's gaze locked onto Miranda's and he raised her hand to his lips. "Is Mr. Phineas Tempest. And I am at your service."

Miranda's eyes widened, her face paled and she snatched her hand from Chapman's. "Tempest?"

Chapman smiled in an altogether too charming manner. "We meet at last, Lady Garret."

"You're *my* Mr. Tempest?" A horror akin to Win's own sounded in her voice.

Chapman chuckled. "One can only hope."

For a long moment Miranda stared at the man. Win held his breath.

"I see," she said slowly, considering the investigator. Win had seen that look before. Miranda was obviously trying to determine exactly who this man was and what he might want. At last, she cast Chapman a brilliant smile. "This is indeed an unexpected pleasure then. Dare I ask why you are here?"

"Recently, I have come to the realization that I have been remiss in my responsibilities." Chapman shrugged in an offhand manner. "I've been quite selfish and allowed first Lord Garret and now you to bear the burden of management of the firm."

"Have you?" Her words were measured.

"It's past time I took a greater part in this company than simply sitting at home, creating my plans and blueprints, in my own little world." He paused. "I'm not certain how much your husband told you about me."

"Very little," she said cautiously.

"Ah yes, well, not surprising, is it? It was business after all and not of interest to a lady."

Win winced.

"Perhaps I should explain," Chapman said.

Miranda nodded. "That would be most appreciated."

"Shortly after your husband and I started the firm I was taken ill. I shan't go into all the details, but it was the sort of debilitating illness that saps a man's strength. I much preferred to keep my health difficulties quiet, which is why I led everyone to believe I was too eccentric to meet with people." Chapman shook his head in a regretful manner. "I was able to work but only within the confines of my own home. Which is why, even after Lord Garret's regrettable death, I was not able to assume the duties of management of the firm in the way in which I should have."

Win couldn't help but admire the way the lie flowed easily from Chapman's lips. He wondered if the man had made all this up alone or if this was Adrian's fabrication. Either way, Miranda knew it was a lie. Still, she couldn't confront him as doing so would reveal her own deception. It was little satisfaction to know that Waterston had been wrong about his sister's reaction to coming face to face with the *architect* she had invented. She was entirely too intelligent to call the man's bluff. No, she was obviously going to play this out until she knew exactly what this *Mr. Tempest* wanted.

"Understandable," Miranda murmured.

"There was a time when I assumed I would never be recovered enough to take my place in the world outside the doors of my house again let alone my full position at Garret and Tempest. But recent treatments have proven most effective." He drew in a deep breath as if drawing strength from the very air itself. "And so here I am."

"Yes, I can see that." Miranda studied him closely. "But why are you here? At Millworth Manor, that is?"

"Why, I called on you in London first, which seemed appropriate, and was told that you were residing in the country at the moment. So I thought why not come and see the progress for myself, as well as pay a call on Lord Stillwell? After all, it is his home we are reconstructing." Chapman inclined his head toward Miranda. "It did seem wise to determine if he was pleased with my work and the progress at Fairborough Hall."

Miranda's jaw tightened at "my work," as well it should. Here was a complete stranger taking credit for her work and preparing to take over management of her business. Win had to give her brother credit. It was a clever, if convoluted idea. Indeed, there might well have been a time when Adrian's youngest sister would have faltered when confronted with her own imaginary creation come to life. But this Miranda was made of sterner stuff.

"I couldn't be more pleased," Win said quickly.

Miranda cast him a grateful if somewhat absent glance. Apparently, Win was the last thing on her mind. Damn it all. If Chapman had not shown up, she would even now be in his arms and they would be well on their way to resolving the differences between them. Now, the idiotic actions of her well-meaning brother had put another obstacle in their path.

"I assume you wish to see the progress at Fairborough for yourself?" Miranda said. "Perhaps Lord Stillwell would care to accompany us?"

Wise of her not to offer to go with this stranger alone. Not that Win would have allowed her to do so even if she knew the true identity of the fraudulent Tempest.

"I'm afraid Lord Stillwell is right." Chapman shook his head. "I have miscalculated the amount of time I had to linger here and I do have to return to London at once."

"We would hate to keep you." Win again attempted to steer Chapman toward the door.

"I shall see you in London then, Lady Garret." Chapman smiled pleasantly.

Miranda nodded.

"I believe we have a great deal to discuss about the firm and the future."

"Indeed we do, Mr. Tempest." Miranda paused, obviously to choose her words carefully. "I had planned to go into London next week. Perhaps we could meet Thursday afternoon?"

"Excellent, Lady Garret. I look forward to it." Chapman stepped toward the door.

Win breathed a sigh of relief, although his relief would be short-lived. He was going to have to tell Miranda the truth about, well, everything. Why Chapman had pretended to be Tempest. What Chapman had learned about her. Why Win had hired that blasted man in the first place. She would be furious about all of it, of course. Indeed, her deception about her work did seem to pale in comparison with all he had kept from her. But if there was to be trust between them, he would have to make a clean breast of it and hope for the best. At least he had until Thursday next.

"Good day, Lady Garret, Lord Stillwell." Chapman nodded and reached for the door. It abruptly swung open.

"Welcome me home, cousin." Gray strode into the room, a wide grin on his face. "I can't say I ever want to make another trip to America and back that quickly, but there is something exhilarating about . . ." He paused in mid-step, his gaze shifting from Chapman to Miranda. "Am I interrupting?"

"Does no one knock anymore?" Win snapped.

"Welcome home, Grayson," Miranda said with a weak smile.

Chapman threw Win a warning look.

"It's good to be home," Gray said cautiously.

"Gray." Win met his cousin's curious gaze. "I don't believe you've met my architect, Mr. Tempest." He turned toward Chapman. "Mr. Tempest, this is my cousin, Mr. Grayson Elliott."

"I'm honored to meet you, Mr. Tempest," Gray said, as coolly as if he met investigators pretending to be imaginary architects every day. "I'm a great admirer of your work."

"Thank you, Mr. Elliott. And I do need to be on my way." Chapman cast a smile at Miranda and Win. "Good day." With that, he finally took his leave.

"What an unexpected . . . pleasure." Gray's smile was noncommittal, but laughter danced in his eyes.

"Not exactly," Miranda said softly, staring at the door.

"Miranda." Win braced himself. "We have much to talk about."

"Yes, of course." Miranda wrenched her gaze from the door and smiled at him. "I am sorry that everything got so terribly out of control. And I do apologize for calling you a twit."

He drew his brows together. "When did you call me a twit?"

"Oh, you might not have heard that." She shrugged. "It scarcely matters now."

Gray's gaze slid from Win to Miranda and back. "Should I leave?"

"Yes," Win said.

"No," Miranda said firmly. "I'm sure you both have a great deal to talk about and I have a great deal to accomplish today. Lady Fairborough and I had planned to spend the afternoon at the hall in preparations for the ball."

Gray's eyes widened. "Is Fairborough complete then?"

"Not entirely. But the wings that were untouched by the fire are again habitable. As those included the family's private rooms, your aunt insists that we dress at Fairborough and spend the day of the ball there. Which makes perfect sense, of course, as there are all sorts of minor details that will still need attention. As for the rest of the work, the finishes—woodwork, trims, plaster details and that sort of thing—will still take well into the autumn to complete. But as most of the destroyed portion of the hall has been rebuilt, the noise, the disorder and mess of construction is essentially over. The family can take up residence again within the next few weeks."

Win stared. "I had no idea."

"You haven't been here," Miranda said pointedly.

Gray's brows drew together. "Where have you been?"

Win waved off the question. "It's a long story."

"However, the ball will be held at Fairborough as it has been for the last 127 years." She turned to Win. "I know you and I have much to discuss as well, but it shall have to wait. I have other matters I need to attend to first."

Win stepped closer to her. "I understand that, but—"

"We have time, Winfield," she said firmly. "All the time in the world, really. This can wait until after the ball, don't you agree?"

"Yes, I suppose, but—"

"But know this." She met his gaze directly. "I do trust you. Now, I must ask that you trust me as well. Can you do that?"

He stared into her eyes, brown today and

flecked with gold and simmering with promise and something else that was surely love.

"Of course," he murmured. In truth, he had no choice at the moment thanks to the farce her brother had orchestrated.

"Good." She turned to leave, then turned back, grabbed his jacket and kissed him fast and hard. Before he could so much as breathe she released him and turned to leave. She nodded at his cousin. "Your aunt will be so pleased you're back in time for the ball."

"I wouldn't think of missing it," Gray said with a stunned smile.

Miranda smiled, cast a last look at Win and sailed out the door, closing it firmly in her wake.

Win stared after her. It was at once a pity and a very good thing she had left so abruptly. Otherwise he wasn't sure he could have resisted the need to pull her into his arms and ravish her right here in the library in front of his cousin and anyone else who might burst in unexpectedly.

"Well, that was certainly interesting." Gray studied his cousin. "I gather a lot has happened in my absence."

"You have no idea." Win sighed and returned to his chair behind the desk.

Gray settled in the chair in front of the desk. "Then perhaps you could enlighten me as to what I have missed." He grinned. "I too have all the time in the world."

Win narrowed his eyes.

"Come now, cousin. It's obvious you and Miranda have resolved your differences. Given her comment when she left, I am curious as to what end."

"That does seem to be the question, and at the moment I'm not sure of the answer. This is a reprieve, Gray, nothing more than a pause in the battle. I suppose I should start at the beginning."

"That does usually work best."

"Usually." Win blew a long breath. "The day you left for America, I was invited to join Miranda's family for dinner. . . ."

Quickly Win recounted all that had occurred since Gray had left, starting with his defense of Miranda at dinner and her subsequent standing up to her family. He did, of course, skip the more intimate details of that night. Win explained Miranda's reluctance to accept an engagement, the questions of trust that had risen between them, his continuing concern about her feelings for her late husband, his sojourn in London, his meeting with her brother and Chapman's subsequent visit today.

Gray stared in disbelief. "I can't leave you alone for a moment, can I?"

"Not all of this is my fault."

"No, not all of it." He shook his head. "But I never thought you were a coward."

"I'm not."

Gray's brow rose.

"I'm not," Win said staunchly.

"What do you call a man who flees before the battle is ended?"

"Intelligent," Win snapped.

"An intelligent man would have stayed here. Once the two of you had calmed down, you could have worked out your differences. Then you would not have met with Waterston and he would not have set this absurd plan in motion." Gray studied him closely. "But you know that, don't you?"

"Of course I know that. I am apparently much smarter than I look. Or less, I suppose." Win ran his hand through his hair. "I'm not certain of anything at the moment. Nor have I been since the moment her ugly shoes stalked into my life."

Gray considered him thoughtfully. "You've always been able to charm a woman into doing very nearly anything you wished."

Win snorted. "With the notable exception of those I have asked to marry me. They seem well able to resist my charming nature."

"What are you going to do now?"

"Obviously, I am going to have to tell her everything."

"When?"

"I don't know. Timing is crucial if I don't want to lose her." Win drummed his fingers on the desk. "I have until next Thursday, when she intends to meet with Chapman. She has to know the truth before then."

"Not that he will actually appear for their meeting."

"There is that." Win brightened. "Perhaps I could simply do nothing and this will all work itself out."

Gray scoffed. "Coward."

"There is a fine line between cowardice and wisdom," Win said in a lofty manner.

Gray laughed. "No, there isn't." He paused. "It will only get worse, you know. The longer you put off telling her who Chapman really is, as well as how long you have known the truth about her work."

"I know." Win thought for a moment. "It seems to me, it might be wiser to wait until after the ball to reveal my, oh, let's call them mistakes in judgment."

"Yes, I'm sure that's what Miranda will call them."

Win glared at the other man. "I know you find this all most amusing."

"Forgive me, cousin, but as I was not here for your first three engagements . . ." Gray snorted back a laugh. "Yes, I do find this extremely entertaining. I must say, I cannot wait to see what happens next."

"Neither can I." Win blew a long breath. "It's ironic, isn't it? I finally found the one woman I cannot live without when I wasn't actually looking at all. And now, it's all so very messy and complicated."

"In my experience, love is usually messy and complicated."

"You could have warned me."

Gray chuckled. "I only recently discovered that myself."

"I'll do what I have to do. Tell her everything and hope for the best. I can no longer imagine my life without her."

"You've never had to fight for a woman before."

"I've never met one worth fighting for. No matter what else happens, I will not give up." He met his cousin's gaze. "I will not lose her."

Miranda closed the library door behind her and collapsed back against it. Who was this man? And more to the point: What did he want? There was, of course, a Mr. Tempest, but he was a silent investor, not the primary architect of Garret and Tempest.

Damnation, she did not need this now. When she and Winfield were so close to resolving their differences. She suspected—no, she knew—he would come to her rescue if asked, but she would much prefer not to have to be rescued. Besides, if she asked for his help now she would have to tell him everything, and while she fully intended to do so, she hadn't planned to do so quite yet.

She would much prefer to reveal that she had, well, misled him after another night in his bed. And perhaps after she told him she did indeed want to marry him. And even possibly after she agreed to an engagement, a short one. Yes, that would be a good time to tell him everything.

Still, the very idea was terrifying. After all, while she didn't consider that her deception had been directed at him—she had fooled everyone after all—he might not see it exactly the same way. He could be most annoying in that respect. Besides, as questions of trust seemed to be the biggest difficulty between them, even if he did love her, he might feel he could never trust a woman who had not been completely honest with him.

She pushed away from the door and headed toward her room. She would have to write to Clara at once warning her and Emmett of this imposter pretending to be Mr. Tempest. There was little else she could do at the moment. She certainly couldn't return to London until after the ball. There was entirely too much to accomplish. With the appearance of this charlatan, it was more important than ever that she receive the bonus Winfield had promised her for having the ball held at Fairborough. Garret and Tempest's days could very well be numbered. Even if accepting that bonus did now seem the tiniest bit wrong of her, it would go for a good cause. She was not about to allow her employees to lose their livelihoods without some sort of financial compensation.

Besides, the Midsummer Ball was a tradition at Fairborough and was important to Winfield and his family. Miranda would do all she could to make certain it was an evening to remember.

Then she would deal with the fraudulent Mr. Tempest.

Then she would confess all to Winfield.

In the meantime, it might be best to keep her distance. The man was entirely too tempting to resist. But then, hadn't someone told her that wicked men usually were?

Chapter 25

"I think it looks quite marvelous." Lady Fairborough gazed around the newly rebuilt grand entry of Fairborough Hall and gestured with the notebook that had become permanently affixed to her hand in recent days. "There's an element of, well, magic about it, I would say."

"Exactly as we intended," Miranda said with a satisfied nod.

"I couldn't be more pleased with the progress here, even if the hall is not completely finished. But, as we do want everything restored to its original appearance, that cannot be helped. It was really foolish of any of us to think . . ."

In the last week, Mr. Clarke's men had been split between work on the house itself and preparations for the ball, as had most of the servants from the manor. Ferns and palms and all manner of tropical foliage had been gathered from the Fairborough conservatory—untouched by any damage from the fire—as well as borrowed from the conservatory at Millworth and arranged to form a sort of living corridor leading guests from the front entry to the grand stairway. Interspersed with the foliage were white painted, simple, tall, square pedestals with chandeliers affixed to them to provide adequate lighting while still being far enough away from the plants to prevent any possibility of fire. Here in the grand entry, as well as on the ground and first floors leading into the ballroom, all the walls were covered in dark blue dyed muslin with silver spangles glued on in a random manner to give the impression of the night sky. Here too the walls, as well as the ceiling, were hidden by blue fabric dotted with spangles. The enormous chandelier that Lady Fairborough had selected in London to replace the one lost in the fire had been delivered some weeks ago but only uncrated and hung in recent days.

But the ballroom was little more than a large open space leading guests to the terrace. While the tall French doors had been installed, they would be taken off their hinges tomorrow and removed.

Guests would freely flow from inside to the out-of-doors, the idea being that one might not be sure if the stars one was under were real or an illusion. Each doorway was flanked by large urns, which would be filled to overflowing with fresh flowers. That was a final touch and could not be arranged until hours before the first guests arrived.

Below the terrace, much of the lawn was hidden by a temporary wooden floor for dancing. Tables and chairs had already been placed on the tennis and croquet courts. Fairborough's kitchen had been cleaned of the lingering effects of the smoke and was now operational. All in all, preparations were very nearly completed for the Fairborough Hall Midsummer Ball.

Something of a pity, really.

As long as Miranda's head was filled with the myriad details of turning a half-finished construction site into the magical location for a century-old tradition she didn't need to consider the implications of the fraudulent Mr. Tempest. For the life of her, she couldn't figure out who he was or what he had to gain from his impersona-tion.

The question of what to do about Mr. Tempest led directly to the question of what to do about Winfield. Yet another thing she could not get off her mind. When she wasn't thinking about Tempest, she was thinking about Winfield. When she wasn't thinking about Winfield she was dreaming about him. Oh bother, it was all so blasted complicated and she had no—

"Miranda? Are you listening to me?"

Miranda's attention jerked back to the older woman. "Yes, of course."

Lady Fairborough arched a disbelieving brow.

"My mind might have wandered for a moment . . ."

"My dear girl, your mind has been anywhere but on the matters at hand ever since Winfield returned yesterday."

"Oh, I daresay—"

"What is even more puzzling"—Lady Fairborough's eyes narrowed—"is that you seem to be avoiding him as well."

"I'm afraid you're mistaken, Lady Fairborough." Winfield's mother was far more perceptive than Miranda had realized. It did seem best, at the moment, to stay as far away from him as possible. Being around him just muddled her mind and made her long to be in his arms. Miranda busied herself adjusting a potted banana tree and adopted a casual tone. "I have simply had a great deal on my mind, that's all. The ball is tomorrow and there is still much to accomplish."

"Yes, that's what I thought." Lady Fairborough started up the stairs and Miranda trailed after her. "I didn't for a moment think that it was because someone was unsure of his or her feelings."

"Lady Fairborough."

The older woman stopped and glanced back at her. Miranda met her gaze directly. "I am not the least bit unsure of my feelings."

"I see," she said thoughtfully. "And Winfield's?"

Miranda shrugged. "That is another question, isn't it? One only he can answer."

"How very interesting. Well, we shall see, won't we?" Lady Fairborough continued up the stairs. She reached the top, looked around and nodded with satisfaction. "One cannot discount the influence of magic, you know."

"Magic?" Miranda's brow furrowed in confusion.

"Look around, Miranda." Lady Fairborough swept into the ballroom, pride sounded in her voice. "We have created nothing less than magic here. Why, anything can happen in a setting like this. Tomorrow night will certainly be a night filled with magic." She sighed. "It's a pity the queen isn't coming, although she would have been a great deal of trouble."

"Are you disappointed?"

"Not at all. I really never expected that she would come. It was scarcely more than a rumor that she would attend in the first place." She shrugged. "Besides, as I said, it would have been a great deal of trouble and we still have more than enough to do without a royal visit." She glanced down at her notebook.

"Lady Fairborough," Miranda said abruptly. "Might I ask you a question?"

"Of course. Anything, dear," the older woman said absently, her gaze shifting from her notebook to the blue spangled fabric on the ceiling.

Miranda drew a deep breath. "Do you think complete and total honesty is important between a husband and wife?"

Lady Fairborough glanced at her. "Complete and total honesty?"

Miranda nodded.

"That was not the question I was expecting." She chuckled. "However, I do think complete and total honesty is without doubt the worst thing that can happen between two people. It leads to comments like him saying your favorite gown makes your waist look wide or you pointing out that perhaps if he had ever learned to drive properly, your carriages wouldn't lose quite so many wheels. That sort of thing."

"I see."

"However, before one marries, relative honesty does strike me as a good idea." She picked a stray thread off the fabric. "Is whatever it is you're hiding so very terrible then?"

"Oh, I didn't say—"

"Did you poison your first husband?" she asked in a casual manner.

Miranda gasped. "Of course not!"

"Are you secretly married to an Italian count?"

Shock widened Miranda's eyes. "Lady Fairborough!"

"Have you ever been employed by or managed a brothel for wealthy gentlemen of society?"

Miranda gasped. "I cannot believe—"

"Have you changed your name after committing a heinous crime?"

Miranda stared at the older woman.

"I thought not." Lady Fairborough shrugged. "If we can eliminate all of those possibilities, then I can't imagine your secret to be at all dreadful."

"I am the architect of Fairborough Hall," Miranda blurted.

"Don't be absurd. He died nearly three centuries ago." Lady Fairborough thought for a moment. "Perhaps a bit less, but I really cannot be certain."

"No." Impatience sounded in Miranda's voice. "I mean I am the architect who designed the plans for the rebuilding."

"Oh, I see." Winfield's mother smiled. "How delightful."

"Delightful?" Miranda stared. "You're not shocked that I am doing work that has always been the purview of men?"

"Perhaps I would have been before I met you. Before the fire, really." She directed a firm glance at Miranda. "Losing much of what you hold dear puts everything in a much different perspective. I might well have been a little shocked if I hadn't known that you don't merely represent Garret and Tempest but you run the firm as well."

Miranda drew her brows together. "How did you know that?"

"Your mother told me." Lady Fairborough checked something off in her notebook, then proceeded across the ballroom floor to the open doorways leading to the terrace.

Miranda hurried after her. "How did my mother know?"

"I have no idea." Lady Fairborough's gaze scanned the terrace. "I have long made it a point not to question where other people get their information, but mothers do tend to know everything. One can rarely hide something from one's mother."

"But . . ." Her brothers, of course! They must have told Mother everything. Her jaw clenched. She would have to kill them. All of them. Slowly and with a great deal of satisfaction on her part.

"Although, if I recall correctly, didn't you say you intended to tell your family yourself?"

"I did tell them." Miranda ignored the slightest twinge of guilt. "Some of them, anyway. When did you see my mother?"

Lady Fairborough cast her a chastising look. "I thought you only had one question?"

"One just seems to lead to another."

"It always does." She waved off the comment. "I saw your mother when I went into London to tell my son he was being something of a . . . of a . . ."

"A twit?"

"Exactly." Lady Fairborough stepped onto the terrace and frowned. She waved her notebook at the scaffoldings still in place on the ground on either side of the terrace. "I assume those will be taken down before the festivities? They're not at all in the spirit of the event."

"They're just finishing up work on the windows. They'll come down tomorrow." She paused. "One more question." Miranda held her breath. "Should I tell Winfield the truth about my work?"

"Under other circumstances, I would say that particular revelation could wait until after the two of you are wed. However . . ." She thought for a moment. "My son has had three fiancées who were not completely honest with him. With them, as it turned out, it was not overly significant. But with you . . ." She smiled. "He is in love with you, my dear. Your deception might well hurt him deeply."

"And he would think I didn't trust him," Miranda said under her breath. "I am willing to give up Garret and Tempest, but I do wish to continue my work."

"As well you should."

"What if he forbids it? As my husband, that would be his right."

"Precisely why you should tell him before you

marry. But I can't imagine him forbidding you to do anything, nor can I imagine you not standing your ground."

"He has very strong opinions on what women should or should not do."

"And I doubt if that has changed. But Winfield is not an idiot. Your love of your work makes you who you are, the woman he has fallen in love with. You have a gift, Miranda, and my son has recognized that. You have proven to him, to the world really, that you can do this as well as any man. And to that I say bravo!"

"Thank you, but—"

"And I would be quite disappointed if you were to abandon work that you love and do so well." She studied the younger woman. "Let me tell you something about myself. I have spent my entire life doing and being exactly what and who I was supposed to be. I married well, as I was expected to do, raised my son, ran my household and I've been a perfect hostess, wife and mother. I never ran off to Paris to live in an attic in Montmartre and create wild, improper works of art. I never had mad, impetuous affairs with foreign princes and counts with unpronounceable names. I never swam nude in a mountain lake while a poet composed sonnets about the color of my eyes."

Miranda stared.

"All of which is far more unforgiveable in the eyes of society than what you have done." She thought for a moment. "Do not take my comments for regret. I have quite enjoyed my life although I do wish I had done more. And once Winfield is settled, I intend to."

"You do?" Miranda said cautiously.

"There are things in this world I will never do, but there are any number of things I wish to see. And I intend to drag my husband along with me. We shall see the pyramids and China's Great Wall and buffalos in the wilds of America. And when we return"—she squared her shoulders—"I intend to vote."

"I'm not sure I would tell your son that. About voting, that is," she added.

"Oh, but telling Winfield will be the most enjoyable part of it." She flashed Miranda a wicked smile.

Miranda laughed, then sobered. "You're right though, I do need to tell him everything. Especially . . ."

"There's something else, isn't there?"

"I'm afraid so." Miranda explained the appearance of the fraudulent Mr. Tempest.

"That is a problem. And I can certainly see why you don't wish to involve Winfield in this. At least not yet. But you do need something of a plan, I think." Lady Fairborough's brow furrowed in a considering manner; then her expression brightened. "I have it. You, my dear, need a professional."

"A professional?"

"An investigator." Lady Fairborough nodded. "You need to uncover the truth about this man as quickly as possible. Although nothing can really be done until after the ball."

Miranda shook her head. "I have no idea how to find an investigator."

"Nor do I, but I would wager Camille does. She can no doubt supply the name of someone who will be both efficient and discreet."

"That is a good idea." She should have thought of it herself. At once, it was as if a weight had been lifted from her shoulders. The moment she disposed of the problem of the imposter, she could tell Winfield everything. Then, of course, she'd probably have to do battle with the stubborn man. Still, there was nothing quite as much fun as arguing with him although this was much more important than any of their previous disputes had been. This one she did not intend to lose.

For both of them, the stakes were entirely too high.

This was absurd.

Win paced the floor of the Fairborough library. It was good to be back in his own home even if it was not entirely finished. The wiring for the electricity had been completed in the family's wing, as well as in the newly rebuilt portion of the house, but would not be operational until the generating system was fully installed. As much as he hated to admit it, the prospect was vaguely exciting. If, of course, it didn't burn the house down. Again. But he had greater concerns at the moment.

He and Miranda had been avoiding one another since Chapman's visit. She had obviously been too busy to give him more than a second thought, which was understandable but no less annoying. Aside from that, the matter of the fraudulent Mr. Tempest was surely weighing on her mind. Win had thought it wise to keep his distance until he decided exactly what his next step would be. But it had proven harder than he had imagined, as all he wanted was to be with her. The days were bad enough, but the nights . . .

Still, he had finally reached a decision. He could wait no longer to resolve things between them. The ball was in a few hours and he would confess everything to her before the guests arrived. It might not be a good plan, but it did seem to him, that no matter how furious she might be, the hours of enforced gaiety at the ball would serve to ease her anger. At least he hoped so.

He had no idea exactly what he would say although he had attempted to rehearse any number of variations on the same theme. Nothing struck him as quite right. Still, he hoped the words would come when he needed them. They always had with women in the past. But this was no ordinary woman. This was Miranda, the one woman, the only woman, who had captured his heart.

The one woman, the only woman, who could destroy it.

"Miranda!" Camille waved from the terrace and started down the stairs toward her.

Miranda stood on the dance floor and waved back. She had been studying the scene laid out before her with a fair amount of pride and more than a little satisfaction. The musicians were setting up on one side of the terrace. The scaffolding was in the process of being taken down. The urns were being filled with flowers. She had just inspected both the tennis and croquet courts and all looked, well, perfect.

She had managed to put her concerns about the imposter aside, as worrying about him could do no good at the moment. She'd had no chance to ask Camille about an investigator, but this was the perfect opportunity.

"Everything looks quite wonderful," Camille said when she reached Miranda. "It's hard to believe when one remembers the devastation of only a few months ago."

"It's amazing what an extraordinary amount of work and a huge amount of money can accomplish."

"But well spent, I would say." Camille laughed. "I have always believed a huge amount of money can accomplish very nearly anything."

"Perhaps not everything." Miranda paused. "Lady Fairborough suggested you might have the answer to a dilemma I have."

Camille's brow rose. "What kind of dilemma?"

"I have encountered a man claiming to be someone I know full well he isn't. I need to find out who he really is." She drew a deep breath. "Lady Fairborough thought you might know the name of a good and discreet investigator."

Camille's eyes widened. "Yes, I do, but—"

"I need to contact him as soon as possible. Not today, of course, but tomorrow. I do have a few days to spare." She had no idea what would be waiting for her on Thursday when she returned to London and that, together with the problems with Winfield, weighed on her mind more and more. She had thought she could put it off, but—

"Miranda, listen to me." A worried frown creased Camille's forehead. "There's something you should know. In truth, I was going to say something to you. I simply hadn't planned on saying it at this moment."

Miranda studied the other woman. She didn't know Camille well, but she hadn't struck her as the kind of woman to be concerned over trifles. "Go on."

"Yes, well, now I'm not sure how to say this. But I wasn't told not to tell you, although when Grayson told me I suspect he assumed I wouldn't mention it. It is rather awkward. Still."

She straightened her shoulders. "I do believe women should help one another."

Miranda stared in confusion. "What are you trying to say?"

"Before I tell you anything at all you should understand that Grayson says Winfield is truly in love with you. It might make what I'm about to say a little more, oh, palatable."

"Go on."

"And men in love do tend to be rather stupid. Especially if they are concerned that the object of their affection is still in love with their late husband."

"That's absurd." Miranda scoffed. "I told Winfield that I have moved on with my life."

"I said men were stupid." She studied Miranda closely. "Are you sure about moving on?"

"I have never been more certain of anything in my life." She blew a long breath. "John is gone and I am not the same woman I was when I married him. Indeed, I am not the same woman I was when he died. And Winfield is . . ."

"Yes?"

"It's difficult to say. It feels . . . disloyal, I suppose." She met the other woman's gaze firmly. "John was my first love. Winfield is my last and, I suspect, the true love of my life."

"Oh, how wonderful." Camille beamed.

"I'm not sure how wonderful it is." She shook her head. "It certainly isn't easy."

"I don't think it's supposed to be." Camille shrugged.

"That said, what did you have to tell me?"

"It does fall in that category of not being easy. . . ." Camille wrung her hands together. "I do know the name of an excellent investigator. But Winfield has already hired him."

"What?" Miranda stared. "Why on earth would Winfield need—" Without warning the answer struck her and she sucked in a hard breath. "To investigate me? *Me?*"

"Actually, he wanted to know more about Garret and Tempest first," Camille said quickly. "And then you."

"When?" Miranda said sharply.

"Right after your first meeting. So you see it's really quite understandable and most forgivable, I would think. Nothing to really upset yourself over." Camille cast her a weak smile.

Miranda narrowed her eyes. "But there's more, isn't there?"

"Mr. Chapman—he's the investigator—is very good. And very thorough."

"And?"

"And he learned the extent of your involvement with Garret and Tempest."

"The extent of my involvement?"

"That you not only run the firm but you are the chief architect."

Miranda gasped. "Winfield knew that?"

Camille nodded.

"How long has he known?"

Reluctance sounded in Camille's voice. "Since before we left for America."

"Since before . . ." Shock coursed through her. "He knew all along? So all his talk about trust and honesty . . ." Anger swept through her and she started toward the house. "If he wants honesty, he shall have honesty!"

"Wait," Camille said. "There's one more thing you should know."

She stopped and turned toward Camille. "I'm almost afraid to ask."

"I don't blame you." Camille paused, obviously to choose the right words. Miranda didn't think there were any. "The gentleman you met the other day, Mr. Tempest."

Miranda nodded. "I already know he's an imposter."

"Actually . . ." Camille winced. "He's the investigator. Mr. Chapman."

"I don't understand. If Winfield had hired him . . ." Miranda stared in disbelief. "Winfield hired him to play the role of Mr. Tempest?"

"Absolutely not," Camille said. "He would never do such a thing. Or at least I don't think that he would, although I could be wrong. But Mr. Chapman was hired to pretend to be Mr. Tempest by one of your brothers. The same brother who funded your husband's company under the name of Tempest."

Miranda stared. "My brother funded . . ." She gritted her teeth. "Which brother?"

"Lord Waterston, I believe."

Miranda snorted in disdain. "Of course. I should have known."

"Still, it wasn't Winfield's doing."

"Oh, that makes it all so much better," she snapped and started toward the house.

"I would think it might make it a little better," Camille called after her.

"Oh, it does." Her jaw clenched. "I shall have the privilege of strangling the lifc out of two men instead of just one!"

Chapter 26

The door to the library slammed open.

"You knew!" Miranda stalked into the room.

"Knew what?" Win said innocently. He had long found it best to feign ignorance rather than admit knowledge until he was certain he knew what he was admitting to. Although he was fairly sure he knew exactly what she was talking about.

"You knew all along that I ran the firm and that I was the architect!"

"Not *all* along."

"Long enough." She advanced toward him in a

threatening manner. "And you went on and on about trust and honesty!"

"I do think honesty is important."

"Apparently only my honesty is important." Her hazel eyes flashed. Hazel? She wasn't nearly as angry as he thought she'd be. "You had me investigated!"

"One does like to know who one is dealing with." He crossed his arms over his chest and assumed what he considered a businesslike expression. "It's good business. And as a woman of business you should understand that."

That gave her pause, as well it should.

"I will grant you that point, so you needn't continue to look at me in that manner. But you did know the Mr. Tempest I met was a fraud."

"That wasn't my idea," he said quickly. "In fact I distinctly recall thinking it was an exceptionally bad idea when it was first suggested."

"By my brother! The same brother who had funded Garret and Tempest in the first place! Why didn't you stop him?"

"I didn't think he'd actually do it." He stepped toward her. "If you recall, I did try to stop Chapman."

"Not hard enough!"

"It was extremely awkward with you—" He drew his brows together. "How do you know all this?"

She waved off his question. "Does it matter?"

"I suppose not." Still, it would be nice to know.

"If we are to have honesty and trust between us, it does have to go both ways."

"I fully intended to tell you everything," he said staunchly. "In fact, I planned on doing so today."

"You were going to tell me you had me investigated? You were going to tell me you knew about my position and my work even while you were trying to pry that information out of me? You were going to tell me that my brother was the investor in my business—"

"Your late husband's business," he corrected her.

"*My* business. And you were going to tell me you knew Mr. Tempest was an imposter?"

"Absolutely."

"So you were going to tell me everything?" Her brow rose in disbelief.

"Not everything, but most of it." He shook his head. "I didn't think you needed to know about your brother's investment."

Suspicion narrowed her eyes. "Why not?"

"I thought it might make you feel, well, weak. As if you couldn't manage on your own, without your family's help. Even if it was your husband who arranged the financing in the first place."

She stared at him. "That's really rather thoughtful of you."

"I can be very thoughtful." He sniffed.

She crossed her arms over her chest. "If you

were going to tell me all the rest, why haven't you done so?"

"You've been busy." Even to his own ears, it sounded feeble.

"Do you have any idea how worried I have been about this imposter?"

"I am sorry about that, but again, it was not my idea." He paused. "Why didn't you tell me the truth about your work? Why didn't you trust me?"

"I don't know." She shrugged. "Probably because you're so dreadfully stuffy when it comes to this sort of thing. About a woman's place in the world, that is."

"I do feel women have a proper place, but—"

"Aha!"

"But." He heaved a sigh of surrender. "You have proven to me that I cannot paint all women with the same brush, as it were." He stepped closer and met her gaze. "You are a remarkable woman, Miranda Garret, and I daresay you can do anything you set your mind to. And, while it's somewhat difficult to admit, I find a certain measure of pride in that."

She stared. "You do?"

"Yes, well, who would have thought?" He rolled his gaze toward the ceiling. "Besides, it's not as if you were doing something completely absurd. Crusading for the rights of women or demanding the vote or anything of that nature."

"Oh, no." She shook her head. "Not me."

"You should have trusted me. Not in the beginning, perhaps, but once we knew one another."

"I probably should have." She nodded slowly. "But I was, well, afraid."

"Afraid?" He stared. "Of me?"

"I am terrified of you," she said in a lofty manner. "You yell at me."

He snorted. "You're not terrified of anything and you yell at me."

"That's entirely different." She sniffed.

"Because you're a woman?"

She shrugged. "Of course."

His brow rose in a smug manner. "Then you want to do the work of a man while being treated like a woman?"

Her eyes widened. "You did that on purpose."

"Indeed I did." He couldn't resist a satisfied smile.

"You manipulated me!"

"It seems only fair. You manipulate me."

She gasped. "I never—"

"And I needn't say more than one word to prove my point." He leaned closer and met her gaze. "Electrification."

She winced. "That was not intentional."

"Nonetheless—"

"Very well then, I will concede that." She paused for a moment, obviously to consider her next point. Not that she had one. "I didn't intend to be this reasonable when I came in here."

"I didn't expect you to be this reasonable either." Reasonable was the last thing he expected from her, but there was apparently something to be said for loving a reasonable woman. He smiled slowly with the sure and certain knowledge all would be forgiven "And yet you are a reasonable woman."

"Nor am I entirely innocent."

"I believe I mentioned that."

"One could say, I suppose, if this were some sort of game—"

"Which it isn't, of course."

"No, definitely not." She shook her head. "But if it were, and if we discount the fraudulent Mr. Tempest, as that was my brother's doing—"

"Oh, absolutely, we should discount that."

"Then one might say, as there were things I didn't tell you and things you didn't tell me . . ."

"Yes, yes, go on." He reached out and pulled her unresisting into his arms.

"That it might be considered a draw. That your misdeeds—"

"Let's call them mistakes rather than misdeeds. Misdeeds sounds so very . . ."

"Wrong?"

"Exactly."

"Very well." She wrapped her arms around him and gazed up into his eyes. "Mistakes then. And yours are not substantially worse than mine."

He grinned. "I never thought they were."

"We should agree not to keep things from one another in the future—in the interest of trust, that is."

"Then, in the interest of trust, I should tell you I intend to kiss you." He lowered his lips to hers.

"Come now, my lord," she murmured against his lips. "I already knew that."

The instant his lips met hers, a knock sounded at the door. It opened immediately.

"I beg your pardon, my lord." Prescott stepped into the room.

Win sighed and released her. Miranda bit back a laugh and stepped away. His good humor faded at the look on the butler's face. "What is it, Prescott?"

Prescott looked from Win to Miranda and back. "I thought you would want to know, my lord, there has been an accident."

Miranda sucked in a sharp breath.

Dread settled in Win's stomach. "What kind of accident?"

"The workers were taking down one of the scaffoldings when it collapsed, sir."

Miranda paled and she reached out to steady herself on the back of a chair. "Is he—" She shook her head as if to clear it. "Is anyone . . ."

"Was anyone hurt?" Win asked sharply.

"Three of the men were hurt, my lord."

Miranda sank into the chair, her eyes wide with shock. "How bad is it?"

"The injuries do not appear to be fatal."

She stared at the butler. "Are you absolutely sure?"

"Yes, my lady." Prescott nodded. "Two of the men were knocked unconscious, but they have come around. Other than that, the injuries appear limited to a few nasty cuts and bruises, possibly a sprain as well. The men are being taken into the village now."

"Thank God. For a moment . . ." Miranda buried her face in her hands.

"Thank you, Prescott."

The butler nodded and left the library.

Win took a step toward Miranda to comfort her and the realization slammed into him like a cold dash of water, stealing his breath, twisting his heart. Of course, this was how her husband had died. Obviously, today's accident had brought back the memories and the distress of the day she had lost him. And just as obviously, it—he— would never truly be in the past. Could Win live the rest of his life with that?

He drew a deep breath and tried and failed to keep the answer at bay. Tried to ignore the awful truth burning inside him.

He crossed the room, poured a glass of whisky and brought it to her.

Her hand trembled when she took it. He was shocked to note his was rock steady. But then, why wouldn't it be? Something inside him had turned cold and empty. No doubt his heart. He suspected that would not last and suspected as well the pain to come.

"Are you all right?" he asked coolly.

"I think so." She sipped the whisky. "It was just—"

"I know what it was." His voice was harsh and he couldn't seem to stop himself. "This is how your husband died. This has brought it all back to you."

"Of course it did. It would be surprising if it didn't," she said under her breath.

He turned away, moved to the window and stared unseeing at the countryside. He had never in his life not known what to do before, but at this very moment, he was lost. "It's growing late. Guests will be arriving in a few hours. You should probably be getting ready for the ball."

"Winfield." Concern sounded in her voice. "What is it? Prescott said the injuries weren't fatal."

Still, was there really any choice? "There are things I can do, Miranda, things I can face and things I cannot."

"What do you mean?"

He turned back to her and smiled in a wry manner. "I cannot give my heart to a woman who has already given hers away. I cannot play second to a dead man."

"But you're not."

"I saw the look on your face, my dear."

"It was the accident, nothing more than that." She stared at him. "Surely, you can understand how this would upset me?"

"I do understand. I understand a great deal. Now. I should have understood it from the beginning. The past is always with us, Miranda." He shook his head. "I can't ask you to change how you feel. It's not your fault. It's not anyone's fault. Unfortunately, this is how I feel."

He started toward the door. She caught his arm and pulled him around. "Stop it, Winfield, stop it at once."

"I wish I could."

"You're being unreasonable."

"Oddly enough, I am well aware of that."

"This has nothing to do with you and me."

"I think this has everything to do with you and me. And it doesn't seem to matter." He stared into her eyes for a long moment, brown now and so lovely, even shadowed by concern and shock. "I know I am not your first love. But knowing that does not make it easier. And I cannot help but wonder if that first love might not have been your true love. Even your soul mate, if one believes in such things. It's a silly, overly romantic concept, I suppose, but there you have it."

"What are you saying?"

"I cannot compete with a dead man and I can never take his place. A few weeks ago I asked you to prove that you had moved on. I'm afraid what you have proved now is my point." He shook his head. "I am truly sorry, Miranda. More than you can ever imagine. But I can't spend the rest of my life knowing I am nothing more than a replacement in the heart of the woman I love. And that's all I can ever be."

"I cannot change my past, Winfield, nor do I wish to. It has made me who I am."

"I understand that as well. Perhaps if I had met you first—"

"No." She shook her head. "I was not the same woman then. We would not have suited."

"Perhaps not." He paused. "It is one of those odd quirks of fate, don't you think? A joke of the gods or something of that nature. When I wasn't looking, I at last found the one woman, the right woman, the love of my life. And it seems I am too late." He removed her hand from his arm and raised it to his lips. "I cannot be less to you than you are to me. I know myself well enough to know that would destroy me. Would destroy us. And you would hate me."

He released her hand, turned and walked out the door. He continued out of the house and didn't stop. His feet moved as if of their own accord, but his mind was as numb as his heart. He didn't want to think, didn't want to feel. He paid no heed to where he was going; he had no destination in mind. At last he found himself at the folly and realized he had been walking for some time. He hadn't intended to come here, yet here he was. Appropriate, really, to end up here at this monument to a doomed love. He sank down on one of the marble benches and tried to think. He had no idea what to do now.

He knew, in a part of his mind that still retained some semblance of rational thought, that he was being absurd and completely irrational and this was not at all his usual nature, but he couldn't seem to help himself. He had never felt this way before. He had never loved before.

He suspected he never would again.

Win had not considered himself the type of man to give up. Now, helplessness gripped him. There was nothing he could do. He could not force Miranda to stop loving her late husband. And he could not live his life as a substitute.

The breeze whispered through the trees, sounding very much like a sigh of heartfelt sorrow. Of course, this was the place for it. He wondered what Thomas and Anne would think of his plight? Would they sympathize? Or would they point out they were ultimately separated by death and anything else could be overcome.

Nonetheless, he didn't see how and it no longer mattered. This was not a question of logic or reason. This was emotion, feelings. Raw and new and awful. A dull heavy weight that settled in the bottom of his stomach and clutched at his breath and caught at his heart.

Win got to his feet and started back toward Fairborough. He had to survive the ball, and then he would do whatever was necessary never to see Miranda Garret again. Gray could handle anything that needed seeing to regarding construction. Win would treat her with polite reserve tonight; he had no choice. And tomorrow, as cowardly as it might seem, he would flee to London or anywhere that she was not.

He had never had to fight for a woman before. And now he understood this was a fight he could not win.

Even if the battle was only with himself.

Miranda stared at the library door.

She'd been too stunned to say much of anything and now it was too late. She had no idea how to show him, to prove to him, that John was part of her past. And Winfield was her future. The only future she wanted. Indeed, while it did feel disloyal and even wrong, she was certain if she met John for the first time today, they would not suit at all. She had loved him, of course, but it had been so easy to do so. And she was a different woman now.

Winfield was not the least bit easy. Nor did she want him to be. Loving Winfield was exhilarating and exciting and completely unexpected. And so much more than anything she'd ever dreamed of.

Miranda paced the library and considered what to do now. She could certainly go after him, but, as she didn't know what to say, that might do more harm than good. It might be best to leave him be for a bit. Perhaps he would come to his senses on his own. She scoffed at the thought. He would never come to his senses on his own. He was far too upset and obviously hurt. Her heart ached for him. She would never deliberately do anything to hurt him. She'd been with the man nearly every day for months now. Surely she knew how to fix this.

She paused in mid-step. There did seem to be only one way to prove to him that she had moved on with her life, and that he was the one she wished to move on with. It might well be a dreadful mistake and result in horrible humiliation for them both, publicly and privately. If she failed, the man would break her heart. It was a risk she would have to take. And hadn't Winfield said the greater the risk, the greater the reward?

Even so, this time, the risk was insignificant compared to the reward.

Compared to the rest of their lives.

Chapter 27

Lady Fairborough was right. It was indeed a night of magic.

The weather was perfect, the food excellent and the musicians superb. Even the stars in the sky twinkled merrily as if trying to outshine the spangles on the yards and yards of dyed muslin covering Fairborough's walls.

Miranda wasn't sure she'd ever seen a ball quite so well attended before. But then the tradition was to invite everyone in the county regardless of wealth or social position. It was a country affair and as such, was a bit less formal than something held in London, but there were any number of guests who had made the trip from the city to attend. Lady Fairborough had said the ball always drew a great crowd, greater this year as she suspected few who had been invited would fail to attend. After all, the rebuilding of Fairborough Hall was a subject of some curiosity in the area.

Lady Fairborough was in her glory. Lord Fairborough was having a grand time. Their son was a different story.

Winfield had done everything possible to avoid her. Indeed, she wouldn't have been at all surprised to have discovered him hiding behind a potted palm. Although she did note he seemed to have no lack of attractive dancing partners. It was most annoying. Fortunately, his sense of responsibility kept him from abandoning the event altogether.

The ball was well under way. It was time.

She took Lord Fairborough aside and explained her plan. The older man studied her for a long moment. "Are you certain you wish to do this?"

"I can think of nothing else that would be as effective." She smiled wryly.

"Very well then." He nodded. "I shall do my part and we shall both hope for the best."

The next waltz started and Lord Fairborough caught Miranda's eye and nodded. She drew a deep breath and approached Winfield, who was chatting with a lovely young blonde thing, no doubt in her first season.

"My lord." Miranda cast him a brilliant smile. "I believe this is our dance."

Win glanced from Miranda to the young lady and back. "My apologies, Lady Garret, it must have slipped my mind. And as the dance is now half over—"

"Then we have no time to waste." She cast the blonde a dismissive smile.

Winfield hesitated, then smiled at the young woman. "If you will forgive me, Miss Robb." He turned to Miranda and offered his arm.

She took his arm and he escorted her onto the floor and swept her into the dance. Their first dance. She would not allow it to be their last.

"A bit young for you, don't you think?" she said pleasantly.

"Not at all." He smiled in a polite manner.

"I suspect she would be willing to marry you should you ask her."

"Most women are."

She drew a deep breath. "I have given a great deal of thought to our recent conversations and I must admit I was wrong."

"Were you?"

"I was indeed." She smiled up at him. "I was wrong when I apologized for calling you a twit as you so clearly are."

His eyes narrowed.

"Let me ask you this: Do you feel a responsibility toward your employees? To keep them out of harm's way and that sort of thing?"

He frowned down at her. "Yes, of course."

"Then surely you can understand how learning that men, who were essentially in my employ, were injured would upset me."

His brow furrowed. "I suppose I hadn't really considered—"

"No, you were entirely too busy reaching the wrong conclusion because you are so concerned about once again making the wrong decision and choosing the wrong woman."

"Don't be absurd." His expression tightened. "And this is not the place for this discussion."

"You've given me very little choice. If we do not resolve this tonight you will probably flee to London to hide. Again."

"I did not . . ." His jaw clenched. "This is not the time."

"Unless you intend to leave me right here in the middle of a dance, it's the only time I have." She paused to choose her words carefully. "You should know, I do intend to continue my work."

"I shall be happy to give you excellent references." He glanced down at her. "And that's no longer any of my concern."

"Nonetheless, I thought you might be interested." She paused as they executed a perfect turn. But then she had heard he danced well. "Although I do think it would be wise to close or sell Garret and Tempest."

That caught his attention. "You do?"

She nodded. "While it is now my business, the firm was started by my husband and I think I would rather start fresh. With my work and my life."

Hope flashed in his blue eyes. "Do you?"

"I have no need to cling to the past. I would much prefer to look toward the future." She shrugged as best she could in his arms. "Besides, I see no other way to prove to you that I have moved on. I cannot change my past, nor can you change yours. I loved John, but that has nothing to do with the way I love you."

"You never said you loved me," he said slowly, his gaze boring into hers. "You could have mentioned that sooner. It's rather important."

"Yes, well, I should have told you the moment I realized it. My apologies."

He stared down at her. "Accepted."

"I cannot conceive of living the rest of my life without you." He led her through a complicated turn and she continued. "Nor do I intend to."

His brows drew together. "You don't?"

"Absolutely not. You are an annoying, obstinate, complicated twit of a man and I will not allow you to stalk out of my life in a huff of foolish pride and misunderstanding."

"Do try not to make me sound so appealing." The corners of his mouth twitched as if he were holding back a smile.

"I told you I have always wanted a wicked man and now that I have found one . . . well . . ."

"Well?"

"You were wrong when you said nothing terrifies me. I find any number of things terrifying. At the top of that list is losing you."

"Miranda—"

"Although there is one other thing I should tell you as it is rather important as well."

The music ended and Lord Fairborough took his place in the center of the terrace to address the gathering as was traditional.

Winfield stared down at her. "What?"

She peered around him. "I believe your father is about to speak."

"What is the other thing?" Impatience rang in his voice.

"That will have to wait. As you said, now is not the time."

"Miranda!"

Miranda bit back a satisfied smile and started toward Winfield's mother, Grayson and Camille, who were standing near the stairs leading up to the terrace.

"It seems to me this is the perfect time," an obviously confused and annoyed Winfield muttered behind her. Good. She did so love annoying him and everything was so much easier when he was confused. This was going quite well thus far.

"Good evening, friends, neighbors and honored guests," Lord Fairborough began. "It has been a long and unusual year, to say the least. It is my very great pleasure to welcome you . . ."

Winfield leaned close to her and spoke softly into her ear. "You are the most annoying creature I have ever met."

"Yes, I know."

"I insist you tell—"

"Shh!"

". . . and best of all," Lord Fairborough continued, "I should like to take this opportunity . . ."

"You might wish to listen to this," she murmured.

"I've heard my father's Midsummer Ball speech before." He glared down at her. "What haven't you told me? This is not the time for games, Miranda."

"Listen to your father, Winfield."

Winfield huffed in frustration and shifted his gaze to his father.

". . . to announce the engagement of my son, Lord Stillwell, to the lovely and enchanting Lady Garret."

At once all eyes were on them. She leaned toward him and lowered her voice for his ears alone. "My darling Lord Stillwell, would you do me the very great honor of accepting my proposal of marriage?"

"Are you sure?" His gaze searched hers.

"I have never been more certain of anything in my life." She paused. "Although you should know all of my engagements end in marriage and you would only be my second fiancé."

He stared at her for a long moment. Her heart thudded in her chest. She wasn't sure what she would do if he had changed his mind. If he didn't want her after all.

"Well? Will you?" She held her breath.

"No, Lady Garret, I will not be your second fiancé." A slow, easy smile curved his lips. "But I will be your last."

He took her hand and raised it to his lips. The crowd applauded.

"Surely you can do better than that," Miranda said softly and gazed into his eyes. "You do have that wicked reputation to maintain."

"Indeed I do. What was I thinking?" He grinned and swept her into his arms, bent her backwards and kissed her as she'd never been kissed before.

The gathering roared its approval and it flashed through Miranda's mind that there wasn't a person here who wouldn't be making a wager on whether or not this engagement of Lord Stillwell's ended in marriage. She did hope those who bet against their marriage wouldn't lose too much.

The noise of the crowd faded and there was nothing in all of creation except him and her and the way their hearts beat together, one in perfect rhythm with the other, as it was meant to be. As it would be for the rest of their days.

The wicked lord and the governess.

Who would have thought?

July

The honor of your presence

is requested at the marriage of

The Right Honorable

The Viscountess Garret

and

The Right Honorable

The Viscount Stillwell

on Wednesday, July twentieth

at eleven o'clock

Fairborough Hall

Epilogue

Three weeks later . . .

It had been pointed out to Win that this was perhaps not the most appropriate spot at Fairborough to hold a wedding as a previous wedding planned here had not taken place. But then, there were few places at Fairborough where weddings planned had occurred as expected. At least not his weddings. But he and Miranda had agreed there could be no better place to vow their eternal love for one another then here at the folly.

His mother had outdone herself, but then she'd had a great deal of practice at planning weddings. The clearing was filled with chairs and tables and a temporary floor for dancing. The folly had been festooned with ribbons and fresh flowers. He couldn't help but wonder if the fairies appreciated it, although why wouldn't they? It was so clearly the perfect setting for magic. The perfect setting for love.

Now, with his wife, his future, by his side, he gazed over the gathering—neither too large nor too small—with all of their friends and families in attendance. And two guests who were not invited but were welcome nonetheless. There had been a collective sigh of relief, which he had found annoying but understandable, when he and Miranda had at last been pronounced husband and wife.

"I can't believe you finally made it to the altar." Gray chuckled beside him.

"Nor can anyone, Grayson." Camille smiled. "Do you have any idea how many wagers there were in London about whether or not this wedding would take place?"

Miranda laughed. "Did you win a great deal?"

"You have no idea," Camille said smugly.

"You didn't." Grayson stared at his fiancée.

"Of course not." Camille scoffed and cast him an innocent smile that didn't fool anyone.

Win leaned close to his cousin and lowered his voice. "And how did you fare in that?"

"Suffice it to say, your wedding has proven most profitable," Gray said quietly. "About the wedding . . ." He paused. "Did you see them? Off to one side. Watching the proceedings?"

Win nodded. "I wondered if anyone else had."

"They looked happy."

"I thought so as well. But then their folly has at last seen a wedding as was intended all along."

"I hope the two of you realize you are not as discreet as you think and we have heard every word you said." Miranda smiled. "And I saw them as well."

"I didn't." Camille nudged Gray with her elbow. "You should have pointed them out to me. I would have loved to have seen them again."

Gray stared at his fiancée. "You've seen them? Thomas and Anne?"

"Goodness, Grayson, one can't grow up at Millworth Manor without seeing at least a handful of the dearly departed. But more to the point—" Her eyes narrowed. "How profitable?"

Win laughed.

"Very profitable." Gray grinned and deftly changed the subject. "Now that you have managed to ensnare in marriage a woman who is obviously entirely too good for you, do you—and Miranda as well, of course—have any words of wisdom as we follow your footsteps to the altar?"

"And Grayson at least can certainly use all the wisdom he can get." Camille directed a teasing smile at her fiancé.

"Trust," Winfield said firmly. "Trust between you is paramount."

"And honesty," Miranda added. "Not complete and total honesty, mind you, but relative honesty."

"Personally, I have always preferred relative honesty," Camille murmured.

Gray raised a brow.

"And do try not to jump to conclusions," Miranda said. "Even if they make perfect sense to you because it's more than likely they do not make any sense at all to anyone else."

"Never allow your family to interfere in your affairs," Win added.

"Oh, that ship has sailed," Gray said under his breath.

"And do be willing to compromise." Miranda smiled at her husband. "What you give up does tend to lose all importance compared to what you gain."

"And give her what she wants, Gray."

"Within reason, you mean?" Gray asked.

Camille scoffed. "Don't be absurd, dear."

"For example, Miranda has always rather fancied a wicked man." Win cast Miranda his most charming smile. The very one women had always considered irresistible. The smile reserved now and for the rest of his days for one woman and one woman alone. "And I was only too happy to give her exactly what she wanted."

Gray nodded. "As any intelligent man would."

"A wicked man? How very interesting." Camille considered Miranda thoughtfully. "It's my understanding that wicked men are nearly impossible to resist. As is reforming them."

"I can be very wicked." Gray grinned.

"I know." Camille smiled a wicked smile of her own. "I like it."

"It does seem that when all is said and done . . ." Miranda turned to her husband and met his gaze. His breath caught at the look in her brown eyes, of the promise of tomorrow and the love that would last until the day they breathed their last. And perhaps, like Thomas and Anne, even beyond. "One can never underestimate the importance of being wicked."

Center Point Large Print
600 Brooks Road / PO Box 1
Thorndike ME 04986-0001 USA

(207) 568-3717

US & Canada:
1 800 929-9108
www.centerpointlargeprint.com